bridge to
FOREVER

OTHER BOOKS AND BOOKS ON CASSETTE
BY RACHEL ANN NUNES:

Ariana: The Making of a Queen

Ariana: A Gift Most Precious

Ariana: A New Beginning

Ariana: A Glimpse of Eternity

Love to the Highest Bidder

Framed for Love

Love on the Run

To Love and to Promise

Tomorrow and Always

This Time Forever

bridge to FOREVER

a novel

Rachel Ann Nunes

Covenant Communications, Inc.

Cover photo © 2001 PhotoDisc, Inc.

Cover design copyrighted 2001 by Covenant Communications, Inc.

Published by Covenant Communications, Inc.
American Fork, Utah

Printed in the United States of America
First Printing: July 2001

08 07 06 05 04 03 02 01   10 9 8 7 6 5 4 3 2 1

ISBN 1-57734-833-8

ACKNOWLEDGMENTS

A sincere thank you goes to Shauna Nelson, managing editor at Covenant Communications, who has been a joy to work with this past year. Her encouragement and helpfulness have been a real blessing in my life. I also want to thank Angela Colvin who edited this book with Shauna. Their sharp eyes and insights were invaluable. Thanks ladies!

For Tami B.
You know why.

CHAPTER 1

Mickelle Hansen started her blue Metro and backed out of her American Fork driveway, past the ancient gold station wagon parked by the curb. Her stomach churned with a mixture of excitement and nervousness. What was she doing getting involved with someone so soon after her husband's death?

She had known Damon Wolfe less than six weeks, but already he had become a regular and vital part of her life. He was continually on her mind, and just thinking about him stirred a range of emotions her deceased husband had never evoked.

Was this really love?

She thought it was, prayed that it was, but she had been mistaken before—with Riley. Neither she nor their children had been happy living with him. Riley hadn't been happy, either, for that matter. A hard knot of anxiety formed in her stomach.

Damon is not Riley. She had said these words so many times, she had hoped to believe them by now.

Her feelings about Damon's two children were not so troubled. She loved them with all her heart, especially smart little Isabelle—Belle for short—who had quickly become the daughter she had always craved. She was grateful for the opportunity to earn money by tending Belle and her older brother after school each day until their father picked them up on his way home from work. When for some reason they didn't come to the house—like today because Damon had taken time off work to spend with his children during the teachers'

UEA conference—she missed them terribly.

Of course, watching his children gave Mickelle the fringe benefit of seeing Damon every day, and more often than not they shared dinner—either a home-cooked meal at Mickelle's or at any restaurant of her choice. Although these evenings weren't official "dates" and the children were always present, she felt loved, needed, and protected as she had never felt during her fourteen years of marriage to Riley.

Damon had actually said the words "I love you" to her several times when he had taken her out alone on real dates, and while she had thought the same about him in her heart and had wanted to say it back to him, she hadn't allowed herself that luxury. There was so much she still needed to know about this widower before she could commit herself and her two sons to his care.

They had discussed marriage, and vaguely talked about their separate temple sealings to their deceased spouses. But as yet they had kept their plans abstract rather than concrete. Mickelle suspected this was mostly due to her own hesitancy, stemming from the fact that the last time she had trusted her future to a man, the results had been tragic. She now believed deep within her heart that the only person she could truly depend on was herself—and the Lord.

Not a bad place to be, but she had quickly learned that Damon *wanted* to be depended on. And Mickelle was beginning to trust him, too—at least a little. Was she ready for the next step?

Damon was. She knew that. The thought made her heart jump.

"Mom, there it is!" Jeremy's thin arm pointed to the beginning of the Wolfe's Alpine driveway, his voice quivering with all the excitement and anticipation of a nine-year-old.

Mickelle glanced in the backseat and smiled at her son in appreciation. His blue eyes danced and his grin was so large it seemed as though it would split his face in two.

"Am I right?" he asked, bouncing on the seat.

Bryan, Mickelle's older son, nodded. "Yeah, that's it. Can't you see that metal arch they put up? See? It says Wolfe Estates. Now stop bouncing my seat." Although the stocky thirteen-year-old was trying hard to act indifferent, Mickelle detected a hint of anticipation in his brown eyes. She knew that meant he was looking forward to visiting the mansion, where Damon's family lived, despite his reluctance to let

Damon into their lives. Except for his blonde hair, Bryan looked like his deceased father more and more each day. This didn't bother her, though sometimes she wondered if he had inherited his father's tendency toward sullenness as well. She prayed that he hadn't, and that his wounds from his father's death wouldn't be permanent.

"You got your towels?" she asked, turning into the long drive lined by tall paper birch trees, their white trunks contrasting with the bright green foliage.

"Of course we got the towels." Bryan's voice was impatient. "You asked us a million times."

"Oh." Mickelle recalled asking, but never remembered hearing any response. She had been too worried about her own attire and wishing she had bought a new swimsuit for the occasion. A few thousand sit-ups wouldn't have hurt her, either. Too late now. Damon would have to accept her as she was.

She brought her attention back to the boys. "Now remember what I said about swimming. I know they have two pools, but I want you two to stay in the indoor one with me."

"Well, of course, Mom," Jeremy said. "It's too cold to swim outside. Gosh, it's almost Halloween already."

"Not for weeks and weeks," Bryan corrected. "And Tanner said the outdoor pool was heated." He referred to Damon's son, who was nearly sixteen. "And it's really not too cold yet. I had to leave my window open last night, and look, I'm wearing shorts. Jeremy, too."

Jeremy must have sensed the worry in her silence. "Don't worry, Mom. Damon said no one can swim by themselves in any of the pools. It's a rule. Nothing's going to happen to us."

Tears burned behind Mickelle's eyes. Jeremy had pinpointed her worry perfectly: she couldn't bear the idea of losing either of her sons. Each night she prayed fervently for their protection. She tried not to be overprotective, but knew she was failing. Once, last week, she had even frantically called the police when Bryan hadn't come home from school on time. They had found him at the school in an extracurricular activity she had given him permission to attend.

Not one of my better moments, she thought.

Yet she *had* come a long way. Riley had died the first week in May, and she would never forget the day the police officers had come to break the news. Though her husband had been verbally and emotionally abusive, she had high hopes for change, and so his death had robbed her of her deepest dreams. It had taken four months for her to get out of bed and face the world. She told herself that meeting Damon almost six weeks ago had only coincided with her decision to get over Riley and make a better life for her children. But had it? A part of her wondered what might have happened if he hadn't come along, if his son Tanner hadn't banged into her old station wagon, the Snail, while he was driving without a license. Would she still be in bed most of the day, a prisoner of the panic attacks that had plagued her?

So am I just grateful to him, or is there more between us?

The question couldn't be answered to her satisfaction, try as Damon might to convince her. When she was with him, all doubts faded; but when she was alone, her fears continued to eat at her.

"I can't believe we're finally getting to swim here. And watch videos after! I'll bet he has some great food for dinner." Jeremy's voice pulled her attention back to her driving. Damon's residence had come into sight now through the lofty trees, and its magnitude struck Mickelle as forcibly as the first time she had seen it.

The mansion was decidedly Victorian, made of gray bricks and white wood, with huge windows and two tall rounded sections on either side that gave the impression of castle turrets. A perfect residence for a princess. (Oh, how she had always wanted to live in a castle!) A covered porch ran the entire length of the house, wrapping around the turret on the right side, and continuing on to the back of the house. Tall trees—black walnut and more paper birch—were scattered invitingly over the sculptured lawns, and beautiful flower beds surrounded the house.

Mickelle checked the mirror, making sure her lipstick still looked fresh, and that her shoulder-length, honey-blonde hair was in place around her oval face. She had used a new eyeliner too, a blue to match her eyes, and she wondered if Damon would notice.

The boys left the car and skipped up the flower-lined walk. Mickelle hefted her canvas bag with her swimming supplies and followed more slowly, eyes roving appreciatively over the groundskeeper's work. Of all the varieties of flowers at Damon's, she loved the miniature roses the best, particularly the way they inched along the white-painted wooden railings of the porch. Roses of all colors still bloomed, holding out against the increasing night cold. But she especially loved the tiny blossoms that were yellow in the center and red on the outer half of the petals. Their colors were still vivid enough to match the vibrant red and gold leaves that clung to the trees. Someday she would look up the name of the miniature roses, buy as many as she could afford, and plant them around her backyard fence.

She had been to Damon's several times before, but coming here was always a jolting reminder of the disparity between them. He was so incredibly wealthy. Her sister, Brionney Hergarter, had joked that everything he touched turned to gold. It certainly seemed so, if Hospital's Choice Incorporated—the company Damon and Jesse, Brionney's husband, had started—was any indication. After only six months of full-time operation, they were already close to paying back their initial three-million-dollar investment.

The fact was, Damon probably paid more in tithing to the Church each month than Mickelle's first husband had made in a year. He was generous, stable, an excellent father, and more than a good catch for any woman. Yet instead of Damon's wealth reassuring her, it made her wonder what he saw in her. Could it be she had captured his pity rather than his love? His charity rather than his heart?

She sighed and hurried up the cement walk, recalling how Damon was planning to replace it with gray cobblestone to match the house. The idea had been hers originally, and Damon had called Old Bobby, the groundskeeper, the next day. That was one of the things she loved so much about Damon: he listened to her.

Mickelle arrived at the bottom of the porch stairs before the front door opened, though she was sure the boys had rung the bell—probably several times. Damon should be answering soon. Her breath caught as she imagined his angular, good-looking face with his strange eyes that were more dark amber than brown, staring at her with that longing intensity that threatened her newly earned self-reliance. Vividly, she remembered the times he had kissed her, the feel of his trim blonde moustache on her skin, and the way his yellow hair, long overdue for a haircut, felt against her fingers.

The last time she had seen him, two days before on Wednesday, they had joked about when he would find time from his busy schedule to get his hair cut. Mickelle had pulled out some shears and offered to do the job. She meant it too—hadn't she cut Riley's well enough?—but kept her voice light in case he refused. The man probably spent more on a haircut than she did on an entire dress. He had laughed with her, and the conversation had rolled on, leaving her with a loss she couldn't name. Perhaps the intimacy was inappropriate, but oh, she had wanted to feel his hair beneath her fingers! Of course, she could have done that by letting him kiss her again, but that would more directly involve her heart. She couldn't even think straight when he held her in his arms.

Now her heart threatened to jump out of her chest as she waited for what seemed an interminable time for someone to answer the door. At last it moved a little hesitantly, then inched open slowly. Instinctively, she ran a hand through her blonde locks to fluff them. She kept hoping that her legs didn't look quite as flabby as they had at home in the stark light reflected in the bathroom mirror.

Damon wasn't behind the door. Instead, little Belle tugged at the heavy wood, using only her left hand. She wore a swimsuit, and under her right arm she carried a large brown teddy bear and a cream-colored plastic horse. "You're here! Finally." She dodged past the two boys and threw herself at Mickelle. "I missed you!"

Mickelle's arms closed around the girl's small body. Belle was a beautiful child, with curly brown hair, a round cherubic face, and brown eyes that held a hint of her father's amber. The precocious five-year-old had skipped kindergarten to enter the first grade, where she often drove her teacher crazy as she struggled to keep Belle's interest.

"Look!" Belle held up her right arm. "See? I got the cast off! Now I can really take piano lessons." The toys under her arms clattered to the wood steps. "Oops, sorry Bear, sorry Horse." As she reached for them with her left hand, she nearly toppled Mickelle over. Her clear laughter rang out, and two dimples appeared in her cheeks. "I keep forgetting I can use my other arm now," she explained. "That's why it took me so long to open the door."

"And because you were carrying Bear and Horse." Mickelle helped her gather the toys. "Let's see that arm."

Belle's smile died. "It's so skinny," she said mournfully. "And white. I just hate it!"

"She cried when they took off the cast," said another voice from the open doorway. It was Tanner, Belle's older brother. His tall frame was clad in oversized shorts and a white T-shirt. Normally, the lower half of his brown hair was close-cropped, with the top hanging all one length an inch above his ears, but he too was in desperate need of a haircut.

"Well, it looked so awful," Belle countered with feeling. "Worse than now. And it had *yucky* stuff on it." She stared down at her arm sadly. "Daddy had to rub it off in the bathtub."

"It was dead skin that couldn't flake off inside the cast," Tanner said, rolling his eyes. "She wacked out about it."

"Oh yeah, I remember that from the two times Bryan broke his arm." Mickelle examined Belle's arm more closely, wishing that she could have been with the child during this small crisis. Damon would have let her, if only she had asked, but she had been worried about seeming too forward. Belle was not her daughter, no matter how much she wanted her to be. *At least not yet,* a voice inside her said.

Mickelle ran a gentle finger over the little girl's arm. "Hmm, it looks like your dad did a good job. I don't see anything wrong with this arm, other than it needs a little sun."

"It doesn't look too skinny to you?" Belle demanded, frowning.

"Nope. And see how straight it is? I think the doctor did a great job."

Belle moved her arm back and forth a minute, then apparently lost interest. "At least I can swim now! Come on inside. Let's tell Daddy you're finally here." She hugged her animals to her small chest, but Mickelle noticed she still favored her right arm. Bryan had done that too for a while.

"Dad went out to the pool house to check if the water is warm enough," Tanner told her as they entered the house. With his brown eyes and hair, only the angular planes in his face resembled his father's. In fact, both of Damon's children had their mother's brown hair. Mickelle mused that if she and Damon had children together, they would likely have blonde hair like her children.

His child?

Mickelle sighed. She was almost thirty-seven and thought she had put those dreams aside. Riley hadn't wanted any more children. Did Damon? She should know that much already, if she was really in love with him.

"He got tired of waiting for you," Belle added, bringing Mickelle's thoughts back to the conversation at hand. "He thought you were going to be here hours ago." She put her hand in Mickelle's and led her through the two-story entryway. The sun shone through the stained-glass window far overhead, washing the walls with a brilliantly lit rainbow of colors. They passed the sweeping main staircase, going in the direction of the kitchen. Mickelle barely had time to glance through the sitting room to the music room where a full-sized Steinway Concert Grand stood in beckoning elegance. Her fingers itched to try it out, though she only knew one decent song, "The Entertainer."

"He's been waiting?" Mickelle said distractedly. Damon had asked her over after lunch and although she and the boys had been ready to go since ten, she had waited until two, so as not to appear too anxious. Now that seemed silly.

As Mickelle remembered from several prior visits, the kitchen and adjoining family room were immense; full of windows, deep hues, and quality furniture. Today, she had little time to take in any details, except a huge bowl of fat red grapes spilling over onto the counter. Belle grabbed a few and popped them into her mouth on her way past. "Dad says these are to eat in the hot tub," she announced. "I don't know why. I think it's something romantic."

"Belle," Tanner warned, but he flashed Mickelle a smile. She knew that he approved of her relationship with his dad.

Bryan glowered at the reference, but Jeremy skipped blithely ahead. "I don't care much if the pool is cold," he announced. "I'm just going to jump right in."

"I'll have to change first." Mickelle had felt awkward about wearing her swimming suit over to the house. Besides, she would need clothes for afterwards.

"Well Damon can watch me until you get changed, can't he, Mom?" pleaded Jeremy.

"I suppose. If he's willing."

"He will be," Belle replied confidently.

The group went outside, across the back patio and along the

covered walkway to the pool house, which was nestled behind a row of pink dogwood trees on the far side of the yard. Behind the pool house lay a tennis court, too, according to Belle and Tanner. Mickelle had always meant to challenge Damon to a game, though neither of them really knew how to play. Perhaps today they would have time for Tanner to show them a few moves.

The warmer air of the pool house hit them as they opened the door. Mickelle wrinkled her nose at the strong chlorine smell.

"Yippee!" yelled Jeremy, gazing at the pool. While not as large as the public pool in American Fork where Mickelle lived, this one was certainly more than adequate for several families to swim in comfort.

Damon was nowhere in sight. Mickelle looked around, eager to be with him after so much waiting. Through the large, floor-to-ceiling windows on the right side she could see the outdoor pool, covered now, and an area for barbeques. Damon wasn't on any of the lounge chairs there.

"Daddy!" Belle shouted.

"He must have gone upstairs or somewhere." Mickelle shot a glance over her shoulder at the house through the open pool house door. She didn't even know where his room was located. She knew the house had two separate wings on the top floor and an entire basement where Tanner and their live-in maid had their rooms, but where Damon slept in all that hugeness was still a mystery.

"He just came out here," Tanner told them. "He said he had something to do before you got here—*besides* checking the water temperature. He acted nervous."

Mickelle's heartbeat, which had finally settled to a normal pace after expecting Damon at the front door, resumed thumping again erratically. Goose bumps covered her skin, and her stomach felt queasy. She pushed past the children, searching the pool with her eyes. "Damon!" she called forcefully.

No answer.

Something wasn't right. She could feel it in the tingling of her spine, in the thundering of her heart.

"You kids check the house," she ordered. She hurried along the side of the pool, praying as she went.

Then she saw him, floating face down in the pool under the

diving board. She must have screamed because the children hurtled toward her. Not waiting for them, Mickelle forced her fright-frozen limbs to work, and rushed toward his unmoving body.

Not Damon, please not Damon!

This wasn't happening! This wonderful, attractive, alluring man couldn't leave her too!

Like Riley.

She heard a splash and realized that Tanner was in the water, swimming at high velocity toward his dad. Spying a lifesaving hook on the wall she dived toward it and reached for Damon at the same time Tanner arrived at the inert form. Together they began pulling him to the side. Belle and Jeremy were sobbing and clutching at Mickelle, making her job more difficult.

"911!" she shouted at Bryan. He glanced at her, eyes wide with shock, as though he couldn't hear. Reaching now for Damon, Mickelle caught Belle's tearful gaze with her own. "Belle, call 911. Your daddy needs help—now!"

Little Belle galvanized into action, racing for a phone on the wall near where Mickelle had found the hook.

With great effort Tanner and Mickelle pushed and dragged Damon from the water. She knelt beside him, trying to remember what she should do.

"Heartbeat!" yelled Tanner. He was pale and shaking as he pulled himself out of the pool.

Mickelle felt for a pulse, and nearly cried with relief. "Yes! He's got one."

Together they rolled him onto his stomach, trying to force water from his lungs. A flood of liquid gushed onto the cement. Still, he didn't start breathing. Mickelle willed him to open those intriguing amber eyes, but they were unmoving beneath the thick, expressive eyebrows.

"Mouth-to-mouth," she said faintly.

With a quick nod, Tanner helped her roll Damon to his back. He was on the tall side for a man, with broad shoulders, but she had never dreamed he weighed so much. She tipped back his head as she had seen people do in the movies, and pinched the end of his slightly hooked nose. *Please let me be doing this right!* Why hadn't she ever taken a course in lifesaving?

She put her mouth to his, and fleetingly recalled those other moments when their lips had met—firmly, passionately, sending heat throughout her body. The heat was utterly missing now. His lips were slack and cold. Oh, so cold! Deathly cold. The coldness slammed into her, made her shiver and gasp for breath. Above all there was the blind urgency and the terrible, looming fear.

"Someone's coming!" Belle called from her place by the phone. "They said to keep doing mouth-to-mouth."

Mickelle didn't look her way, but continued forcing air into Damon's lungs. *I can't do it,* she thought. But she tried anyway.

She hadn't been able to keep Riley from dying. Where had she been when his truck went off that cliff?

It wasn't my fault. She knew that, but sometimes the guilt still ate at her. She had threatened him with divorce.

"Dad! Dad!" Tanner cried, losing his composure. "Don't die! Oh, it's too late! We're too late! Oh, no! Oh, no!"

Mickelle wanted to soothe him, to tell him what a good sign it was that his dad's heart still beat in his chest, but she couldn't stop breathing for Damon long enough to explain.

In. Out. In. Out. Never faltering. And while she worked, she prayed.

CHAPTER 2

It seemed an eternity before four men burst into the pool house, two of them carrying a gurney. Mickelle was so dizzy that their faces looked blurred and distorted as they approached at a run.

She didn't give up. In. Out. In. Out. She tasted salt and knew it came from her tears.

"Please, Damon," she whispered.

"We'll take over," one of the ambulance workers said, kneeling beside her.

Suddenly, Damon's blonde moustache moved against her mouth. His chest rose and fell of its own accord.

"He's breathing!" she exclaimed joyfully, looking up at the children. Belle and Jeremy clung together on her right, while Tanner knelt on the other side of Damon's body. Bryan was still frozen in place several paces beyond Belle and Jeremy, as pale as the white HardRock Cafe T-shirt he wore.

Mickelle fell back, holding onto Belle and Jeremy while the ambulance men checked Damon. "Good work, ma'am," one said. "He's breathing and his heartbeat is strong."

"Then why doesn't he wake up?" Tanner asked.

"I don't know. We'll have to take him in and let the doctor take a look at him. Could be that his body just needs to rest. That happens a lot. Look here. He's had quite a blow to the side of his head. That's probably given him some trauma."

Meaning what? Brain damage? Mickelle didn't voice the words aloud.

She watched as they loaded the unconscious Damon onto their gurney. He wore nothing but a pair of knee-length swimming trunks, and she realized that this was the first time she'd seen him in shorts and without a shirt. His chest was broader than she imagined, and his legs were strong and muscular. She willed him silently to wake, but to no avail.

"Can I go with him?" Tanner asked.

The men looked at Mickelle, obviously assuming she was Damon's wife and Tanner's mother.

"Go ahead, Tanner," she said, not bothering to explain her relationship. "We'll meet you at the hospital."

The men nodded and allowed Tanner inside the ambulance.

"Which hospital?" Mickelle asked.

"That's up to you," one of the men told her. "And your insurance. If he were having heart trouble, and could wait a bit, we'd take him to Provo, but either American Fork or Timpanogos can handle this."

"American Fork then," Mickelle said. Besides being the closest hospital, several women in her ward worked there, and she knew the staff was dedicated.

"I want to go with him, too," Belle complained in a high, wavering voice.

Mickelle knelt down and hugged her. "I know you do, honey, but only one person can go. We'll be there almost as soon as Tanner. Don't worry. Your brother and those men will take good care of him. Come on, Jeremy, Bryan. Let's go."

Now that the immediate danger was over, Mickelle began to shake, but she forced herself into the blue Metro. The drive to the American Fork Hospital was very quiet. Jeremy and Belle wore sad faces as they took turns muttering quiet prayers in the back seat of the Metro. Their faith eased the terror in Mickelle's heart.

The color had returned to Bryan's face, but his eyes were still wide with shock. He hadn't spoken since they had found Damon.

Mickelle put her hand out to touch his. "Are you okay?"

He swallowed and opened his mouth to speak, but the words were difficult in coming. "Is he going to die?"

"No."

He nodded, but didn't speak further.

At the hospital, Mickelle and the children had to wait thirty minutes before someone finally came to talk to them. "We're taking him to a room now," said the intern. He was tall and thin, with brown hair and kind hazel eyes. "He seems to be doing well, and I don't think there's any permanent damage. We want to keep him overnight for observation, however. He was out for quite a while, and it always pays to be careful."

Mickelle's entire body felt weak with relief.

"We do have some papers to check over. Your son has supplied most of the information, but he didn't know about the insurance."

"I don't know about that, either," she said. "We'll have to ask Damon."

Only when the intern eyed her strangely did Mickelle realize that, like the ambulance workers, he thought she was Damon's wife.

"There's no problem with paying," she assured him hurriedly.

To Mickelle's embarrassment, Jeremy added, "Yeah, he's really rich."

"Can I see my daddy?" Belle pleaded. "Please?"

The man smiled. "You can all go see him right now. He's awake and asking for you."

Tanner met them on their way to the room. "Oh good, you're here. He wants to see you." He nodded toward the hall. "Since you'll be with him, I'm going to take a walk. Want to come, Bryan?"

Bryan fell into step with the older boy.

"Come back soon, okay?" Mickelle called after them.

Tanner smiled over his shoulder. "Sure. I just want to check out the vending machines."

Mickelle, Belle, and Jeremy went into Damon's room. Immediately, Belle ran into her father's outstretched arms. "Are you okay?"

"Of course I am, ma Belle." He hugged her tightly as his amber-brown eyes met Mickelle's over the top of Belle's soft curls. Damon had told her that *ma belle* meant "my beauty" in French, and she agreed that it was a perfect description of his beloved daughter.

Jeremy approached the bed hesitantly, "I thought you said no swimming by yourself," he said, his blue eyes accusing.

"I did say that, Jer, and occasionally I have broken that rule because I put it into place mostly for Belle and Tan. But since they pointed out to me that I was also vulnerable, I've begun to obey it. I wasn't swimming today."

"You weren't?" Belle appeared surprised. "But we found you in the water." Her round face grew bleak at the memory.

He sighed. "I fell. It was a stupid mistake." Again his eyes met Mickelle's. "I was trying to do . . . something. It doesn't matter now. I'm all right—thanks to you guys."

"I called 911," Belle said importantly. "I told the ambulance to come and get you."

"Mom breathed in your mouth," Jeremy put in, not to be outdone in the telling.

"So I heard." Damon's eyes still held Mickelle's. He gave Belle another squeeze. "Look, you guys, can I talk to Kelle a minute?" He used a nickname for Mickelle as he did for everyone special in his life. According to Belle, Mickelle's nickname was the most special because it rhymed with hers.

Belle smiled widely, showing her twin dimples, her fears forgotten. "Sure. I bet you want to *kiss* her!"

"Ew, gross!" added Jeremy as they headed to the door, making smooching sounds.

"Maybe," Damon teased. The laugh lines that gave his angular face so much character deepened as he grinned.

"Stay just outside the door," ordered Mickelle. "I'll be right out."

She approached the bed with even more reluctance than Jeremy had shown. Damon was alive and she was glad—more than glad. But she never wanted to go through such horror again.

Like with Riley.

"What is it?" Damon asked, his voice gentle. He sat up a little higher in the bed and reached for her hand. The electricity of his touch flooded warmly through her entire body and she longed to throw herself into his arms and weep out her relief.

"You scared us." She was unwilling to explain how utterly terrified she had been; she simply couldn't.

His strong jaw clenched with compassion. "I'm sorry. I know that was tough on you. And I'm thankful you and Tan knew what to do."

"I didn't really, I . . . ." Her voice trailed off. They had come so close to losing him. What an unbearable thought! And deep inside, she felt that his death would even be worse than Riley's had been for her. And why was that? She had loved Riley enough to marry him. What did that say about her feelings for Damon?

Damon squeezed her fingers more tightly. "Where's Bry?" he asked.

"He's with Tanner."

Silence fell between them, but it was uncomfortable and tense. Mickelle shifted nervously, feeling oddly alienated from this man she thought she loved.

Slowly, without taking his eyes from hers, he held up his free hand and opened it slowly. Mickelle followed the movement with her eyes, but it took some time for her brain to process what she saw.

"This is what I was trying to do," Damon said softly. "I was putting this on the end of the diving board for you to find, only I slipped or something and hit my head. Tan found it still clenched in my hand in the ambulance." He laughed. "Not even unconscious would I give it up."

She barely heard him, her attention rivetted on his hand where the largest heart-shaped diamond she had ever seen stood out sharply against the white skin of his palm. The band that held the diamond was thick, and glistened like only fine gold could. As she stared at the obviously precious ring, a desire to possess it—and all it represented—grew in her heart until she was almost bursting with the feeling.

But she didn't allow herself to take it from him. Sometimes safety was only an illusion.

"I hope it's not too big," Damon said earnestly. His overlong hair had swept forward, making him seem younger than his thirty-eight years. "I know you're not into showy things, but the heart shape was perfect, and I didn't want to wait for them to put in a smaller diamond. It's only three carats, so it's not unreasonably big . . . I hope. Oh . . ." His voice sounded frustrated. "This isn't at all as romantic as I'd planned. I should have kept it in the bowl of grapes— would have if you'd come a little earlier . . . forget all that. Please, Kelle, I've been waiting to ask you for weeks—will you marry me?"

He was so sincere and stared at her with so much love that the fear almost left.

Almost.

"I love you so much," he continued. "And I'll do my best to take care of you and be a father to your boys. Everything I have is yours."

Mickelle's heart rate increased and her vision dimmed. The room seem to whirl, as she struggled for breath. Fear loomed over her, as tangible as anything else in the room. A panic attack! She hadn't experienced one of those for weeks—for as long as she had known Damon.

She pulled from his grasp and backed away from the bed until she felt the solid wall behind her. "Damon," she managed. "I—I'm sorry, but I can't marry you!" Then, before he could demand a reason, she turned and fled from the room.

* * * * *

Damon looked from the closing door to the ring in his hand. Mickelle's refusal had nothing to do with the size of the diamond, he knew, but with the fear showing so plainly in her eyes. It twisted his gut and made him ache to take away her pain. He felt that her response would have been quite different, if only he hadn't been such a clumsy fool.

A lovesick fool, he amended silently. And that was good enough reason for him.

He loved Mickelle, loved her every bit as deeply as he had loved his wife, dead now these past two years from cancer. With Mickelle, he had found the companionship and physical attraction he hadn't known with a woman since Belle's birth and Charlotte's regression. While he still wondered what it might have been like for him and Charlotte under different circumstances, Mickelle had filled every remaining emptiness within his heart.

He had asked his children only this morning if they would support his decision to ask Mickelle to marry him. They had both been more than supportive. Tanner liked Mickelle, and Damon knew he envied his friends who had mothers. And Belle—well, she had never been close to Charlotte. By the time she could understand who her mother was, Charlotte was bedridden and too sick to mother a baby. Charlotte had died when Belle was three. In Mickelle, Damon knew Belle had found the mother she needed, and he thought Mickelle needed Belle every bit as much.

But not me, he thought bitterly.

No, she's just scared. No matter how damaged his ego, he refused to be thwarted or to give into the petty hurt that filled his heart. He loved Mickelle with his entire being and he would somehow make this relationship work. He would make her happy.

Even as these thoughts filtered through his mind, he was picking up the phone, dialing his partner Jesse's home phone number. Jesse's wife, Brionney, had always given Damon good advice; perhaps she could help him. It didn't hurt that she was also Mickelle's sister.

"Hello?" answered a woman's cheerful voice.

"Hi Bri," he said. "Look, I'm sorry to burden you like this, knowing you have all your kids home, but could you come down to the hospital and talk to Kelle?"

"The hospital?" Bri's voice went up an octave.

"Well, it's a long story, but somehow I ended up here. They want to keep me for observation overnight. Don't worry, though, I'm perfectly fine. Although this has put a big kink in my relationship with your sister."

"But you two were getting along so well."

Damon's chest tightened. "That's what I thought. But after this accident today . . . well, I proposed and she got all scared on me. Turned me down flat. And now I'm worried about her. Remember those panic attacks she used to have? Well, I think she had one here. I'm afraid for her to drive home alone." He wanted to say more, but felt too stupid to continue. Of all the idiot things to do; how could he have fallen off a diving board?

"I'll be right there. I can leave the three oldest with my neighbor, but I'll have to bring the terror twins. They're too much for anyone just now, especially Forest. He's teething again."

Damon thought that Forest, barely a year old, was always teething. Or at least acted like it. But he thought it best not to voice this thought aloud. "The more, the merrier," he said instead.

"Yeah, right," she replied dryly. "You don't have to watch them, since you're in bed. Lucky you. But before I come, you have to tell me what happened. I can't take the suspense a minute longer!"

Damon quickly outlined the accident and Mickelle's subsequent rescue. "That's so romantic!" Brionney said with a sigh. "And I gotta see that ring. I bet it's fabulous. You always did have great taste."

"Uh, thanks." Weariness settled on Damon. He had offered Mickelle his heart; she had refused. But he wouldn't allow that to be her final answer, not yet.

Brionney seemed to sense his thoughts. "Don't worry, Damon. It's not over until it's over. Mickelle's been through a lot this year. She deserves a chance to wig out on you a time or two. Her husband's death was very hard on her. You might have to give her time."

Damon knew that, but it felt good to have the thought voiced aloud by someone other than himself. Someone who knew and loved Mickelle as much as he did. Or almost as much.

He hung up the phone, still feeling depressed. One thing was sure: he *had* almost died by being so careless. No one could blame Mickelle for being disturbed by this event. *He* was disturbed by it. He had almost lost her forever through his own clumsiness.

He closed his eyes and saw her again, the honey-blonde hair, stormy blue eyes, the classic features of her fine-boned face—not to mention the slender curves of her shapely body. She was intelligent, witty, and so . . . vulnerable. He thought about her almost constantly, even at work, and sometimes the intensity of his love for her frightened him. What if she could never return these feelings?

But she had. At least he thought so.

Until today.

Damon abruptly swung his feet out of the bed. Dang it all, he was going after her!

A wave of dizziness caught him off-guard just as a gray-haired nurse entered the room, followed closely by Tanner and Belle. "Oh, no you don't," she said, firmly pushing him back into bed. "You need to stay right here until tomorrow morning. And then in bed for the weekend, if you want to get better." Her hands were like iron bands from which he couldn't escape.

"But I . . ." he held his hand open to reveal the ring.

"Don't worry, Dad, I'll give it to her."

Before he could protest, Belle snatched the ring out of his hand and disappeared from the room.

"Are you okay, Dad?" Tanner's worried voice came to him through a blurry haze.

"Yes, just a little dizzy." He wasn't worried about the ring. It was insured, like everything else he owned—except his heart.

"That's because you got up too soon." The nurse gave him a smile. "Now, what would you like me to bring you for dinner?"

Damon managed to choose something from the limited menu and then watched as she squeaked out the door in her white nurse's shoes.

"So did she say yes?" Tanner asked him excitedly. He glowed with anticipation.

Damon frowned, not wanting to disappoint him. "Not yet," he said with determination, "but she will."

* * * * *

Mickelle sat numbly on a stiff chair down the hall from Damon's room, wondering what she should do. Her pulse had returned to normal, and she could see properly again, but the fear from the panic attack was still with her. Why had the panic returned?

The trauma, of course, she told herself, but knowing a reason didn't ease the fear.

She couldn't believe she had just turned down Damon's proposal. The hurt in his eyes had been obvious; she had seen that even with her sight dimmed from the attack.

I must not love him, she thought.

But it wasn't that exactly, at least if she could judge by the terrible loss she felt in her heart.

Then what was it?

Her troublesome thoughts ceased abruptly as Belle's rosy-cheeked face appeared in front of her. "Mickelle, you forgot this." The child shoved something into Mickelle's hand, kissed her cheek, and went to see what Bryan and Jeremy were looking at in a magazine.

Mickelle stared at her hand and saw the beautiful diamond ring. She picked it up between her forefinger and thumb, studying the design. Her heart began to race again. Damon was nothing if not romantic. The thick band met the heart-shaped diamond on each side in a dramatic sweep. *Three carats,* she thought. How could she ever wear something like this? It belonged in a vault, and what fun would it be if you couldn't wear the symbol of your husband's undying love?

Seemingly of its own accord the ring slid on her finger, exactly where she would be wearing it if she hadn't turned Damon down. Only a few weeks ago she had finally removed the slim gold band Riley had given her for their wedding. The simple band had been all they could afford, and she had cherished it. When she had finally taken it off it left a white circle around her finger, a remnant of her long hours in the garden.

Damon's thick ring completely covered the white, as though it had never existed at all. She marveled at the brilliance of the diamond and the elegance of the setting. She had never been a person to desire such things, and yet suddenly she wanted that ring more than she had ever wanted *anything*.

Her heartbeat had now built to a pounding crescendo in her ears, and her eyesight blurred. Forgetting the ring, she clasped her hands to her chest and bowed her head, struggling to breathe evenly. She could no longer hear the children talking, only the furious beating of her heart. *I'm dying!* she thought, but knew it wasn't true.

"Please, Father," she whispered. She knew she had spoken the words aloud, but couldn't hear them. Her panic increased, and she pulled her knees up to her chest. Her limbs felt numb.

She had no concept of how long she stayed in that position, but at last she felt a hand touch her shoulder, and then a pair of caring arms surrounded her. In that warm embrace, Mickelle felt the panic gradually ebb.

"It's all right," said a familiar voice. "Mickelle, everything is all right. Just take some deep breaths. Come on. In and out. You can do it."

The words "in and out" made Mickelle remember how she had breathed air into Damon's lungs.

He had lived!

In. Out. Slowly, her vision cleared and she could hear normal hospital sounds again. Her sister, Brionney, sat in the next chair, her arms still wrapped around Mickelle.

"There, that's better, isn't it?" Brionney had white-blonde hair that went to her chin, and eyes the color of sky on a clear day. She was shorter than Mickelle, slightly heavier, and her face was pale as though she didn't get out of the house much. Mickelle had always thought her sister beautiful, but never more so than at that moment.

"I'm okay," Mickelle managed. "Thank you."

Brionney let her hands fall slowly down to her side. "I'm glad I could come."

Mickelle glanced across the room to see her boys and Belle staring at her with concern. Forcing a smile, she nodded at them. "Don't worry, I'm fine." She lifted her hands to her face to wipe away tears she didn't remember crying.

Reassured, Jeremy began to play with Brionney's twins, who had recently learned to walk, but Bryan and Belle continued to watch her solemnly.

"I heard you had a tough day," Brionney said sympathetically.

Mickelle turned her face back to her sister. "Yes, you could say that."

"Thank heaven you got there in time. The Lord has really blessed us."

Mickelle didn't reply.

"I guess it was a pretty frightening experience and that's what brought on your panic attack." Brionney rubbed Mickelle's shoulder. "But you did it. I'm so proud of you."

Mickelle didn't feel proud. She swallowed hard. "I didn't know what to do when I saw him there. If it hadn't been for Tanner's help . . ." The thought was too chilling to consider.

"But Tanner was there—you all were." Brionney's blue, blue eyes looked deeply into her own. "And you're all okay. Now you and Damon can just go on with your lives."

"You don't understand!" Mickelle shrugged her sister's hand from her shoulder, but kept her voice low so the children wouldn't hear. "When I saw Damon in that pool today, I realized that I can't do it again. I can't love . . . care about someone and have them die like that. I just can't!"

"Damon's not going to die."

"He almost did!"

Brionney chewed on her lip for a moment. "He didn't, though. The Lord protected him by sending you."

"And who will be there the next time?" Mickelle answered in a vehement half-whisper. "And who was with Riley?" She stood, feeling slightly disoriented, as though her balance was off. "Oh, I know the answer to that, I really do. I'm not losing my faith or anything. But it's my husband who died at the bottom of that ravine last May, and you know how I reacted to that—I quit living. I simply can't go through it again."

"You'd rather be alone?" Brionney asked quietly.

Mickelle clenched her jaw. "Yes."

Brionney's eyes went beyond her to the children, and Mickelle followed her gaze. They were all playing with the babies now, and appeared to be having a great time.

"Besides," Mickelle said, "I'm not alone, I have the kids."

"You have *your* kids. Damon's are only on loan."

Mickelle's heart constricted. "He wouldn't . . ." She hadn't considered that turning down Damon's proposal would make her lose Belle and Tanner, too.

"No, he wouldn't. Of course he wouldn't. Not only because you need the money, but because the kids love you. But have you ever asked yourself why they mean so much to you? Could it be because of the feelings you have for their father?"

Mickelle wanted to tell her that she was wrong, at least where Belle was concerned. She and Belle were *connected*. Mickelle was almost certain she was the girl in the dream she had experienced the night of Riley's funeral. *I was meant to be a part of her life!* After the dream, Mickelle had thought she was expecting a daughter, but now she understood the Lord had been preparing her to love Belle. And she did.

But it seemed that telling Brionney this would work against her at the moment. She looked at Brionney where she still sat on the stiff green chair. "My children need me as an active part of their lives, not hovering under my covers trying to stave off panic attacks brought on by losing another husband."

"Is that what this is really about? Or is this more of the same thing with that cop? You dated him 'cause he was safe, and you knew you wouldn't love him. Unlike with Damon."

Mickelle thought about that, remembering how the intensity of her reaction to Damon's first kiss had made her vow not to become further involved. At the time, she had not been ready to trust another man, to lose her new sense of self. She never wanted to have to rely on a man again . . . and yet Damon was dependable. She knew she could trust him. He wasn't going to belittle her yearning for education, her efforts around the house, or her looks. He would give her everything, and expect everything in return.

A fair deal, but not one she could fulfill. Because now she knew that the one thing he couldn't give her were guarantees—that he would live, that they would be happy together forever. She could marry him if they were only friends, joined together because of the children, but she knew he wouldn't settle for simple friendship. And she wasn't willing to risk more.

She met her sister's steady gaze. "I would trust Damon with my life, but I can't trust him, or *anyone*, with my heart."

There was a flash of undefined emotion in Brionney's eyes. "Damon's fall was an accident," she said, accentuating each word. "He's not like Riley. Riley chose to drive off that cliff."

The old pain surged through Mickelle. How had her husband committed suicide when their lives were just getting back on track? She knew the question would never be answered, not in this life. Over the months, she thought she had learned to live with his choice, but maybe she was wrong.

She turned back to the children. "Come on, guys. Belle, go tell your dad good-bye. You and Tanner can stay over at my house tonight."

"Can you drive?" Worry etched lines across Brionney's brow.

Mickelle lowered her voice. "You tell Damon I took them, okay? I'll be fine as long as I don't have to see him tonight."

"All right. But promise me you'll stop if anything starts to happen—right in the middle of the street if you have to."

"I promise."

Looking only partially satisfied, Brionney headed down the hall with the children. Only Bryan stayed behind.

"Don't you want to see Damon?" Mickelle asked, remembering how pale and silent he had been earlier. She laid an arm over his shoulder.

Bryan shook his head. "Naw, I don't want to see him. I mean, I'm glad he's going to be okay, but I don't even like the guy."

"Bryan!"

"It's true!" He shrugged and walked away.

Mickelle watched him, wondering if he really didn't like Damon or if he was putting on an act.

Like you? an inner voice mocked.

Mickelle didn't have an answer.

CHAPTER 3

When Mickelle awoke the next morning, her thoughts immediately went to Damon. A quick call to the hospital assured her he was fine. "In fact, he's being released as soon as the doctor signs him out," the nurse told her.

She digested that information slowly. Of course, she had known Damon would be released today, but how would he get home? *I should pick him up,* she thought, but decided to call Jesse instead. Since today was Saturday, Brionney could stay with their five children, while he escorted Damon home. With any luck, she could have him swing by and collect Tanner and Belle first. That way she wouldn't have to face Damon until Monday morning when he brought Belle on his way to work.

Mickelle surveyed her small kitchen. The walls were painted white, with only a few inexpensive crafts adorning them, and the curtains were ones she had made when she was first married. The bright blue had faded to a dusty color and the dust had made permanent stains on the material. The counter was patterned yellow on white—pale enough to coordinate with almost anything, but utterly lacking in imagination. The square table, atop the beige, vinyl-tiled floor, was small and worn; the bar even smaller, barely long enough to fit three tall stools. The fourth stool, where Riley had sat, had always been positioned on the opposite side of the counter where the drawers were located. *Him against us,* she couldn't help thinking, although she knew he had sat there only to make more space.

Yeah, for himself. The thought was bitter.

She had stored Riley's stool in the basement because it was in the way, and now they used the table, often bringing the other stools around it to make extra seats for Damon and his children.

Throwing her hands up at this train of thought, Mickelle headed for the basement, where only last week Damon had helped her move the television set. Her father and brother-in-law Joe had framed and finished a TV room for her this past month. She didn't have the money for it, but her father had insisted on providing everything. She was very grateful to have the upstairs living room free of the noise and mess a television generated. Of course the carpet in the living room still needed replacing, and the curio cabinet where she kept her collection of roses begged for repair, but those things could wait—would have to wait until she could afford them.

Damon could afford them.

She sighed. Marrying Damon for his money was not an option.

Unbidden, a vision of the ring he had given her flashed across her mind. It was only when she had arrived home last night that she realized the ring was still on her finger. Tanner had seen her staring at it, and while the other children scrambled out of the back seat, he stayed in his place in the front.

"So Belle gave you the ring," he had said.

Mickelle had felt herself flush. "Yes, I forgot I had it. I should have given it back to your father."

"Why? He bought it for you."

"Because I can't marry him."

Tanner's face became solemn. "Because of us?"

"Goodness, no!" Mickelle touched him lightly on the arm. "Tanner, you're an admirable young man, and I'm glad my boys have you to look up to. And Belle, well, she's the daughter I never had. The reason I can't marry your father is between him and me. You and I will always be friends."

He gazed at her for a long moment. "I don't think it's between him at all," he said slowly. He pushed open the door and climbed out of the car before adding, "But I'm glad we're still friends."

Noise from the television brought Mickelle back to the present. She had arrived in the basement family room, where all four children stared at the blaring set with a rapt expression, even Tanner who had claimed to be too old for cartoons. Bryan, Belle, and Tanner sat on the long couch; it was the only furniture in the room besides the TV set. Belle lay with her head against her brother's arm, clutching her special brown teddy bear that Mickelle had retrieved along with pajamas and a change of clothes from their house the night before. Jeremy sprawled on the floor, a few Star Wars action figures forgotten in his hands.

"Hi kids," she said brightly. The only one who noticed her was Tanner. He nudged Belle, and the little girl jumped off the couch to hug Mickelle.

"I like those pajamas." Belle ran her small hand over the dark blue velour of Mickelle's outfit. "It's soft and snugly."

"They're warm," Mickelle said. She had purchased the lounge wear only last week on clearance at Shopko because they were comfortable enough to wear to bed, but modest enough in case she was still wearing them when Damon came in to drop off Belle in the mornings. She had even seen women wearing similar velour outfits in the nice restaurants where Damon had taken them to eat.

Belle's eyes wandered back to the TV. She sank to the carpet next to Jeremy.

"I'm making breakfast," Mickelle announced loudly, "and then Uncle Jesse's coming to get Tanner and Belle." At the mention of food, her sons glanced up.

"Can we have pancakes, Mom?" Jeremy asked.

"I think I can manage that."

Bryan regarded her for a moment without speaking before letting his attention drift back to the TV. His color had returned to normal today, but his eyes seemed haunted.

Sighing, Mickelle trooped back up the stairs. She hated the television set, and in the past month had stopped allowing the children to watch it except for Saturday-morning cartoons and an hour or so on Friday or Saturday nights. Riley would never have permitted her to limit their watching, but she was glad she had. The boys' grades were higher than they had ever been and their chores were getting done.

I wonder if Riley would at least approve of the results, she wondered. The thought was recurrent. Often she would ponder what her husband would have thought about this or that; more often than not, she didn't know. For the life of her, she couldn't say why it even mattered. How long would it be until she didn't wonder? The funny thing was that she knew exactly how Damon would react, what he would say about children and television; but not what the man to whom she had been married for over fourteen years would think.

Pushing the thought aside, she lifted the phone to call her brother-in-law.

"Sure, I'll pick him up," Jesse agreed immediately. "I'll just give him a call and see when he's being released." Relieved, Mickelle began mixing her pancake batter.

She had just finished cooking the first stack of pancakes when the doorbell rang. "Kids!" she yelled down the stairs. "Come up and eat fast! Uncle Jesse's here to pick up Belle and Tanner. Hurry kids, your dad's waiting at the hospital!"

She paused at the top of the stairs until she heard the blare of the TV fall silent. The children came tromping up the stairs, still in their pajamas. "Oh well, Jesse'll have to wait," she muttered.

"He can eat some pancakes," Jeremy suggested.

With the spatula in hand, she went down the narrow hall that bordered the living room. Once, the door had opened directly onto the living room, but someone had added a short wall between the door and the living room, making a small but adequate entryway. She enjoyed the added privacy, although it made the living room somewhat smaller.

The smile froze on her face when she opened the door and saw Damon, dressed in black pants and a gray and black long-sleeved polo that emphasized his yellow hair. She stared, drinking in his presence, happy to see that apart from being slightly pasty, he appeared all right. "But you're . . . how . . . ?"

He smiled easily, his eyes roaming over her face, traveling the length of her lounge outfit. Suddenly she was sure the pants were too tight and revealing, though the shirt was decidedly a little large. Why hadn't she asked who was at the door before opening? She vowed to have a peephole installed as soon as she could afford it.

"I threatened them with unlawful confinement if they didn't let me out," Damon explained, a teasing lilt to his voice. "I actually feel pretty good. They wanted me to wait for someone to pick me up, but

I just called a taxi. I was going home first to get my car, and then to come get the kids, but I figured I'm not quite up to driving."

"Well, come on in," Mickelle invited, waving the spatula. "You should sit down. The kids were going to eat breakfast, but they can just go with you. I'm sure they won't miss my pancakes."

"Blueberry?" Damon asked, stepping into the entryway next to her, where it was suddenly more cramped than it had been before. "I wouldn't want to deprive them of that. Belle talks a lot about your pancakes. Maybe I could ask my taxi driver to wait."

"Taxi . . . ?" She stared over his shoulder where the taxi waited at the curb. "Goodness, let's just pay the man off. I can take you home." She could have kicked herself as the instinctive frugality tumbled from her lips.

He gave a self-deprecating smile. "Well, the problem is, I don't have any cash on me. I don't usually carry it in my swimming trunks, and Jesse brought me some clothes last night, but not my wallet. I told the guy I'd pay him when I got home."

Mickelle didn't hide her exasperation. "If you had just stayed put at the hospital you wouldn't be having this problem. Jesse was coming to pick you up."

"Jesse? Not you?"

She didn't answer his question, but handed him the spatula and pushed him toward the kitchen. "Go sit down while I talk to the taxi driver." Grabbing her purse from the hall closet, Mickelle sped out the door, down the cement stairs on her tiny porch, and over to the curb.

"He'll be staying here," she told the man. "How much does he owe you?"

Mickelle paid the driver and walked slowly back to the house, her anger growing. How dare he come here when she hadn't asked him! How dare he be so handsome and nice? Not to mention terribly rich, *and* the father of two great kids. Would he demand an explanation of her refusal? What could she say when she didn't understand it herself?

She was halfway up the stairs before the attack hit, abruptly and without warning. She slumped to the middle stair, clutching her chest and closing her eyes tight against the terror. Her heart pounded as though she were running at full speed.

This is Damon's fault! she told herself silently. *His fault, his fault.* She clung to the words as though they were the only thing keeping her afloat in an ocean of fear.

The next thing she knew, comforting arms had encircled her. For a moment, she resisted, then let herself relax against his chest.

Damon made a noise in his throat. "I'm sorry, Mickelle. I know yesterday wasn't easy for you, but it's going to be okay. Whatever happens, I will always be here for you. Understand? I don't want to take more than you are willing to give." He wiped the tears gently from her face.

She didn't reply, but after a long time her trembling gradually ceased. She became conscious of his closeness: the aroma of his after-shave, the familiar scent of his body that was his alone, the strength and warmth of his embrace. For a moment all was right with her world. He wasn't questioning her motives, or demanding anything. This she could deal with.

Then why the lurking feeling of disappointment?

Taking a deep breath, Mickelle straightened and his arms released her. "Thank you," she said, not meeting his gaze.

His hand reached to touch her chin, as though to force her to look at him, then paused as he reconsidered. Finally, he let it drop. "You're welcome."

"The pancakes . . ." Mickelle bolted to her feet, still feeling faint.

"Whoa, careful. Tanner's taking care of them. Don't worry about it. We've made pancakes a time or two at our house. He can handle it."

Sure enough, at the kitchen table everyone was eating happily, except Tanner who was at the stove with Mickelle's spatula. Belle laughed when she saw Mickelle. "Tanner makes pancakes almost as good as you."

"They *are* hers," Tanner inserted.

"No they aren't, you're making them!"

Tanner rolled his eyes, while Damon laughed. Mickelle felt the smile return to her own face. No pressure here.

"So does this mean we can go swimming today?" Jeremy said to Damon.

Mickelle tensed but Damon didn't even hesitate before replying. "Not today, Jeremy. I'm not up to facing water again so soon."

"It's like a horse," Jeremy insisted. "You have to get back on."

"I will. I will. But not today."

"I'm going to get a horse," Belle announced. "Well, not right now, but in a month or two. Daddy says I've been responsible about telling people where I'm going, so I'm not grounded from having a horse anymore."

"Almost not grounded," Damon corrected. "I must be quite convinced."

Belle's lower lip protruded becomingly, but she didn't argue the discrepancy. That told Mickelle she was growing up.

In the first few weeks of school Belle had twice gone somewhere after class without telling her father, solely for the purpose of upsetting his dating schedule because she hadn't approved of his date. But that had been before Mickelle had become her sitter, and Belle had been a perfect angel since. She had even encouraged Mickelle to go out with her father.

The breakfast was nearly over when Jesse arrived on Mickelle's doorstep. His short, dark hair was ruffled and his brown eyes worried. "I called the hospital, but they said Damon already checked out—alone."

"He's here," Mickelle said sheepishly. "He took a taxi, if you can believe it. I'm sorry, I should have called."

Damon appeared in the kitchen doorway, looking unquestionably tired. "Hey, Jesse. I thought I heard your voice. Mickelle told me you were going to pick me up. If you don't mind, I'd like to take you up on that. The kids and I have imposed on Mickelle enough for one day."

Mickelle wanted to say it wasn't an imposition, but found it difficult to think coherently with Damon's amber-brown eyes staring at her. Besides, it *was* an imposition. She wouldn't have experienced another panic attack if he had stayed where he belonged.

"To tell you the truth, I am kind of tired," Damon continued. "I might not be in on Monday after all."

"Just so's you're still here." Jesse clapped Damon on the back. "I'm glad you're all right."

"Me too." Damon raised his voice. "Kids, let's get going."

"But I'm still in my PJs," Belle protested.

"So? You can change when you get home."

Belle gave her father a disgusted stare, but she obediently picked up her bear and the little pink overnight bag she had brought from home. She grinned at Mickelle. "Bye. I'll see you on Monday!"

"I'll see you." Mickelle turned to Tanner. "You too. I'll try to be on time when I pick you up from school." Belle attended first grade at Forbes Elementary in American Fork with Jesse and Brionney's daughter, but Tanner attended high school in Highland, close to where the Wolfe family lived. He took the bus there each morning after Damon left for Mickelle's with Belle, and then Mickelle picked him up after school. This schedule would only last for a few more months until he received his driver's license. After the accident where he had slammed into Mickelle's car, the juvenile judge had threatened to delay his driving by as much as a year, but when Tanner had fixed Mickelle's car himself, the judge had reduced his sentence to three months. Since he turned sixteen in November, that meant he would be behind the wheel in February.

Jesse, Tanner, and Belle filtered out the door, with Damon bringing up the rear. Bryan and Jeremy yelled good-bye from the kitchen, where they were still downing blueberry pancakes.

From her porch, Mickelle watched Damon leave, his body moving much slower than usual. She hoped he would go right home to bed, and made a mental note to ask Brionney to check up on him. Then she remembered the ring.

"Oh wait!"

He looked up from the front walk expectantly, almost eagerly. "Yes?"

"You, uh, forgot something. I'll go get it." She turned to go back inside, glad to free herself from his intent gaze.

"I can get it Monday." His voice was soft and his face strained with weariness.

"It's the ring," she blurted.

A smile came to his lips, hovering as though unsure whether or not it would stay. "I was wondering if Belle lost it." He didn't sound as though that was important.

"It belongs in a safe," she replied a little sharply.

He looked at her for a long moment. "No, Mickelle, it belongs with you . . . like my heart."

"I don't . . . I can't . . . yesterday . . ." she babbled.

"Keep it." Then his smile grew bigger, and his eyes twinkled. "You're going to wear it someday anyway."

"What!" She didn't know whether to be touched or angry at his audacity. The latter seemed the safest, and she might as well choose it. "I told you how I felt yesterday."

He shook his head. "No, you didn't. And your beautiful eyes didn't agree with what little your equally beautiful mouth *did* say."

Okay, now I'm really angry! Of course, it was hard to be angry at a man who said you had a beautiful mouth and beautiful eyes. She glared at him anyway, but he turned on his heel and strode toward Jesse's truck, where the others were waiting.

Mickelle watched them drive away, her heart beating erratically. This time it didn't have anything to do with a panic attack.

"Who does he think he is?" she said aloud. "He is so annoying."

Intent on her thoughts, she didn't hear Jeremy open the door behind her until he spoke. "Mom, Brenda's on the phone. I told her you were outside, but she says she just *has* to talk to you." He thrust the phone into her hand.

Mickelle lifted it to her ear and spoke. "Hi."

"Hi? That's all you have to say? Tonight's the night, don't you remember? I am so excited that you're finally going."

Mickelle didn't know what Brenda was talking about. "Uh, tonight might not be good," she stalled.

"What? But you *told* me you'd go! I simply can't go alone—that looks too needy. Of course I *am* needy, but I don't want them to know that. *If* there's anyone there to impress in the first place, which I'm hoping there will be. You simply have to go!"

Now Mickelle remembered—faintly—what she had promised. Brenda, a new ward member and also a divorced mother of four daughters, had asked her to attend a single adult activity nearly three weeks ago. A dance, to be exact. Mickelle had planned to invite Damon, but yesterday's events had driven the thought from her mind. Now there was no way she could ask him.

"I can't go," she said flatly.

"But you said you would," Brenda wailed. "I got a baby-sitter and *everything*. Besides, I hear there are some new men, and it would be nice to meet them *before* they're married."

"I don't want to get married."

"No, but I do. Not everyone has a handsome millionaire widower wooing her. Is it him? Is he why you won't go tonight?"

"Damon and I are just friends."

"That's not what you said last time. But if he's not a keeper, you may as well toss him back into the pot for the rest of us to fight over."

Mickelle was silent a moment, not at all appreciating this mental picture. The truth was that she and Damon *were* more than friends, and had been since a week after they had met. But all that was over now, especially since he was so infuriatingly sure of himself.

Well, I'll show him! "I'll go," Mickelle said.

"Oh, thank you, thank you," Brenda gushed. "My future children thank you."

"Future children? You've already got four. How many do you want?"

"At least three or four more. I love kids."

And she did. Brenda was one of the most attentive and thorough mothers Mickelle had ever known. When her husband had begun stepping out on her and refused joint counseling, she had finally gained the courage to leave him. She had confessed to Mickelle that she had done it for the children. "I couldn't allow them to think that such behavior was appropriate," she had said. "I didn't want my daughters to endure what I've endured."

Now, two years after her divorce, Brenda was happier than she had been in her entire life. She worked as a general building contractor and provided for her daughters better than her husband with his fancy corporate job ever had. But she was still searching for the perfect eternal mate. "I'm going to be darned sure he's the right man this time," she had assured Mickelle. "And he'd better love children."

Mickelle had also once entertained the thought of having more children, possibly with Damon. But now . . . She forced her thoughts back to her friend.

"I'll pick you up," Brenda finished.

Mickelle hung up the phone after agreeing to be ready at six-thirty for the dance. She knew that for Brenda, who was notoriously late for everything not related to her job or her children, that meant at least six-forty.

Humming, she made her way back to the kitchen, wondering if there were any more pancakes left. Another thought also entered her mind. How would Damon react if he knew where she was going?

Well, she certainly wasn't going to tell him.

CHAPTER 4

Damon arrived at his home in Alpine, where Tanner and Belle promptly urged him to bed. He compromised by lying on the couch in the game room, in front of the wide-screen TV. There he could rest and keep an eye on Tanner and his friends as they played pool.

A vision of Mickelle sobbing on the porch tormented him. He had comforted her and had promised friendship, hoping that this would release her from the pressure she was obviously experiencing. The plan had worked, at least until he had told her to keep the ring.

Had he had done the right thing? Would she be angry at him for not allowing her to return the diamond? Probably. But everything he had told her was true. He only hoped his words didn't trigger another panic attack.

He had questioned Belle privately during breakfast to find out where the ring was, and had been content for Mickelle to keep it. The diamond's heart shape represented his love for her. His heart. As long as she didn't give it back he had a chance to convince her to keep it forever. Apparently, it would take more time than he expected, but he wasn't going to desist. Bridges that withstood time sometimes took years to build; though he hoped he wouldn't have to wait that long.

He worried about her until he fell asleep. When he awoke it was dark outside and Tanner and his friends were gone. Belle was gazing down at him with a worried expression, her face only inches away from his own. He blinked in surprise.

"Dinner's been ready for a long time," she informed him gravely, adjusting the brown teddy bear and the plastic horse in her arms.

"But you just keep on sleeping."

"What?" He looked at the wall clock. "Seven already?"

"Brionney's in the kitchen." Belle thumbed over her shoulder. "She said for me to leave you alone, but I didn't want you to starve. You didn't eat lunch, either."

Giving her a smile, Damon gathered her into his arms. She sighed with contentment. "Did you eat lunch?" he asked. Cammy, their part-time cook wasn't on duty today. In fact, she had recently married and given up her room in the basement to move into an apartment in Provo, where her husband was going to school. Now she came only on weekdays to make dinner, which she left in the oven or the refrigerator. Since Damon and the kids had been eating with Mickelle, they usually had a lot of leftovers.

Belle made a face. "Tanner cooked me a corndog in the microwave. I don't think I like those anymore. But I ate it."

"Good girl." Damon pulled her close, breathing in the scent of her hair. It badly needed combing, but it smelled clean. Mickelle must have given her a bath the night before.

Sorrow hit him deep inside his chest as it always did when he thought about how desperately Belle needed a mother. He did as well as a father could, but the little things often escaped him—the how-to of braids and ribbons, the nuances of dress. And what would he do when she began dating? When she had problems at school with her girlfriends that were just too tender to share with a man—even a father? He ached to think that Belle wouldn't have a woman to whom she could turn.

Mickelle, she'll have Mickelle.

He held onto this hope, not only for his daughter but for himself. Mickelle filled his life when he hadn't even known there was anything missing. He stifled a heartfelt sigh.

As if she sensed his mood, Belle's tiny arms went around his neck, evoking a warm feeling of fatherly love. She was a wonderful child. He hadn't done so shabbily after all!

"I'll go tell Brionney you're awake." Belle's voice lowered conspiratorially. "And don't tell her I came in here, okay? She didn't want me to, but I had to make sure you were breathing."

"All right, Belle," Damon agreed, wincing at her obvious preoccupation. He silently thanked God that he had not drowned.

Funny how things can change so quickly, he thought. A diagnosis of cancer and Charlotte was ripped away from him; a slip in the pool and the walls around Mickelle's heart were firmly back in place. But he would not sit around and mourn yesterday. He was going to talk to Mickelle; urge her to visit her doctor, or to resume seeing the grief counselor she had talked with after Riley's death. Most of all, he would be her friend, no matter how much self-control or time it took.

He dragged himself to a sitting position on the couch, reached for the phone on the side table by the lamp, and punched in Mickelle's number. While he waited for someone to pick up, he gingerly felt the lump on his head. It ached painfully, but he was no longer dizzy.

"Hello?"

Damon recognized Bryan's voice. Of everyone in the house, Damon had hoped not to talk to him. Despite repeated attempts to befriend the boy, Bryan refused to respond to his efforts. Damon was at the end of his wits trying to reach him, though they had found some connection when they played basketball or soccer together at Mickelle's. Other than this, Bryan seemed to want nothing to do with him.

"Hi, Bry. Damon here."

"Oh, hi."

"How're you doing?"

"Fine."

"Good. Is your mom there?"

"Nope. She went out."

"Out?" Damon was disturbed at the hint of smugness in his reply.

"Yeah."

"Could you tell me where?"

"I don't know, some dance."

A dance? That didn't make sense. The feeling he had received from Mickelle was that she wasn't ready for any relationship, not just one with him. "Uh, who'd she go with?" Damon tried to make his voice casual.

"A friend, I guess. I didn't see her leave. They picked her up." Bryan's voice had a tinge of amusement now, and Damon wished he could ask to talk to Jeremy. The younger child would shed a considerable amount of light on the subject. Had Mickelle actually gone with a man?

He grimaced at the thought. When they had first started dating, she had also been dating a baby-faced cop, some years her junior. She had stopped dating him soon after meeting Damon, even calling off their last date in favor of one with him. That seemed like a lifetime ago now.

He did some fast thinking and said, "Is there a place I can reach her?"

"Some church. Not sure where."

"Oh." That explained it. The only dance he was aware of tonight at a church was the multi-stake singles' dance. As one of the most eligible LDS bachelors in Utah Valley, he had been invited, of course, but hadn't given a second thought to attending. Not with marriage to Mickelle already on his agenda.

All at once, the relief he felt at knowing where Mickelle was changed to a feeling of consternation. At that dance there would be a number of men searching for spouses, and Mickelle was a beautiful, funny, intelligent woman who was more vulnerable than she liked to admit.

One thing was certain: Damon wasn't getting much help from Bryan. "Well, thanks, Bry. See you Monday."

"Yeah, okay."

The phone went dead. Damon tried not to be angry or hurt by either Bryan's or Mickelle's actions, but the image of her dancing the night away in someone else's arms was almost too much to bear.

"I'll go myself," he said suddenly.

"You're not going anywhere," came a voice from the door.

He glanced up to see Brionney carrying a steaming plate of food on a tray. "Oh, hi. Belle told me you were here."

"And I told her to stay out of here. You need your rest."

"I'm fine," he countered tersely.

"That lump on your head doesn't look so good. And then there's that small matter of you almost drowning."

"Okay, so I'm not exactly fine, but I'm still going."

She shoved the plate into his hands. "Eat," she ordered. "And tell me where it is you want to go."

He stared at her, unwilling to admit anything.

"Better hurry. I left the twins in the kitchen, and any minute now they might find their way into your study. They know how to climb."

Defeated, Damon swallowed the food he had shoveled into his mouth. "A dance. I'm bored and I need to go to a dance."

"What?" She spied the phone next to him on the couch and scooped it up, pushing the redial button. "Hello, Bryan. It's Aunt Brionney. Is your mom there? No? Where? Oh, I see. No, just tell her I called."

Brionney tossed the phone onto the couch. "You are so transparent."

He shrugged and continued eating. "I'm going."

"No you aren't, because you need to rest for at least two days, doctor's orders. There's too much risk of blacking out while you're driving."

"You drive then."

"What about the twins? Besides, I have to get home to my family."

"I'll take a taxi."

"What about Belle? She needs you now."

He knew that, but . . . "I have to talk to Mickelle."

"So. There's always tomorrow."

"Tomorrow may be too late."

"You can't force her," Brionney stated. "Give her some space. When she realizes what she's missing, she'll come around. You certainly won't help anything by showing up tonight. She told me today that she just can't go through what she did when Riley died. You need to prove to her that you can take care of yourself so you *will* be around. She needs reassurance; guarantees."

Damon froze. "I have more money than I could use in a hundred lifetimes," he said in a choked voice. "I can give her anything she could ever want. Except that. Nobody can give her that."

Brionney reached out to pat him on the hand. "I know. And she knows, too. But it's hard to tell that to her heart. I think this is something only time can heal. She has to love enough to be willing to take the risk."

"Are you saying she doesn't love me?"

"I'm only saying that right now the idea of *not* loving you seems safer than loving and losing again. But don't feel so bad—this actually shows she cares. If she didn't, she might just marry you for your money."

"I'd settle for that, at this point."

A smile played on Brionney's lips. "No you wouldn't."

Damon settled back onto the couch, pondering his options. Brionney was right about everything. All his instincts told him to go after Mickelle and fight for the woman he loved, but Brionney's womanly intuitions had never led him astray. Maybe he could use a different tactic. "Could I at least send flowers?" he asked, rubbing his jaw.

Brionney nodded approvingly. "Now you're talking. I'll go get you the phone book."

CHAPTER 5

Mickelle spent the first few moments at the dance hoping to see Damon walk through the door. The idea was ludicrous, because if he had, she would have been furious at him for not taking care of himself. None of her feelings made sense, but she was not going to analyze them now.

Since Damon left her house that morning she had been free from panic attacks. She hoped they had been triggered only by his accident and would no longer plague her. If not, she would have to return to the doctor, much as she disliked admitting defeat.

She sighed loudly.

"Oh, I know just what you mean!" Brenda whispered emphatically, running a hand through her mid-length brown hair. Her small green eyes gleamed with excitement.

They were siting in a prominent place by the door to the cultural hall where they could see everyone who entered. And *be* seen. Mickelle felt awkward, as though she had suddenly been thrust back into high school. How did Brenda handle this? Mickelle began to wish she hadn't come. *I did it just to prove I can be without Damon,* she admitted. And he wasn't even here to see it.

Mickelle sighed again.

"Don't just sigh about it, go meet him!"

"What?"

Brenda's attention was on a man who had paused at the entrance, head moving slightly as he surveyed the group. He was drop-dead gorgeous, with sleek black hair combed neatly to the side, perfect facial features tanned to a light bronze, and blue eyes that could rival

Brionney's for their unusual beauty. Except for his average height, his figure was also the epitome of a perfect male, with broad shoulders tapering to a trim waist, and arms strong with sculpted muscles. His short-sleeved polo was open slightly at the neck, showing a tuft of dark curls that somehow reminded Mickelle of Damon.

"He is one good-looking guy," she admitted.

Brenda giggled. "And guess what? I know him! I've told him all about you and he wants to meet you!"

"Me?" Mickelle was confused, but before she could protest more, Brenda dragged her from the metal chair and propelled her in the man's direction. Everything was happening too fast.

"Colton!" Brenda called. Mickelle tried to stop their movement, but Brenda was substantially heavier. Instead, she struggled simply to maintain her balance.

The man called Colton caught sight of them and smiled. "Hello, Brenda," he said, his blue eyes gleaming like sapphires under water.

"Colton Scofield, meet Mickelle Hansen. Mickelle, this is Colton. We met at the last activity."

"Hi, Mickelle," Colton took her hand, and inclined his head. "I've heard so much about you."

"You have?" Mickelle cast a bewildered glance at Brenda. The women hadn't known each other long, so how on earth had she told him so much?

He saw her glance. "Oh, not just from Brenda here, but from another friend of mine in your ward. She works at the hospital."

"Oh." Mickelle still didn't know why they would be discussing her.

"It's because of my job, you see," Colton confessed, flashing her a brilliant smile that took her breath away—despite her determination not to be impressed by his appearance. "I work for a life insurance company, checking out cases to eliminate fraud."

Mickelle tried to hide her grimace. Her only experience with a life insurance company was when Riley's insurance had denied her benefits because of the suicide policy. Three weeks. He had killed himself three weeks before the suicide clause on his policy would have expired. The resulting lack of insurance had forced her to struggle for months to make ends meet, until she began watching

Damon's children. She knew he paid her more than she deserved, but she had accepted the offer to be at home when her children might need her. Eventually she intended to complete college and find a job, perhaps teaching somewhere.

Colton's hand rose to her shoulder, sending warmth throughout her body at the unexpected contact. "I know about your case. And I thought it darned unfair. If you want I can look into it. I don't work for the same company, but I bet I know someone who does."

Mickelle shrugged. "My father checked into it. I'm sure he did everything that could be done."

"Sometimes it helps if you know someone." Colton's smile was warm and full of confidence, and Mickelle felt a burgeoning hope. There was a deep dimple in his left cheek that was extremely attractive. She wanted to keep making him smile so that she could study it.

"Well, I suppose it can't hurt, if you don't mind."

"I don't mind at all. Now, would you like to dance?"

"Sure."

Mickelle let him lead her to the dance floor, wondering why he would pick her over all the many beautiful women in the room. She glanced over her shoulder at Brenda, who gave her the thumbs-up signal. She did not seem the least bit depressed that Colton had chosen Mickelle for a partner.

"Do you know Brenda well?" she asked as she began dancing, feeling awkward again. How long had it been since she had actually danced with a man? Much too long. She tried to copy the other dancers without being too obvious about it, but her movements were jerky.

"Not really." Unlike her, Colton was a beautiful dancer; she could have enjoyed just watching him move. "I met her at the last activity. Another time I went out to lunch with a group of singles, and she was there on her lunch hour. That woman has so much energy, I get exhausted just watching her."

Mickelle chuckled. "She does at that. But she's a wonderful person."

"Pretty, too," he agreed. "But not really my type." The remark seemed to be a compliment, although Mickelle wasn't sure why.

The music was louder than she had expected, and Mickelle fell silent, except for a few exchanged comments with Colton. She found herself enjoying the rhythm as she loosened up and her movements became more natural.

The music changed to a slow song, and Colton moved closer, opening his arms in an endearing gesture that Mickelle couldn't refuse. She nodded and brought one hand to his shoulder and placed the other in his. Colton's hand slid around her back, pulling her closer, but not uncomfortably so. He smiled so engagingly that she forgot to be nervous.

"You have any children?" she asked, glad they could talk now without the loud music.

"No." His voice sounded regretful. "I mean, I did, but they . . . uh, died. It's a bit of a story that I won't go into right now, but after my sons died my wife and I broke up. Losing our sons was just too much for our relationship."

"I'm sorry," Mickelle said, mentally kicking herself. Trust her to choose the one topic he was sensitive about.

"So am I, but we go on. It's been a long time—ten years."

"And you're still single?" That surprised her. She imagined that he would have a whole entourage of women suitors.

"Yeah. I've dated a few women, but haven't found the right one yet. What about you? Do you have any children?"

"Two boys."

"Sounds fun." Since Brenda had warned her about single men and their aversion to children that weren't theirs, his wide grin took her by surprise. "Do they like soccer?"

"You kidding? Of course they do. Basketball, too."

"Can't help you there. I was just a bit too short for the basketball coach, but soccer, that's what I was good at. Even played on my college team. Thought about going professional, but decided to serve a mission instead."

"Where'd you go?"

"Canada."

The talk drifted from one subject to another, with Colton constantly asking questions about her life, and then sharing a story from his own. They had a lot in common. He loved soccer, cookies, and Chinese food just like she did, and he was really interested in the boys and in her extended family.

"So your husband didn't have any family?" he asked when they were well into the second slow song.

"Not really. His parents died early, and he was never close to his siblings. They don't live in Utah."

"But you are close to yours, I take it?"

"Yes. My family's great."

He frowned briefly, but it was gone so quickly Mickelle though she had imagined it.

Suddenly, Mickelle noticed that they were much closer than they had been, so close their bodies brushed occasionally. She took a discreet step back, not wanting him to mistake her intentions.

What were her intentions?

She didn't know, but she had enjoyed herself thoroughly from the moment she had met Colton. He was funny, nice, and *so* good-looking. She admitted to herself that his appearance was the real reason she was attracted to him. Never in her life had such a beautiful man paid her so much attention.

Except Damon, of course. But Damon was handsome in a much more rugged sense, and his face had sharper planes. By contrast, Colton's good looks were of fairytale proportions. Not to mention that there was none of the tension she had felt with Damon since his accident.

Colton pulled her close again. "I've never met anyone like you, Mickelle," he said in her ear. "I know that sounds like a line, but I don't know how else to put it." His breath was warm in her hair and smelled slightly of mint.

She didn't know what to say except that she was flattered. Colton didn't seem the type to pursue a commitment, especially with a woman like her—who was too flabby in certain places. Maybe this flowing black skirt and matching blue-and-black jacket became her more than she knew. Or maybe it was the lighting.

You're crazy, she thought.

But she had to admit there was something magical about the night. Her problems with Damon and his proposal were forgotten, and she had become the princess in a fairytale. Tonight she would play make-believe; tomorrow, she would return to her life.

"Would you like a drink?" Colton asked. He didn't release her, though the music had changed.

"Sure," she replied breathlessly, though there was no reason to be winded.

With a hand under her elbow, he led her to the table covered with refreshments, and poured her a drink. "Good punch," he stated, his blue eyes never leaving hers.

Brenda broke in on them. "Can I talk to you for a minute, Mickelle?" Then to Colton, "I promise I'll bring her right back." She practically dragged Mickelle out the door and down the hallway near the bathrooms. "So, how's it going?"

"Fine," Mickelle said, faking nonchalance. "He's a nice guy."

Brenda appeared eager. "Any electricity?"

"Not that I noticed. I mean, he's really good-looking. It's hard to see beyond that."

"Just watching him makes me breathless!" Brenda agreed, green eyes sparkling. "What does he say about kids?"

"Likes them, I think. He had some, but they died."

"I heard that, but there does seem to be a mystery about the situation. He hasn't told anyone the details."

Mickelle was surprised. She had thought that Brenda, with her finger on the pulse of Mormon single life, would know. "Well, it must be painful for him."

"I think he really likes you."

Mickelle shrugged, though she felt pleased.

"Why aren't you more excited?" Brenda asked, arching one eyebrow. "This doesn't have anything to do with that millionaire, does it?"

"No." But even as she said it Mickelle knew that Damon *was* the reason she wasn't enjoying herself fully. She kept expecting him to appear. She even felt guilty, as though she were going behind his back.

We've only dated five or six weeks, she rationalized. *He doesn't own me.*

And she didn't owe him anything, other than the truth, and she had tried to give him that yesterday.

"Oh, look! Here comes Colton!"

Mickelle saw Colton emerge from the cultural hall, head moving as though searching for someone. His eyes brightened when he spied Mickelle.

"He's looking for you!" Brenda squealed in her ear. "You go, girl!"

Mickelle had already resigned herself to finding Colton dancing with some other lucky woman by the time she returned, and was surprised to have him come after her. She grinned at Brenda. "Well, this Cinderella is going back to the ball."

She danced with Colton for the next half hour, marveling at how well they seemed to get along. He was funny, gracious, and listened attentively when she spoke.

"This is really fun," he said, when they stopped for another drink. "Listen, would you excuse me a minute? I saw someone I need to talk with. Do you mind?"

"Of course not."

Mickelle knew he wouldn't be back. Her Cinderella act was over, but she had enjoyed every minute of her time with the good-looking prince. Even so, she turned down another man who asked her to dance. "I'm sorry, I'd love to, but I'm waiting for someone."

To her surprise, Colton returned shortly, carrying a large vase of roses whose petals were a yellow so dark and lustrous they were almost the color of gold. "For you," he said, offering them to her.

"They're beautiful!" She breathed in the luscious fragrance. How could he possibly know how much she loved roses? In her curio cabinet at home she had roses made of everything from metal to wood. She even had a real rose dipped in twenty-four karat gold that Damon had given her shortly after their first kiss. She had been so touched that he knew her well enough to find such a perfect gift— offered without strings.

Tears gathered in Mickelle's eyes, both from the memory of Damon's gift and this new offering from Colton. "How did you know how much I love roses?"

"It just felt right. They're my favorite too."

"But when . . . you didn't have time . . ."

"I ordered them when you went with Brenda earlier. There's this all-night place I know. And then I went out just now in the parking lot to get them from the delivery guy."

Impulsively, Mickelle leaned forward and kissed him on the cheek. "Thank you. You shouldn't have, but thank you."

He grinned. "Beautiful flowers for a beautiful woman."

"Hey, you two!" called Brenda, hurrying over to them. She buried her face in the roses and took a deep breath. "Wonderful! There must be three dozen here." She glared teasingly at Colton. "Where're mine?"

He laughed. "Oops, they haven't delivered them yet."

Brenda rolled her eyes. "Right. Good save, Colton." She sighed. "Anyway, I just called home and my youngest daughter isn't feeling well. I have to go home to be with her."

"Is it bad?" Mickelle asked.

"No, but she needs her mommy. You know how it goes."

"I'm sorry. I know you were looking forward to this dance."

"Oh, don't be," Brenda said flippantly. "See that guy over there?" Mickelle followed her gaze to a group of people talking near the refreshment table, including a dark-haired man Brenda had been dancing with earlier. "He's asked me out for next week, and I really like him. He's a banker. Responsible. Nice-looking, too—he's got that distinguishing sliver at the temple which I find irresistible. Who knows?"

"Well, I guess I have to be going," Mickelle told Colton. "I came with Brenda."

"I could take you home," Colton offered.

"Well, I would hate to impose."

"I wouldn't mind, really. And that way we could dance some more."

"Go ahead, stay," Brenda urged. "There's no reason for both of us to leave early."

"All right, I will."

For the next hour and a half, Mickelle alternately danced with Colton and talked with the other single adults. Many were divorced, others widowed like herself, and a few had never been married. Yet it seemed everyone present had baggage of some sort that set them apart from the other families in the Church. For the first time in a long time she felt welcomed and appreciated—and understood—by an entire group of people.

Mickelle wondered where all her fears had gone. Each time she had thought about Damon since the accident, she had seen his death, but with Colton there was only life. How was she supposed to interpret that?

As the dance ended, her nervousness returned. What did she really know about Colton? He seemed well known and popular in the single arena, but for all she knew, he could be an escaped convict. Her heart constricted, and for a moment, she thought she was going to have a panic attack.

"Is something bothering you?" Colton asked. They were walking toward his low-slung sports car that glowed a brilliant white under the lights in the parking lot.

Mickelle breathed in the smell of the yellow roses in her arms. "Well . . ."

"Tell me. I'm easy."

Mickelle wondered what that meant. "It's just . . . I realized how little I really know you. I mean, no offense, but if a daughter of mine went to a dance—even a church dance—and came home alone with someone she had never met before . . ."

Colton gave a low chuckle. Because of the dark, she could barely see the dimple in his cheek, but he was still gorgeous. "I see what you mean. Good thing you don't have a daughter."

Mickelle started. She had been thinking of Belle when she had spoken, but Colton was right; Belle wasn't her daughter. "I'd like to, though," she told him, without meaning to. "It was the one thing I really regretted with my . . ." She trailed off awkwardly, wishing she had kept quiet.

"I want a little girl, too," Colton said softly. "I always have. There's something special about little girls. And I'll bet any daughter of yours would be extra beautiful."

Mickelle smiled but remained silent. She took a deep breath of the roses in her arms.

"Anyway," Colton continued, taking her elbow. "I've got just the thing for you."

"What?"

"Wait, you'll see." Colton released her arm, unlocked his car door with a beep from his pocket, and opened the passenger side door. After rummaging for a few minutes in the glove compartment, he came up with a small bottle which he offered to Mickelle.

"What is it?" she asked, shifting the vase of roses so that she could take the offering.

"Pepper spray." The light overhead illuminated his face at just the right angle and she could see the endearing dimple again. Whew, he was so gorgeous!

"That way, if I get out of hand—whoosh!" He made a spraying motion.

Mickelle laughed, feeling her immediate worries evaporate. He wouldn't be giving her this, if he was going to attack her. But she shook it just in case, to make sure it was full, and even tested the spray a little while he was occupied arranging the flowers in the back seat.

They arrived home shortly after ten, Mickelle having declined his offer to go out for hot chocolate and pie. She used the boys as an excuse, although the real reason was that she was nervous about being alone with him. If she wasn't ready for a relationship with Damon, she certainly wasn't ready for one with Colton, even if he looked like a prince. Besides, she might never see him after tonight.

He bought me roses! She couldn't imagine him doing that if he didn't plan on calling her. Or would he? Maybe he had money to burn like Damon.

Colton walked her to the door, and her heart thudded dully in her chest. *Please don't try to kiss me*, she thought. If the idea of marrying Damon or being close to him sent her into a panic, how would she react to kissing a near stranger?

Balancing the heavy vase of flowers in one hand, she inserted her key quickly into the door and opened it. Keeping her voice bright, she said, "Good-bye, Colton. It was nice meeting you. Thank you for taking me home."

"I enjoyed tonight." His hand darted out and grabbed hers, holding her in place. Mickelle felt brief panic, and prepared to use the roses as a weapon, but he only planted a soft kiss on her cheek. "I'll check up on that insurance business for you," he promised, going back down the porch stairs, "and let you know."

"Thank you," Mickelle called after him. He held up a hand in farewell as he opened his car door.

The boys were still up, watching television in the basement family room. Mickelle paid the babysitter and walked her to the door. She greeted the boys with hugs and sat down to watch with them for a moment. The room seemed oddly vacant, as though someone was missing.

"Anyone call?" she asked, thinking of Damon.

Bryan didn't take his eyes from the TV. "Nope. No one called."

What had she expected? Mickelle didn't know why she should feel depressed that Damon hadn't called when she had spent all evening with a very nice Prince Charming look-alike.

Later, after saying evening prayer with the boys and sending them to bed, Mickelle went to her room to remove her outfit. In her top drawer where she kept her pajamas, her fingers closed upon the heart-shaped diamond ring Damon had bought for her.

"His heart," she said softly, knowing that was what he had meant the ring to represent.

A vision of him lying lifeless on the cement near his pool shot through her mind. Her breath quickened and her heart pounded wildly. She sank to the bed, squeezing her eyes shut against the sight. He had almost died in front of her very eyes! What if she had arrived too late?

She pulled her pillow over her head and cried.

When she awoke the next morning, Damon's ring was still clutched in her hand.

CHAPTER 6

Early Monday morning Mickelle was up and dressed long before Damon arrived with Belle. She took extra care with her hair, telling herself it was *not* for Damon, but for her own esteem. Besides, even though she wasn't going to marry him, they were still friends, and for reasons she couldn't begin to fathom, she still wanted him to find her attractive.

Damon didn't come into the house, but paused on the porch. His eyes roamed appreciatively over Mickelle. "You look beautiful this morning. And is that a new color of eyeliner?"

She nodding, feeling both pleased and uncomfortable with the compliment. Riley had never complimented her unless he wanted something. "How're you feeling?"

"Good," he said. "Brionney made me stay in bed almost the whole weekend. Great woman, your sister, but she can sure be bossy."

"Well, with five kids it's a matter of protection," Mickelle returned.

"Yes, well, I appreciate her help." For an instant, his amber eyes told her more than he was saying, like how he wished she had been at the house instead of Brionney, and how much he wanted right then to take her in his arms. Then the fleeting look was gone and his face became rigid.

Mickelle averted her gaze.

"So how was your weekend?" he asked, his voice achingly polite. He stared at a place behind her, and she saw that he could see into the kitchen, where the golden roses Colton had given her sat in plain sight next to the sink.

Mickelle felt her face flush. She didn't owe him an explanation for the roses. For all he knew, she had bought them herself—not that she would ever spend so much money on something so temporary. Now, if it were a rose she could keep in her curio cabinet . . .

Her blush deepened as she recalled the golden rose Damon had given her. Of all her roses, she loved that the most, except perhaps for the wooden one Bryan had made her in school.

"That good, huh?" he asked dryly.

She blinked at him in confusion. "What?"

"I asked you how your weekend went and you turned, well, red. Are you all right?" His voice was casual, but underneath she sensed something more.

"I'm fine," she assured him, with a touch of arrogance. She must keep him in his place. "I haven't had a panic attack all weekend."

"It must just be me, then."

Mickelle regarded his familiar face thoughtfully. He had a point.

He glanced again into the kitchen, mouth parted as though to speak, then shook his head and turned to go down the stairs. "Better get to work. See you tonight."

"See you." Mickelle shut the door instead of watching his lean body saunter toward the dark blue Mercedes he customarily drove. She had always loved watching him—but that was before he had almost died.

Behind the closed door, she pondered the cool politeness between them. It was the one result of her refusal that she hadn't counted on. Perhaps she had grown too dependent upon his warm friendship. Would they be able to keep it alive? Or had their friendship died when she rejected the rest of what he offered? The thought cut her to the core.

Mickelle's chest tightened with a familiar onslaught of panic. She walked quickly, almost blindly, to her room, where she sank to her bed and sprawled out with relief. Tears escaped from under her tightly closed lids until her face was wet. But she didn't sob, and she didn't feel like she was dying.

In only a few minutes, Mickelle was able to gain control of her emotions. She splashed her face with water in the bathroom and plodded to the kitchen where the boys and Belle were gathered at the small table, eating a generic bagged version of Fruit Loops. Or rather, the boys were eating. Belle was stringing the round cereal on a piece of green yarn Mickelle recognized as coming from the odds-and-ends drawer.

"I'm making a necklace for my new friend," Belle announced, dimpling with excitement.

"New friend?" Mickelle slid into the last vacant chair.

"Yes." Belle bent back to her task. "We got a new girl in our class. Her name is Jennie Anne, and I'm going to be her assigned buddy."

"When did all this happen?" Mickelle asked.

"Last week."

"I didn't see you with anybody new at recess," Jeremy said. He was in the fourth grade at the school and Mickelle knew he liked to check up on Belle and his cousin Camille, who were in the same class. "Wasn't Jennie Anne there yet?"

Belle's eyes were wistful. "She was, but she was with Morgan. Or it might have been Pamela."

"But don't they usually just assign one helper for every new child?" Mickelle asked.

Belle shrugged. "Yeah, but the others didn't get along."

Mickelle tried not to jump to wrong conclusions, but what was so difficult about this new child that she had already gone through two assigned friends?

"I don't really blame her," Belle added. "At least not for Lorene. She's mean."

Make that three assigned friends, corrected Mickelle.

"And Morgan's not very patient."

"And you are?" Jeremy said with a snort.

"Better than you," Bryan retorted.

Belle held up her chin. "That's right, I am. At least more than Lorene and Morgan and Pamela. Besides, I can help Jennie Anne read because I can read better than anyone in the whole class."

"Jennie Anne can't read?" Mickelle thought that perhaps for the teacher it was convenient to pair the smartest child in the class with the one the furthest behind, but she didn't think it would do Belle any good to be held back by a student who couldn't read. Should she call Damon to discuss it?

She nixed that thought even as it came. No, this was not a problem—yet. And she was making excuses to contact him. Parent-teacher conferences were in a few weeks, and meanwhile she would question Belle and keep track of the situation. She could even go to the school and meet this Jennie Anne herself.

Once the children had left for school, Mickelle went out into her backyard to feed the dog and work in her garden, bringing the portable phone in case one of the children should call.

"Hi Sasha," she crooned to the yellow Labrador as she opened the pen, allowing the dog to rush wildly around the backyard. "Come 'ere girl! Come 'ere!" Sasha skidded to a stop and panted exuberantly while Mickelle scratched her thick yellow coat.

She filled Sasha's food dish and gave her fresh water from the hose, rubbing her own hands vigorously under the water to remove most of the dog's scent. Allowing Sasha to stay loose in the backyard, Mickelle turned to her garden.

Her tomatoes were thriving in the middle of the abundant greenery, soaking up the sun. The nights were colder now, and Mickelle knew that the weather would hasten her harvest. She picked a big juicy tomato and rubbed it gently on her jeans before biting into the firm, acidic flesh. "Hmm," she murmured with a sigh.

As she ate, she observed the pumpkins growing in a disarray of tangled, twisted vines. A smile came to her face as she thought about their annual Halloween pumpkin seed fight. It was a yearly ritual of which Riley had disapproved, but she and the boys had indulged anyway. Mickelle was sure that Damon and his children would enjoy it, and she had just enough pumpkins for them each to carve one.

She stopped chewing and swallowed hard, realizing that she wouldn't be spending Halloween with Damon, Tanner, or Belle. At that moment of realization, she couldn't have missed him more than if he *had* drowned in that pool.

The vision of him floating in the water returned with force. *I do not need him,* she told herself unconvincingly.

Her thoughts were in such a turmoil that the ringing of the phone clipped onto her back pocket came as a welcome relief. Across the grass, Sasha perked her ears.

Mickelle lifted the phone. "Hello?"

"Hi, Mickelle," said a masculine voice that was familiar, but that she couldn't quite place.

"Who's this?"

"Colton," he said. "Remember Saturday night?"

She was glad he couldn't see how her jaw fell open. "Hi, Colton," she managed.

"I did some checking at the insurance company as I promised, and I have news."

"You do?" She hadn't really expected anything.

"Look, I'm on my way over there right now, okay?"

"But . . ."

"Don't worry, it's good news. Oops, gotta go. I'm getting another call. But I should be at your house in about five minutes."

Mickelle was nearly consumed with curiosity. What had Colton discovered? He certainly couldn't change the fact that Riley had died three weeks before the suicide clause on his policy would have been up. The policy stated that the insurance money would not be received in the case of suicide within two years of the effective date. If Riley had planned his death three weeks later, she would have a right to the money. But he hadn't.

She returned the reluctant Sasha to her pen. Inside the house, she placed the phone in its recharging cradle and washed her hands. Then she changed into a blue dress she had recently bought because it matched her eyes, checked her hair, and added another coat of lipstick. Was she too dressed up? Probably. But the dress made her feel good.

She had scarcely finished when the bell rang, and Mickelle practically flew to the door. Colton Scofield was just as good-looking as she remembered. He wore a black double-breasted suit that made his shiny hair appear even blacker. Mickelle wondered what he put in his hair to make it shine. She was glad she had changed her clothes.

The dimple in his left cheek deepened when he saw her. "You look absolutely ravishing today."

Mickelle smiled and lowered her eyes, embarrassed for the second time that day. "Come in, please." She led him to the sitting room.

"Nice place," Colton said, settling onto the couch. Mickelle wondered what kind of a background he had come from that he thought her small house was nice. Though it was clean, there were obvious repairs to be made, items that should be replaced. Or had she been to Damon's so often that she had become ashamed of her own modest lifestyle?

She sat across from him on the bench of the family piano her parents had recently given her. She felt nervous, having him here when she was alone in the house, something that had never bothered her with Damon.

Colton's blue eyes seemed to read her discomfort. "I don't bite," he told her, patting the cushion next to him. "Come over here, would you? I'd like to show you something." He put his black briefcase on his lap, clicking it open.

She crossed the few steps between them and sat on the couch. The aroma of his aftershave swirled around him, rich and pungent. "What's this?" she asked, glancing at the documents he had withdrawn.

"These are copies of your husband's life insurance policy. This is also a copy of the check he gave to the agent."

Mickelle studied them skeptically. "Yes. But forgive me if I don't see anything different about them. It still has the two-year suicide clause, the date is the same. There's nothing new here."

"Check the date on the check."

Mickelle looked, and her heart leapt. "April thirtieth," she read. "How odd. The date on the policy is later."

"Exactly. Your husband obviously paid the agent and then the paperwork was done later. Why, I don't know. Usually, it's done at the same time. But apparently, this agent was doing a lot of traveling to people's houses and had a backlog to enter. So the contract was made up later."

"And signed later," Mickelle pointed out.

"But the check is proof of coverage." Colton's eyes were warm on hers. "Legally, your husband was covered from the day he made out the check."

Mickelle's eyes opened wide. "That means . . ."

"It means you will be receiving one hundred thousand dollars this week from the insurance company." He grinned at her, and she knew there was more. "I went to visit them this morning, first thing. I told them I represented you and that if they didn't have the money to you this week, we planned to go to court to sue them for fraud." He paused for effect. "I believe they'll be prompt."

Mickelle was amazed. One moment she was a struggling single mother surviving on social security benefits and baby-sitting, and now, while she definitely wasn't rich, she could be independent to a good extent. She could afford to fix the old fence in the yard, at least, and even pay off the mortgage altogether!

She beamed at Colton. "I can't believe this!"

"Believe it. You just need to sign these papers here, so that they can set up a checking account on your behalf. Then you can take the money out as you please when you decide what you want to do with it."

Mickelle scanned the papers before signing them, scarcely able to believe her good fortune. "Thank you so much! How can I ever repay you?"

He caught her hand. "Go to lunch with me. Come on, my treat." He gazed at her so entreatingly that she agreed, blaming her surrender on that adorable dimple.

"Okay. Just let me get a sweater." In the coat closet near the front door she took out a long, thick black sweater that buttoned up the front. It wasn't quite as warm as her coat, but more dressy.

He took her to Chuck-A-Rama in Orem. She was surprised because he didn't seem the type of man who enjoyed serving himself in a restaurant. "The truth is," he confessed when she teased him, "I like choosing what I eat."

"Well, I love it here," she said. "I know the boys can fill up on things they like." For herself, she enjoyed Souper Salad or even McDonald's, because it was often cheaper. She grinned to herself. Of course now she wouldn't be worrying over pennies.

Lunch was marvelous. Colton was an excellent conversationalist, and there were no awkward silences as he launched into one narrative after another, recounting cases he had worked on. "I see a lot of fraud in the insurance business," he told her. "And not just regular people, but the insurance companies. Many will purposely cover things up if they can get away with it."

"Like in my case?"

"Exactly. Although that may have actually been an oversight." He sliced a piece of beef that was too rare for Mickelle's taste; she was glad she had chosen the chicken instead. "You wouldn't believe what I've seen. Why, last month in Alabama, I saw a case where the insurance company tried to pin a murder charge on a poor woman whose husband was killed in a car accident. When I heard about it, I just had to step in. I had investigated enough true frauds to believe that this one was made up. Luckily, the case was thrown out, and she got her money."

"Who exactly do you work for?" The picture he painted wasn't very clear.

"Oh, actually I work for a private law firm that helps people obtain their funds from insurance companies."

With difficulty, Mickelle swallowed the mouthful of green beans she was chewing. Finally, this explained his interest in her. "How much do you charge?"

"Up to fifty percent in some cases." He looked at her and his eyes widened. "But you're not a client, Mickelle. What I did for you was a favor. I hope you understand that."

Relief washed over Mickelle. Now that she had been promised the money, she didn't want to give it away. "Thank you," she said apologetically.

He smiled at her and she suddenly wanted to touch his dimple, just to see what it felt like. She was surprised at the thought—and flustered. "So, if you worked in Alabama, what brought you here?"

"I came back here because I missed Utah, you know, being with the Mormons. I was born in California, but I went to school here. My parents don't live here, but I still feel like it's home."

"So where exactly do you live in Happy Valley?"

"In Provo," he said vaguely. "You want to get some more grub?"

She laughed. "Maybe a little."

Colton ate more than any man she had ever seen—even Riley, who had been quite stocky and had eaten triple helpings of every meal. Either Colton had a high metabolism to keep so fit, or he was famished from lack of eating regularly. "I can't wait to tell the kids about the money," she confided, as she watched him finish his fourth plate of food.

"I wish I could see it."

An invitation was on the tip of her tongue—until she remembered Damon. If Colton stayed too long, they would meet, and the ensuing questions would be awkward.

Damon doesn't own me, she thought, resentful that she had begun to worry about it. She had promised herself after Riley's death that she would never change her plans for a man. But then, was having Colton at the house when the boys returned her plan or his? Hadn't he hinted to be invited? What did *she* want?

Not waiting for her response, Colton pushed forward his plate and slid from the padded booth. "Okay, I'm finally ready," he announced, looking slightly abashed. "I haven't had time for a good meal lately."

With her suspicions confirmed, Mickelle felt sorry for Colton. He was new in Utah and didn't have any family here. But what about female companionship? Most of the single women Mickelle knew would give up a month's salary to go out with someone so drop-dead gorgeous. They should be making him dinner by the droves.

Once inside his car Colton didn't start the engine. He turned his head in her direction, but seemed to stare right through her. "So you have two sons," he said, his voice full of melancholy. "How old are they?"

"Nine and thirteen."

"Ah. A good age. I wish . . ." He shrugged and turned the key.

"Wish what?"

"I wish my boys were alive," he said, sorrow etched across his face.

"Do you want to talk about it?" Mickelle was more curious than she wanted to admit. What had happened to his children?

He studied her for a long minute without replying. She felt as though he were weighing and measuring her. "You don't have to if you don't want," she offered quickly.

His answer came slowly. "I think I would like to talk about it. But I'm not sure you'll like it. Or if you'll even understand. Yet I think . . . given the way I feel . . ." He stopped completely, as though searching for words. "You are unlike any woman I have ever met," he said finally. "Maybe you would understand."

"I can try." Mickelle was flattered. What kind of women did he usually date? The glamorous beauty queens? Yes, she could easily see him with women like that.

He slid the car into gear. "Do you mind if we go somewhere less crowded?"

Mickelle thought about the pepper spray she still had in her purse. She had meant to give it back, but now . . . "Sure." After all he had done for her, she could spend a little time comforting him in his time of need. Heaven knew she had once been in a similar situation.

Instead of returning to Mickelle's house, Colton drove up American Fork Canyon. Mickelle hadn't been to the canyon since Riley had died. She didn't even know the exact place where he had purposely driven off the road and plunged to his death. Her stomach suddenly felt queasy and her heart raced, but she didn't have a panic attack. Just in case, she deliberately breathed in an even pattern. At least Riley hadn't taken anyone over that cliff with him.

The leaves on the sea of trees were changing colors, leaving brilliant patterns of gold and red as they undulated gently in the light breeze. The beautiful sight was enough to hold her attention. She wondered briefly if the leaves changed color like this in Anchorage where Damon had lived before coming to Utah. Or in Alabama where Colton had been.

Colton sighed and pulled over to the side of the road next to the river. "Want to go for a walk?"

Mickelle nodded. She thought about taking the pepper spray, but decided against it. They wouldn't be going far, and Colton was a nice man. She could feel it. Maybe they could be friends. She would certainly need one if Damon couldn't come to terms with her decision.

They walked along the river. There was no real trail, so they meandered along. Neither were dressed for the occasion, and Mickelle was glad that at least her pumps were low and had a wide heel. The breeze here was colder than in the valley and she buttoned her long sweater with stiff, cold fingers. The scent of pine was strong, as was the smell of the wet leaves now beginning to stack on the rich earth.

They came to several fallen logs and Colton took her hand to help her over them. Afterwards, he continued to hold her hand. Mickelle told herself that he was just trying to ease her path over the terrain, that it didn't mean anything, did it? His skin felt warm against hers.

"Look at this." Colton indicated a place that descended close to the rushing water. There was a tiny clearing, surrounded by small trees that kept out most of the breeze. Mickelle couldn't hear the cars from the road over the sound of the river, but knew they were there. She and Colton seemed to be in a separate world from the rest of humankind.

Colton released her hand, and it felt suddenly cold. He bent and picked up several stones from the dark, rich earth and tossed them into the river. One sent up a spray of water that hit the ground at his feet. He turned to her and grinned, but Mickelle could see something more important lurking in his blue eyes.

He didn't speak; neither did she. For a long time, all that was between them was the sound of the river and the rustling of the colorful leaves.

"I told you I had two sons," he said at last.

Mickelle could barely hear him over the rushing water, and she stepped closer. He was less than an inch taller than she was, she noticed, though this was certainly not a drawback when coupled with his looks. She nodded encouragingly.

He squeezed his eyes tightly shut, and for a moment Mickelle was sure he had changed his mind about sharing his story. A single tear slipped out of the inner corner of his left eye, trailing down the side of his nose before angling outwards near his dimple. Instinctively, she reached to wipe it away, but stopped herself in time.

Mickelle looked swiftly down at the ground. She wanted to comfort Colton, but didn't feel she knew him well enough. Wasn't there anyone he could turn to?

When she glanced back at him, he had opened his eyes. He blinked a couple of times. "We had twins, my wife Terry and I." He smiled slightly, but the sorrow in his face was still evident. "They were beautiful and perfect, and we doted on them. My favorite memories are of them." He paused and the smile vanished.

"What happened?" Mickelle asked, unable to bear it any longer.

His eyes held to hers as though to a lifeline. "One evening when they were a year old Terry went to the store. She'd had a difficult day with the twins and I volunteered to watch them. Told her to take her time, that I'd get them to bed." Again he stopped talking. Mickelle was anxious now to hear more. In her mind she pictured her nephews, Forest and Gabriel, Brionney's twin boys. Just last week they had celebrated their first birthday.

"I was giving them their bath." Colton's voice had become tragic. "The phone rang. There was just a little water in the tub." He showed her a space of about six inches with his fingers. Mickelle swallowed with difficulty, sensing what would come next. She had never left either of her boys in the bathtub alone until they were five, and even then she had allowed them only a little bit of water and kept within earshot.

"I thought I could just run down the hall and grab the phone," he began again. "It was such a short space and I would be fast. The boys played together well in the tub. I didn't feel they were in any danger. So I ran, but it took me longer than I thought because I couldn't find the portable. I heard them laughing, so I kept looking. I found it, but it had stopped ringing. I went back and . . ."

He drew in a breath, obviously unable to continue.

"I'm so sorry," Mickelle murmured, her initial outrage at his carelessness tempered by the evident torture he still endured.

"I tried to revive them." He was crying now, in earnest, his eyes frantic as he relived the horror. "I know it's no excuse, but I was so inexperienced as a father. I didn't know what to do. I called 911, and I kept trying to breathe air into their lungs. I didn't know who to help first. I'd go to one, then the next . . ."

Mickelle could imagine vividly what he must have felt. Hadn't she felt a similar terror when confronted with an unconscious Damon. What if her sons had been in the water? What if she had to choose which one to save?

Colton stepped closer to her, and Mickelle put her arms around him. "They died," he cried into her shoulder. "And it was all my fault. I should never have left them. Not even to grab the phone. I shouldn't have left them for anything. Terry blamed me too. We couldn't be together after that. She couldn't love me after I had done something so horrible. And I don't think anyone ever will."

Mickelle let him cling to her. She massaged his back and held him while the emotions raged. She marveled that her own emotions seemed steady, when his experience so closely mirrored that of hers with Damon.

But Damon had lived.

After a long time, Colton drew away. "I hope you don't hate me now," he said, voice barely audible.

She shook her head. "No." Then she gave him a sad smile. "You're looking at a woman who asked her husband for a divorce a few days before he went out and drove himself purposely over a cliff. There's enough guilt to go around; somehow we have to forgive ourselves and go on."

"My boys can't go on," he muttered.

She wondered if he had meant her to hear this last comment. That he had perhaps hoped the sound of the river would cover the bitter words.

"You're wrong," she told him. "They do go on. And whatever awful stuff they passed through on earth, they're in their Heavenly Father's arms now, anxious and waiting to see you again."

His eyes filled once again with tears, but this time they didn't fall onto the tanned cheeks. "Thank you for reminding me of that, Mickelle. Sometimes I forget that they have another Father who loves them even more than I do."

She smiled and he smiled back. For a long moment they stared at each other silently. Then without warning, he leaned forward and kissed her hard on the mouth. Mickelle responded before she could help herself. In his warm lips she could feel him asking absolution and understanding. His kiss was different from Damon's, less demanding and heart-stopping, but very enjoyable.

At last he pulled away. "I'm sorry," he said, not looking it. "I shouldn't have done that. But I've been wanting to since the moment I saw you at the dance." He paused and reached to run a gentle finger over her cheek. "Thank you for listening, Mickelle. Thank you."

She stepped away, gradually, so that it wouldn't be noticeable. "No, I need to thank *you*. You're the one who tackled that insurance company for me."

He waved the words aside. "That was nothing."

"Not to me, it wasn't. Or to my boys."

Something flickered in his eyes. "I hope I can meet them sometime."

Mickelle hesitated only an instant. "Then why don't you come over for dinner tonight?" Colton obviously needed company, and she needed someone who wasn't going to pressure her about making a commitment.

"I'd love to." He grinned at her with unconcealed pleasure. Once again his striking appearance hit her, made her feel weak inside just gazing at him. What did he see in her?

Of course, there was the tragedy in his life. *That* was hard to swallow, especially for someone intent on keeping what was left of her family together. But then, Mickelle had always been a bit paranoid about her sons' safety, and her protectiveness had grown since Riley's death. She still checked to see if Bryan and Jeremy were breathing at night, checked out the families of their friends, made them wear seat belts . . .

Riley had never been a stickler for seat belts. It had driven her insane when the boys were small. She had given up on him and had focused on training the boys instead. For the most part, they had obeyed. The thing that had saved her most, though, was the fact that Riley had rarely taken them anywhere alone. And by the time he did, they were old enough to put on their belts of their own free will. It was no surprise to her that Riley hadn't been wearing a seat belt when his smashed truck had been recovered from the canyon. The police suspected that he might have survived if he had clipped it on. But then, he hadn't meant to survive.

One thing was sure: Mickelle would have never left Riley to bathe the boys when they were small. He simply hadn't known enough about their abilities to do it safely. And didn't care about them enough to learn.

Wrenching herself away from this vein of thought, Mickelle smiled at Colton. "I have to get home. I have to go pick up one of the children I baby-sit at school in Highland."

Again Colton helped her over the fallen logs and rough terrain, perhaps touching her hands and arms more than necessary. Mickelle didn't mind; she enjoyed the human contact.

But what about Damon who was willing to give her his whole heart?

No—too much involvement there. She thought she had been ready for a relationship, but Friday's accident had proven her wrong. Now she didn't know if she would ever be ready.

CHAPTER 7

When they were finally back in Colton's car, with the doors shut firmly against the roaring of the river, the silence was so loud that Mickelle laughed.

"What?" he asked, inserting the key into the ignition.

"Just that it's positively quiet in here after being by that river. Gives a new meaning to the term 'deafening silence.'"

He chuckled. "Why so it is. I wondered if there was something wrong with my ears."

They chatted casually all the way back to Mickelle's. She was actually sorry to see him go, but it was high time she picked up Tanner. By the time she returned from Highland, Bryan would be home from the junior high and she would leave to collect Belle and Jeremy. Ordinarily Belle and Jeremy would walk home from school with the neighbor children, but Mickelle wanted to catch a glimpse of the new girl Belle had been assigned to befriend. Something about the way Belle had talked made her uneasy. *It's just my overprotective state,* Mickelle thought.

"Penny for your thoughts," Colton said as they pulled up in front of her house.

"Only a penny? They're worth *way* more than that."

He grinned. "You went quiet all of a sudden. If it's something you'd rather not share . . ."

"Oh, it's just the little girl I watch. She's having some stuff happen at school that I need to keep an eye on."

"Can't her father handle it?" Colton asked. "Uh, or her mother," he added hastily.

"Well, it's not a problem—yet. It might not become one. And their mother died from cancer a few years back. That's why I'm watching them."

"That's too bad."

She nodded. "Anyway, thank you for lunch."

"Wait." He jumped out of the car and hurried around to open her door. He helped her out carefully, as though she were made of fragile porcelain. His hand lingered long after she was out of the car, and she suspected he was going to try to kiss her again.

"Colton, what happened up there . . . after . . ." She wanted to tell him that she wasn't looking for a relationship, that she welcomed him only as a friend, but suddenly she couldn't do that. If she brought it up now, he would suspect that she held his sons' deaths against him. Hadn't he hinted that women had reacted that way before?

"Yes?" he prompted.

She made a show of eyeing her wristwatch. "Oh, I've got to get going. Look, about dinner. Is seven-thirty too late?" She wanted to be sure Damon and his children were gone before he arrived.

And why was that? a nasty little voice wanted to know.

"I know that might be a little bit later than you're used to eating," she added hastily, "but the kids I watch don't leave much before that and I'll need time to cook."

"Sure." Then his brow creased. "Is there a problem with this being a Monday? You and the boys probably have family night."

Mickelle had forgotten. Like most members of the Church, she and the boys had set aside Mondays as a special family togetherness night, but it wasn't as if Colton would be staying the entire evening. She could have family night after he left, and the boys could simply go to sleep an hour later. "That's fine," she said. "The boys'll be so excited about the insurance money that they won't complain too much." She rolled her eyes to show him she was teasing. What he couldn't know was that recently Bryan had been trying to get out of having family nights. She hadn't shared that information with anyone other than Damon.

Damon would have laughed and commiserated with her comment, but Colton only shrugged. "Okay then. I'll see you tonight."

Mickelle watched him drive away before she pulled out the keys to her car.

* * * * *

Later, as she drove up to Belle's school, Mickelle had all but forgotten the incident between her and Colton. The kiss they shared had only been inspired by the deep feelings of his sad past, nothing more.

Mickelle reached the classroom before the bell rang, and she stood at the open door, allowing her eyes to run over the numerous students, who were grouped in twos throughout the room. The teacher, Mrs. Palmer, was reading from a book, and most of the students were listening avidly. Mickelle's niece Camille, near the back of the class, spotted her and turned to wave.

Belle didn't notice Mickelle. She was too busy leaning over to whisper to the child next to her. Mickelle couldn't see the girl's face, but she was thin, too thin, and her long dark hair—a shade darker than Belle's—hung straight and stringy from her scalp. Her oversized jeans were ragged and her short-sleeved, striped top was too tight.

Was this the mysterious Jennie Anne? If so, she didn't seem like much of a threat, at least not from behind. She was as little as Belle, who was small for her age and even smaller compared to the rest of the class since she had skipped a grade. From her posture, Belle's new friend appeared to be doing most of the listening, not the talking. Around her neck was the remainder of the Fruit Loop necklace Belle had put together that morning, a few pieces of cereal still intact on the green yarn.

The two dark heads—one with shining, gently curling locks, the other dull, unbrushed, and limp—touched as the girls whispered together. Belle was also writing something on a paper lying on the other girl's desk. Every so often her friend gave a little nod or a whispered reply.

The bell rang and the teacher closed the book. "We'll read the rest tomorrow," she announced. "Have a good evening. Don't forget to take home your math tests to show your parents."

Mickelle smiled at the teacher before approaching Belle. She was intercepted by Camille. "Aunt Mickelle!" the girl shouted with excitement. "Can I see the ring? Belle said her dad gave you a BIG ring that looks like a heart. Do I get to wear a pretty dress for the wedding?"

Mickelle frowned. No doubt about it, she had to give back that ring as soon as possible to stop these speculations. In a quiet voice, she told her niece, "I'm *not* getting married, Camille, but if I ever do, you will certainly get to wear a pretty dress."

"Cool!" Camille wasn't daunted in the least by Mickelle's denial. She gave Mickelle a hug and a peck on the cheek. "Gotta go. I got a hundred on my math test and I have to hurry and tell Mom! Every time we get a hundred we get to put our name in the jar, and when we get it full of names we're going to Disneyland!" Then she was out the door before Mickelle could marvel aloud at her good fortune. Camille was usually the most quiet of her sister's five children, and Mickelle was glad to see that she was beginning to open up more now that she was growing older. Or perhaps it was simply because Camille was away from her more voluble sisters.

Belle and her friend were still at their desks, but Belle spied Mickelle and smiled. The other girl glanced over at the same time and Mickelle saw a thin brown face covered in splotchy freckles. She had large brown eyes framed within dark lashes, but they were overshadowed by an ugly green-brown bruise splayed over her cheekbone. Her eyes moved quickly away from Mickelle's, and meekly down to the paper Belle had been writing on. Was this the girl who had gone through three other assigned friends? It didn't seem possible that such an apparently unassuming child could cause a problem.

Mickelle hurried over. "Hello, Belle."

"Hi, Mickelle!" She folded the paper on the other girl's desk, as though she didn't want Mickelle to see what was on it.

"I decided to come get you. I wanted to meet your new friend."

Belle dimpled. "This is her." She pointed to the other girl, who didn't lift her face at the introduction. "Her name's Jennie Anne."

"Hi, Jennie Anne. It's nice to meet you."

At that Jennie Anne did look up, just a glance, and then stared downward again. She sat unnaturally still.

"Say hello to Mrs. Hansen," said their teacher, appearing beside Jennie Anne. Mrs. Palmer was very young, with short blonde hair, hazel eyes, and a soft look about her face. She placed a hand on the girl's shoulder. Her touch appeared gentle, but Jennie Anne flinched. Mrs. Palmer withdrew her hand, her brow wrinkling briefly. In worry? In anger? Mickelle couldn't say. She had always liked and respected Belle's teacher, but she couldn't help wondering now if her perception of the younger woman had been accurate.

"Hello," Jennie Anne repeated obediently.

"That's a big bruise you have there on your cheek," Mickelle said. "I bet that hurt."

"I got hit by a ball," Jennie Anne answered, this time without prompting.

Mrs. Palmer continued as though there had been no interruption. "Belle is helping Jennie Anne get used to our class."

"So I heard." Mickelle was careful not to put any inflection into her voice since she didn't know enough about the situation to make a judgment.

"They're doing very well. I appreciate both of them." Mrs. Palmer smiled her sweet smile and moved away to talk with another parent.

Mickelle slid into an empty desk across from the girls. The squeeze was tight, but she managed to fit. "So, did you have a fun day?"

Jennie Anne averted her eyes again, but Belle nodded excitedly. "Jennie Anne and I had fun. We got to have our own reading group, just her and me. And you know what? We found out that Jennie Anne is like a genius in math. No lie." Her voice lowered. "I haven't told Mrs. Palmer yet. We were working on math during reading because Jennie Anne didn't get a very high score on her test. But when I asked her the problems out loud she got them all right, didn't you, Jennie Anne?"

The girl nodded. She glanced over at the paper Belle had folded and reached for it, slipping it inside her desk—out of sight.

"That's wonderful," Mickelle said.

"Ask her, Mickelle. Ask her anything. She can do it."

"Okay." Mickelle was up for the game. "What's five plus five?"

"Tell her, Jennie Anne," Belle urged when the other girl remained silent.

The answer came reluctantly, "Ten."

"Eight and eight."

Belle sighed in exasperation. "Aw, do harder ones Mickelle. Not doubles. Those are easy."

"Not for your grade they're not."

"Sixteen," answered Jennie Anne.

"That's right. But what's five, plus four, plus eight?" asked Belle.

"Seventeen."

"Very good!" Mickelle was impressed.

Jennie Anne smiled for the first time and Mickelle was amazed at the transformation in her homely face. She was pretty!

"Mom!" Mickelle turned to see Jeremy coming into the classroom. "What are you doing here?"

"Oh, I thought you two could use a ride home."

"We're testing Jennie Anne," Belle informed him importantly. "She's better at math than you are."

"No way, I'm a fourth grader."

Belle lifted her chin, undaunted. "Oh yeah, watch. Jennie Anne, what's eight plus three plus . . . thirteen . . . plus . . . twenty one!"

"Forty-five."

Jeremy blinked. "Well, I bet you can't do times. You're only in first grade. Hah! But I can do them. What's eight times four?"

"Thirty-two."

Mickelle laughed at her son's chagrin. Belle giggled and pulled a face.

Jeremy glared at her. "Okay, then what's forty-nine times sixteen."

"Jeremy," Mickelle warned. This was going too far. "You shouldn't ask any question you can't answer yourself."

"I can do it," he protested. "I just need some paper."

"Yeah, or a calculator," taunted Belle.

Mickelle stood. "Come on, guys, it's time to go. Would you like a ride, Jennie Anne?"

The girl didn't reply.

"Yes, your aunt won't mind, will she?" Belle said, taking her friend's hand. Jennie Anne continued to stare at the floor, but Belle bent her head to look at her face. After a minute, she straightened and nodded at Mickelle. "She'll come."

Mickelle wondered how she knew, but didn't ask the question. She needed to get home to Tanner and Bryan. "Let's go, then."

With Belle prompting her Jennie Anne gave directions to her home. Shortly Mickelle parked in front of a small, run-down house surrounded by an overgrown lawn made up of more weeds than grass. Weathered papers, chunks of shingles from the roof, plastic sacks, and soft drink cans peeked out of various hiding places in the long grass and scrubby bushes that marked the line between the neighboring properties. A huge willow tree sprouted desolately in the front yard, looking as though it wept for times gone by.

Mickelle frowned in dismay. Her own clapboard house had been in sore need of repainting until the task had been undertaken recently by her brothers-in-law. The shingles on her roof curled, and the wobbly black railing on her porch needed replacing; in all, there was still much work to do. Yet her home had never, even in its worst state, projected this air of despair, this complete and utter neglect—the same neglect that was reflected in little Jennie Anne. Even studying it carefully, she wasn't sure what color the original paint had been. Grey? Yellow? Impossible to tell. The only positive thing Mickelle could determine about the house was that the weeping willow hid much of the shocking disrepair.

Mickelle had a sudden desperate wish not to let Jennie Anne leave the car. This was no place for a child.

"See you Jennie Anne," Belle shouted as her friend exited the car.

Jennie Anne nodded, unsmiling. She paused on the gravel outside, shifting her feet as though itching to run away. But instead she met Mickelle's pitying gaze. "Seven hundred eighty-four," she said, a bit breathlessly. Without another word she turned on her heel and ran across the weed-infested lawn, up the single cement step, and disappeared from sight behind the battered door.

A full minute passed before Mickelle realized that Jennie Anne had given her the correct answer to Jeremy's equation.

"Are you sure Jennie Anne can't read?" Mickelle asked Belle, staring at the closed door thoughtfully.

"Yep. I'm sure. She's got some words memorized, but if you show her a word she doesn't know, she can't say it. But she's a quick learner. I taught her all the ABC sounds today. You know, like they do on that video Camille's little sister watches."

"She didn't know the sounds?"

Belle shook her head. "No. A few of the kids don't know all of them, but Jennie Anne didn't know *any*. The kids laugh at her because they think she's stupid, but she's not. She just never learned it before. I don't think she went to kindergarten or preschool. She's afraid of the kids and the teacher, but she's not afraid of me 'cause I'm littler than her. And I can help because I'm the best reader in the class. Mrs. Palmer gives me big books from the third grade."

"I'm a good reader too," Jeremy put in. "And today I read a Halloween story. The house in it was just like this one, all old and crumbly. I wonder if Jennie Anne's house is haunted."

"It might be." Belle bounced on her seat with excitement. "She's got an aunt who I bet's as wicked as an old witch!"

"Now kids," Mickelle warned.

"Well it could be," Belle insisted.

Mickelle felt reluctant to drive away. Whoever did take care of Jennie Anne was doing a very poor job of it. She chewed on her bottom lip. Maybe it was time someone found out just what was going on in that house.

* * * * *

"Did you hear?" Bryan met them excitedly as they came through the side door into the kitchen.

"Hear what?" Jeremy asked, puzzled.

Mickelle had been so preoccupied with Belle and Jennie Anne that she had forgotten her wonderful news. "I haven't told him yet."

"We're rich!" With uncharacteristic joy, Bryan grabbed Jeremy and twirled him around.

"Mom's marrying Damon!" Jeremy shouted happily.

An abrupt silence filled the small kitchen, and Tanner, who sat at the small table, quickly focused on his homework, frowning fiercely.

"No!" Bryan shouted. "It's Dad's life insurance company. They're giving us a hundred thousand dollars!"

Jeremy's eyes grew big. "We *are* rich," he said with awe. "Does this mean we can go to Disneyland with Aunt Brionney?"

"Maybe." Mickelle laughed and hugged her sons. "We'll have enough money for piano lessons and soccer, if you want, and I can go to school. But we're not exactly rich. We have to save as much as we can so it can make interest. I'm not sure exactly how it'll work; I'll have to look into it. Maybe we can ask . . ." She had been going to say "Damon" but with their relationship the way it was, she didn't know if she dared. "Maybe we can ask Uncle Jesse to help us. He knows a lot about investing."

"So does my dad," Tanner volunteered.

Mickelle realized she wasn't fooling him for a minute. "Yeah, he does." She decided to change the subject. "So, how about an afternoon snack while we do our homework?"

"I don't have homework," Belle said, with a touch of arrogance. "And I'm not hungry. Isn't it time for my piano lesson yet?"

"In about fifteen minutes. Why don't you practice your songs one last time before you go next door?"

"All right." Belle dropped her backpack on the table and started for the living room. "But I know them all perfectly. Didn't you hear me when I practiced this morning?"

Mickelle had heard. In fact, she had made a mental note to ask Belle's piano teacher to find more complicated books. After having her cast removed, Belle had been so anxious to finally use both hands, that over the weekend she had gone through most of the books she already owned.

While the boys worked on homework at the table, Mickelle started dinner. She hummed as she worked, content. Life wasn't uncomplicated, but it was going tolerably well. At one point in the preparations she turned to see Tanner staring at her. There was a subtle longing in the fifteen-year-old's gaze, and also a memory. Mickelle wondered if he still felt deeply the loss of his mother, or if he felt guilty because he didn't miss her enough. She often felt this about Riley.

There was a big difference. Tanner's mother had been sick for years before she died, and she suspected that his memories of her when she was healthy were very faded in his mind.

Mickelle met his brown eyes. "Tanner?" she asked.

He shook his head. "I just . . . for a moment I remembered . . . my mom used to hum as she cooked. I only remembered that just now."

"I'm sorry, Tanner."

He held her gaze. "Why? I know she's happier than she was here. And we have you." He reddened, as though he hadn't meant to say the last sentence aloud.

Why did he say that? Mickelle thought. *Why not, "and we have our dad"?* Suddenly she felt very confused, but her compassion for this motherless child glossed over the confusion, making it unimportant. "I'm glad, Tanner," she said simply.

Then she caught sight of Bryan's face where he sat at the table across from Tanner. He was a bright red, a sure sign of anger, an anger Mickelle believed came from jealousy. "So, boys, shouldn't we call Grandma and Grandpa and tell them about the money?" she asked, trying to defuse the situation. Bryan practically worshiped Tanner, and she didn't want that to change.

"Yes!" shouted Jeremy.

"I get to call first!" Bryan, his color returning to normal, lunged for the phone on the counter.

Mickelle sighed and turned back to her dinner preparations, feeling Tanner's eyes still following her.

CHAPTER 8

Damon had tried to call Mickelle to let her know he'd be late to pick up the children, but her phone was busy. He made a mental note to try again later, and promptly forgot. Now as he drove from his Orem office to her house in American Fork, he remembered that he had never reached her.

He shrugged the worry aside; Mickelle had never minded when he was late. Of course, after Friday's dramatic events, things were very different.

His hand reached up to twirl his blonde moustache, though he now wore it much too short to do so. He had been trying to break himself of the habit for months, and thought he had until now. Instead, he rubbed his jaw. He could feel the tiny hairs growing there already; a five o'clock shadow.

Or seven o'clock, he amended, glancing at the clock on the CD player in the dashboard. He ached to see Mickelle again, but feared it at the same time. Would she try to return the ring again? And why the heck wouldn't she marry him anyway?

He sighed loud and long. *Patience,* he told himself. It was so difficult when all he wanted was to take her in his arms and show her how much he loved her.

Another thought had plagued him all day. Why hadn't she mentioned the roses? He had spied them on her counter by the sink, and she had seen him looking at them. Yet she had said nothing. Her reaction went against everything he knew about her. Maybe she really did want him out of her personal life.

Then why did he feel so strongly that they were meant to be together?

Belle was waiting for him on Mickelle's porch when he drove up in his Mercedes. He still preferred this car over the new forest green Lexus he had recently bought. He wanted to give that car to Mickelle once they were married—he knew she wouldn't accept it before—or the Mercedes if she preferred. Darn it all, he would buy her any car she desired, if she would just leave behind the fear he believed was holding her back.

Silently he cursed the man who had left that legacy. Of course, if Riley Hansen hadn't killed himself, Mickelle might still be enduring the emotional abuse.

No, he protested, *she had begun fighting back. That's why Riley did what he did; he could no longer control her.*

Even as the thoughts came, Damon wondered if he was any better than Riley. *No! I just want to take care of her!* But it had to be her decision, or it wouldn't be enough on which to base a relationship. An eternal relationship.

These torturous thoughts filtered away as Belle raced across the lawn toward him. "I'm getting new piano books! I'm too good for the other ones! Can you believe it?" She launched herself into his arms.

He held her tightly, breathing in the flowery scent of her hair and the earthy scent of the rest of her. She, at least, was all his.

"I really was Jennie Anne's friend today, Dad. And I like her. The kids say she's dumb, but she's not. She has all sorts of ideas. And she's a math whiz."

"That's wonderful!" Damon knew she had been a little nervous about her important job as an assigned friend.

"And Mickelle's rich. This guy went and got her money for her husband dying. And now they've got just tons of money! Though not as much as we do. Come on and see for yourself."

Belle pulled him into the house, where the delicious fragrance of roasting meat made his mouth water. His hopes reared to life. Maybe Mickelle had reconsidered her decision. Maybe even now, she would come toward him, wearing his ring and . . .

Mickelle did come toward him, but she wasn't wearing his ring or even a smile. "You're late." Her face was worried, but she looked even better to him than she had that morning, if possible. Her honey-blonde hair was shiny and styled, curled slightly under and full on the top the way he liked it. She wore a blue dress that made the blue of her eyes even more prominent, and which accented the womanly curves that drove him to distraction.

"I meant to call," he said apologetically. She went back into the kitchen and he followed her. "Actually, I did once, but the line was busy."

"We were probably talking to Grandma," Jeremy offered, glancing up from the Game Boy in his hands. Damon knew Jeremy's mother had given him a daily limit on the handheld computer game, so his using it was a sure sign that his homework was done. He glanced at Bryan and Tanner who also had their homework stashed in their backpacks. Maybe he could interest the boys in a game of basketball. Mickelle might play with them as she often did, though she would have to change out of that very becoming dress. At the very least she might invite them to stay to dinner as she had so many other times. Never mind that their own cook would once again be upset that they hadn't eaten her prepared meal.

"That's what I was telling him," Belle said. She tugged on Damon's hand. "They're rich now, Daddy."

"Yep," Jeremy confirmed. "And we were telling Grandma. Or Bryan was. I only got to talk to her after." A wide grin filled his thin face. "Mom says now we can get a trampoline for Christmas like the one you guys have. I've always wanted a tramp."

Damon could make no sense of the conversation. "What?" he asked, directing the question to Mickelle.

Mickelle folded her arms and leaned against her refrigerator. "A guy—a friend of mine—did a little research and found out that Riley had paid his life insurance with a check dated before the contract so the insurance company has to pay us a hundred thousand dollars." She spoke quietly, but excitement radiated from her face. "I know it's not a lot of money compared to what you're used to, but if I invest it . . ."

"Uncle Jesse can help with that," Bryan put in.

"Jesse?" Damon nearly laughed. "Jesse doesn't know beans about investing. He just puts his money where I tell him to."

Mickelle stiffened. "Well, I'm sure I'll find a way to make it work, and meanwhile, I'm going to celebrate by getting a few things that we've needed. And I'm going to school . . ."

Damon wanted to be happy for her, but with each passing minute he felt her growing more independent, more able to live without him.

Don't you want her to be independent? a voice asked in his head.

The truth was he would give her ten times a hundred thousand dollars if she would only agree to marry him. All the money in the world meant nothing without someone to share it with. That much he had learned.

He slowly clenched and unclenched his fists. "I'm happy for you, Mickelle. I really am. And I would enjoy helping you with investment opportunities if you'd like."

"Thank you," she stated politely, but she didn't ask him to help.

He tried to smile, resisting the nervous urge to twirl his moustache. "I hope that doesn't mean you plan to make us find another sitter." He spoke the words casually, though his heart thumped unevenly in his chest, so thunderous he was sure everyone in the room could hear.

Her face paled, and her eyes went immediately to Belle, who gaped at them, and then to Tanner who sat at the table frowning. "Of course not," she said. "I enjoy having the children here." The sincerity with which she spoke partially filled the gnawing emptiness inside his soul.

"Well, that's good because we don't know what we'd do without you." He glanced at the boys. "So, is anyone up for a quick game of basketball?"

Tanner shot to his feet and Jeremy cheered. Even Bryan managed to appear pleased. But not Mickelle. She shook her head. "Not tonight." She paused, as though suddenly nervous. "Look, Damon, I've got company coming over tonight for dinner. They'll be here soon and I have to check the boys' homework and . . . stuff."

Meaning she didn't want him around.

"Aw, Mom," Jeremy wailed. "Just a short game. I gotta practice and we haven't played since way last week."

"No," Mickelle's voice was firm. "Besides, Damon bumped his head pretty badly and . . . well, he shouldn't be jumping after balls."

"But he could just watch."

"Jeremy." Mickelle's blue eyes flashed.

As much as he wanted to stay, Damon reluctantly supported Mickelle. "Your mother's right. Besides, we need to have family night."

"But we always have family night together," Belle protested.

Damon hadn't realized they had fallen into a custom, but his daughter was right. "Not tonight," he told her. Mickelle cast him such a grateful smile that he was almost angry at her. Why had his accident made them near strangers? Did she really not care about him any longer? How could he know what was in her heart if she wouldn't tell him? Last Saturday he had been so sure that she would come around, but now he didn't know what to think.

"Besides," he added. "I am feeling pretty bad right now. My head's pounding and I don't know if I should be out of bed after what happened. I think I might have to go in and see the doctor." He darted a glance at Mickelle and was gratified to see worry spring to life. So she wasn't as indifferent as she pretended.

She twisted her hands. "Do you need a ride home?"

"No, I can make it, thank you." He felt remorse for even suggesting that he was feeling sick—although come to think of it, he did have a headache. He wished he could shake Mickelle, beg her to talk to him, but he had promised her all the time she needed.

He grabbed Belle's hand. "Come on, ma Belle."

Reluctantly, the children followed him outside. Mickelle came with them as far as the porch, looking down the street as though expecting a disaster.

What was it she was hiding?

He paused at the door. "Nice roses."

"What?"

"The ones by the sink."

She flushed a deep red. "Oh, uh, thanks."

Not exactly the effusive response he had hope for. Hadn't she noticed that they were nearly the same color as the gold-dipped one he had given her last month?

She said nothing more and he had no choice but to join Tanner and Belle, already waiting in the Mercedes parked halfway down the driveway. "Well, see you tomorrow."

"See you." Her voice was abruptly strained. He followed her gaze to watch a white new-model Nissan Z pull up to the curb behind Mickelle's old gold station wagon. A man with dark silky hair climbed out, wearing a double-breasted suit with an expensive cut. Though Damon was not a fanatic for clothing, he would bet it was an imitation. This joker looked like a corporate version of the stereotypical used car salesman—and Damon had dealt with enough of those types to know one when he saw one. In his hand the newcomer held a single gold-yellow rose, the same color as the ones Damon had sent Mickelle on Saturday.

This was . . . interesting. Damon stayed right where he was at the bottom of the stairs, though he could see from the glance he had given Mickelle that she wanted him to leave.

The man registered no surprise to see him there, and Damon could almost swear this man *knew* him. But try as he might, Damon couldn't place him in his memory.

"Hi," the man said with a hearty confidence that Damon knew was faked. In fact, everything about the man was faked, including that stupid greasy smile and that cover-boy dimple.

"Colton," Mickelle mumbled, sounding as though she would faint. "Uh, Colton, meet Damon Wolfe. Damon, Colton Scofield."

"Hello," Damon presented his hand.

The other man took it, grinning. "I guess you heard the good news."

"About the insurance money? I guess that means you're the friend who figured it all out."

"That's me." Beauty-boy beamed until Damon wanted to punch the grin right off his face.

"Nice going," Damon said casually. "We—her family and friends—sure appreciate it. So where did you meet Kelle? I've never heard her speak of you."

"We met for the first time on Saturday at a singles' dance," Colton replied. "One glance and I couldn't dance with anyone else."

This answer wasn't one Damon had expected. His head swivelled to Mickelle and he read the truth in her eyes. They *had* danced together.

Burning jealousy consumed him. And a crushing hurt—a hurt that made it so he could scarcely breathe. All this time he had thought Mickelle's refusal of his marriage proposal was connected with her fears, but apparently she had no fears in relation to Mr. Cover Boy here. "I see," he managed with a modicum of composure. "Well, good evening." He didn't even look at Mickelle. He was so furious that he feared he would not be able to control his emotions.

He sprinted angrily to the Mercedes, and pulled the door shut behind him. Inside, he slammed the palm of his hand against the steering wheel.

"What's wrong, Dad?" Belle asked from the back seat.

Tanner stared at him, brown eyes full of worry. "Is it that guy?"

Damon forced himself to calm down. He hadn't felt so angry since he had learned that Charlotte had cancer. Was he losing Mickelle as he had lost Charlotte? *Please, dear Father,* he prayed. *Don't let that happen.*

He was grateful for this relatively new aspect of his life—the praying. While he had always believed in God, he had never really believed prayers were heard until joining The Church of Jesus Christ of Latter-day Saints in Anchorage little more than a year ago. Now the prayers were habit and immediately comforting.

"I'm okay," he said after a while. His voice broke only a little bit as he added, "I'm just having a hard time convincing Kelle that she's supposed to marry me."

"Is she going to marry that guy instead?" asked Belle. "I mean, he's really cute, but you're cuter."

"Looks don't have anything to do with it!" Tanner nearly shouted. There was a loss in his face that Damon could read too clearly. They all needed Mickelle, more than she knew. And her boys needed *him,* despite Bryan's antagonistic attitude.

But maybe he was wrong. Maybe he should cut his losses and give up before his heart was trampled on too badly.

"But you can't give up," Belle urged.

He hadn't realized he had spoken that last part of his thought aloud. "I'm sorry, kids. I'm just a little frustrated." The reality was that he would never give up until Mickelle had remarried someone else. Perhaps this doggedness was what made him such a successful business man.

"He even brought her another rose like last time," Belle said disdainfully. She scowled at Mickelle's porch, although Mickelle and her friend had already disappeared inside.

Damon held his breath. "Like last time?"

"Yes. Jeremy told me his mom met some guy on Saturday—it must be this guy—and he gave her that bunch of roses on the counter. Didn't you see them?"

"I saw them." Damon's anger drained slowly away.

They were still parked at Mickelle's curb, but Damon drew out his cell phone and dialed her number. Mickelle answered, sounding happy. "Hello?"

"The roses," Damon said without preamble. "Did *he* give them to you?"

There was a brief pause and Damon half expected her to laugh and tell him that he knew very well who had sent the flowers.

"Yes," she answered softly. "It doesn't mean . . . well . . ." He sensed there was more she wanted to say, but wouldn't. Whether because of Colton Scofield's presence or because of the strain between them, he didn't know.

"Enjoy them," he growled, and hung up. He shouldn't have done it, but he felt better.

At least now the oiliness of the man's appearance made sense. Somehow he had intercepted Damon's gift and passed it off as his own. Damon punched another set of numbers on his phone. "Hello, Keith? Damon here. Yes, I've got a little job for you. No"—he glanced at his children—"can't really discuss it over the phone. Could you come to my house, say around eight? No? Okay, nine. Good deal. See you then."

"Can he bring his daughter?" Belle asked. Keith was Damon's new attorney and he had a little girl just Belle's age.

"Not tonight," Damon told her. "He's going to have family night with his kids and then they have to get to bed."

"Rats!" She settled back in the seat. "Oh, Dad," she said as he started the engine. "Do you mind if I clean out my closet? There's a whole bunch of stuff that I can't wear anymore. It's just taking up room."

Damon chuckled at how grown-up she sounded. "Do you need some bigger clothes?"

"Maybe."

"Let me know." He had recently given a fashion consultant he knew a hefty amount of money to outfit the kids for school, but she may not have covered it all. Mickelle would know; maybe he could ask her to check over Belle's wardrobe. She would probably agree—if she was still speaking to him tomorrow. At worst, he could take Belle to the mall and turn her loose. He sighed. At least Belle wouldn't be wearing a bra any time in the near future.

And soon Damon would know the truth about Mr. Cover Boy. Keith with his connections would see to it for him, even if they had to use his investigator to do the legwork. He would get to the bottom of this mess.

* * * * *

Mickelle stared at the phone in her hand. Damon had sounded angry. She knew he had been hurt by the realization that Colton was interested in her as more than a friend, and she wanted to let Damon know that she wasn't interested in pursuing a relationship with Colton. That if she had been ready, she would choose Damon.

Of course, by staying quiet she knew Damon would have no choice but to back off. Meanwhile, Colton was good company.

He had the boys charmed in a few minutes. Mickelle wasn't surprised that Jeremy liked him—he liked everyone—but was amazed that Bryan did. He insisted upon hearing the story of the insurance money three times, and hung on the man's every word.

He was also in awe of Colton's sports car. "Can I ride in your Z?"

"Sure, why not?" Colton said. "If it's okay with your mom." He gave Mickelle an appreciative smile. "Honestly, this is the best roast beef I've ever eaten. You're a wonderful cook."

He was full of similar compliments that made Mickelle's color rise. She constantly searched his face to see if he was teasing, but saw only sincerity.

After dinner, Colton took them for a ride, stopping for ice cream. When they returned, it was later than she had expected and she knew the boys had to go to sleep soon or they would never wake in time for school.

"Go inside and get ready," she told them. "I'll be there in a minute," she added, so that Colton wouldn't come inside again. It had been a nice evening, but she was exhausted and wanted to sleep. She was also irritated that she hadn't given the boys the lesson she had prepared for family night, though it was really her own fault for inviting Colton. But what else could she do? He had seemed so lonely.

Colton insisted on walking her to the door. "I had a really wonderful time, Mickelle," he said when they arrived on the lighted porch in full view of any peering neighbors. "I feel so comfortable with you, as though I've known you my entire life."

"It was fun," Mickelle agreed, not buying the line.

"You know what?" He caught her hand, rubbing it with his thumb. "I'm so grateful to the Lord that you were there Saturday night. I believe I was placed there at that time so I could help you."

"I'm very grateful," she admitted with a laugh. "Now all I have to do is figure out a way to invest the money."

"Any ideas on that?"

He seemed genuinely interested so Mickelle answered, "Well, my brother-in-law has a few mutual funds. I thought I'd look into that." Then, remembering Damon's comment, she added, "I'm not sure how successful he's been."

"I know a guy who's been fabulously successful for me." Colton pointed to his car. "I bought that new from the proceeds of two months. It was a little bit of risk, so I wouldn't recommend something that bold, but he has plenty of other options. I could give you his name, if you want. Even go with you. He doesn't charge for consulting."

"Thank you." Mickelle was glad to accept his offer. If she could begin to understand investments she wouldn't need Jesse . . . or Damon. She could prove to them once and for all that she could take control of her own affairs.

"Well, I'll give him a call and see what he's got open tomorrow. I doubt you'll have your insurance money by then, but at least you'll be prepared."

"You don't have to come," she said quickly, her free hand on the door-knob. Her other hand was still in his. "I'm sure you have a job to do."

"I can work it in. Don't worry about it."

"Thank you." It seemed like she had repeated those words a dozen times.

"No, thank *you*." He paused and tears welled in his eyes. "I appreciate what you did for me this afternoon. I needed to talk. Sometimes I miss my family so much that I don't know what to do. I wonder if I will ever have such a wonderful thing again, or if my mistake with my boys will keep me from ever being truly happy."

Compassion filled Mickelle. "I think you will. The Lord knows you and loves you. He'll have someone prepared."

"You're right." Colton brought her hand to his mouth and kissed it like one of the knights of old. "And you know what?" Now his voice was husky. "I think that someone is you."

Mickelle felt shocked, although in the back of her mind she suspected they had been heading down this road since he had given her that wonderful bouquet of golden roses. And besides, she liked Colton. She liked how she felt when he was with her. There was no uncertainty, no fear of loss. Why was that? And his terrible past only made her want to help him, to ease his loss. But a relationship? She had tried that with Damon and now she could barely see the man without having a panic attack.

"I know you're confused," Colton said. "I'm not a very patient man, but I am willing to wait for you." He kissed her hand again gently before releasing it and going down the steps. "See you tomorrow!"

She watched him drive off into the night.

Inside the house, she found the boys waiting for her, dressed for bed. "Colton's nice," Jeremy said, looking at his brother for confirmation. "He even told us he'd play soccer next time if he remembers to bring a change of clothes." He frowned. "Damon never cared what he was wearing."

Mickelle was also thinking of Damon, of his terse voice on the phone when he asked about the roses, and the hurt in his eyes earlier. She remembered their long talks. Oh, how she missed them already! She wished they could go back to where they had been before last Friday.

Before she realized that she could lose him.

But by pushing him away, wasn't that exactly what she had done?

One thing was certain: as flattering as Colton's interest in her was, she would have to tell him the truth about her relationship with Damon. She didn't know where she and Damon would end up in the long run, but Colton's presence was only complicating matters. She felt gratitude toward him for obtaining the insurance money and, yes, sorrow for his loss, but that was all. *I hope he understands.*

She sighed, feeling better about the whole subject. Picking up the phone, she almost dialed Damon's number to tell him she was thinking of him. But what would that mean? She couldn't do it, not yet.

Instead, she waited until the boys were in bed and then she called her sister, Brionney, recounting the events of the past three days.

"Mom told me about the money," Brionney said. "I wondered when you'd get around to calling me. Dang it all, you have to call me first! I'm your sister."

"Well, I've been a bit busy."

"So it seems. But I don't know about this Colton character. Are you sure you can trust him?"

"I'm sure of that much. But I'm afraid he's going to end up hurt." Mickelle told Brionney about his boys and how she wished she could help him.

"That's too sad. Hold on a minute; the twins are asleep, but I just have to check on them after hearing that."

Mickelle chuckled. "That's okay, I'll let you go. I only wanted to talk to you for a minute. Thanks."

"Any time." Yet Brionney didn't hang up. "What about you and Damon?"

Mickelle swallowed hard. This was what she had called to talk about, but now her pride—and her fears—were getting in the way. "I'm not sure," she said honestly. "I think I might have hurt him too much. And I'm still afraid."

"Damon doesn't give up easily. Do you want me to talk to him?"

"No." Mickelle's answer was quick. "Hey, I'll talk to you later, okay? I know you want to go check on your babies. I'll call you again tomorrow."

Mickelle went into her room, still carrying the phone. She dialed Damon's number, but hung up before it could ring. *I need a psychiatrist, not a husband,* she thought. Then she laughed. Damon would have loved that joke, and she was being an idiot. A complete idiot. And had been since last Friday. More than anything she wanted to talk to Damon, to hear his voice. She called his number again, but the phone was busy. She dialed his cell, but he had turned it off, and leaving a voice-mail just wasn't the same thing.

In her dresser she found Damon's ring and slipped it on her finger. Since she had removed her old wedding band her finger felt naked. Not so when she was wearing this ring. It was much heavier and larger than she would have chosen, but it felt right because Damon had given it to her.

That didn't mean she was going to marry Damon, but it did mean she had to confront her fears, and search out the possibility. Tomorrow she would talk with him. Her heart beat a little faster at the prospect.

Would he forgive her? And what would she do about Colton?

CHAPTER 9

The next morning Mickelle awoke early and took special pains to get ready for her talk with Damon. But Damon didn't come to the door when he dropped off Belle. Instead, he waited in his car to see that she got inside all right and then drove away. Mickelle was irritated all morning because her plan had gone awry.

The boys steered clear of her instinctively, but Belle chattered away as if nothing were wrong. Mickelle was reading the obituaries in her renewed subscription of the *Daily Herald,* a morbid habit she had developed after Riley's death, but something she hadn't indulged in during the past month or more, and Belle's chatter was interrupting her focus. Finally, Mickelle asked her—a bit more sharply than intended—to wait out on the porch for the neighbor children so they could walk to school.

"Aren't you going to take us to school?" Belle asked, her dark eyebrows drawing together in consternation.

"It's not cold today." Mickelle glanced out the kitchen window to her garden, thinking that an hour or two of work there should improve her mood.

"Yeah, but I got a heavy load."

Mickelle set down her newspaper and hefted Belle's bright red backpack. "Criminy child, what on earth do you have in here?"

Belle shrugged. "Just a few little outfits."

Mickelle investigated and found a beautiful off-white satin and black velvet dress that she had only seen Belle wear once, two skirts, several pairs of designer jeans, and a dozen tops. Hardly "a few little outfits."

"What did you do, clean out your closet?" she asked, stuffing in several pairs of socks that had fallen out, and handing the backpack to Belle.

"Yes, I did."

"Does your father know?"

"Yeah, I told him last night."

Mickelle stared hard at Belle. For all her apparent innocence, the child could tell a fib better than anyone she had met. But she also knew that Belle was on her best behavior because she wanted a horse for Christmas, or before then if possible.

"Well, I don't know if I like the idea of you changing clothes at school," Mickelle said, because she couldn't see any other reason for Belle wanting to bring the clothes. Most likely, showing off outfits was the latest fad during recess.

"If I do, I'll go into the bathroom and lock the door. Don't worry." Belle put her backpack on her shoulder and smiled. "So, you gonna take us?"

"Sure." Mickelle didn't know how Damon could deny this child anything. *She* certainly couldn't. "Go get in the car."

* * * * *

Damon was in a foul mood. He wanted to shake sense into Mickelle by telling her about the roses, and then kiss her until she clung to him with desire.

Yeah, right. He worried that she had already fallen in love with Mr. Cover Boy. But how could she?

Every time Damon had kissed Mickelle he knew that she loved him, even though she wasn't prepared yet to say the words. He slammed his hand against the steering wheel, wincing as he hit the bruise that had developed from hitting it in the same place the night before. Well, at least he wasn't twisting the ends of his moustache.

He arrived at his office in Orem, sneaking in the back door so that he wouldn't have to see anyone. During normal hours he wouldn't have succeeded, but since it was only seven, most of the employees hadn't yet arrived. They were crowded into every nook and cranny and would stay that way until the new building near Utah Lake was finished. He hoped it would be soon.

Glancing at his clock, he saw that he was late in calling Tanner to make sure he left in time for the bus. He rang the house in Alpine, but there was no answer, so Damon was sure his son had caught the bus.

The morning dragged by. Twice he found himself nodding off, and more than once he found himself thinking of Mickelle. By noon he could stand it no longer. He was going over to her house and talk to her whether she wanted to listen or not!

He met his partner Jesse in the hall with Brionney. They pulled apart a bit quickly and Damon knew he had interrupted a kiss.

"Hi, Damon." Brionney smiled at him, her blue eyes sparkling. "Don't mind me, I'm just leaving."

Jesse watched her leave, shaking his head. "Fastest lunch we ever had. I never thought we'd go to a McDonald's drive-in for a lunch date." He lifted the McDonald's bag in his hand. "Mickelle told her a story about a friend of hers who had twins drown in the bathtub, and it really scared Brionney. She left the twins with my mother, but because of that story, she's afraid to be without them for long."

"Even with her mother?"

"It'll wear off after she warns everyone about giving them baths." Jesse grinned. "Actually, I'm glad she's worrying about it so I won't have to. That story *was* pretty tragic. Don't know what I'd do if I lost my boys."

Damon clapped his hand on his partner's shoulder. "It's probably just a story. You know how these things go around. Some woman must have made it up to warn her husband about leaving the kids in the bath."

"Yeah, could be. But it seems I remember reading about a similar incident in the newspaper. Been awhile, though."

Damon could smell the aroma coming from the fast food bag and his stomach growled so loudly that Jesse heard it. "Here," he said, shoving the bag at Damon. "Sounds like you need this more than I do." He started for the exit where his wife had disappeared.

"Where're you going?"

"To take my wife and sons out for a real lunch," Jesse threw the words over his shoulder. "After all, I just signed up two more hospitals for our program while you were taking it easy last weekend. I deserve a break."

Damon felt an intense rush of jealousy. But Jesse had given him an idea. Surely if he arrived on Mickelle's doorstop with a lunch invitation, she couldn't refuse. Better yet, he'd show up with Chinese food. She loved Chinese, and, knowing her, it was unlikely that she would send him away.

Removing the burger from the bag, Damon took a bite. No use in letting this food go to waste.

As he waited in the drive-up for the Chinese food, he called his attorney to see if he already had the goods on Mr. Cover Boy. He didn't, but promised to have something later in the day. Damon was sure it was just a matter of time.

* * * * *

When the doorbell rang just before lunch Mickelle was still in her gardening attire—an old sweatshirt and stained jeans with rips in the knees. She opened the door anyway, expecting a neighbor or the mailman.

"Damon!" She was ashamed for him to see her this way, especially in light of the conversation she wanted to have with him.

Or did she? Now that he was standing in front of her, her heart was racing so quickly she couldn't think straight. She longed for him to take her into his arms, yet at the same time that feeling frightened her.

No, I'm through all that fear, she told herself. But her thundering heart told another story.

As though sensing her nervousness, he held up a large bag in his hand. "I brought lunch. I hope you haven't eaten."

She glanced down at her clothing. "Not yet. I was in the garden." As she spoke, she stepped back from the door and let him in. She passed through the short entryway and entered the kitchen. "Want a tomato?" On the counter, next to the three dozen golden roses, sat a huge wicker basket full of red tomatoes.

He laughed, but his eyes were focused on the roses.

Mickelle knew she had to speak. "About the flowers," she said. The bag in his hand froze halfway to the counter. "About my friend Colton . . ."

Damon set the bag on the counter and faced her, his amber-brown eyes uncommonly rigid. "I've been meaning to talk to you about him, Mickelle. Look, I know you like this guy, but I don't trust him. He's hiding something. I *feel* it."

This tactic took Mickelle by surprise. It also made her angry. "I think I'm old enough to choose my friends," she remarked acidly. "There is something in his past that was very traumatic, and his twin sons died because of it, but he's a good man. I've enjoyed getting to know him . . . as a friend. And he's been nothing but help with my insurance company."

Damon glanced again at the bouquet of roses. His nostrils flared slightly as he took a deep breath. "I think you should know that I'm having someone check into his background."

"You're what?" She couldn't be hearing him right. Riley would have done something like this. He would assume that she didn't know what she was doing. He would try to control her life.

"You heard me," he stated. "I'm having him checked out."

"You're jealous!"

"Dang right, I'm jealous." Damon's face was heated now, his amber eyes fierce. He folded his arms obstinately over his chest. "And I don't know what sort of story Mr. Cover Boy has told you, but I know his type—so oily, you can't get him off you. He wants something, mark my words."

The insinuation increased Mickelle's own anger. "Is it so hard to believe that he would be interested in me?"

His bushy eyebrows rose, as did his voice. "Hard? Not a bit. Any man in his right mind would be lucky to have you. But that pretty boy isn't worth the fake designer clothes he wears, and I don't think you're in any position to recognize it."

"Why, because I'm not as smart or as rich as you are?"

"It has nothing to do with money!" he bellowed. "And in case you haven't figured it out, I'm doing this because I care about you. I *love* you."

"Well thank you for spelling that out Mr. Billionaire!" Mickelle shouted back. "You certainly have a funny way of showing it!" She was trembling with rage, as though all of her pent up emotions in the past week were bursting forth in one huge explosion.

"Then how's this?" He pulled her to him firmly and kissed her passionately on the mouth, his lips molding against hers as though they had been created to be this close. "Did he kiss you like this?" he murmured hotly, his moustache brushing her skin, and sending a shuddering warmth over her entire body. "Does he make you feel the way I do?" Cupping the back of her head with one hand and placing the other on her back, he kissed her neck, cheeks, and eyes. Then he found her mouth again and his kiss deepened, urgently seeking. For a delicious moment Mickelle reveled at being kissed so thoroughly, at being held so firmly in his arms. When at last he drew away, she moaned softly.

She opened her eyes and found him watching her, smiling gently, knowingly. She hated that he could read her need for him so plainly. "Please leave." Keeping her voice steady and devoid of emotion wasn't easy.

"I love you, Mickelle," he said earnestly. "I will always love you." In his eyes Mickelle now saw a sadness, a deep longing for something that went beyond mere intimacy, but she stifled the urge to reach out to him. She was still angry that he was checking up on her, and angry that he should kiss her that way. And even more livid at herself for responding.

Without another word, he sauntered to the door. She stayed where she was, unmoving. On the back of her head and neck she felt the imprint of his fingertips where he'd held her to him during their kiss. Her face tingled where his lips had touched her skin.

At once, she missed him, wished desperately that she could tell him what was in her heart—both her fears and her growing feelings toward him. Her eyes went to the large white bag Damon had set on the counter. Slowly, she opened it, and tears threatened when she saw the chopsticks and cartons of Chinese food. He knew her so well!

But she was too angry to let this realization stem the flow of her frustration. She took the bag and shoved it into the refrigerator. When Damon came to pick up his children that evening, she would have them give it to him.

So there, Mr. Smarty Pants Billionaire.

Mickelle had scarcely finished changing into a clean pair of jeans and a bright blue, long-sleeved, ribbed turtleneck when the doorbell rang again. This time it was Colton. She raised an eyebrow in surprise, trying to switch gears. Her emotions with Damon had been running high, and it was a decided letdown to see Colton standing there instead of Damon. "Hello. What's up?"

He waved something in the air. "I got it! One hundred thousand dollars, and it's all yours." He handed her something that looked like a checkbook.

She glanced inside at the balance with all those zeros, and hugged him. "Oh Colton, thank you!"

"Well, now all we have to do is get it invested for you. I've asked my friend to come over, if that's all right."

Mickelle felt an abrupt, sick feeling inside. "I think I'd rather go in to see him. You know, check out his office, the company. I know you trust him, but I'm new at this. And to me this is an awful lot of money."

Darn that Damon! She knew it was because of him that she was being so cautious. Damon seemed to forget that if it weren't for Colton, she wouldn't even have this money.

"I don't have a problem with that." Colton was suddenly very close, too close for comfort, especially after her encounter with Damon. Mickelle stepped back into the entryway as he continued, "I can just give him a call and we can schedule an appointment tomorrow. Meanwhile, I'll give you the name of his company so you can check out their reputation. I'll write down his number too, so you can call and talk to him personally. I'm confident we can safely get you at least sixteen percent return a year from your money. That's what . . . about sixteen thousand a year?"

Mickelle shook her head in amazement. Given those numbers, it might be better not to pay off the house, but to make mortgage payments with the interest earnings. Was this how Damon's wealth kept multiplying?

She grinned at Colton, feeling happy. He smiled back and said, "You're beautiful when you smile." There was a tenderness in his eyes that she couldn't mistake.

"Colton, look," she began.

He shook his head. "I know what you're going to say, and I don't want to hear it. It's because of what happened with my boys, isn't it?"

"Oh, no!" Mickelle put a hand on his arm. "Don't think that for a minute. It's just that I've been dating a man—the father of the children I watch—and last Friday he asked me to marry him. Well, right now I'm angry with him, and—" She recalled for a clear second her response to Damon's urgent kiss, and had to shake her head to clear it. "It's not fair to let you think I'm interested in a relationship with you. Heck, I don't even know if I'm ready for *any* relationship, but I have to resolve whatever it is between him and me. Do you understand?"

"Is this an excuse?" The words were obviously painful for him, and for a moment he resembled the wounded hero in a romance film. "I know it's a hard thing to take, my past. Would it help if I tell you I've learned from my mistakes? That I would be a good father if given another chance?"

Mickelle was dismayed at this turn in the conversation. "Wait. Stay right here. I'll show you." She ran down the hall to her room and found Damon's ring. Quickly, she brought it back to Colton. "See?" she said, showing it to him. "He gave me this ring."

Colton let the air rush out of his lungs. "Wow, that is some impressive stone."

"I know."

"Unless it's fake."

"I don't think so."

"That's probably worth more than your insurance money." The scowl on Colton's face reminded her of Bryan. "I hope that's not a factor in your decision."

"Of course it's not!" Yet she wondered, remembering how marvelous Damon's house was, and how she had felt like a princess there.

Colton's eyebrows drew together in annoyance. "I think you should quit watching his kids. I think he's using them to get to you, and that's unfair."

"I enjoy taking care of them."

"I know you do." He reached out and captured her hand, rubbing the back of it with his thumb. "You have a wonderful, kind heart, but maybe it's time to find out what's best for *you*. I'm here, Mickelle, and I'm willing to give my all for this relationship."

She tried to pull away from him, but his grip tightened. "What relationship? Colton, we've known each other just a few days. This is only the fourth time I've even seen you!" Surely he was blowing everything all out of proportion. Of course, she had felt completely smitten with Damon after seeing him that many times. Or fewer, even. Her knees had gone weak at the very sight of him—they still did.

"Mickelle, I—"

"Colton, let go! You're hurting me!"

Instantly, the anger in his expression vanished. "Sorry. Please forgive me, Mickelle. I've just never felt so strongly for a woman as I do for you. It seems like I've known you forever. I can't explain it. There's a bond between us. Maybe it was how you listened to me up in the mountains, or how you let me kiss you. I don't know. But just don't write me off so easily. Please."

She didn't answer. He was making her feel distinctly uneasy, but she owed him so much for all the help with her insurance money. Because of him, her children would have a college education.

"Just give me a few days, okay?" he pleaded, giving her a dimpled smile. "I promise to behave myself."

"All right," she agreed reluctantly. Maybe by then she and Damon would be back to normal, and he could help her convince Colton that she wasn't interested.

"Now how about some lunch?"

She grinned and waved the new checkbook. "Only if you'll let me pay."

"No way. I may not be as rich as your *other* boyfriend, but I do have means." He laughed and so did she, and the tension between them completely vanished.

* * * * *

Mickelle returned from a short but enjoyable lunch with Colton just as Brionney drove up to her house with the twins. Colton helped Mickelle out of his car and stayed for a moment to meet her sister. He made a fuss over the little boys, casting a bleak expression at Mickelle. She couldn't imagine how his heart must be breaking as he compared

Brionney's twins to those he had lost, and her heart grew more tender toward him.

Brionney shook her head as Colton drove away. "I've never, ever, seen such a perfectly gorgeous man up so close. He's really something. A little shorter than your usual idea of a movie star, but tall enough for me."

"Wait a minute, I thought you were happily married." Mickelle picked up Gabriel and followed his brother Forest, who was already heading toward the front porch on his wobbly legs.

Brionney tossed back her white-blonde hair with a laugh. "Of course I am. And I wouldn't trade Jesse for any man, not even one that gorgeous. Still, one can't help but wonder why he's not married."

"He thinks it's because of his boys."

They had caught up to Forest and Brionney picked him up in her arms, while Mickelle opened the door. "Maybe so. But I still don't think he holds a candle to Damon. Now there's a man with pure masculine appeal!"

"Him!" Mickelle's earlier anger returned with force. "Do you know that he's insane? He's having a background check done on Colton. Can you believe that? What a waste of money."

Brionney smiled thoughtfully. "I think it's sweet."

They put the boys on the kitchen floor with a basket of toys Mickelle kept under the counter for their visits. "It's not sweet at all, it's obsessive."

"Maybe he has a reason."

"He doesn't even know Colton. Just because I won't marry him he's got to try and control my life."

Brionney slid onto a stool at the counter. "Control. That's what you're really worried about, isn't it? You're still afraid that Damon's trying to control you the way Riley did. But he's not like that!"

"Then how do you explain this obsession with Colton? It's not like I'm planning to run off with the man. We're friends, that's all. And he did me a big favor."

"Well, there is something kind of oily about him, you have to admit," Brionney said, ignoring her frown. "He's just so perfect-looking. What do you bet he's got some big flaw, like he's afraid to get dirty or something. I'll bet he's never put his head beneath the hood of a car."

"And Damon has?"

"Yes, when he first started out. And even more recently. Who was it that changed your wipers on that old junk heap you still have out front? And wasn't that right before he found you the deal on your new car? Don't you remember any of that?"

Mickelle did, suddenly, and a warmth suffused her body, vying with the heat of the anger. Damon had fixed the wipers without telling her he had done it, and without her asking. And that happened before they had ever gone out on a date.

With this recollection she had to struggle to remember why she was so angry at him. "Well, if he thinks that a passionate kiss and a little Chinese food can make up for the fact that he doesn't trust my judgment, he's mistaken!"

Brionney's eyes widened eagerly. "He kissed you! Today? But I thought you and he were . . . Well, how was it? Tell me all the juicy details."

Mickelle kicked a toy back to Forest who had thrown it at her feet, and sank to the stool next to her sister with a long sigh. "It was fabulous. Absolutely and perfectly fabulous." She heaved another sigh. "I was married for fourteen years and I never had a kiss affect me that way. I don't even have words for it. How can it be so wonderful when I'm so angry at him?"

"You're in love."

Goose bumps rippled over Mickelle's flesh. "But—"

"Come on, admit it," Brionney said earnestly. "I know you're terrified of losing someone you love again, but I've seen you together. You love him and he loves you."

"He says he does. It just seems too good to be true. A rich, good-looking, upstanding man, nice kids, an incredible house . . ."

"Well, sometimes dreams do come true."

"Maybe he just sees me as a mother for his children." Deny it as she might, Colton's words had stayed with her.

"If you had seen him Saturday night, all set to go to that dance to find you, despite the fact that he was so dizzy he could barely stand, you wouldn't doubt his motives." Brionney lifted Gabriel from the floor where Forest was trying to steal his toy. Over Forest's wails, she continued, "I finally convinced him that sending you flowers would suffice. He called about a dozen places—personally, mind you—before he found one that was open and that carried the right color." Brionney's gaze found the golden roses on the counter. "I guess these are it, huh? Very nice." She stood and leaned over them, breathing in deeply. Gabriel reached for a rose, but Brionney held his hand back, helping him smell the flower instead. Forest saw the exchange and lifted his arms, demanding with screams to see the flowers too.

Mickelle felt the blood drain from her face. Suddenly, a few things she had thought odd fit into place: Damon's covert glances at the roses, and his abrupt question on the phone about them. No wonder he suspected Colton!

There had to be some mistake. Perhaps Damon's flowers had never made it—though the golden color of these had him written all over them. Maybe Colton had mistaken them for the ones he had ordered.

Strange there had been no card.

"Mickelle," Brionney said, waving a hand in front of her face. "Hello, Mickelle, are you listening?"

"Yeah, what?"

"I said that no matter how nice this Colton fellow is—or how good-looking—you really ought to be careful. You know that women get taken advantage of all the time. For all we really know, he's a crook in disguise."

"Now you sound like Damon." But the anger she had felt toward him had vanished. If she hadn't been so quick to judge his motives and be offended by them, he might have confided his suspicions. Even if Colton had a perfectly good excuse for the flower mix-up, there were definite grounds for questions.

Brionney shrugged. "Well, he's a smart guy and we both care about you." She let the twin in her arms—Forest now, Mickelle noticed, though she hadn't seen Brionney trading twins—slide to the ground next to his brother.

"When I even think about that, I start to have a panic attack," Mickelle said, though that wasn't quite true. She hadn't experienced one since yesterday morning.

"Well, I think you and Damon have a chance at something wonderful. You have to give that a chance, no manner how many panic attacks you have. They're probably linked to your anxiety about Riley's death anyway, not to Damon. Have you thought about seeing your doctor again?"

"Yes. In fact, I think the man I really need in my life right now is a psychiatrist."

Brionney chuckled. "I'll tell that to Damon. What do you bet he changes occupations?"

Mickelle laughed with her sister. She couldn't help herself. No matter what protest she made, Brionney had an answer—one she desperately needed to hear.

"You win," she gave in. "I'll talk to Damon. But I still think he's gone too far. I'm Colton's friend, nothing more, and it's not like he wants anything from me. He didn't even charge me a fee for getting my money." Again she was stretching the truth. Colton did want a relationship.

"Then tell that to Damon. But I think you'll have a hard time convincing him that Colton doesn't want something. I've seen the look in Colton's eyes, and it makes me uncomfortable."

"You're reading too much into it. He might be a little zealous, that's all."

Brionney rolled her eyes. "Wow, are you defensive! Now I see why you and Damon fought." She grinned wickedly. "Then again, if it leads to such a wonderful kiss as you described, maybe you should fight more often. Heck, I might go home and pick a good fight with Jesse tonight."

Mickelle felt her face turn red, but she laughed anyway.

"Oh no!" Brionney gaped at the clock on the wall. "Goodness, help me get the twins in the car. I was supposed to pick up Rosalie at preschool five minutes ago! And then I have a hair appointment at Chloe's."

After Brionney left, Mickelle went back inside the house, pondering her options. Then her eyes spied the paper on which Colton had written the number of his financial consultant. Maybe it was time to do a little investigating of her own.

CHAPTER 10

D amon had blown it with Mickelle. He knew he shouldn't have argued with her, but rather discussed his suspicions calmly, even when she had become defensive. He most certainly *shouldn't* have kissed her when they were both angry. But she had been so beautiful at that moment, her head held high, her blue eyes storming as she defended Mr. Cover Boy.

What a kiss! Even just thinking about it made him long to be with her.

He still shouldn't have done it.

What had he expected to prove? He only wished that he could make Mickelle understand the foreboding that filled him when he had met Colton Scofield. He had been in business too long not to recognize a crook when he saw one—no matter what kind of sheep's clothing he wore.

So help me, if he hurts her I'll . . .

Stop it!

Damon busied himself with work. He was already far behind because of his preoccupation with Mickelle. His stomach growled, unsatisfied with Jesse's hamburger. He thought of the Chinese food he had left at Mickelle's with more than a little longing. Yet he stifled the urge to run back to her house. She had made it clear that she wasn't interested in hearing his opinions on Mr. Cover Boy.

No, better not to talk to her again until he had something solid to present.

What about my flowers?

He grimaced at the thought. The flowers were proof of a sort, and he wanted to tell her he had been the one to send them, yet at the same time he remembered the hurt in her eyes when she had asked him if it was so hard to believe that Colton was attracted to her. The look stopped him from telling her the truth. He would rather have her not know he had sent the roses than to cause her more pain.

He wished now that he had not rushed his official marriage proposal. She had been so scared of trusting him in the first place, and his near death had added to her worry. He should have let more time pass before giving her the ring. *We need to talk about it,* he thought.

But would it only frighten her away further?

Damon raked his fingers through his hair, and stared at the papers on his desk. This was getting him nowhere.

A tap at the door revealed Jesse, with another sheaf of papers. "Look at this, look at this! We're doing it! The Jackson group has agreed to sign up! Everything you touch really does turn to gold! Only problem is, they want a conference call. Tonight."

Damon stifled a sigh. "I'd better ask Juliet if she can pick up the kids then. I'm fairly sure Kelle has a meeting at her ward tonight— Enrichment, or whatever they're calling it." He made a mental note to talk to Juliet, their receptionist, who was always willing to help out in a pinch.

"Have them walk over to my house. Brionney can keep an eye on them until we get done. Bryan and Jeremy are going over there anyway."

"I hate to do that to Bri. That's a lot of kids."

"She won't mind, honest. And if she does, she'll let me know. The girls'll have a ball with Belle."

Damon smiled, regaining some of his good humor. "If she doesn't boss them to death. But I'd really rather get Juliet to take them home. Our cook will appreciate having them home to actually eat her meal. And that means they can get ready for bed. Less work for me when I get home."

In a way, he was relieved. By having to work late tonight he wouldn't have to deliberate over what he would say to Mickelle. Instead, he would concentrate on the business at hand and give Mickelle the room she seemed to need.

"Let me see what questions I've got to prepare for," he growled, reaching for the papers. "If I remember correctly, these guys are not easily satisfied."

* * * * *

Mickelle made a few calls in the moments she had left before she needed to pick up Tanner at school. After talking to Colton's investor friend, the front office at the investment firm where he worked, and the apartment manager where Colton had said he was staying, she still had nothing on which to base an accusation.

Except the flowers.

Mickelle chewed on her lip, deep in thought. Colton seemed to be all he was supposed to be. And yet . . .

Something didn't feel right. Was it only Damon's suspicions crowding in on her, or was the Lord trying to warn her? The truth was, she had been so out of touch with spiritual things in the aftermath of Riley's death, that she wasn't as practiced at using the gift of the Holy Ghost as she had once been.

It's time for that to change, she thought. Slipping onto her knees next to her bed, she prayed that she could come to a decision about Colton, that somehow she could find out if he should be trusted.

At least his investor friend seems to be on the up and up.

Impulsively, she went to the kitchen and dialed Brenda's cell number. Since she had been the one to introduce her to Colton, maybe she held the answer.

Her friend answered quickly, her bubbling personality filling the space between them. "Mickelle, it's good to hear from you! How's it going with Colton?"

"Well, that's exactly why I'm calling." Mickelle said, feeling awkward.

"What is it?"

"Did you by chance see Colton receive the flowers he gave me at the dance?"

"Nope. But that was so sweet, wasn't it? If a man did that for me, I'd be tempted to marry him."

"How's your daughter?" Mickelle picked up a cloth and began to wipe the counter.

"My daughter?"

"Yes, your daughter. Wasn't she the reason you went home early from the dance? I didn't see you at church and I wondered."

"Oh, we went to visit my parents—didn't I tell you? But Mickelle, I thought you would figure out that my daughter being sick was an excuse to let Colton take you home."

Mickelle froze. "Whose idea was it?" she asked carefully. "Yours or Colton's?"

"Well, his. Isn't that just *precious*? I would have done it myself, if I'd thought about it first. He beat me to it. I think he's quite smitten with you."

"He knew all about my not getting the insurance money."

There was a brief pause. "Yes, some of us talked when we went out to lunch that day. Don't be mad. We just wanted to help. I know how difficult it can be to survive on social security. When he told us what he did for a living, we all thought the Lord was working in His mysterious ways."

Or maybe in Colton's mysterious ways, Mickelle thought.

"He seemed sure he could help you."

And why was that? How could he have been so sure?

Brenda's voice became apologetic. "Did something happen? Is something wrong? I'm sorry if I said something I shouldn't have."

"No, everything's fine. Colton did go to bat for me with the insurance company." Mickelle was reluctant to tell Brenda everything. "I'll let you know how it goes."

"Why don't you let me pick you up for Enrichment meeting tonight? We can talk more then."

Mickelle was hesitant, but she had no real excuse not to accept. The boys were going over to Brionney's, and Belle and Tanner would be in Alpine by then. Besides, it might be good to get out with a friend.

"Okay, but don't be late." Of course, that was like telling the sun not to rise, but they would likely only miss the opening song, and going with a friend was better than going alone.

She hung up the phone, feeling pensive. Confusion was foremost in her thoughts, and she didn't know how to change that. A swift glance at the clock told her she didn't have time to dwell on her problems. Tanner would be waiting at the high school.

After picking up Tanner and seeing that he and Bryan were started on their homework, Mickelle went to Forbes Elementary for Belle and Jeremy. After all, Belle would still be struggling under her heavy load of clothes; yet that was only an excuse. The real reason Mickelle wanted to go the school came from a pair of large, dark eyes in a thin, freckle-covered face. A face marred by bruises. Jennie Anne. Had Belle talked to the teacher about her mathematical ability? And how had the child gotten those ugly bruises?

She told herself it was none of her business, but that didn't stop her from going to the school. During the months after Riley's death, when she had been obsessed with the obituaries and depressing head-lines, she had read too many times about children suffering because no one interfered. Often, she would stay awake nights thinking and praying for those unfortunate children. Perhaps that was why she was so protective of her own.

Of course, Jennie Anne might have a perfectly wonderful family, but Mickelle wasn't going to rest until she was sure.

Belle looked relieved when Mickelle appeared at her classroom door. Her classmates streamed past her, but she stood near her desk. Jennie Anne was with her, hair as unkempt as before, but today her clothes looked surprisingly new. She carried a faded yellow backpack that was stuffed to the bursting point. Mickelle smiled, grateful the homely little girl had been included in whatever game Belle and her friends had been playing.

"I'm so glad you came," Belle said. "I was worried Jennie Anne'd have to walk home with her backpack so heavy."

Mickelle thought how sweet it was that Belle seemed to be worried more about her friend than herself. "Hi, Jennie Anne," she said with a smile. "Does your aunt care if I give you a ride home?"

Jennie Anne smiled at Mickelle shyly. Her dark hair barely moved as she shook her head, as though held in place by weeks of dirt and grime. The large bruise on her cheek was now a mottled gray-green, edged with yellow. "She don't care."

"You mean she *doesn't* care," said Mrs. Palmer, emerging from another group of students. She looked slightly worn from a day with twenty-three first-graders, but her smile was still in place.

"Oh, yeah." Jennie Anne flushed. She didn't look at her teacher or

Mickelle.

"She never cares about nothin'," Belle added. "Jennie Anne's aunt, I mean."

Mrs. Palmer put a slender hand on Jennie Anne's shoulder. As on the previous day, the girl cringed silently, her eyes going bright with unshed tears. An odd protectiveness kindled in Mickelle's heart. Was this child so afraid of Mrs. Palmer that even a touch from her evoked fear? Or was there something else going on, something even more sinister?

"May I talk to you a few moments?" Mickelle asked. She glanced at the attentive girls and added, "Alone?"

"Sure, come on over to my desk. I have a few minutes. Belle and Jennie Anne can work on the alphabet."

Belle grinned at her teacher and willingly pulled a piece of paper out of her desk. She took a short pencil from behind her ear and began to write.

Mickelle felt nervous as she tried to put her thoughts in order. "It's not about Belle, really. It's about . . . Jennie Anne."

"A nice little girl," Mrs. Palmer said, but her hazel eyes were troubled. "Most of the children can't see beyond her . . . her outer appearance. I know it's sad to say, but . . ." She brightened. "Belle has been a real friend. The first two children I assigned to Jennie Anne caused her not to talk for the whole day. The next two said that she . . . well, smelled bad and they didn't want to be with her. Only Belle became her friend. She's a very special child, Belle is. I keep thinking maybe she overlooks all the outer stuff because she's younger, but she's so precocious in all the other areas that theory seems to be off. I certainly have my hands full trying to keep her learning." She broke off, smiling self-consciously. "But then you know that better than I do. Belle's a wonderful student. A teacher's dream come true. She lights up my life, the whole room, really."

"Well, she has her moments," Mickelle offered, pleased with the comments. "But she does love to learn. And I have to admit that I was a little concerned when I learned that you were pairing her with someone who couldn't read, but then yesterday I saw how smart Jennie Anne was—"

"She really is smart," interrupted Mrs. Palmer earnestly. "I know she can't read, but that's because she's never been in school before. When they tested her verbally she was off the charts, but when we handed her a pencil, she did absolutely nothing. By rights she should have gone to the kindergarten class, but they are already so full. Besides, putting her there would just hold her back even more. I thought I'd be able to work with her if she was in my class." She sighed, as though embarrassed that her youthful ideals were so clearly showing. "If I could work alone with her more, she'd be caught up in no time. There are simply too many students."

"Then you knew about the math."

"That she gets the problems right when you ask them verbally? Yes, I knew that. And now I just need to help her translate that to paper."

Her calm answer didn't seem to go with the amazing times table display Mickelle had witnessed yesterday. Had the children faked the scene for her sake? Once she might not have doubted that Belle would try, but she had been on her best behavior for weeks, determined to earn her promised horse. "But don't you think doing multiplication is exceptional in someone that age?"

The teacher blinked in confusion, and two bright spots appeared on her pale cheeks. "Doing multiplication?"

"Well, yes." Mickelle described what had happened the day before.

"I've never tested her on them. It never even crossed my mind." Mrs. Palmer stared across the room at Jennie Anne and Belle in amazement. Jeremy had arrived in the classroom, and he gave them a little wave before taking the pencil from Belle and writing something on the paper.

"Maybe we should. . ." Mrs. Palmer's expression turned from amazement to eagerness. She appeared about to call Jennie Anne to the desk, but remembering how the girl had reacted to the teacher, Mickelle put a restraining hand on her arm.

"Please, can it wait? I wanted to ask you about something else first."

Mrs. Palmer turned back to Mickelle, raising her thin eyebrows in question.

"It's just that . . . the bruise on her cheek . . ." Mickelle suddenly felt tongue-tied. "And then when you touched her shoulder yesterday and again today, she sort of . . . well, cringed . . . as though . . ." Mickelle took a deep breath. "She seemed afraid . . . or in pain."

Mrs. Palmer's gaze changed from confusion to horror. Her eyes flew to the two dark heads and one blonde that bent close together over the paper on Belle's desk. "Do you think that she has a—a bruise there, too?" The way she said the words made Mickelle silently repent for having suspected her of any undue harshness.

"I knew her home life wasn't good," Mrs. Palmer went on, "but I believed her about getting hit by the ball. I never dreamed that . . ." Her wide eyes turned to Mickelle. "I've never had to deal with something like this, never. What do I do?"

Mickelle wasn't sure either. She let her eyes stray to Jennie Anne, whose face wore a small smile. The brown eyes, which had once appeared ordinary, now shone with intelligence.

"When she looks like that you can see how smart she is. But she turns it off just like that." Mrs. Palmer snapped her fingers.

"What's her aunt like?"

The teacher gave a half-shrug with one shoulder. "Her great-aunt, really. She seemed rather ordinary."

She was silent, but Mickelle waited for more.

"Apparently Jennie Anne's mother died some years back and Mrs. Chase inherited Jennie Anne. From the way she spoke, I don't think there was any love lost between Mrs. Chase and Jennie Anne's mother."

"So why didn't Jennie Anne attend kindergarten?"

"I don't know." She leaned forward as though to share a confidence. "It was the neighbors who brought the situation to the attention of the school officials, but the aunt didn't seem to mind if Jennie Anne came to school just as long as—"

"As she didn't have to deal with the arrangements."

Mrs. Palmer grimaced. "Yeah, something like that. I felt sorry for Jennie Anne, and when the kindergarten teachers protested an extra student I volunteered. But if her aunt is . . . I'm going to have to talk with the principal."

"Well we don't know anything—yet," Mickelle said. "But to look at Jennie Anne, well, something's not right."

"It will take weeks to find the truth. I've heard some awful stories from some of the other teachers. You'd think that here in Happy Valley we wouldn't have the problems of the outside world, but we do. And they are increasing."

Mickelle knew that only too well. The mental abuse she had suffered behind closed doors was an ever-present reminder that all was *not* well in Happy Valley. At least not for everyone. For Mickelle, the idea that a small, helpless little girl could be enduring both mental and physical abuse—practically in her own backyard—was unthinkable. Someone had to stand up for her. Someone.

I will! Mickelle was surprised at the vehemence of the thought.

She took a deep breath to steady the flow of images coming from her brain. "I'll go over to her house and meet this aunt. And I would also like to work with Jennie Anne. I could come in during the day. I'll be starting school myself, but not until January, and until then I can come in for a while to work with her."

"That would be wonderful!" Mrs. Palmer's pale eyes sparkled with gratitude. "You don't know what this will mean to her."

But she was wrong. Mickelle did know. Someone had also thrown a lifeline to her in her time of need. And that someone had been Damon. "Well, I guess I'd better get going."

"Thank you for coming in."

They walked over to the children, who were still intent upon their paper. Jennie Anne had the pencil and was copying the word CAT. "Good!" encouraged Belle. "Now write hat!" She sounded it out, exaggerating the sounds of the letters, "Hhhh-aaaa-tttt."

Jennie Anne painfully printed the word.

Jeremy did a drum roll on the desk. "Now you can do rat, fat, sat, and, uh, mat, and . . ."

"And pat," Belle inserted.

"Bat!" Jennie Anne's face was transformed. She bent to her work.

Jeremy studied the ABC cards surrounding the wall. "That's all, I think. No, vat. Vat's a word, isn't it, Mom?"

Jennie Anne's hand immediately went still. Mrs. Palmer reached out to her shoulder, but hesitated and withdrew her hand at the last moment. "Go ahead, Jennie Anne," she urged gently. "That's wonderful you've learned all the sounds."

For a moment, the girl paused, as though torn. Then she slowly and methodically set her pencil on the desk and folded her hands in her lap. She stared at her hands wordlessly. No one spoke for a long time, not even talkative Belle, though Jeremy's mouth hung open in confused amazement.

Mickelle saw that Mrs. Palmer had a sheen of tears in her eyes. "Well, maybe tomorrow we can work on it some more." Her gaze went to Mickelle in a silent plea.

"Yeah, we have to go now," Mickelle said, thinking fast. "I only have sixty times three minutes before I have to go to my meeting at the church."

"Sixty times three minutes," repeated Jeremy. He was accustomed to her games, though she hadn't used them much lately. "Let's see that's, uh . . ." He grabbed Jennie Anne's discarded pencil. "Three times zero is zero. . ."

"Three hours," Jennie Anne said, as though the words were ripped from her mouth of their own accord. "One hundred and eighty minutes."

"Uh . . . three times six is eighteen, add them together." Jeremy paused. "Yes, it's a hundred and eighty minutes!" he shouted.

"Jennie Anne already told us," Belle answered in disgust. "And she doesn't need any paper, either."

Jeremy looked wounded. "Fine," he huffed.

Mickelle laughed. "Good job guys, both of you. But come on, we really have to go."

Mrs. Palmer watched them thoughtfully as they walked out the door. Mickelle felt triumphant that she had succeeded in getting Jennie Anne to show her ability, but she hoped Mrs. Palmer could also reach the child. After all, she was the one who had fought for Jennie Anne's education in the first place. So why had Jennie Anne stopped writing in front of the teacher? Did the adults make her nervous. Scared?

Mickelle drove to Jennie Anne's place listening to Jeremy and Belle exchange stories of their day. Jennie Anne kept silent. When they arrived at her home, the overwhelming neglect of the place once again demanded Mickelle's scrutiny. It was more than neglect. Perhaps even abuse.

Abuse.

"Can I come in to meet your aunt?" Mickelle asked as Jennie Anne slipped from the car, nearly losing her balance under the weight of her yellow backpack.

Jennie Anne darted a fearful glance past the willow tree at the shabby house, but when she looked back, she only shrugged.

"She's probably not there," said Belle, helpfully. "She usually isn't."

"There's a car." Mickelle eyed the rusty old automobile next to the house.

She shut off the engine and slid out of the car. She went around to where Jennie Anne waited, staring at her feet, clad in tattered sneakers that would be no protection against the coming snow. "Is it true that your aunt isn't home much Jennie Anne?" Mickelle asked, not because she disbelieved Belle's story, but because her young charge often exaggerated.

Jennie Anne didn't reply.

"You can tell Mickelle," Belle said through the open car door. "You can tell her everything like I do. She doesn't tell on you."

Jennie Anne sighed, the weight of the world on her shoulders. When she spoke, the words came reluctantly. "She's home some-times."

"Was she home yesterday when I dropped you off?"

"No."

"What time did she come?"

Jennie Anne shrugged.

Mickelle had always prided herself on getting to the truth when dealing with her boys, but this was proving difficult. "Was it dinner time?"

Again a negative shake.

"At bed time?"

Another shake.

A feeling of unease grew in the pit of Mickelle's stomach. "Jennie Anne," she asked softly, "did you see your aunt last night at all?"

"No." The forlorn word broke Mickelle's heart.

"Was anyone home at all besides you?"

Jennie Anne shook her head.

The idea of a six-year-old coming home alone, finding something to eat, and getting herself to bed was beyond belief, and yet Mickelle felt that the child hadn't lied, though she had been tempted to do so.

And now Mickelle shared Jennie Anne's burden. She had to do something to help her, but she also had to make sure she didn't betray the child's trust or make the situation worse.

Somehow she didn't think the responsibility would be easy.

CHAPTER 11

"Come on." Mickelle reached for Jennie Anne's hand. The child began to pull away, but then relaxed and left her hand in Mickelle's.

"I'm coming, too!" Belle shouted.

Jeremy followed her out of the car. "Me too!"

Mickelle wanted to order them back into the car, but didn't want to blow the circumstances out of proportion. Surely if Jennie Anne's aunt was there she would at least be civil to them.

They walked up the remains of a concrete sidewalk, barely discernible under the layers of fallen leaves and overgrown grass and weeds. Mickelle stumbled once on a broken chunk of cement, but regained her balance in time to prevent a fall. Now that she was closer, she decided that the nondescript paint had probably been yellow at one time. The single window in front was dirty, as though covered by a hundred years' worth of dust. One side of the curtains was open, but Mickelle couldn't begin to see through the glass pane. There was no porch, just a single cement step that led up to the house. With growing unease, Mickelle followed Jennie Anne up the step.

Jennie Anne opened the door with a turn of the knob and a swift nudge with her hip. Mickelle stood squinting just inside the door, blinking in the dim light. The carpet—or what there was left of it— was green shag. The pathway from the door was worn bare, and the curtain, the one Mickelle had thought was open, was missing. These things in themselves weren't bad signs, because Mickelle had never believed that poverty was a sin, but the clutter and neglect of the front room were inexcusable. Boxes, magazines, and piles of clothes filled every corner. Only a path leading to the battered couch was free of everything but several scraps of paper. The couch itself was relatively clear, holding a muddle of thin blankets and a meager stack of folded child's clothes near the end.

"We'll wait here," Mickelle said to Jennie Anne. "Why don't you see if your aunt is home?"

Jennie Anne walked around the tall stacks of boxes and clothes to a narrow path that led to the couch. She slung her heavy backpack down and then disappeared through a doorway into what Mickelle assumed was the kitchen. It was hard to tell with all the stuff jammed on top of every available space. Mickelle glanced into an open box near her and was startled to see rusty pans, a single dirty sock, and a scattering of dried mouse droppings.

"Mom," Jeremy whispered loudly, "this is sure messy!"

She put her hand on his shoulder. "Shhh." The last thing they needed to do was alienate Jennie Anne's aunt.

Besides, having a house stacked full with boxes and . . . stuff did not mean abuse. In her one year of college Mickelle had become close friends with a woman whose mother had filled her entire house in the same manner, leaving only a narrow path weaving through the house. Every surface, be it countertop, piano, or floor, had been piled at least waist—and often shoulder—high. Yet the family had been clean, talented, and very loving, and Mickelle had enjoyed knowing them. So for now she would hold off judgment . . . despite the mouse droppings.

She took a tentative sniff. There was a dusty taint to the air, but no foul odors. Perhaps this cluttered disorder was simply brought on by a move to a smaller house. There could be many reasons.

Yet Mrs. Palmer had said that the children at school had complained of Jennie Anne's smell, and she herself had noticed that the child's hair was unwashed. But what about the new clothes she was wearing today? Obviously someone cared about her enough to buy them for her.

Jennie Anne came out of the kitchen and disappeared into another room, whose entrance was nearly obscured by the odd collection. She emerged within another minute. "She's getting out of bed," she muttered. "She'll come in a minute." Her face was frightened and her voice low. She opened her mouth, as though wanting to say something, but shut it again. Her eyes became dull and shuttered.

"Is this where you sleep?" Belle asked, going down the short path to the couch. "I didn't imagine your house was like this, even though you told me. There are great places to play hide and seek here!"

"I'm not allowed to play in this stuff."

"But you get to sleep on the couch." Belle bounced on it a little. "Where's your pillow?"

Jennie Anne shrugged. "I don't like pillows." She froze abruptly and Mickelle turned to see a woman come from the other room.

The aunt was much older than Mickelle had expected, more near her own mother's age. She was short and rotund with a haggard face that drooped like a hound's. Her hair was blonde—*dyed blonde,* thought Mickelle—with finger-sized curls that curved under toward her scalp. She had blue eyes that appeared small in her drooping face, and a stubborn square jaw. Her flower-patterned dressing gown was old, but no older than something Mickelle might wear around the house. Except for the haggardness in her face, she was average-looking, someone Mickelle wouldn't give a second glance to at Wal-Mart.

"Hello," Mickelle said, forcing a smile she did not feel. Her heart began pounding and she prayed she wouldn't have a panic attack. But Damon wasn't here, was he? So she should be safe.

She thrust the ironic thought to a deep part of her mind.

"Can I help you?" The aunt's eyes were wary as they contemplated Mickelle.

"Yes, uh, my name is Mickelle Hansen. Our girls are friends at school, and I—" She broke off. She had been going to say that she had given Jennie Anne a ride several times, but didn't want to get the child in trouble. "I thought it might be nice to meet you. The girls get along really well."

The other woman relaxed slightly. "That's good. Jennie Anne don't get along with too many kids."

"Well, maybe—" Again Mickelle had to stop herself. She had been going to point out that perhaps Jennie Anne had lacked an opportunity to know many children yet as she had never attended school before. "I think they'll be good friends," she said instead. With a brief pause, she continued, "So you're Jennie Anne's aunt."

"Yeah. Well sort of." The woman looked around. "I'd offer you a place to sit, but you can see . . ."

"I don't mind standing." Mickelle glanced over the piles at Jeremy and Belle, who sat on the couch with Jennie Anne, hoping they wouldn't say anything rude. "So what's your name?"

"Nedda Chase. Jennie Anne's mother was my niece. She and my boy grew up together, but she died a couple of years back, and there was nobody but me to take Jennie Anne. I always told my sister that Donna May would get into trouble. No sirree, my sister shouldn'ta had a child so old. That girl did anything she pleased, and in the end, it killed her."

Mickelle opened her mouth to ask what had happened, but Jennie Anne's aunt continued with barely a pause. "It's a hard thing, raising someone else's child. I couldn't do it at first, and she had to stay with some other people. But they help me out now—the state—so I can keep her with me."

"But Jennie Anne's mo—"

"My Troy's an ungrateful boy," Nedda went on. "But at least he's smart. Not like Jennie Anne's mother. She was an actress, you know. Thought she was real hot stuff at one time, but she never really made it. She had to work nights as a waitress. Worked herself to death, I guess. Got sick and died."

Finally the answer. Mickelle saw that Jennie Anne was no longer watching them, but staring at her hands clutched tightly in her lap. Mickelle's heart ached for her. She wanted more than anything to give the child more than this squalor and neglect around her. There certainly seemed to be no love in this old woman's heart.

"Well, I wanted to know if it would be okay for our girls to play together." The words slipped out before she could remind herself that Belle was not technically "her girl."

The eyes narrowed and the wariness reemerged in Nedda's drooping face. "I'm really busy."

"They can play at my place. I can help them with their homework and then they can play. You see, Belle has no one but boys around the house, and it would be good for her to play with Jennie Anne."

Nedda frowned and her eyes grew hard as stone. "Jennie Anne has work to do here. We stuff envelopes and put on labels for a company.

She has her share to get done."

Mickelle blinked, stunned for a moment at the idea of Jennie Anne sitting for hours at a table stuffing envelopes, hours that she should have been in school. Was this why Nedda had to be forced into putting the child in school? Because someone found out?

"Well, I, uh . . ." Mickelle floundered. How could she come up with a way to give Jennie Anne a little desperately needed care? The child had trusted in Mickelle and yet she could find nothing to save her. There was no backing down; she had to try again. "It doesn't have to be every day. And the girls could do homework together. Jennie Anne's great at math. You should see her. And they work well together . . ."

"So Jennie Anne is helping your girl." Nedda's voice was flat, calculating.

"Uh . . . yes. That's it! Jennie Anne's a great help." Mickelle stifled her guilt at her misinterpretation. How else could she take care of Jennie Anne? Besides, it *would* do Belle good to have a girl around. She glanced at the children, praying they wouldn't interfere—especially Belle, who hated the idea of needing help from anyone.

"And I think that's a job in itself," Mickelle continued. "We'd be willing to pay Jennie Anne. For all her time at our house. Aside from school work, Belle needs a girl her age around."

"Sort of like a paid companion, huh." Nedda's gaze swung toward the girls, taking in Jennie Anne's downcast face and Belle's frank, curious stare. "Well, she seems normal enough. Can't think why she can't get her some friends without paying for them."

Mickelle bristled at the statement, but she bit her tongue. "Jennie Anne can eat dinner with us if you're willing, since she'll be there anyway. And if you were going out of town or something, she'd have somewhere to stay." Had she gone too far? Would the other woman perceive Mickelle's belief that Jennie Anne was being both physically and mentally abused?

Nedda's eyes came back to hers, glinting in the dull light. "How much?"

Mickelle wondered how many envelopes Jennie Anne could stuff and how much she was paid for them. Damon paid her generously to watch the children, but . . .

Then Mickelle almost started laughing. What was she worried

about money for? Hadn't she just received a hundred thousand dollars? If needed, she could use some of that money to help pay Jennie Anne.

"How about five dollars a day?" Mickelle suggested. "Jennie Anne and Belle can, uh, work on homework, and then play. After dinner, I can bring her home."

"I don't know," Nedda hedged.

Mickelle knew her offer wasn't a lot of money, but did this woman really believe that her great-niece, who had never been to school, was really going to tutor Belle? "Dinner's included," Mickelle reminded the other woman. "And we have a lot of extra clothes that we can pass on to Jennie Anne. My sister has three girls." The clothes alone should tempt the old woman.

"All right," Nedda agreed. "I usually have most of the envelopes done before she gets home anyways." Then, as though realizing what she had said, Nedda straightened her pudgy figure as tall as possible and added, "Of course that means I'll have to clean up here alone, and eat alone."

Mickelle refused to be manipulated further. What cleaning did Nedda do besides throwing more piles of junk onto already teetering stacks? And no way would she would start bringing the woman food. "We'll pay her each week," she said sweetly. "Twenty-five dollars."

"Twenty-five? Oh, yeah, guess there won't be no tutoring on the weekend."

Mickelle suddenly felt desperate. She wanted to offer thirty-five to have weekends included. But what was she doing, trying to buy a child? And what was the great-aunt doing letting Jennie Anne spend so much time away from home? What if someone else offered more money for something else?

She wished she knew if what she was doing was right. "Well, maybe the girls could play on the weekends. Let's see how it goes." Of course, Belle was with Damon on weekends, and since Mickelle had refused his proposal, she wouldn't be with him.

Unless they had their talk.

Mickelle knew she had to do just that. Not only because she loved Belle and Tanner, or because he had brought her Chinese food, but because she loved him. She really did. In spite of the way he made her crazy with fear and anger, she wanted to be a part of Damon's life.

Tonight when he comes to pick up the kids, we'll talk. And I'll tell him about Jennie Anne. He can help me decide what to do.

"Well, okay then," Mickelle backed up a couple of steps, her hand behind her as she searched for the doorknob. "Kids, let's go."

Belle arose and padded down the path from the couch. The piled up boxes, clothes, and papers were well above her head. Her little nose wrinkled as though she wanted to sneeze or was smelling something disgusting. She didn't look at Nedda, but cast a sad glance toward Jennie Anne.

"Go on, girl," Nedda told Jennie Anne. "I'll see you tonight."

Mickelle's heart leapt in her chest. She hadn't expected the old lady would allow the tutoring to begin tonight! Jennie Anne moved rapidly from the couch and stood near Belle. Mickelle noticed that she didn't have her backpack or any homework, but she was too anxious to leave the house to care.

Nedda didn't hug Jennie Anne. Nor was there any hint of kindness or love in her attitude toward her great-niece. An urge to weep sprang up in Mickelle's heart. For an instant she was immobilized by an emotion that was more a vision than anything she could describe. She *knew* that she had been sent to help Jennie Anne, and that she could only do it in this way.

For now.

She smiled at Nedda, who watched her with glittering blue eyes. Calculating. That she didn't care much for Jennie Anne was obvious. What guardian would allow her child to go home with a complete stranger without first doing a little investigating?

Back in the car, Mickelle's tense muscles relaxed, leaving her shaking. She cast a last glance at the house—the willow weeping its continuous tears, the sagging house, the overgrown yard, the missing curtain. She shuddered. How could she allow Jennie Anne to return to such a place? Surely there were laws about putting a child in a home where a narrow pathway between piles of junk was the only way through the house! It might be different if the old woman loved Jennie Anne.

"I don't like your aunt one bit," Belle announced, clipping on her safety belt.

Jennie Anne didn't reply, but when Mickelle glanced in the rearview mirror, the girl's eyes bored into hers. They were bright again, not dull as they had been inside the house.

It was a beginning.

Mickelle drove home in silence, while Jeremy and Belle chattered. Jennie Anne remained quiet.

"I'm sure Dad's giving me a horse soon," Belle said. "I hope it's a cream-colored one. Do you think he'll find one like that?"

Jeremy laughed. "I bet he will. He's good at doing stuff."

Mickelle heard the admiration in his voice, and softened further toward Damon. He *was* a good man. Maybe if they talked things out . . .

She didn't let herself finish the thought. Driving was not the best time to have a panic attack, and thinking of Damon often brought them on.

What a crazy relationship!

When they arrived home, Tanner and Bryan were playing basketball on the driveway slab instead of kicking the soccer ball in the backyard. Jeremy turned to Mickelle. "Please let me play a little before I do my chores. Tanner'll be going home soon since we spent so long at the school and at Jennie Anne's. Please." His blue eyes begged, popping out at her from his thin face.

"What about homework?"

"Don't have any. I did it all in class. Well, I have to read a bit, but I can do that in the morning. Please. I want to practice my long shot."

"Okay, okay." Mickelle shooed him away. She was more interested in getting Jennie Anne in the house. Would it be too soon to suggest a bath? How could she work it in without making it seem to obvious?

"I wanna play basketball, too!" Belle said.

Mickelle grabbed her before she could join the boys. "No way, young lady. Are you forgetting that you are recovering from a broken arm? No basketball for you for at least another few months."

"Oh drat!" But Belle came into the house docilely enough. "So what are we going to do then? I don't have any homework. See? My backpack is empty." She was accustomed to either playing with the boys or working on one of the project books Mickelle checked out from the library. Her eager mind never seemed to find enough challenge at school, and Mickelle had taken to supplementing her education as a way of keeping her occupied and content.

Mickelle was learning right along with her. Last week they had been reading about the parts of an atom, and had filled in another section of the map they were making of Alaska. Mickelle admitted to herself that she was curious about where Damon had spent so much of his life before he came to Utah, and that was why she had suggested that particular study. Belle had been only too happy to agree. After all, she had been born there.

Jennie Anne would likely be interested in their educational discoveries, but first things had to come first; Mickelle had taken a casual whiff of Jennie Anne's hair and knew that somehow she had to find a way to wash it.

"We'll play a game in a minute," she told them, "but first let's see if the boys left us any of those pumpkin cookies I made yesterday."

The girls followed her into the house and to the kitchen. Belle threw her red backpack on the table and climbed on a stool. Mickelle frowned at it. There was something odd about the backpack, but she couldn't think what it was. Probably nothing serious. It would likely come to her later.

As Mickelle took out the cookies and milk, she watched Jennie Anne survey the kitchen. There was nothing on her freckled face to show pleasure or displeasure at what she saw, but Mickelle sensed a wonder about her. Despite the disinterest Nedda had in Jennie Anne, the child apparently hadn't been away from home enough to see how a regular family lived.

A regular family. Yes, that's what Mickelle supposed she and the boys represented. Her house wasn't much, but it must seem a lot to Jennie Anne. What had her life been like with her mother? Did she even remember?

All in good time, she told herself. A lack of patience had never been one of her greatest faults, but suddenly she hated not knowing.

Mickelle put the spaghetti casserole she had mixed together that afternoon in the oven while the girls ate. The cookies and milk went down in a flash, and they were ready to play. Belle had plenty of computer and board games that she had brought from home, and a few dolls, but Mickelle was still hoping to get Jennie Anne into the water. If it was summer instead of mid-October, she would fill up the swimming pool and have a water fight.

With soap?

Damon had a pool. And chlorine would kill almost any germ.

Kill.

She swallowed hard and pushed the memory of Damon's inert frame from her mind. *I can't deal with that right now. Think of this little girl.*

She thought up idea after idea, quickly discarding most of them. A water fight in the kitchen was not a good choice, though it probably wouldn't damage the inexpensive vinyl tile or the ancient grime-caked cupboards. Neither was filling up the plastic pool in the unfinished part of the basement. But washing the dog in the bathtub might be the basis of a good idea.

Maybe . . .

Mickelle snapped her fingers. She knew exactly what to do.

"Girls, come on, I have a plan. Let's practice our ABCs in the bathroom."

"What?" Belle gaped at her in surprise.

Mickelle smiled at her innocently. "You've never learned ABCs in the bathroom? Well then, you are in for a treat. I used to do it all the time when the boys were little. We *lived* for this game."

"How do you play?" Belle followed her down the short hallway, bursting with curiosity.

"I have some of Jeremy's old T-shirts and shorts that should fit you—somewhere." Mickelle ignored Belle's question and rummaged through a box of old clothes in the closet at the end of the hall, ones she had intended for rags. "Here, girls, change into these, while I fill up the bath. You can use my room."

Belle pulled Jennie Anne along. "Oh, this is so exciting! Didn't I tell you Mickelle's fun? So fun!"

Mickelle didn't hear a response, if there was any, because the door shut behind them. Hurrying into the small bathroom, she began filling the tub with warm water. She plucked a can of shaving cream from the windowsill and then searched under the vanity for another. She had usually stocked up on them when they were on sale, but she hadn't checked her supply in months.

Under the sink four cans stood in a solemn row, little soldiers ready for their task. Next to them was only one wrapped bar of soap, and two bottles of Flex shampoo, also purchased on sale. Of course she would have more of the shaving cream; she had always been careful to have plenty on hand for Riley, and since his death she had not even used a full can. The lime smell reminded her of him, and she wondered if it always would. She didn't mind.

By the time she had placed the shaving cream and the bottle of shampoo on the edge of the tub, the girls came in—Belle dancing excitedly, and Jennie Anne more quietly, though her face also showed anticipation.

"Grab a can of shaving cream," she told the girls. "I'll be back with towels." In the hall closet again, she found only two clean towels, but a stack of flannel sheets would do just as well for her task. *Good thing Jeremy stopped wetting the bed.*

That had come about because of Damon's attention; one more thing she was grateful to him for.

When she reentered the bathroom the girls each had a can of shaving cream in their hands. Belle was experimenting with the nozzle. Suddenly, cream exploded from the end, blasting into the wall. Belle screamed with laughter, but Jennie Anne looked frozen into place, as though too frightened to move.

"Good job, Belle!" Mickelle said, wiping the cream off the wall. "You figured out how to use it. But come on over here to the bath. First let me turn off the water—looks like we have about enough. Put your feet in. Don't worry, it's warm. Now that wall is yours, Belle," she pointed to the left, "and that side over there is Jennie Anne's. Don't worry, that's ceramic tile to keep out the water from the shower. The cream won't hurt it."

"We get to write letters!" Belle laughed in understanding. "Oh, this is gonna be so fun!"

And it was. Belle sprayed her cream over the wall in the shapes of huge letters. Jennie Anne followed suit, her shyness fading away. When they had filled the walls, they lifted water in their hands and wiped the white cream away. Soon they started drawing pictures and then spraying each other, giggling as they went.

Mickelle had forgotten how different the exuberant joy of a five- and six-year-old could be, compared to the older wisdom of her nine-year-old, who claimed to have outgrown this type of activity. But oh, how easily it came back! She remembered doing this very thing with her own mother, and then with the boys. How joyful it was! For the moment, the cares of the day were utterly banished. She rolled up her jeans, took her own can of shaving cream into the bath, and began to draw a design under the window.

"Mom! Mom!" Jeremy appeared in the open doorway. He stopped, jaw dropping. Mickelle thought she saw a little longing in his eyes.

"What is it Jeremy?"

His eyes went to hers. "Oh yeah, Belle has to go. They're here to pick her up."

"Already?"

She glanced at her watch, which she had removed from her wrist and placed on the low shelf above the back of the toilet. It wasn't even six yet, and Damon usually didn't come until six-thirty.

I should have known, she thought. Damon always appeared when she was dirty from working in the garden, sweaty from playing soccer, or wet from an accident with water.

She grinned, unable to stop herself. Maybe if she could get him to come in here, he could join them, and she would spray him with the shaving cream. Maybe that would break the ice enough for them to talk.

"I don't wanna go home," Belle wailed.

"It's Juliet," Jeremy said. "That's who's come to take you home. She says she is supposed to take you to your house. Your dad's working late." Jeremy frowned, and Mickelle knew that he had hoped to play basketball with him.

"Well, I like Juliet," Belle said in only a slightly aggrieved voice, "but I just wish you'd hurry and marry my dad, Mickelle. Then we could all go live at my house." She turned to Jennie Anne to explain. "Juliet works for my dad. She sometimes baby-sits me." She turned back to Mickelle, her round, cherubic face standing out more clearly with her wet hair matted down. "Do I have to go? And if I do, can Jennie Anne come with me?"

"Let me go talk to Juliet." Mickelle's words were forced and seemed to burn the back of her throat. She couldn't believe that he hadn't come. All day she had been preparing herself to talk to him, to confess her fears and possibly her love. To even apologize for getting angry at him.

And he hadn't come.

She was hurt, though she knew logically the feeling didn't make sense. He hadn't known that she was preparing to talk to him, that she had decided not to throw his Chinese food back in his face, but to invite him to share it with her. Her disappointment was almost tangible, like a sudden cold shower.

CHAPTER 12

Mickelle stepped out of the bath onto one of the flannel sheets she had put down to catch their spills. "While I'm talking to Juliet, you girls might as well wash your hair. You're full of shaving cream, and this way you won't have to do it later. Here's the shampoo. I'll help you rinse when you come back. No, don't worry about your clothes. We're not really taking a bath. Just wash your hair."

She was rewarded for the comment by a look of utter relief from Jennie Anne. That made Mickelle wonder about the bruise on her cheek and the possible one on her shoulder. Who had given them to her?

Juliet was waiting for her on the porch, wearing low heels, black dress pants, and a multi-colored sweater. There was a new chill in the air, one Mickelle hadn't noticed before. *Winter is coming,* she thought.

"Hi, Mickelle." Juliet's wide smile made Mickelle relax. The young, dark-haired receptionist had that effect on people. Her light brown eyes were friendly, and her short hair so cute, that every time Mickelle saw it she experienced a strong urge to cut her own in the same style and dye it brown.

"Come on in." Mickelle pushed the door open wider. "Belle's not quite ready yet. I wasn't expecting Damon—you, so soon."

"Well, Damon had to work late and he told me to come get the kids before the usual time since you have Enrichment meeting tonight at the church. It is tonight, isn't it? Men aren't that great at remembering things. At least my fiancé isn't."

The hurt in Mickelle's heart abated. So Damon hadn't been trying to avoid or punish her.

He's not Riley!

"He got the right night. But frankly it slipped my mind until just now." She sighed. "I have to go help the girls in the bathroom. Make yourself comfortable, okay? It'll just be a few moments."

Belle had already finished washing and rinsing her hair in the bathtub and was scrubbing at Jennie Anne's mass of dark brown. "You'd better get changed," Mickelle said, stifling a laugh at her clothes which were now completely soaked instead of damp. "I told you I'd help you."

Belle beamed. "Yes, but this was fun because I never get to take a bath at home in clothes!" She giggled as Mickelle helped her out of the bath and wrapped her in one of the large towels.

"Your clothes are still in my room," Mickelle told her. "Be sure to bring the wet ones back in here."

* * * * *

"I don't think they're getting married," Tanner said as Jeremy went inside to tell Mickelle that Juliet had arrived.

Bryan scowled. "What does that have to do with our game?"

"I think they love each other."

That made Bryan mad. Tanner had the basketball, but Bryan suddenly threw himself at the older boy. Tanner stepped out of the way. "Watch it. You'll foul me."

Bryan grunted and dove for the ball once more, knocking it out of Tanner's hand. "Ha!" he said triumphantly. He shot the ball at the basket but it fell short. Fury surged through his heart. He rammed Tanner with his body and grabbed the ball to try again.

Tanner fell on the cement. "Gosh, Bryan, why're you being so crazy? It's just a game. Play fair."

"I am." Bryan shot for the basket, felt the tears come as he missed again. Tanner didn't even try to get the ball, but stared at him oddly. In a blind rage, Bryan shoved the ball at Tanner, not caring if it hit him in the face. "Humph!" Tanner said as the ball made contact with his gut.

Serves him right, Bryan thought. Tanner glared at him and he felt better, knowing he had made the other boy angry. He had never done that before, and it felt good making someone else as miserable as he felt. Especially Tanner, who kept talking about all that love nonsense.

At least Colton was on Bryan's side. Though the man hadn't said so aloud, Bryan knew by his attitude that he would help keep Damon and Mickelle apart. But what if his mom started liking Colton instead? Bryan shook his head, not wanting to think of that possibility. *Dad wouldn't want her to marry anybody.* That much he knew. *And I don't want her to marry anybody, especially Damon.* He didn't know why that was, but he didn't care to examine his thoughts too carefully.

Jeremy came out of the house as Bryan stomped from the driveway. Bryan didn't look up as he passed his brother. He sat on the porch, shoulders hunched, listening as Tanner and Jeremy started to play without him. Instead of easing, his fury mounted.

He reached through the cast-iron stair railing and tore off a few heads of his mother's nearest roses. One by one he let the pink petals fall to the ground. He grabbed more, choosing the brightest and biggest blossoms still alive on the bush. Slowly, methodically, he ripped them apart as his brain rehashed the game with Tanner. A puddle of pink grew at his feet.

The door opened again behind him. "Time to go," called a voice. It was Juliet, Damon's receptionist. Normally, Bryan liked to see her because she was so friendly and pretty, but he didn't feel like talking to her today.

"See ya, Bryan," she said.

He didn't respond, but reached for another rose. Tear, rip, squish, let them fall. Repeat. Someone sat beside him. Out of the corner of his eye, he saw Belle. "I love that game," she said, leaning over him to pick off a rose. "He loves me, he loves me not, he loves me, he loves me not . . ." She continued until all the petals were gone. "But see, you can make it end up however you want. If the last petal is 'he loves me not,' then you just throw this middle part and say 'he loves me.' But if the last petal is 'he loves me,' then you don't use it. See? That way you always win. I *hate* losing."

Bryan couldn't help but smile, and his anger oozed away. "I do too," he admitted.

"I bet Tanner made you mad." She rolled her eyes. "He always makes me mad."

It felt good that she understood.

"And boy is he boring. And he hates it when I talk. Like he thinks I'm stupid or something. But I know a lot of stuff, and you do. I bet you know a ton of stuff if you felt like talking about it. And you're nice, too. You always listen to me. Tanner tells me to shut up, even though Dad says that's a bad word."

Belle didn't stop talking. She rolled on as though she didn't expect anything of him; she just accepted him. Bryan loved hearing her talk because for some reason it always made him feel better.

"Belle!" Juliet called from her tan car. She was parked in front of his mom's old Ford station wagon, the Snail.

"Gotta go," Belle said mournfully. "I wish I could stay here. Look at Jeremy hanging on the car window like that. Wouldn't it be cool if we could trade me for him?"

Bryan smiled again. "He's okay, for a kid."

"Yeah, it's Tanner I'm trying to get rid of. Remember last week when he wouldn't let us watch our show? We gotta stick together."

Bryan thought about this. While he really liked Belle, he didn't want his mom getting wind of any cooperation between them. That wouldn't get rid of Damon. Bryan didn't really have it out for Tanner, either. *I just got angry today,* he thought.

"Yeah, we'll keep sticking together," he told Belle in a low voice. "Only we have to keep it cool. Quiet. Like we've been doing. Or they'll all gang up against us."

"Yeeeeaaaah!" Belle's eyes grew huge. "It's our secret. Like a spy movie." She leapt to her feet. "See ya tomorrow." She hesitated before adding with a grin, "Jerk." Giggling, she ran across the lawn.

Bryan stifled a laugh, and called out, "Yeah, twerp, whatever."

She waved, eyes sparkling. Bryan watched the car drive away.

Jeremy plodded up the walk, sighing. "Darn it all, I was hoping Damon would play with us. And you shouldn't call Belle a twerp. I heard you."

Bryan's anger seeped back as though it had never left. "Oh shut up!"

"I'm telling Mom. Shut up's a bad word."

"You do and I'll tell everybody you still pee the bed," he sneered.

"I'm not going to talk to you anymore. But I wish Tanner was my brother, not you!" With that final shot, Jeremy fled past him into the house.

Tears came to Bryan's eyes. Why had Jeremy's words hurt him so much? Why did he care what that skinny little idiot said anyway?

Bryan plucked off several more roses, rubbing and squishing them until his fingers became moist. The crushing feeling gave focus for his anger, made him feel in control. The bush was empty now, except for a few dead blossoms, and he stared guiltily. His mother would have a fit. Carefully, he swept the pink petals off the porch and into the dirt, hoping she wouldn't notice. It wasn't that important—all the blooms on every bush would be dead soon, away. Winter always killed them.

Wiping his stained fingers on his jeans, he went into the house to find something to eat.

* * * * *

When Belle had shut the door behind her, Mickelle turned back to Jennie Anne. "Can I help?" she asked tentatively.

A single nod gave permission, and Mickelle began to wash the oil and dust out of her hair. The ends were uneven and split as though she had never had it cut. "There, almost done." Mickelle massaged the girl's scalp with increasing pressure, glad that she had bought shampoo with conditioner to calm down Jeremy's flyaway hair.

With no warning, Jennie Anne's hand crept up to Mickelle's as she scrubbed, and held tight. Mickelle stopped, wondering if the child had a sore or lump she hadn't noticed.

"My mother used to wash my hair, I think," Jennie Anne's voice was soft and hesitant. "I remember this . . ." Her hand dropped and Mickelle continued her washing, her heart full of an emotion she could not name.

"Jennie Anne," she said simply. "I'm glad you're here." Before yesterday, she had never seen this child; yet already she had a place in Mickelle's heart.

After washing Jennie Anne's hair twice and then rinsing with fresh water from the tap, Mickelle retrieved Jennie Anne's clothes from her bedroom, spying Belle's discarded wet ones on the carpet. Shaking her head, she picked them up in her other hand and returned to the bathroom. "Here are your clothes," she told Jennie Anne. She took note of the shoe size as she placed them on the floor by the door, vowing to buy her new ones for winter.

Belle and Tanner had already left when she reemerged, and Mickelle felt a distinct loss. She hadn't said good-bye. *How silly,* she thought. *I'll see them tomorrow.*

Her boys were in the kitchen searching the cupboards for food. "Dinner's in the oven," she said. "Spaghetti casserole. If you'll set the table, we'll eat."

Bryan slammed a cupboard door shut, his dark eyes brooding. "I thought we were going to Aunt Brionney's."

"After dinner. She has enough kids to feed as it is. I can drop you guys off there after I take Jennie Anne to her house. Then I'll go over to the church. I hope Jennie Anne likes spaghetti casserole."

"I thought you said you were going with Brenda." Jeremy used a stool to reach the plates in the cupboard.

"Oh, that's right. I'll have to come back here then. It's getting dark too early for you guys to walk to your cousins' house. Not to mention cold."

Bryan frowned and his dark brows creased. "I don't know why we have to go to Aunt Brionney's anyway. We're old enough to baby-sit ourselves. At least I am. Lots of thirteen-year-olds baby-sit."

"I know that, but I just feel more comfortable knowing you're with my sister. It's the same reason Tanner comes over here. He's almost sixteen; he certainly doesn't need anyone to tend him."

Bryan nodded, seemingly appeased. "Tanner says you're not going to marry his dad. Is that true?"

Jeremy paused with a stack of plates in his hands. His eyes, full of questions, dug into hers. Mickelle picked up her hot pads, crushing them apprehensively in her fists. "I don't know. Damon and I care very much for each other. You both know that. He and I are having a little trouble now—mostly it's me, but we're going to talk about it and maybe . . . I hope we'll work things out." She felt a peace in her heart when she said it.

Her younger son appeared relieved, but Bryan scowled. "I don't like him."

"What?" She was honestly surprised. There had been reservation on Bryan's part toward Damon—increasingly so recently—but she had always believed that he liked Damon at least a little. "Why don't you like him?"

He gave a sullen shrug. "He's not Dad." The brown eyes that so reminded her of Riley's challenged her, with no sign of yielding.

She threw the hot pads onto the counter next to the stove, and said earnestly, "Bryan, your dad's gone. I know that hurts, but there's nothing I can do to bring him back. If I could, believe me, I would."

Bryan erupted like gas near a flame. "You didn't even love him!" he shouted, his face contorting with the sudden rage that had often consumed his father.

"I did!" Mickelle raised her own voice. "You can't even *begin* to imagine what I felt for your father!"

Bryan glared at her. "You were going to get a divorce!"

"Who on earth told you that?"

"He did. He wanted me to watch you when he was gone."

Fury at Riley welled inside Mickelle. She fought it down and spoke as calmly as she could. "I loved your father, but I did tell him that I would no longer accept his treatment of me—or of you guys. He understood and was changing. We would have made it, but *he* chickened out. *He's* the one who left us. Not because he didn't love us, but because of the emotional problems left by his seizures. End of story. Now help your brother set the table, please."

Bryan had reached for a plate, but at her words, he slammed it on the counter. She was amazed that it didn't break.

"I'm not hungry." Bryan stalked from the kitchen.

Mickelle watched him go, and saw Jennie Anne in the doorway, not looking at them, but down at the floor, her small fists clenched in tight, hard balls. Her hair hung wetly down her back, but newly combed, and the freckles and green bruise on her face stood out in harsh contrast against the white skin.

"Come on in, Jennie Anne," Mickelle said, making her voice friendly. "We're about ready to eat. I'm sorry Belle had to go home. You don't mind being here with us, do you? You look so nice with your hair combed like that."

"Oh, I didn't do my math!" Jeremy said, hitting his palm flat on the counter. "I forgot!" He dived for his backpack, hung on a hook by the back door. "Can I do it while I eat, huh, Mom? Jennie Anne can check it without even a calculator. You'll help, won't you Jennie Anne? I can read you the numbers after I'm done with the problem."

Jennie Anne nodded.

"Come to the counter then. Or the bar, rather." Mickelle indicated a stool and the little girl slipped over to it and climbed up. "We usually eat at the counter when Belle and Tanner aren't here."

After putting the meal on the countertop, Mickelle left to check on Bryan, but he wasn't in his room, or anywhere else. Her heart started the erratic beating that was all too familiar. Where could he be? He knew that he had to notify her when he went out. He knew better!

She went to his room again, searching for a clue. The door eased partially closed behind her and she gasped as she spied the huge hole in the inside bottom of the door. The damage looked as though someone had kicked the door, breaking completely through the outer layer and revealing the hollow core. When had this happened? Had it been now? If not, why hadn't she seen it before?

And what made him so angry?

She thought she knew the answer to this, but didn't know how to help Bryan deal with his emotions. She would have to discipline him better. She would have to make him understand her growing feelings for Damon. But would he ever accept the idea of a stepfather?

Her eyes fell once again to the jagged edges of the hole. Riley, too, had been mad at her that last day. Before he had taken himself from her life permanently, he had ruined many pieces of her rose collection and damaged the curio cabinet. His last jab at her heart.

Mickelle stumbled to her room, knelt by her bed, and uttered a heartfelt prayer. The beating in her chest gradually slowed to a normal level as her panic faded. Still, she stopped in the living room to check on her curio cabinet and its contents. All was normal—except the missing glass, and the cracks and gouges left in one of the side panels from when Riley had pushed it onto the TV set that fateful day last May.

She sighed with relief and returned to the kitchen. "Bryan's not eating with us," she said with false brightness. "Who would like to say a prayer for the meal?" She stared at Jeremy pointedly, unsure if Jennie Anne knew how to pray.

"I will," Jeremy volunteered obediently.

Dinner wasn't quiet, with Jeremy doing his math and asking Jennie Anne to verify his answers, but it was odd without Bryan. Even so, Mickelle derived pleasure seeing Jennie Anne eat two helpings. The child was too thin.

They were finishing up as the doorbell rang. Mickelle was surprised to see Colton standing there for the second time that day. "Hi," he said. "I came by to see how you were doing."

Mickelle was annoyed, but tried not to show it. He had left only four hours ago—what was he doing back so soon? She had too much to do before going to her meeting to talk to him.

"Hi," she replied. "We're just on our way out. I have to take home one of Belle's friends and I have to find—" No, she didn't want to tell him about Bryan. "I have to take Jeremy to my sister's."

"I'll drive you," he offered, smiling at her so winningly that she forgot to be annoyed. "Come on, we'll talk as we go."

"Well, all right. But we'll have to hurry. I'm going to Enrichment meeting in less than a half hour." *And I have to find Bryan first,* she added to herself.

"Mom," Jeremy shouted from the kitchen. "Aunt Brionney's on the phone. She called to tell you that Bryan's over there already. She knew you would worry!"

"Bryan was missing?" Colton asked.

"Yeah," she answered reluctantly, "we had a little argument."

"About what?" When she didn't answer, he said, "Come on, what are friends for? I may not know much about being a father, but I've been thirteen before."

The faint underlying bitterness in his words forced her to answer. "We fought about Damon. Bryan seems to feel that he's somehow coming between me and his father."

Colton's face was the picture of sympathy. "I'll talk to him, if you like."

"It's okay, really."

"Well, just so you know that I'm willing."

They drove to Jennie Anne's first, and Mickelle walked her to the door, leaving Colton and Jeremy in the car. She felt apprehensive as she approached the ramshackle house. What would she do if Jennie Anne's aunt wasn't home? She wouldn't leave her here alone.

I'll call the authorities, that's what I'll do.

She stopped halfway down the walk and faced Jennie Anne, crouching so she could see directly into her face. "Jennie Anne, look, I want you to know that I'm only a phone call away. If you're ever alone and scared, or sad, or if you just need someone to talk to, call me. I know you're good with numbers, and I bet you can remember mine if I tell you." She repeated the number several times until Jennie Anne could repeat it back. But the little girl did so stoically, her eyes returning to the dull, vacant stare she had worn when talking to her aunt. Mickelle's heart felt heavy. What more could she do? Until Jennie Anne trusted her, she wouldn't be able to make a judgment as to what was going on in her house. She would get to the bottom of it soon, though, and until then, she wouldn't desert Jennie Anne.

Mickelle almost hoped Nedda Chase wouldn't be home, but she was. The old woman had changed from the dressing gown to a pair of stretch jeans and an oversized green sweater. Her cheeks and the skin beneath her eyes still drooped like a hound's but the effect was alleviated by a smile. "Did you do good?" she asked Jennie Anne.

The girl nodded.

"Yes, she even helped my fourth grade son with his math." Mickelle saw that Jennie Anne's hair was still damp, and hurried to add. "The girls and I practiced ABCs and spelling with shaving cream on the tile in the bathroom. I let them wear old clothes—and they got a little wet and covered in the shaving cream. The girls washed their hair so they could get it all out. I hope you don't mind."

"That's okay." Nedda looked Jennie Anne over. "Saves me the trouble."

Yeah, I'll bet.

"Well, thanks again. Jennie Anne was a big help." Mickelle wished she could go in to make sure Jennie Anne was all right, that someone would read her a story and tuck her into bed. It was one of the hardest things she had ever done to walk back down the overgrown sidewalk alone, leaving Jennie Anne behind.

"Homely little girl, isn't she?" Colton said pleasantly, when she was once more in the car. "Splotchy freckles, straight hair, brown eyes, thin."

Mickelle had once thought so too, but she had seen those eyes bursting with intelligence and curiosity, and in those moments Jennie

Anne had been the epitome of a cute, bright little girl. "Did you see the bruise on her cheek?" she asked a bit tersely.

"No, I didn't notice."

Mickelle explained how she had met Jennie Anne and her suspicions about her treatment.

"So what now?"

"I don't know. But I'm not going to let her fall through the cracks. I don't know if her aunt is abusing her, but . . ."

"No, I meant, where are we going next? Your sister's, right? How do I get there?" He smiled and for the first time the dimple in his left cheek reminded Mickelle of a crater similar to those she had seen in pictures of the moon. "I mean, I'm glad you're not giving up on the girl, but you sure get involved, don't you? You don't worry much about yourself. Maybe it's time you did." He paused before adding pointedly, "Or let someone else do so. I'm sure that little girl is just fine."

Mickelle stared at him, feeling as though he were speaking a foreign language. "I guess I'm used to looking out for children," she answered slowly. "I like children—I care for children. Even those who aren't mine."

"I know, and that's why you're such a great mother."

But his words didn't placate her. Had he been alone so long that he had forgotten what it meant to live in a family? *Or how about the human race?* She scowled, but Colton was listening to Jeremy and didn't question her expression.

" . . . to my aunt's. Go back down that way."

Colton glanced at Mickelle for verification. "Yes, let's take him there. And I'll have to go in and talk to Bryan for a minute."

"Let me talk to him, please?" Colton asked. "I've been thinking about it and maybe if I tell him a few things about my own life, it might help. I lost my own father at a young age you know, and my mother remarried."

Mickelle hadn't known that. In fact, he had told her that both his parents were still living. Of course, he could have been referring to his stepfather.

"All right," she agreed finally. Whatever Colton said to him, it certainly couldn't hurt.

Brionney lived in a new two-story house, with vaulted ceilings and gabled windows. The outside was rock and stucco, and basically maintenance-free when compared to the boards on Mickelle's house that required painting every few years. Brionney's front lawn and cement-lined flower beds were coming along nicely, due mostly to Damon's loan of Old Bobby, his full-time groundskeeper.

"Nice place." Colton's eyes roamed over the house and yard appreciatively. "I'd like to buy something like this soon."

Mickelle didn't comment, too anxious to see her son. Should she yell at him? How else could she impress upon him the seriousness of what he had done?

"He's down in the family room playing Nintendo with Savannah," Brionney said when she opened the door. "But he's acting funny."

"May I go down?" Colton asked, giving Brionney his best smile.

"Sure go ahead." She turned to her six-year-old. "Camille, show him the way, okay?"

The women watched the pair disappear into the kitchen. Mickelle expected Jeremy to follow, but he gasped, "Oh, no, Mom! I forgot my Game Boy in Colton's car. I can't leave it there!"

"Well, go get it. I don't think he locked the door."

Jeremy was out the door in a flash. Mickelle turned back to her sister, shaking her head. "I didn't want him to bring it, but he said he had to show Savannah something."

Brionney laughed. "At least he's growing out of that Pokémon stage. I was getting to hate those little creatures." She gave a surreptitious glance around her, but only the twins were in sight. "So what are you doing with Mr. Gorgeous? Are you ditching your Enrichment meeting young lady and going out?"

Mickelle's cheeks flamed. "No, I—"

"I'm kidding." Brionney tossed her blonde head more exuberantly than normal, and the short, feathered locks rippled around her face becomingly. "I think it's good you're going out. I just think you're with the wrong man."

"I am going to the church tonight, actually. He just happened along when I was about to take Jennie Anne home and then—"

"Jennie Anne?"

"Yes—oh, you don't know about her." She launched into an abbreviated explanation, which nevertheless had Brionney wanting to adopt Jennie Anne herself. How different from Colton's reaction!

". . . so Colton happened to come by right at that time and here we are. I think he has some news for me, or something—probably about the insurance money. We haven't gotten to it yet—not that it matters since I've decided not to go through his friend anyway. So here I am trying to rush everything. Brenda is picking me up on her way to the church tonight, though I should have just gone on my own; she's always late."

"Well, if it's that long-winded lady in your ward who's teaching, you might be glad for that." Brionney laughed again. She lowered her eyes playfully at Mickelle's reproving glance. "Yeah, yeah, I know. You always find something important in the talks. You're who I want to be when I grow up." She ran her hands through her hair, fluffing it, batting her blue eyes rapidly.

"Oh, right," Mickelle said dryly. "And what's with your hair today? You keep tossing it around and . . . Oh, yeah, you got a haircut this afternoon."

"Actually, yes. How kind of you to notice." Brionney flipped her hair again. "And I got a little lighter color woven into it at the same time."

"But you've always been so blonde."

"Well, I've noticed some darkening since I had the twins, and I thought, why not?"

"Looks really cute. I'm sorry I didn't notice before."

"Don't worry about it; Jesse hardly ever does. He says that's because he loves me so much no matter how I look, and so I let him off the hook—if he'll do the dishes."

They laughed again, and Mickelle mused aloud, "I wonder if Damon would notice if I did that to mine."

"Damon and not Mr. Gorgeous? Hmm. That's odd."

"Oh . . ." Mickelle glared at her sister in mock frustration. Why couldn't anyone seem to call Colton by his right name? Mr. Gorgeous, Mr. Cover Boy—really!

Jeremy came into the house, and Mickelle was relieved to end her conversation with Brionney. Or was until she saw the troubled expression on his face. "Mom, I think you should see this." He handed her a small black notebook.

"What is it?"

"I found it under Colton's seat. I wasn't snooping, honest, I was just looking for my Game Boy so I could show Savannah my new Tarzan game on it, but it was on the floor, and I saw this book. I . . ." His thin face flushed, but his eyes remained on hers. "I opened it. It has all sorts of stuff about us in it."

A chill shuddered up Mickelle's back. "Thank you, Jeremy," she said. "I'll take care of it. You go on and find Savannah."

"She's downstairs," Brionney called as he disappeared into the kitchen.

For a moment neither woman spoke, as they stood uncertainly in the entryway. Then finally Brionney said, "What do you think?"

Mickelle sighed. "I probably should give it back to him."

"But you're not going to, right?"

"No." Mickelle opened the book. It was probably harmless, but she didn't exactly trust Colton—didn't trust any man. She knew that was Riley's legacy, but at the moment it was necessary for her survival.

Her name was at the top of the first page, along with her birth date. The boys' names were next, with birthdays also noted, and a short description of each child: Bryan—husky, blonde hair, brown eyes, frowns a lot, good at soccer, okay at basketball; Jeremy—skinny, blonde hair, blue eyes, always smiling, clumsy at most sports, okay at basketball, likes to read.

Brionney stared over her shoulder at the words. "Could be quite innocent. He doesn't want to forget anything about you guys. Kinda sweet, actually."

"Maybe." Mickelle had an odd feeling about the whole thing.

The next page held a list of Mickelle's favorite things—gardening, reading, playing soccer with the boys, taking walks with the dog, tending her rose bushes, collecting wood and ceramic roses. The list held even a few of her dreams—going back to college, getting new cupboards, having another child . . .

Where did he learn all this? Mickelle felt strangely as though he had pried into her life, although as she thought about it, she realized that she had told him all of these things herself. Was he only being sure that he didn't forget her needs and desires? Or was this something else?

Steps coming from the kitchen made her shut the little notebook. Fearing that it would make an odd bulge in the pocket of her jeans, she slipped it under her blue turtleneck, wishing she had thought to put on a sweater or coat. She folded an arm over the notebook and glanced up as Colton entered the room, with Bryan in tow.

Colton's smile was dazzling. "I think Bryan has something to say to you." He turned his smile on Brionney. "That is an amazing quilt you have hanging in the kitchen. Did you make it?"

Taking the hint, Brionney followed him into the kitchen saying, "Actually, a friend of mine made that for me when my twins were born. I've taken really good care of it because . . ."

The voices faded and Mickelle and Bryan stared at each other, Mickelle still holding the notebook under her shirt with her arm, and Bryan with his hands in the pockets of his jeans. In his face and stance Mickelle saw no signs of the anger and belligerence she had seen earlier. Despite her suspicions of Colton in regards to the notebook, she was impressed. "I was worried," she said, seeing that he was having trouble knowing how to begin.

Bryan hung his head. "I'm sorry. I was mad." He glanced up at her. "But I'm not anymore. I won't do it again. I'm really sorry." He paused and gripped something unseen in his pocket.

"The door in your room . . ."

His face flushed. "It was last week. I'll ask grandpa to help me fix it. Or I'll earn the money somehow. I didn't mean to. I was just mad." He sneaked a peek at her face. "I'm sorry," he repeated.

"I accept your apology, and the offer to fix the door. Thank you." Mickelle's voice was only a whisper as she struggled to swallow the sudden lump in her throat. She held out her arms and hugged him; he clung to her like a small boy. "I love you, Bryan. So very much. I know life sometimes is hard, but we will always make it if we do it together."

He nodded and drew away, a serious expression on his face.

"Well, I'm going now, but I'll be back in a few hours. Enjoy yourself."

"I will." Bryan smiled sheepishly and walked with an air of nonchalance into the kitchen, as though glad to have everything in the open.

Colton and Brionney returned from the other room. "I'm sorry to run, Brionney," Mickelle told her sister, "but Brenda will be picking me up in a few minutes."

Brionney opened the front door. "Hey, don't worry about it. I understand. Have a fun time at your meeting. Nice to see you again, Colton."

Mickelle didn't remember the black notebook until Colton pulled up to her house. With a sinking feeling, she casually checked her shirt and the area around the passenger seat. She found nothing but the house keys she had left in the drink holder between their bucket seats.

"Lose something?" Colton asked.

"Uh, no. I guess I didn't bring my purse."

"Nope."

Had she dropped the notebook at Brionney's? The last time she remembered having it was just before she hugged Bryan.

With both arms.

An imaginary vision of the black notebook on Brionney's tiled entryway made Mickelle anxious. She had wanted to see what else had been inside. Maybe she and Brenda could even stop by Brionney's before Enrichment meeting and retrieve the notebook. She would call Brionney now and have her put it in a safe place for them.

Colton hurried around to open her car door, and together they walked up to the house. Mickelle paused on the porch. "Thanks for coming by. I really appreciate what you did with Bryan. Whatever you said seemed to work."

"You're welcome." His dimpled grin was back, and she was relieved to see it no longer resembled a crater, but was once again a very becoming feature on his handsome face.

"Good-bye then." She put a hand on the knob.

"Oh, but I almost forgot what it was I came to tell you."

She paused, waiting, but didn't invite him in.

"Do you mind if I get a drink of something while we talk? Brenda doesn't seem to be here yet, and I might as well wait with you."

She almost didn't hear him. Her eyes had focused on the rose bush next to the porch, one that only this morning had held large, beautiful pink blossoms. They were missing now, every one of them. What had happened? Surely they hadn't all dropped off at the same time. Leaning forward, she saw a mound of pink petals in the dirt next to the cement porch. *That didn't happen naturally,* she thought. *Someone did that. But who?* Her mind said it was Bryan—who else would damage something so precious to her? *No,* she told herself. *There must be some other explanation. Maybe Belle and Jeremy were making rose mud pies . . . or something.*

"Mickelle?" Colton's voice demanded attention.

"What?"

"I asked whether you minded if I get a drink of something while we talk. And I might as well wait with you until Brenda gets here."

There didn't seem to be any way to refuse his request; she would have to call Brionney later. But what if she had dropped the notebook on the cement outside? What if she . . .

". . . and he also said he'd be glad to meet you and talk about your investments," Colton was saying as she poured him a glass of cold orange juice from the refrigerator.

Colton's words dragged Mickelle back into the conversation. "Look," she said, settling on a stool on the opposite side of the counter where Riley had always sat. There wasn't room for her legs under the counter on this side, but she preferred that to sitting close to Colton. "I've done a lot of thinking and I don't think I want to go to your friend. I know he works for a good company, but I want to do this myself. Check into things and all. I hope you understand." What she didn't say was that she had decided to talk to Damon about where to invest. He was obviously experienced . . . and she knew she could trust him.

Trust him? Where did that come from?

She couldn't take time to decipher the thought because Colton stood up, face flushed with anger. "I wish you would have told me that earlier because I have an appointment set up first thing in the morning."

"I'm really sorry."

He took a deep breath. "Well, the least you can do is go and see what he says. Can you do that much?"

Mickelle was reluctant. "Colton, I'm feeling a lot of pressure here. I appreciate all you've done for me, but this . . . I—" She broke off as he came around the counter. There was a predator glint to his eyes she hadn't seen before, and his face was set in hard lines of determination.

She had never been more afraid.

CHAPTER 12

Mickelle backed away from Colton as he approached, until she felt the edge of the sink counter jab into her back. Her hands came up between them. "Colton!" Her voice was sharp and warning. She pushed against his chest, but he grabbed her hands and held them in a grip like iron, forcing them slowly to her side.

"I think you should come with me tomorrow." He spoke slowly, darkly.

Mickelle could see the clock above the table, and already it was ten after seven. Where was Brenda? Of course she was late; she was always late.

Mickelle forced herself to be calm as she had done so many times with Riley when he was angry. Yet he had never hit her, never gripped her so cruelly. Had this been the real reason Colton's wife had left him? Or was this what he had become after the devastating death of his twins?

Compassion filled her heart, but did not completely overcome her outrage. "Colton," she said, trying to strike the perfect balance between reason and righteous anger. "You're hurting me."

"Am I?" The amusement in his voice mocked her. "I'm so sorry." His perfect face moved closer as though to kiss her, but she turned away. He released one hand and brought it up to her face, his nails biting into her flesh as he forced her to look at him.

Mickelle was afraid. So afraid that she could hardly think. She knew he was going to kiss her, or worse, and there was nothing she could do to stop him.

Except pray.

Where are you Brenda? Hurry. Please dear Lord, send her quickly!

She put her free hand up and pulled his hand from her face. "I think you should leave. Now."

"All I'm asking is for you to come with me tomorrow. That's not much." There was no mistaking the determination in his face. Again he forced both her hands to either side of her hips.

"You are *not* asking," she rejoined tightly. "And the last time I checked, forcing someone was Satan's role."

He didn't even blink, but she continued. "If you don't leave, I'm going to call the police."

"And why would you do that?" The dimple in his cheek was a crater again, rough and hideous. His hands held hers like twin vises. His pretty face, now stretched into the mask of a dangerous stranger, came nearer.

The doorbell rang at that moment, and before Colton could react, Mickelle called out, "Come in, the door's open!"

He kissed her, but she turned her face away, and his lips fell on her cheek. She was so furious at him she would have slapped him if her hands had been free. As Brenda entered, he released her and stepped decorously away.

"Oh, am I interrupting something?"

"Well, sort of." Colton smirked indulgently.

Brenda grinned at Mickelle. "I can wait outside,"

"No!" Mickelle moved toward her. "Colton was just leaving."

Brenda didn't seem to notice her vehemence. "Oh, there are those beautiful roses," she gushed, coming into the kitchen to smell them.

"Aren't they, though?" Colton said. "And Mickelle here was just showing me how grateful she was for them."

Mickelle scowled. "Yes, but it was so strange that I didn't see the card. My friend, Damon, who also gives me flowers, always sends along a card. It comes with the purchase, you know. They must have shorted you."

"Sometimes they get lost," Colton said with a shrug.

"So it seems." Mickelle could read in his eyes as clearly as if he had spoken that he hadn't sent the flowers. There was no doubt in her heart that they were from Damon, and that Colton had stolen them.

"I guess I'll be on my way," Colton announced. "I'll call you later."

"There's no need," Mickelle replied sweetly. "I think we've said all we need to."

To her surprise, Colton appeared contrite. "I'm sorry about the misunderstanding we had, Mickelle. You have to know it was just that—a misunderstanding. It's hard for us guys when we're in love with a beautiful woman. Hormones you know. We're built differently. I'm sorry. I know it makes us too human sometimes. But I really care about you, and I want to make you happy."

Mickelle had a desire to laugh at the trite words, but his seriousness stunned her. What *was* he talking about? After this little scene did he really expect her to believe him?

"I'll drop by soon," Colton promised. With another crater smile for Brenda, he was gone. Mickelle breathed a sigh of relief.

"Hormones?" Brenda shook her dark head. "You know, I'm having second thoughts about this guy. When a man starts using his hormones to make excuses for his actions, something's wrong. Reminds me of my ex-husband: 'Oh, I just couldn't help fooling around with my secretary, it's the way I'm built.' Humph! As if the Lord didn't give him a brain in his head. He couldn't see that the natural man had to be overcome. That the Lord could make him strong and that *I* could make him happy, if he put enough effort into the relationship." She sighed, and for the first time since Mickelle had known her she looked depressed.

Mickelle put her arm around her friend. "I'm sorry."

"So am I," sniffed Brenda. "I've come so far without him, spiritually and emotionally, and the children are much better without his constant deceit. But I still wish that he had been the kind of man I thought he was back then. I wish we could have worked it out, that we could have had an eternal family. I don't love him anymore. I don't long to be with him. In fact, I sort of hate him. But even so . . . it's hard. I wish he would take more notice of the girls. I wish they had a man in their life that they could respect."

"What about that banker you met at the dance?"

Brenda smiled, though tears glittered in her green eyes. "He's nice. Very cautious, but nice. It's too early to tell. He likes kids, but I'm not getting my hopes up."

"I know what you mean," Mickelle said with a grimace. "Colton seemed so nice up front. He talked a good talk, and he helped me get my money. But it just seems so odd for him to discuss the gospel one minute and then . . ." Mickelle trailed off, not wanting to explain how Colton had treated her.

Brenda reached up and squeezed Mickelle's hand that was still draped over her shoulder. "The gospel is true, Mickelle. It's the one thing I've learned through this whole mess—I know it with all of my heart. It's just unfortunate that some men choose to use an outward piety to hide what is really inside their hearts. That's not the Lord's plan, we know that. Women just have to remember that they are entitled to their own revelation and that we don't have to marry a man just because he said he had a confirmation."

Mickelle knew that had happened to Brenda. Her husband had told her that he knew they were supposed to marry, and that the revelation would come first to the man. She had trusted him before trusting in her own communication with the Lord.

"I was so naive when I married," Brenda remembered with a sigh. "And so young. I didn't understand that I was entitled to my own answer."

"Or that you didn't even *have* to ask the Lord if you didn't like him," Mickelle said dryly. "After all, the Lord gives us brains and intuition. He expects us to use them." Of course, sometimes even those things didn't stop a woman from being blinded—like with Colton. But he had shown his true colors now, and she refused to be fooled again.

Brenda shrugged. "Oh, I liked my husband well enough. I just wasn't sure that we should get married. I should have seen that he wasn't truly committed to me or to the Lord." She sighed again and then said, "Shall we go now? Or not."

Mickelle frowned. She didn't feel like going anywhere. Not now. What she wanted was to talk to Damon. "You go ahead," she told Brenda as they walked to the door. "We've missed the lesson anyway, and after Colton . . . well I'm not feeling up to talking with the other ladies tonight. You can all manage tying that quilt without me."

"Are you sure?" Brenda smiled skeptically. "You always love doing that. You're faster than anyone."

"It'll give someone else a chance."

When Brenda looked as though she would offer to stay, Mickelle added, "I think I really need to talk with Damon."

"So . . . that's how it is. You should have told me."

"I didn't know." Mickelle felt herself blush. "I mean . . . I knew, but I was fighting it."

Brenda hugged her. "Good luck. You deserve a dream come true."

A dream come true.

Was that what Damon was? Maybe she would go right in and call him on his cell phone. His late meeting should be over by now.

As Brenda was pulling away a white van drove into her vacated spot, behind the ancient gold station wagon Mickelle had nicknamed the Snail. A man emerged from the van, and sauntered across the grass, a paper in his hands. "Hello, I have a service order here. To look at a damaged cabinet."

"What?" Mickelle stared at him suspiciously. His sandy blonde hair was a bit longer than she liked, but his hazel eyes were earnest. "I didn't call anyone to fix anything."

"Uh . . ." He consulted his paper. "I talked to a Damon Wolfe. Does that ring a bell?"

"Yeah, it's starting to chime."

He grinned. "Good one. Well, this Mr. Wolfe said he'd meet me here. I was to wait if he wasn't here yet."

"You won't have to wait long." Over his shoulder, Mickelle saw Damon drive up in his dark green Lexus. She felt a pang at not seeing him in the familiar dark blue Mercedes, but that was because she had grown attached to it when he had lent it to her for a week when Tanner was fixing the damage to the Snail—her only car at the time.

Damon was out of the Lexus in a flash, and jogging across the lawn toward them. "Kelle," he said in greeting. She could tell he was a little unsettled by the way he rubbed the shadow growing on his chin.

Her heart was doing funny things in her chest at the sight of his beloved angular face, and she wanted nothing more than to throw herself in his arms. But, "Hello, Damon" was all she allowed herself.

"I thought you'd be gone by now."

"Apparently."

"Is it okay? I just wanted to do something for you . . . I know how much that curio cabinet means to you, and I thought tonight would be the perfect time to fix it since you were going to be gone. Even if you're mad at me for today. Your sister lent me her spare key. Well?" He gazed at her anxiously, while next to him the repair man laboriously studied his paper.

"Come on in," Mickelle said softly.

The repair man started up the cement stairs, but Damon held back. "You too," she invited. "We've got some Chinese food to finish."

He grinned, and she caught a glimpse of a gold tooth. She almost laughed, recalling how he had confessed that the tooth was a whim he succumbed to when the need for a cap had coincided with the making of his first million. As he matured, he had meant to have it replaced with something less eye-catching, but never seemed to have the time—or the desire—to go to the dentist. "I'm a little bit of a wimp about going to the dentist," he had admitted.

"Well, at least it's not a tattoo," Mickelle had replied. "And you can only see it when we're close."

Close! Right where she wanted to be!

Without warning, her entire being filled with light. She had missed that tooth, darn it all!

He took her hand as he came in. Mickelle started to close the front door, but paused as a car down the street caught her attention. White and low-slung, it reminded her of Colton's. But no, that was ridiculous. There was no reason for him to be hanging around. If he did keep his promise to call, she was *not* going to talk to him.

After surveying the damage, the repair man said, "I could fix it here like we agreed, but I could do a better job back at my shop, if you don't mind. And I can return it by the end of the week."

"Well, it's no longer a surprise." Damon smiled at her, asking for a decision. "Kelle, what do you think?"

Mickelle removed her precious roses from the cabinet, and then Damon helped move the curio cabinet out to the white van. All too soon they were alone.

"Well . . ." He let the word hang in the air between them.

Mickelle's heart was once more knocking about oddly. She had forgotten how broad his chest appeared at this close range, how neatly his short moustache combed just over the top of his upper lip. "We need to talk. Can you stay?"

"Of course." His amber eyes held hers in an almost physical embrace. Never had the innocent words "of course" sounded so alluring, so completely breathtaking—electrifying.

This time he didn't take her hand as he followed her up the stairs. She knew why. It was too important. What they said now might mean more than anything they had ever said to each other. She couldn't explain it even to herself, but *not* touching at this moment was right, just as holding her hand *had* been right moments earlier.

Mickelle checked for the white sports car before going into the house, but it was gone. For some reason, that made her feel a lot better.

Damon sat at the counter as Mickelle warmed up the sweet and sour chicken, vegetable spring rolls, and fried rice. The smell made her mouth water; she had only picked at her food when she'd eaten with the children earlier. She took out some plates before sitting and offering a blessing on the food. As she had done with Colton earlier, she took the stool on the opposite side of the counter from Damon.

They ate in silence for a few minutes, until Damon threw down his chopsticks. "Darn it all, I'm too hungry to use these."

She laughed and tossed him a fork from the drawer. He took a few more bites, watching her warily. Abruptly, he let the fork drop to the counter. His amber eyes gazed intently into hers, and the deep laughter lines in his face stood out more prominently on the sides of his slightly hooked nose. He was so ruggedly handsome—especially compared to Colton—and his face was honest, his expressions open and unfeigned.

"I can't eat with . . . What happened to us, Kelle?" His brow furrowed, making his thick blonde eyebrows run together. "I thought you loved me. I was sure of it. But it seems like the day I fell into that pool, I lost something more precious than my life: you."

It was true. Had he *not* nearly died, she wouldn't have felt such a need to protect herself.

Is that what I'm doing?

Even if she was, maybe it was necessary. Who else would do it? She had ceased believing in white knights when Riley killed himself.

"You've done so much for me," Mickelle began. "Giving me a job, helping me find the car. And for the boys. Jeremy hasn't wet the bed for weeks, he loves playing ball with you, and your kids are wonderful. I'm so grateful—"

"You're worried that you don't really love me, aren't you?" he accused in a raw voice. The muscles in his jaw rippled beneath the skin. He seized her hands and leaned across the counter until they were so close that she could smell his breath, spicy from the Chinese food. "You remember that kiss we shared this morning?" he asked huskily. "Was that gratitude? Is what you feel in your heart right now gratitude?"

The nearness of him filled all her senses, and more than anything at that moment she wanted to feel his lips against hers. As though reading her thoughts, he leaned over farther and his lips came down on hers, but instead of the urgent demanding kiss of that morning, his touch was gentle and searching, full of a tenderness she could not name. She wanted it to continue forever. Her heart thumped heavily in her chest, but all the other signs of a panic attack were missing. Maybe confronting the issue head-on was what she should have done from the start. Certainly kissing him didn't seem to be part of the problem!

He drew away reluctantly. "Is that gratitude?" he asked softly. "I don't think so. Gratitude is something you feel for your child when he cleans his room, or your neighbor for not allowing his dog to use your lawn as an outhouse. But not what's between us." He kissed her again, briefly. "Or is it? You tell me."

"It's not gratitude," she said, glad that he had left his hands cupped gently around hers. She couldn't bear it if he retreated now. "I mean, I have wondered occasionally, but not anymore. It's . . ." *Tell him,* she ordered herself silently. "I'm afraid."

"Afraid," he repeated, sounding thoroughly dejected. "Afraid of trusting me? Afraid of losing your freedom like you did with Riley?"

Her grip tightened on the chopsticks that she had not released during their kisses, or even though his hands still held hers. "Losing my freedom? No! Would you just let me talk? That's not it at all! I mean, it was when we first met, but you're not like that—I've learned you're not like that. It's *you* I don't want to lose! I'm afraid of losing *you*!"

He stared at her, jaw opening slightly as understanding dawned.

"Kelle, I—"

She wasn't finished. "I can't go through that again," she said, shaking her head, her voice agonized. Her heart thumped painfully and her sight and hearing grew dim, but she forced herself to continue. "I just can't! And I didn't even love Riley half as much as I love you." Tears spilled down her cheeks, but amazingly the effects of her panic attack didn't deepen.

Damon gave a swift intake of breath. "You love me more than Riley?" he asked tentatively.

She nodded, and sniffed loudly. "I tried so hard not to."

His lips twitched as though making a great effort not to smile. Then he freed the chopsticks from her death-grip and came around the counter, encircling her with his strong arms. For a long moment he searched her face with a sober expression.

"I'm afraid of losing you, too," he said gravely. "But you know what? I'm even more afraid of wasting any time we may have left together. I told you once that I believed we would be together forever— now and after this life—and I meant it. And I can't promise you that I'm not going to be in an accident that might take me away, but I can promise you I will never leave you through my own will. *Never.*"

"When I saw you lying there . . ." She shuddered and closed her eyes, and was glad when he pulled her even closer.

"I'll never go near a pool again, if that's what you want. But please don't let me live without you! I love you, Kelle, more than I have ever loved anyone—even my children."

She opened her eyes again. "I love them too."

"A good thing, because they need you. Sometimes I think as much as I need you."

That's just it, she wanted to say. *I need you too, but I don't want to!* But that was her fear talking again. She forced herself to breathe evenly.

"And, uh, Mickelle," he continued, "I think it's only fair to tell you that my kids, well, they *are* yours." His expression was suddenly half apologetic, like a little boy who was uncertain if his homemade gift would be well-received.

"What?"

He grinned sheepishly, arms still clasped around her. "I had my will changed last week—when I bought the ring. If I had died in that pool, I'm afraid, the kids would have gone to you, along with everything I own—lock, stock, and barrel. I told you that day in the hospital that all I had was yours—and I meant it."

The enormity of what he was saying struck her. He trusted her enough to give her not only all his millions in money and assets, but also his children, whom she knew he loved more than life. "Damon, I . . ." But she didn't know what to say.

"Please marry me, Kelle. Please." His gaze was pleading, but there was none of the sadness she had detected before, none of the uncertainty that had made him so miserable. Her heart leapt a little within her breast, knowing that he was finally aware of her true feelings.

That she loved him.

How could she say no?

"Okay," she whispered, "but I'm still afraid." Again her heart knocked painfully against her rib cage and her breathing quickened. She leaned into him, trying to breathe through the rising panic.

"I know," he said, holding her to him firmly. "But you are stronger than you think." He paused before continuing even more earnestly than before, "And I think that if we get down on our knees and pray with all our hearts, the Lord will bless us with peace. He knows the future and can comfort us. It is the only answer I know."

Damon was right! She had been going about this fear issue all wrong. Why hadn't she remembered that such paralyzing fear did not come from the Lord, but from the other side?

The Lord is my strength and my salvation, she told herself, *whom then shall I fear . . .*

The panic faded slowly, as the tide receding from the shore. She would ask for a priesthood blessing later, but for now she would hold onto Damon. And let him hold onto her. The joy in her heart was all-encompassing.

Then, for no reason at all, she remembered the white car down the street that had so resembled Colton's. She remembered the determination and cruelty in Colton's eyes before Brenda had interrupted them, his promise of return. She shivered. Something was not right with that man. But what?

It doesn't matter. I never have to see him again. But if that was the truth, why did she feel such dread?

CHAPTER 13

She loves me more than she did Riley! The words echoed through Damon's head as he held Mickelle. He wanted to do a victory dance, but he refrained. Later, maybe, when Mickelle was up for teasing. The warmth of her in his arms, the smell of her hair and skin, the taste of her lips, was everything he had dreamed of this past week when they had been separated by her fear.

Her fear of losing me, he corrected. That made all the difference.

"When?" he asked between kisses. He knew he shouldn't push, that it hadn't been even a year since her husband had died, but he couldn't resist.

"When, what?"

"When will you marry me?"

Her face went still, but her smile didn't fade. "How about in December so that we can spend Christmas together?"

He was relieved that it wasn't farther away, but at the same time he wondered how he could possibly wait any longer than another day.

"The ring!" She pulled away from him and disappeared into the hallway. When she returned, she was wearing the ring he had given her.

"It's not too showy, is it?" he asked, bringing up her hand to look at the ring.

"Actually, it is, but I think I can force myself to get used to it."

He laughed. "Good." He brought his head down to kiss her hand, and it was then he noticed the dark marks around her wrist. "What's this?" he asked, tracing the mottled area with a gentle forefinger. He was almost certain they hadn't been there earlier.

Her eyes widened in surprise. "I didn't notice . . ." She concentrated on the bruises, keeping her blue eyes averted. He took her other hand swiftly and examined it. Caught unaware, she had no choice but to allow him to see the single bruise on that wrist: a large thumbprint.

"Kelle?" he asked. Her face flushed, and she tried to pull away. He let her go, but he wasn't finished. "Who did this to you?" These marks weren't natural, and were obviously not self-inflicted.

She sighed and turned from him, sitting on one of the stools near the counter. "I've been so stupid. I didn't see . . . Colton—"

"He did this to you?"

"Don't sound so angry."

He sat next to her, willing himself to be calm. "What happened?"

"He was mad at me today. He set up an appointment for me to talk to his financial wizard friend and I turned him down. He was upset. I—I think he must have gotten a commission or something." She grimaced. "It seems you were right all along about him not being what he seemed."

"Tell me exactly what happened . . . please."

She sighed. "Okay."

Damon's anger grew as Mickelle recounted the scene with Colton. He felt her fury and helplessness as though it were his own. "What was the name of that guy he referred you to?" he asked. "And if you'll give me his number I'll call Mr. Cover Boy to make sure he won't be coming over ever again."

He did just that. As soon as he left Mickelle's—even more reluctantly than usual—he placed the call to Colton Scofield on his cell phone. He let it ring a dozen times before hanging up in frustration. He hit his hand against the steering wheel, wincing with the pain and wishing it was Mr. Cover Boy's face. How dare he treat Mickelle that way!

At his home in Alpine, he found Belle and Tanner in the game room playing pool, and he told them the good news of Mickelle's acceptance of his marriage proposal. Belle squealed and hugged him. "I'm so happy, Daddy! I'm so happy!" she kept saying.

Tanner also appeared content, though a little worried. "What about that other guy? Bryan seems to think he's there to stay. And no offense, Dad, but Bryan likes that guy more than you."

"You leave Mr. Cover Boy to me. As for Bry, he's going to need a little time, but I think we'll win him over yet." Damon tried to sound confident, though Bryan's attitude left him confused. He had done nothing but try to be a friend to that child. What more could he do? Mickelle had told him about the door he had kicked in, and Damon wondered silently at the anger building inside Bryan. What could he do to stop it before Bryan seriously hurt someone?

Life was certainly bound to become more complicated when Bryan learned of their pending marriage. Damon knew his love was strong enough to see the storm through, but was Mickelle's? She was strong, and he knew that she could survive anything, but he understood that their relationship would have to be secondary—at least for now—to her relationship with her son.

Damon grabbed his phone and punched in the numbers of his attorney. If Keith hadn't found anything, maybe it was time to hire someone who could.

* * * * *

Jennie Anne was ready for bed. Not that she had to do anything in particular. She always slept in her clothes. Tonight she was looking forward to sleep because that meant tomorrow would come faster. Besides, now that her aunt had given her two more blankets, she wasn't cold at night. Just in case, she was wearing three pairs of her new socks, and her feet were actually hot. She could barely contain her yawning.

In the summer she found it hard to sleep because of the light, and she had passed many late hours stuffing envelopes with her aunt or thumbing through one of the magazines in the stacks of stuff around the house. She had always wondered what the words said.

But now I can read! Or almost.

Upon arriving home from Mickelle's she had sounded out a few words in a magazine and many had made sense. The ones that didn't, she would ask about. She couldn't ask Mrs. Palmer because her aunt had warned her not to talk to the teacher, but Mickelle would know. A warm, wonderful feeling grew in Jennie Anne's heart. For no reason she could fathom, Mickelle liked her! Jennie Anne knew instinctively that she could be trusted, just like Belle had said.

Jennie Anne fingered her thick hair, still slightly damp from her bath. What fun she'd had! How good her hair felt! She had worried that Mickelle would make her change in front of them, and was relieved when she had let them change in her room instead. Belle had turned her back, and hadn't seen the bruise on Jennie Anne's shoulder. It still hurt, but not nearly as bad as before.

She grinned. Boy, she liked Mickelle. She could hardly believe that she could go over there every day.

I have to make sure I do everything exactly right, she thought. *I don't want them to hate me.*

The happy feeling in her heart dulled slightly, but it was still strong. Jennie Anne straightened her new clothes and snuggled into her blankets.

When the knock came on the door, Jennie Anne was almost asleep, though it was still early. She heard her aunt come from the kitchen, muttering something. The overhead light went on, making her blink at the sudden brightness.

"Hi, Mom," said a masculine voice that sent dread into Jennie Anne's heart.

"What do you want, Troy?"

"I just come to visit. Come, give me a hug, Mom."

"I don't have any money."

"Just need a place to sleep."

As he spoke, Jennie Anne was gathering up her things, trying to keep the panic from slowing her movements. She stored all her treasures except her backpack and her blankets in her special spot under the wooden-frame couch, blocking it from sight with several stacks of musty-smelling magazines. She would come back to move the stuff later, but this would do for now. Her throat felt dry and her heart beat crazily. Less than a week had passed since she had felt this pounding fear in her heart. Now, it seemed it had never left. She thought fleetingly of Mickelle and her promise to call her. Would this be reason enough?

No, it would make her aunt mad. Troy, too.

"We don't have room for you," Nedda whined.

"Sure you do. I'll sleep on the couch." There was silence for a few minutes, then a loud curse. "Mom, this place gets junkier every second. Why don't you get rid of this stuff?"

"I may need it."

"Yeah, right." There was disgust in his tone.

Jennie Anne froze, knowing that they were coming closer to the path that led down to her couch. The couch where Troy would now sleep.

To her relief, Troy said, "Got something to eat?" Nedda mumbled a reply and they passed on into the kitchen.

If it were summer Jennie Anne would wait outside until he was asleep, and then settle herself under the table in the kitchen on a mound of comfortable blankets. But October got cold outside. She contemplated the risk of sneaking into her aunt's room to wait until Troy was settled for the night. Troy might not even see her.

"What happened to your big deal?" Nedda was saying. "Thought you was gonna be gone a long time."

"Had a change of plans," Troy grunted, his mouth full.

Jennie Anne should have known. Troy always ended up back here sooner or later. It was just her luck that it was sooner this time.

"So you come back here." There was a bitterness in her great-aunt's voice that Jennie Anne hadn't noticed before, perhaps wouldn't have noticed at all if she hadn't been listening so hard.

She crept down the hallway between the piles of stuff, nearly jumping when the doorbell rang again. She ducked back toward the couch as her aunt passed. "It better not be one of your friends."

"It ain't. Nobody knows I'm back."

"Good, 'cause I'll send 'em packing. I got enough to worry about."

"Yeah, Donna May's brat, you mean," Troy supplied, his voice surly.

Nedda retorted, "You and her are two of a kind."

Jennie Anne didn't know if her great-aunt meant that her mother and Troy were two of a kind, or if she meant Jennie Anne was like Troy. *I won't believe either one,* she promised herself. *I'm not like him, and my mother wasn't either.* She had heard Nedda lie several times now, and no longer believed her. It gave her much consolation to allow herself not to believe. She would pretend to go along with what they said, but they could never see into her heart.

Only her best friend Belle might be able to do that.

"Hello," said a voice at the door. "I was here earlier with a friend of mine. Dropped off a little girl."

"Did she leave something?" Nedda asked.

"Well, not exactly, but . . . well, maybe she did. I found this twenty-dollar bill in the back where she was riding. Could it be hers?"

Jennie Anne stood on the couch, daring to peer over the stacks. She saw her great-aunt grab at the money she had never seen, much less left in his car. "I told her not to leave it lying around," Nedda said.

"Can I come in?"

Jennie Anne recognized the man from Mickelle's. He was probably the most beautiful man she had ever seen.

"Well, my son's home. I don't think—"

"I've got a proposition for you. A way to earn a lot of money. Are you sure you don't have a little time?" The voice was so sweet and convincing that Jennie Anne wanted to run to the door and let him in herself.

"Well, it don't hurt to listen, I suppose." Nedda stepped back, and allowed him to enter.

The man's eyes met Jennie Anne's, and she felt herself color. He glanced away without acknowledging her. "Could we have a word in *private*?"

"Jennie Anne, get outside and wait," her aunt ordered, her plump fingers raking through her curly hair, as though she were one of the preening robins that visited the weeping willow in the summer.

Jennie Anne needed no second invitation. She darted down the pathway, past the adults and out onto the solitary cement step, now crumbling at its edges. She rubbed her arms, clad only in a thin long-sleeved shirt. In dismay, she realized that she had forgotten a blanket.

Thoughts of Mickelle again came into her mind. Could she find her way there in the dark? Would it do any good?

Jennie Anne massaged her arms more vigorously, before wrapping them around herself. The white car she had ridden in earlier sat outside by the curb, glinting in the moonlight. She sighed. How long would she have to wait?

Long minutes passed until she heard someone approaching the door from the other side. She leapt to her feet and ran around the house, just in case. To her surprise, Troy and the beautiful man walked out to the white sports car and drove away.

Jennie Anne felt like dancing. Anyone who could take Troy away was all right!

"Jennie Anne?" her great-aunt's voice called.

She hurried forward. "Good," Nedda said. "Better come inside to bed. You got school in the morning."

So she did! Jennie Anne loved school. School meant seeing Belle.

She started down the narrow pathway to her couch, nearly bumping into the tall stacks of boxes. Her aunt's voice stopped her. "Better sleep in my room," she said. "Troy might come back. Get what you need for tomorrow and clear out a place under the couch. He has to put his stuff somewhere." She paused, her hand coming to grip Jennie Anne's upper arm. "And don't say nothin' to your new friend about that guy coming over. If you do, you ain't ever going there again. Got it?"

Jennie Anne nodded. She tried to maintain an outer calm, but inside she was singing. She got to go home with Belle again tomorrow!

As she snuggled in her blankets on the far side of her aunt's bed, she recalled the way their beautiful visitor had stared right through her. Who was he and what did he want with Troy?

Suddenly, Jennie Anne was afraid.

* * * * *

Brionney Hergarter glanced at the clock in the kitchen. It was nine, and her sister would soon drop by for the boys. Not that she minded having them over. They actually helped keep the older girls entertained. But Jesse had been home late from work and had only just relieved her of the twins. Once he had them asleep and Mickelle had come for her boys, he would help her get the others in bed. Then she could fill up the bath with lilac-scented oil and water so hot it would nearly scald her skin, and read a few chapters of the novel she had received from Mickelle on her birthday.

Ahhh, hot water and silence—a kind of heaven for a mother of five. Of course, afterwards she would peek in on all the children, making sure they were breathing and covered . . . even Savannah, who insisted she was too old for such things. Yet she wasn't but a year older than Jeremy, who would have slept in his mother's bed every night if she let him. That was the difference between an oldest child with an anxious foot pointed toward adulthood, and a youngest child with a foot clinging to babyhood.

She sighed again, and began picking up toys the twins had strewn throughout the house, following a trail to the entryway. A corner of a tiny black notebook caught her eye, half hidden behind the grandfather clock where someone must have kicked it. She knew what it was at once, and hesitated only an instant before opening it. There she flipped through the pages she and Mickelle had seen before. And more.

Much more.

There was a page for Damon's family—addresses, birthdays, even a list of household help. Mickelle's neighbors each had a page, as did several of Mickelle's friends, each complete with personal information and their observations of Mickelle. There was even a page for Brionney and her family.

Then followed a detailed list of Mickelle's schedule, from church meetings to the time she had to pick up Tanner from the high school each day in Highland. Colton even knew what time her mail arrived. There were also three entire pages of notations about Riley's insurance policy and names of people he had discussed it with in the neighborhood. Mickelle had only known Colton Scofield for less than a week, and yet he had collected an entire notebook full of information.

Like a stalker, Brionney thought. Her hand trembled. What did he want? Could he have been trying to impress Mickelle with his thoughtfulness?

She looked again on the page where the names and ages of her own children were written in a precise male hand. Next to the names of the twins, Forest and Gabriel, was the notation: *Identical twins. Maybe use twin story with Mickelle?* Brionney felt a sinking feeling as she remembered what Mickelle had told her about Colton's boys and their death. Why would he tell such a story if it wasn't true?

Even more curious were several pages of terms that were unique to Mormon culture, like sacrament meeting, Relief Society, and home teaching. And another page of colloquialisms followed. Apparently he had done a thorough research of Utah Mormons. But why would that be necessary for a man who worked in the insurance business?

Jesse was still in with the twins, so Brionney didn't want to disturb him. Should she tell Mickelle? She retraced her steps to the kitchen and dialed her sister's number. She let the phone ring repeatedly before remembering that Mickelle was still at the church.

She laughed a little at her mistake, reminding herself that her nephews were still in her family room with her girls, playing games and staying up later than they ordinarily would on a school night. Mickelle would be back any minute now and then she would give her the notebook.

But the odd feeling she had upon discovering the contents of the black notebook persisted.

She paced the kitchen floor, spying dirty spots on the ceramic tile beneath the two highchairs that she had missed during cleanup. Grabbing a rag, she crouched to remedy the situation. The little black notebook was still in her left hand, pressing into her palm, seemingly branding her with the contents.

Leaving the wet rag on the floor, she tiptoed down the hall and into the nursery. Jesse was sitting in the rocking chair, a sleeping twin over each shoulder. He sighed with relief when he saw her. "Thank heaven!" he whispered. "My muscles are cramping up. I didn't dare move for fear of waking them. I was praying for you to come in and help me get them to the cribs."

Brionney chuckled, a pleasant feeling replacing the odd fear she had felt only seconds before. "No matter how many times I show you the trick, you never seem to master it," she teased. As she spoke, she deftly removed Gabriel from his father's shoulder and laid him in his crib, tucking a quilt around him. His breathing pattern momentarily changed at the transfer, but quickly resumed.

"Hey, holding a kid while putting the other in bed is a talent I simply wasn't given. Forest *always* wakes up when I try it, no matter who I put down first. At least I've learned how to rock the two of them to sleep." He gingerly slid Forest under his own quilt, patting his stomach rhythmically until he was sure the child hadn't awakened.

Then he pulled Brionney into his arms, kissing her soundly.

Brionney responded, loving the feel of her husband's touch, both the passion and security he offered, until a loud slap jolted them both.

"What?" Jesse searched the darkness, eyes going first to Forest's crib since he was usually the most difficult. The boy slept soundly.

"It's a notebook." Brionney picked it up from the rocking chair cushion where it had landed after hitting the bare wood of the armrest. "It's what I came to talk to you about."

With another glance at the twins, Jesse took her hand and they left the room. As soon as they were in the hall Brionney began explaining the situation. "So I was going to wait for Mickelle—she should be here any minute now—but I just feel . . . unsettled about it all."

"Let me see the notebook." Jesse accepted it from her hand. He seated himself at the kitchen table and began to thumb through it. "Man, this is creepy," he said, his brown eyes troubled. "Like a stalker or something."

"That's what I thought. What should we do?"

Jesse shook his head. "I don't know. I really don't. But I guess it really isn't up to us anyway. It's Mickelle who needs to make a decision."

"Yeah, I guess, but I just feel so . . . anxious." Brionney snapped her fingers. "I know, let's call Damon."

"Damon? What's he got to do with this?"

"Well, Mickelle told me earlier that he's having this guy checked out, and she got mad at him, and then they kissed . . . Well none of that really matters, but maybe Damon knows something about this." Brionney felt a warm relief seep through her body, as though the Spirit testified of her decision.

"By all means, let's call him then." Jesse reached for the phone on the table where Brionney had left it, but she grabbed it first.

"I'll do it." She pushed the button where Damon's number was preset, and waited for the dial. "Hi, Belle," she said after a few minutes. "Aren't you in bed yet?"

"Oh, Brionney, it's so wonderful. Daddy and Mickelle are getting married!"

"They are? Why that's great. Really great!" She covered the lower part of the phone and explained to Jesse, "Belle said Damon and Mickelle are getting married!"

He raised his eyebrows in surprise. "Wonder when that happened. Didn't you say she's been at the church?"

Brionney had been thinking the exact same thing. She shrugged and uncovered the mouth piece. "Hey, Belle, can I speak to your daddy? It's kind of important."

"Okay, but then can I tell Camille about Daddy and Mickelle?"

"Sure."

After a brief lapse, Damon was on the phone. "Calling to offer congratulations already?" he joked. "How *do* you keep tabs on everything, Bri. I swear you must read minds."

"Congratulations," Brionney offered. "Actually, I didn't know. Belle just told me. I was calling for something else. But this is amazing news, and I'm glad to hear it. When did it all happen?"

"Just tonight. I went to Kelle's to show the repair guy the cabinet, like I told you, only she was home. Apparently, she'd had a run-in with Mr. Cover Boy and didn't feel like going to the church for her meeting. So we talked."

Brionney laughed aloud at his name for Colton Scofield, but something he said made her uneasy feeling return. "Well, that's great, but she must have decided to go after you left. I just called her and there was no answer. I've been waiting for her to come pick up the boys, and then I found Colton's notebook, and I just got so worried . . ."

"What notebook?" Damon demanded. "And she should be there. She said she was leaving to get the boys."

"Well, maybe that's why she didn't answer. She could be on her way."

"Tell him about the notebook," Jesse urged. Sometime during the conversation he had disappeared and returned with the other portable phone, which he held to his ear. Between them, Brionney and Jesse explained.

Damon made angry noises, but when he spoke, he was calm. "Look, I called the guy I have on Colton's case and he's going to call me right back. He was on another line. He has some information for us. When Mickelle gets there, just keep her there, and I'll call as soon as I hear from them."

"Okay." Brionney felt distinctly better, even knowing that most likely her plan of a long hot soak was evaporating into the realm of dreams.

At least they would be getting to the bottom of this mystery.

CHAPTER 14

Mickelle had planned to pick up the boys immediately after Damon left, but somehow she found herself sitting on a stool and leaning over the counter, admiring the heart-shaped diamond Damon had given her. Outside, night had fallen, but the diamond picked up the overhead light and reflected it back at her.

Married to Damon, she thought, enjoying the delicious shivers that ran up her arms and down her neck and back. *It's like a fairytale.*

Of course, running a house like Damon's would be a task. She knew he had a cook for the weekdays, a groundskeeper, and a live-in housekeeper. Mostly, she approved. She couldn't possibly clean the entire house herself and keep up the yard, but she could do the cooking. In fact, she *enjoyed* cooking. Then again, if she were going back to school . . .

The possibilities were endless. Sometimes when she thought about it, Damon's wealth frightened her. However could a woman like her, accustomed to barely scraping by to make ends meet, step into his world? He had assured her that she would do so easily, and yet there was that lingering fear inside that someone might laugh at the poor little pauper turned princess.

Not that Damon moved in snooty circles. During the short time they had dated, she had learned that he didn't waste nearly the amount of money on luxuries that many of the people in his income bracket were accustomed to spending. He employed no butler or chauffeur, his garage held only four cars instead of ten—two of which weren't even his—and his list of charities was almost as long as his investments.

She laughed softly at her thoughts. *He's a good man. A little impatient, a little arrogant even, but he loves me.* Mickelle stared at the ring, lost in the joy of her love.

The sound of a breaking window jolted her from her reverie. She listened, but heard nothing else.

Had it been her imagination? She rose to her feet and peered out the kitchen window into the night, remembering the time Sasha, as an exuberant, overgrown puppy, had fallen into a window well, breaking a basement window in the process. Luckily the Lab hadn't been hurt.

The darkness told her nothing, and Mickelle decided the sound had been in her imagination. She would just get her jacket and drive over to Brionney's for the boys.

She found her jacket and purse in the closet off the tiny entryway and was reentering the kitchen with them in her hands when something barreled into her, knocking her to the ground. A heavy weight crushed the air from her lungs, and hands roamed over her body as though searching for something hidden.

Fighting the terror that gripped her, Mickelle managed to roll out from under her attacker and put her arms up to defend herself. A figure clad in tight-fitting black sweats and a ski mask lashed out at her with a gloved fist. Mickelle dodged the first blow and managed to block another. Desperately, she pushed herself away from this black-clad stranger, and fled down the hall toward her room, realizing too late that she should have tried for one of the outside doors.

Shut the door quick! she ordered herself. *I can do it, I can do it.* Scarcely breathing, she slammed the door, sobbing when the attacker's foot wedged inside and put an immediate stop to her efforts.

"Go away!" she yelled, throwing all her weight on the door. "I'm calling the police!" In reality, the portable phone was in the kitchen, far out of her reach. In her peripheral vision, she saw that glass from her bedroom window had shattered over the carpet like her newfound peace, and clothes from her dresser were scattered on the floor, the drawers hanging open haphazardly.

He must have come from in here, she thought numbly.

The door groaned under the onslaught of the forces pushing

against it. Fear clogged Mickelle's throat, coating her mouth with a sickening taste that made her want to gag. Still she leaned against the door, praying for release.

With a sudden burst of strength, the attacker flung the door open, tossing Mickelle into a heap on the floor by her bed. Her head cracked against the bottom of the ancient box spring, and her senses whirled. In an instant, he was on her, lifting her onto the bed, shoving her down. Hands again searched her body, and Mickelle fought prying fingers, bringing her knees and feet against her opponent. He struck her twice in the face, open-handed, and then again with his fist. Mickelle was helpless to move away from the assault.

But she would *never* give in easily. From what she could see he wasn't armed, and that meant she had a chance.

She fought, using her nails, her feet, her teeth, everything she could enlist. At one point, she shoved Damon's ring into the eyehole of the ski mask, hoping to do some serious damage, but the assailant only wrenched the jewel from her hand and made it disappear inside a pocket.

Mickelle fought on, though her strength was weakening. Her blue turtleneck had been viciously torn from her body, though her under-clothes were intact. She knew now that this person wanted more from her than just her jewelry or goods. He was going to hurt her—and badly.

Another aching blow landed on her chin; another, less painful, to her stomach. She threw up then in a sudden motion, spraying the remains of her Chinese food onto her attacker. He cringed, but only for an instant. That was all Mickelle needed. Seeing the opening, she shoved her foot between his legs, using all the force she could muster.

With a growl of rage, the assailant lashed out, pounding his hurt and anger into her body in one violent motion; then mercifully he fell to the ground in agony. Mickelle knew she should run, knew that she had to get out of the house before he recovered. But every inch of her body ached, and moving made her feel as though fire leaked from her pores.

Mickelle lay panting on the bed, dragging in much needed air. She had no concept of how long she laid there, fighting to breathe, telling herself to hurry. Faintly, she heard her phone ringing and ringing, calling plaintively for her to answer. The sound forced her to a sitting position. Gritting her teeth against the pain, she stretched out her feet. There was no reaction from the curled figure, who lay clutching himself in anguish. Encouraged, Mickelle inched forward until her feet touched the floor. She took a step.

An iron grip closed around her ankle, and Mickelle tripped, sprawling atop her attacker. She heard an evil chuckle. "What I'll do to you," a gravelly voice muttered. "You will pay for this."

"Let me go!" she demanded.

"I will—eventually." Hands closed around her throat. She couldn't even scream.

* * * * *

Damon hung up the phone with his attorney, reeling from the information he had learned. "I would have called you sooner," his friend had told him, "but I was on the phone with my informant when you rang."

With hands feeling ridiculously clumsy, Damon dialed Jesse and Brionney's home phone number. "Hi, it's me," he said. "This is more serious than I thought. You'd better keep Mickelle there until I come over."

"She hasn't arrived yet," Brionney told him anxiously. "I even called some of her friends who attended Enrichment meeting, just to make sure that she hadn't changed her mind, that maybe she ran on over to the meeting. But one of her friends—a woman named Brenda—said that Mickelle never came and, get this, she also said that she witnessed a really odd scene between her and Colton earlier."

"Yeah, that was the run-in with Mr. Cover Boy I mentioned, the reason she didn't feel like going to the church in the first place. Look, I'm going over there right now. We can talk about Scofield later."

"Shouldn't we call the police?"

"I'd like too, but we have nothing to tell them—yet."

"I'll have Jesse meet you there," Brionney said worriedly. "You still have Mickelle's spare key, don't you?"

"Yeah." Damon paused before disconnecting, wanting to say something to comfort Brionney. "Don't worry too much. Kelle's tough."

"Yeah. She probably decided to take a nice hot bubble bath and forgot the time." Brionney's laugh sounded forced.

"See you soon."

Damon hung up the phone, and ran toward the door. He had already talked briefly with Tanner and Belle when he had sent them to bed before his phone conversation with the attorney. They knew that he might have to go out, and they would be fine on their own.

Checking to make sure that his cell phone was in his suit pocket, he hurried to the garage, choosing not his new Lexus, but the trusty dark blue Mercedes instead. He wouldn't be driving it much longer. In their conversation that evening, Mickelle had mentioned that she much preferred the Mercedes; it would soon be hers. He would need to start becoming accustomed to the Lexus, but tonight he wanted something familiar, something he knew would get him there safely and quickly.

How much time had elapsed since he had left Mickelle's? Since he had first talked to Brionney? And where was Mickelle? Was she all right? He prayed that she was home safe, that perhaps she had fallen asleep or was taking a bath as Brionney suggested.

It wasn't like her to forget the boys—ever. And why wasn't she answering the phone?

Damon's anxiety mounted until the beating of his heart filled the entire car. *Have to get to Mickelle,* it pumped. *Get to Mickelle.*

Jesse was already at Mickelle's house when Damon arrived in record time. "Wow, you got here fast," he said. "I didn't expect you for another ten minutes. And by then I would have everything figured out."

Damon didn't dwell on the miracle of his quick arrival. Didn't that only mean that Mickelle was in serious trouble? His mind churned with the things he had learned about Colton Scofield, a.k.a. Jonny Garvey and Simon Holm.

"Looks quiet," he said, walking toward the house.

Jesse shrugged. "I went around to the back and didn't see anything unusual. There are a few lights on. I was about to knock."

The men sprinted up the last few steps. Jesse rung the bell, while Damon pounded with his fist.

Nothing.

Damon produced her spare key from his pocket, and within seconds they opened the door.

* * * * *

Just when Mickelle thought she would lose consciousness, the pressure at her throat lessened.

He was on top of her now, hands biting cruelly into her flesh despite the black gloves. Mickelle's fear increased. So did her anger. Her thoughts changed from *Why, why, why?* to *How dare he!*

His mouth closed on hers and Mickelle bit him hard, tasting blood, but was unsure if it was his or hers. He swore and pummeled her again. She tried to lift her leg, to kick him as she had before, but she was pinned under his heavier form.

Would no one help her?

Everything in her life had boiled down to this one moment. She was alone and she was the only one who could save herself.

* * * * *

In moments, Damon and Jesse determined that no one was in the living room or kitchen. Damon strode down the hall, afraid that he would miss something in his hurry. He heard sounds now, coming from Mickelle's bedroom. Sounds of a struggle.

As he plunged through the door, he saw Mickelle straining under a figure in black. She lifted her head in a sudden motion, slamming her forehead into the face of her attacker. The person moaned and drooped slightly to the side. Mickelle brought up her newly freed foot . . .

"Mickelle!" Damon shouted. The few steps between them seemed like an ocean.

The black-clad figure leapt up and darted toward Damon. Caught unaware, Damon couldn't grab him as he escaped into the hall.

"Jesse!" Damon yelled. But Jesse was also unprepared as the intruder slipped past him and out into the night.

Damon, torn between needing to go to Mickelle and catching the man, was only slightly behind. He jumped from the porch, tackling the black-clad figure. They rolled once, then twice, as one struggled to get away and the other to hold fast. Out of the corner of his eye, Damon saw the other man reach for a stone frog in Mickelle's rose garden. Saw, but couldn't stop him from slamming it into his head. Desperately, Damon grasped at his opponent as his world tilted crazily.

In a violent wrench, the intruder was gone, leaving only his black ski mask behind as evidence that he had ever been there at all.

"Did you see him?" Jesse yelled from the porch.

"No. Too dark."

Jesse helped him to his feet. "Sorry I didn't get out here sooner. But you were both fast. By the time I got out here, he had that rock. Boy, that must hurt."

Damon was too angry to reply. He should have managed to keep hold of that punk, to punish him. "Mickelle," he said, pushing off Jesse's hands.

Mickelle lay on the floor in her room, unmoving. Her shirt had been torn from her body and the rest of her clothes were ripped or askew. Damon gathered her into his arms. "Get the blanket," he ordered Jesse.

Tenderly Damon tucked the worn quilt from the bed around Mickelle. It was only then that she began sobbing.

"I thought no one would come. I thought no one would save me."

"I'm here, Kelle. I'm here now. No one is ever going to hurt you again."

"How do you know?" her voice was shrill, hysterical.

He tightened his arms around her, trying to make her feel safe. "Because I'll make sure of it." It sounded stupid, even to his own ears. Sure, he could quit work and stay with her every second, but would that make either of them happy in the long run? Living with fear wasn't a life he relished.

"I thought no one would come," she muttered again, burrowing her face into his chest, not even wincing at the pain of the cuts and bruises on her skin. Blood from her face stained his expensive suit, but that was the least of his worries. He felt like an utter failure.

He rocked her slightly, as he did Belle when she awoke with a nightmare. "I'm sorry, Mickelle, I'm sorry."

"No one would come," she sobbed.

He stroked her hair, rocking her. "I'm here. Don't worry. I'm here."

His voice seemed to calm her, if not his words, and soon her sobbing drained away. She clung to him, though, and he was grateful for that much. She didn't seem to blame him as he blamed himself.

"Better call the police," he told Jesse as he dabbed a rivulet of blood from a nasty gash in her forehead.

"And Brionney. She'll have my head if we don't."

When Jesse left the room, Mickelle spoke, "It was him—Colton."

"You saw him?" Somehow Damon didn't think Scofield had the guts for something like this.

"I didn't see him, but it was Colton. It *had* to be him. He was searching for something in particular." Her voice broke. "He took my ring." Her left hand pushed up out of the blanket, looking white and incredibly frail. Along the ring finger were darkening bruises and raw scrapes. "I tried not to let him have it, but . . ." The words were drowned by another sob.

"The ring isn't important. You are. I can always buy another ring."

She rested felt him for a long time. Then, "Why did you come? How did you know?"

Damon cleared the lump in his throat. "Well, it was mostly Brionney. She felt unsettled after finding that black notebook Jeremy took from Colton's car. She and Jesse called me. Meanwhile, I was waiting for a phone call from my attorney to see what he'd found out about Colton."

"And what did he say?"

Damon wished he didn't have to answer, but Mickelle had a right to know. "So far the guy has pulled off several dozen insurance thefts, his target mainly being young widows. First he tracks down a likely target, joins their church or civic group, finds out everything he can about them, and then goes in for the goods."

Mickelle said nothing. She only closed her eyes. A tear dripped out of the corner, and Damon wiped it away with his fingertip.

"Apparently, he has some friends in different investment groups who help him. Somehow he gets the women to sign over their funds, and boom, he's gone. They never track him down."

"I'm glad he's not a real Mormon," Mickelle said.

"Hey, the people aren't the religion."

"I know." She sighed. Tears again leaked out of her eyes, but they were silent tears. The kind that hurt the most.

Damon rocked her. "I'm sorry, Mickelle. I really am."

"It's not your fault."

"I love you so much." His whisper fell into her hair.

"I love you, too."

His heart ached at the sight of her battered face, but he became really upset when she added softly, "He said he'd be back."

"You won't be here."

Again she said nothing, but let her head rest on his chest.

The police arrived, and Brionney and Mickelle's sons were on their heels. Bryan and Jeremy rushed past the officers to their mother.

Mickelle had recovered enough to put her arms around them and assure them she was all right. "It looks worse than it is," she insisted.

"Your mom's strong," Damon agreed, trying to support her statement for their benefit. "I arrived just as she head-punched the guy. In another minute she would have had the best of him."

"Way to go mom!" Jeremy cheered.

Mickelle smiled faintly, but there was an emptiness in her eyes. "No one was coming," she stated in a small voice. Damon tightened his hold, wishing he could do something more to comfort her.

Brionney took the boys to the kitchen while the police began to ask questions, but she returned shortly to hold Mickelle's hand. Finally Damon said, "Look, are you through with your questions? I think she may need to go to a doctor."

Mickelle started to protest, but Brionney interrupted. "No buts about it. You might need stitches or something."

"Come on, I'll take you," Damon said.

"I'm going too," Bryan insisted, almost sullenly, from the doorway.

Damon stared at him. "I think that would be a good idea. Your mother needs us all right now."

Bryan's face appeared slightly repentant, but Damon didn't feel any satisfaction.

If only he hadn't left Mickelle!

As though reading his thoughts, she put a hand to his face. He felt an overwhelming feeling of gratitude that she was safe, and that he wouldn't have to watch her whither away as he had Charlotte. He bent his head and whispered. "Oh, Kelle, I couldn't live without you."

She put her finger over his lips, saying nothing, but her eyes communicated volumes. And Damon understood what they were saying, for as terrifying as losing her might be, it would be infinitely worse not to have loved her at all.

* * * * *

Mickelle answered what seemed like a million questions from the police and her family. And from Damon. Poor Damon, who blamed himself for what had happened. But she knew it wasn't his fault. She had been too trusting, too busy running away from her fears to recognize the signs Colton had given her.

At the hospital she did receive stitches on her forehead, but after cleaning her wounds, there was little more they could do. Damon insisted she stay overnight for observation, and then for good measure, he stayed by her side most of the night. Brionney and Jesse took the boys to their house, but not before Mickelle hugged them and assured them for the millionth time that she was all right.

In the silence of the dark hospital room, she found it difficult to sleep. Several times she would close her eyes, only to find that she couldn't breathe, as though the attacker were once again on top of her, squeezing the air from her throat.

All alone!

She cried silently, not wanting Damon to hear, not wanting to hurt him further. Tears trickled down her face and into the pillow. Though Damon was in the room, she still felt as alone as when she had faced the intruder.

I was there.

It wasn't a voice exactly, but a thought, appearing in her head. And in that seemingly brief expression, she felt a multitude of feelings, a lifetime of conversation between spirits. Pure knowledge, pure love and compassion, flowing from one heart to another—from one soul to another. Immediately, her inner wounds were eased, her understanding complete. She had never been alone. Never! The Lord had been her silent companion during this experience and throughout her entire life, giving her strength and determination when she had needed it most. It was so clear to her now.

"Damon," she whispered.

Instantly, he was out of the armchair and next to the bed. "I'm here. Do you need something?"

"No. I just wanted you to know that I wasn't alone tonight. I thought I was, but I wasn't. He was there, helping me. And He will always be there for both of us . . . no matter what happens."

Damon's lips gently caressed a spot under her left eye that had been left remarkably untouched in the attack. Then he laid his cheek even more gently against hers. "Did I ever tell you how much I love you?"

"Yes, you did."

"Well, now I love you even more than that."

She knew without explanation that it helped him to know how she had been helped during the attack. "And you were right," she whispered. "I am stronger than I knew."

"Does that mean you'll still marry me?"

She put a hand on his cheek. "Yes, I most certainly will."

CHAPTER 15

When Mickelle was released from the hospital early the next morning Damon announced, "You are *not* going back to that house!"

"Well, I can't stay here," she told him with a smile that looked as though it hurt her bruised face.

Damon tucked her carefully into the Mercedes. "I'm taking you home."

"To the palace?" Mickelle asked. "I mean, your place?" She colored so adorably that Damon had to laugh.

"Is that what you call it? And yes I mean my house, where else? You'll be safe there. We have an alarm, and—" He stopped, unwilling to confess that he had already contacted a security man to keep an eye on her and the house.

"I can't live there with you. I hate to remind you, but we're not married yet."

"Bekka lived with us," he protested. "We've got several wings. It's not like we'll be in the same room."

"Rebekka was your nanny. I'm your fiancée. There's a big difference there, and if my lips didn't hurt so much, I'd show you that right now."

His eyes ran over her swollen lips. "I guess I'll have to take a raincheck."

She laughed. "Keep sounding so disappointed. It's good for my ego."

"Seriously though, you can stay at my place with the kids, and I'll stay at yours."

"No!"

He blinked at her with exaggerated surprise.

"He could come back," she explained.

"We can't live in fear."

"I'm not, Mr. Come-to-my-house-and-live. Who's the one afraid? What I am is being careful. If it's not safe for me to live there, then you certainly can't."

"Then we agree it's not safe."

"Oooh . . ." Mickelle shook her head in mock frustration. "Somehow I think you planned this conversation."

"Sort of," Damon admitted, taking her hands.

"So I'll go stay with Brionney and Jesse."

"No, *I'll* stay with them. One person will be less of an intrusion for them, and believe me, I'd feel a lot safer with you at my, um, palace." He grinned at her. "I'm actually going to beef up security." That much he would tell her. "It was long overdue, and this just gave me the opportunity. Besides, you might as well get used to the house. After all, it's going to be yours."

Her eyes dropped demurely to her hands, still tucked firmly in his own. Her lashes left delicate shadows on her cheeks. "What's wrong?" he asked.

"Nothing . . . I . . . it's just so wonderful. And I am a little nervous about . . . I mean, you're so rich."

He hugged her then, as well as he could in the car, finding it difficult to remind himself that she was still in a lot of pain. "Mickelle, we are perfect together. There are going to be a lot of adjustments, but I believe we can do it."

"Bryan," she said with a sigh.

"Yep, Bry."

Mickelle's tongue wet her lip thoughtfully. "Maybe it would be a good thing for the boys to stay at your place. Like a trial run."

"Maybe things will go so smoothly, you'll agree to marry me sooner." He put on his best beseeching face.

She giggled. "You're crazy, you know that? Simply crazy."

"There are worse things. You could hate me 'cause I'm so good-looking."

"Oh, Damon," she moaned. "Belle's right, that saying has got to go!"

Smiling, he started the car and they drove in comfortable silence to her house. On the porch, she hesitated, eyes resting on her rose bushes next to the steps. "Is something wrong?" he asked.

She gave him a half-smile. "No. Not really. It's just my bush . . . lost all its blossoms . . ." She shrugged and led the way into the house.

Gratefully, Damon saw that the shattered glass on her bedroom floor was gone, and the room had been straightened. The window had been temporarily blocked by cardboard and tape. He knew Jesse and Brionney were responsible.

Mickelle's eyes fixed on the broken window. With a sympathetic grimace, Damon said, "When I called your parents from the hospital your dad told me that he was going to take the afternoon off and fix the window. He insisted."

She sighed, and began haphazardly throwing clothes into a suitcase she removed from under the bed. "Good old Dad—always there when you need him."

"He's also going to take a stab at the door in Bryan's room. I'm not sure when. He's going to talk to Bryan about helping him. Hope you don't mind me telling him about the door."

Her answering smile was tight. "No, I don't mind. I just wish it wasn't necessary."

Damon nodded sympathetically. Mickelle had grown steadily more pale since their arrival, though he was unsure if that was because of her injuries or the memories of the attack. Either way, he believed she needed time away from this place. "You about ready?"

"We can come back with the boys to get whatever else we'll need," she said, shutting her suitcase.

"I can stop by when I pick them up from school." Damon hefted her suitcase and started down the hall. "You know moving to Alpine will require more driving on your part. Do you want to find a nanny to help?"

"Heavens no!" Her blue eyes opened wide, and a flush of color returned to her face. "And here I was trying to think of a good way to fire your cook!"

Damon laughed. "Not for a few days at least, Kelle. You need your rest."

"You keep up with all of this," she said, motioning in the air, "and maybe I *will* marry you sooner!"

"Good! Now hold that door, would you? So I can get this suitcase out."

"I really should go see the boys before they leave for school," Mickelle told him, once they arrived at his car. "Could we stop by Brionney's?"

Damon didn't like the exhaustion on Mickelle's face, or the way she moved so gingerly. "Sure, whatever you want. But we need to get back to see Belle soon. She's called me three times on the cell phone already this morning. Tanner says she keeps watching for us through the window."

Bryan and Jeremy were happy to see Mickelle. They met her in Brionney's entryway, along with Brionney and her three daughters. From Jesse's absence Damon assumed he was already at work. Good thing, since Damon had no plans to go in today, not even for a scheduled meeting at one. Jesse could handle it.

After their initial greeting Brionney and her girls returned to the kitchen for breakfast. Bryan and Jeremy remained in the entryway. "Gosh, Mom," exclaimed Jeremy, "you look kinda bad, you know. All bruised. Do you think I could take you for show and tell? I mean, if you're feeling okay."

"She can't go to show and tell, dummy," Bryan growled, rolling his eyes. "Sometimes you're the biggest baby."

"Am not! Janine Gibson brought in her brother who's a blackbelt and he had a big bruise right across his face. The kids loved it. But Mom's is even cooler."

"It hurts, stupid!" Bryan shouted. "It's not something to be proud of."

"Bryan!" Mickelle put a hand on his shoulder. "Just because your brother doesn't understand doesn't mean he's stupid. Please don't use those words."

Damon was pleased to see that Mickelle was up to the task of disciplining her son. He would do it himself, but felt Bryan would resent him even further.

"Now, before I leave," Mickelle continued, "I want you both to know that we are going to stay at Damon's house until we catch this guy."

"At Damon's?" Bryan shot him a dark stare. "Why can't we stay here?"

"Well, they really don't have room. The three of us can't squeeze into one guest room, and I'm reluctant to ask Aunt Brionney to put up with you boys sleeping in their family room for so long. Besides . . ." Mickelle paused, reaching for Damon's hand. "We have other news for you."

The increasingly angry expression on Bryan's face stopped further explanation. Damon wished that he had not been so quick to tell Belle and Tanner of their pending marriage. Maybe it would have been better to work up to informing Bryan.

Mickelle glanced at him, as though thinking the same thing. She grimaced and then sighed. "Look, boys, come on and sit down." She led the way into Brionney's spacious sitting room.

"Do you want me to leave?" Damon asked her. "I could go join them for breakfast." He pointed in the direction of the kitchen where he could hear Brionney and her children at the table.

Mickelle smiled at him. "No, I think maybe you'd better stay." A heavy weariness passed over her face.

He nodded and helped her sit in a padded chair with Queen Anne legs. With his hands resting lightly on her shoulders, he stood behind the chair, hoping to be a silent, comforting presence.

Mickelle waited until the boys were seated on the love seat across from her. "Now, you know that Damon and I have been close these past weeks and we've done some serious talking. We love each other." Her eyes begged them to understand. "Very much. And we want to get married—eventually—and we thought that since we'll be living at his place anyway, that we could get a head start on moving in."

"Yay!" squealed Jeremy, jumping up from the love seat and launching himself at Damon. After a heartfelt hug, the boy broke away to do a victory dance on the handwoven carpet covering the wood floor. "Oh, yeah, uh-huh! Oh, yeah, uh-huh! Cool!"

Bryan sat back on the couch and folded his arms tightly to his chest. "I guess I have no say in this."

"Well, you can't change my love for Damon," Mickelle said gently, "but just because I love him, it doesn't mean that I don't love you. You and Jeremy will always come first with both Damon and me."

Bryan glared at her. "Yeah, right."

"It's true," Mickelle leaned forward, but Bryan seemed to collapse inside himself, as though trying to escape her.

"Well, I'm glad!" Jeremy declared. "I've been waiting a long time for this." He smiled at Damon. "Do you have a room for me? I mean one for my very own."

"I have about a dozen rooms for you to choose from," Damon told him. "But first your mom needs to take a look at them and decide which ones would be best. I happen to know that she likes to check on you at night, and we can't have her going from one wing to the next at night, you know."

Jeremy laughed as though that were the most ridiculous thing he had ever heard. "And I can't be too far away from the kitchen," he joked, "or by the time I get to bed after dinner, it'll be time to wake up! This is great!" Exuberantly, he hugged Damon again. "And we can play basketball with you any old time we want."

Damon felt his heart turn tender from the acceptance in this sweet child. If only Bryan could be so supportive! "I won't be staying at the house, though, until after the wedding. It's not appropriate. But I'll be around a lot."

"Well, I think you shouldn't marry another man," Bryan growled at Mickelle. "Dad's barely dead."

Damon heard Mickelle's sudden intake of breath. He waited to see if she would turn to him, silently asking for help, but she simply stared at her oldest son. "We've talked about how little you knew what was between your father and me," she said slowly. "And there's a lot I won't tell you until you're older, but I will say that I know your father wishes me and Damon well. I *know* that."

"How?" Jeremy asked, interested once again in the conversation. Bryan said nothing, but he was listening.

Mickelle cleared her throat. "Well, one day soon after Damon and I met, I went to the cemetary to talk to him. Your father, that is."

Damon recalled the day well. He had followed her to the cemetary. He had been afraid that day; afraid that she would not be able to let go of the past, but instead, whatever she had experienced there had given her peace. He had always wondered what had happened.

"I felt your father," she continued, her battered face bright with the memory. "I could tell that he was sad for the way he had lived his life. I told him about Damon, and I felt that he wished us well." Mickelle paused, before rushing on. "Now how you react to this situation is up to you, Bryan, but I love Damon. I *need* him. I can't tell you how happy I am to have discovered someone who loves me and you two as much as he does. I know we can make it work if we try."

For an answer, Bryan stood and walked stiffly from the room.

Damon's jaw tightened at the rude response, and he started after him, but Mickelle's hand on his halted the movement. "He'll be more reasonable later," she told him. "He always reacts like this." Then she added in a softer voice. "Just like his father."

Damon conceded to her wishes, though he wanted to talk some sense into Bryan. Mickelle deserved all the happiness she could find, and this child was not making it easy for her. A part of him wanted to love Bryan so entirely that he would have to forget his anger; the other part wanted to turn him over his knee and spank him. But he was not Bryan's father, not yet, and he doubted that the boy would listen to him anyway. He had no choice but to let him go—for now.

After making arrangements to stay with Brionney and Jesse for a few weeks, Damon drove Mickelle to Wolfe Estates, where Belle was indeed waiting at the front window. Damon waved at her before taking the car around to the garage.

Belle met them in the mudroom, where Damon and Mickelle removed their shoes before going into the kitchen. "Are you okay, Mickelle?" she asked. "Oh, you look awful! I mean, I wish I could have been there to help you. I was so worried!" She began to cry, and Mickelle hugged her tightly.

"I'm okay, honest. Don't cry Belle. And guess what? Now I get to stay with you!"

"I know!" chirped Belle, her tears instantly forgotten. "You get to stay forever and ever. And Dad says my piano teacher will come to the house and we'll get to take piano lessons on the Steinway now! It sounds so great! Wanna come see?"

"Belle!" her father warned. "Kelle should be resting."

"That's probably a good idea," Mickelle said tiredly. "Belle, we'll look at it later. My knees are a bit shaky." She leaned heavily on

Damon as he led her into the family room adjoining the kitchen. He helped her settle into one of the plush, blue leather couches.

"I can go pick out a few books for you in our library," he offered.

"We have lots of books," Belle informed her. "My mom read a lot."

Damon grinned apologetically, but Mickelle wasn't offended. "I would love to read some of your mother's books," she said.

"I'll bring you a stack and you can pick!" Belle disappeared before the words were out of her mouth.

"And what about you?" Mickelle asked. Her bright eyes peered out at him, from the bruised wreckage of her face. Damon steeled himself not to grow angry again, but the thought of her enduring such a nightmare still made him furious inside.

He forced his voice to remain calm. "I'm not going anywhere. I have a meeting at one, but I think Jesse can handle it."

"I'll be fine," she insisted.

He went to the built-in wall unit and retrieved a wool blanket. As he spread it over Mickelle he said, "I guess I do need to take Belle to school. And I have a few documents to give to the police."

He felt her stiffen, and rubbed her shoulders lightly, so as not to hurt any of her wounds. "You're safe here. I have a guy coming any minute now to work on the alarm system."

"I don't think Colton'll be back. At least not here."

"Are you sure it was Scofield?"

She hesitated, then nodded once. "He's the only one who knew about the ring. Anyone who was mad at me, anyway."

Damon didn't speak. He still didn't see the man who had bested him the night before as Cover Boy Scofield. To his thinking, the man would be too concerned about his hair to learn how to throw a punch.

There were tears in Mickelle's eyes. "I've been thinking . . . about the money—my insurance money. I wonder if it's there at all."

"You think he took it?"

She lifted her shoulders. "Why else did he bother to get it for me? Isn't that what he does?"

"Well, the police haven't found him yet, or they would have called." He sat on the couch, gently taking her in his arms. "And the money isn't important. You are."

She laid her head against his chest. "You wouldn't say that if you had to scrape by as I have these past years, but I appreciate what you're trying to say."

"All that's over now, Kelle," he said, wanting to wipe the sadness from her face. "I'm going to take care of you. I am."

"I know that." She hesitated before continuing. "And I hope that you also understand that I have to depend on myself a bit."

"I do." He rested his chin on her head, his heart full of love and another feeling he couldn't describe.

They sat in silence for a moment, which was broken when Tanner entered the room, hands deep in the pockets of his baggy pants. "Hey, Tanner," Mickelle greeted him with a smile.

He smiled back, but his brow furrowed. "Boy, I'm sorry about what happened."

"Me too," she said, grimacing. "Thanks."

"But I am glad about you and Dad. I wanted you to know."

"Thank you, Tanner. I know it's going to be an adjustment, but I think we'll have a lot of fun, too."

"Yeah. Except for Bryan."

This was the opening Damon had been waiting for. "Maybe you can help there."

Tanner appeared doubtful. He took a hand from his pocket and pushed the hair out of his eyes.

"He does look up to you," Mickelle said helpfully.

Tanner shifted uncomfortably. "I'll try."

"Thank you." She paused before adding, " Hey, do you need a haircut?"

Damon examined his son and saw that his hair was a little long. Like his own. But he understood that her real reason for asking was to change the subject, to help Tanner feel at ease.

"Yeah, kinda." Tanner pushed his hair back again. "Would you cut it? I like the way you did Bryan's."

Mickelle laughed. "I was copying your style—really short on sides, longer on top."

Tanner grinned and shrugged. "I guess that's why I like it."

"You really cut hair?" Damon asked Mickelle.

"I cut my boys' hair."

"I thought you were just teasing when you offered to cut mine the other day. I really did."

"I know." Her response was too quiet and he sensed that she had been hurt by his earlier refusal.

"Well, I'd love it if you . . . I mean when you feel better . . . Only if you want to . . ."

She reached up to run a hand through his hair. "I'd love to cut your hair, Damon." She laughed, sounding really happy. He kissed her, and Mickelle returned the kiss, adding only a soft, "Ouch."

"Sorry," he apologized. "I keep forgetting."

"I'll be better soon."

Tanner's face reddened. "I, uh, missed the bus waiting for you guys—didn't want to leave Belle before you got here." He thumbed toward the kitchen as though Belle were there. "Do you think you could take me, Dad?"

"Sure. No problem."

"Thanks," he mumbled, turning away.

"Uh, Tanner, just a minute." Mickelle sat up a little straighter.

"Yeah?"

"I've been wondering . . . about the Snail. You did such a nice job repairing her, and she works really well but . . . since we got the Metro we just haven't been using it as much. Station wagons are such gas hogs—at least the Snail is. But I was wondering if maybe we should donate it to the National Kidney Foundation. They can sell it and get some money for whatever they need. It seems sort of appropriate with Rebekka going back to France to marry Marc, you know, with his kidney problems and all. Maybe the Snail will help someone like him."

At the sound of Rebekka's name a wistful look came to Tanner's face. Damon knew too well that he had cultivated a major crush on his former nanny, and still wasn't accustomed to the fact that she was marrying the love of her life, a man who was *her* childhood crush.

"I don't mind. That's nice." Tanner thought a moment, a wide grin covering his face. "As long as I don't have to ride in it."

They shared a laugh so spontaneous and familiar that Damon's heart sang with happiness. This was the life he had imagined with Mickelle. Despite last night's events he was determined they would all be happy—and safe.

"Go get your books," he told Tanner. "When you're ready, I'll drive you to school."

He watched the boy go, feeling a measure of pride in his son. That was one good kid.

Mickelle echoed his sentiments. "I thank Heavenly Father for him quite regularly, you know. He's been good for Bryan and Jeremy. And me."

Damon refrained from kissing her, but only just. Instead, he contented himself with caressing her hand.

Belle soon returned, not with a few books, but with her Little Tikes plastic shopping cart full. "I wasn't sure which ones you'd like," she said, parking the yellow and orange cart in front of Mickelle. "I liked the covers on these." She began shoving them into Mickelle's lap.

"Later, later." Mickelle held up a hand. "First I think I'll take a whack at your hair while your Dad takes Tanner to school. Would you like a ponytail? A French braid? I'll need a brush."

"French braid," Belle answered immediately. "I have my brush in my backpack." Books forgotten, she rushed over to the bar in the kitchen, where her red backpack stood next to an empty bowl of cereal. She lugged it over, obviously unaccustomed to such a heavy load. Once back at the couch, Belle pulled out her pink brush, but not before also bringing to light a shimmering green dress and a pair of yellow socks, both of which stuck to the brush.

"Trying on clothes again, Belle?" Mickelle asked.

"Again?" Damon repeated. "Why are you taking extra clothes to school?" From the corner of his eye, he saw Tanner enter the kitchen with his own backpack. Damon held up a hand, signaling him to wait. He needed to get to the bottom of this.

Mickelle's stitched brow wrinkled in dismay. "Belle, I thought you said your daddy knew about the clothes."

"He does." She blinked innocently at Damon. "Remember, Daddy? I told you I was going through my clothes?"

"Oh, yeah, but you said nothing about taking them to school."

"Well . . ." Belle paused, as though carefully choosing her words. "I thought that maybe since I can't wear those clothes anymore, maybe some other kid could and—"

"But this dress looks like it fits you great!" Mickelle exclaimed, holding the shimmering forest green dress up to Belle. "And so would

that one you had in your pack yesterday—" She broke off so
suddenly, Damon glanced at her to make sure she was all right. "I
knew there was something odd about your backpack yesterday after
school—and there was. You didn't have anything in it! Belle, you've
been giving things to Jennie Anne, haven't you? You're the reason she
has new clothes. And that's why her backpack was so full yesterday!"
Mickelle didn't sound angry; more amazed, and, if Damon read her
correctly, a trifle proud.

Damon wanted to know more. "Please explain," he demanded,
more gruffly than intended.

Belle's bottom lip quivered, and her huge brown eyes filled with
tears, making the slight amber color in them stand out more noticeably. "It's just that . . . well, they all laughed at her 'cause of her
clothes. It makes me feel so bad. For her, I mean. And for us too,
'cause people shouldn't say those things to other people."

"So you decided to share?" prompted Damon.

"I got so many, and she doesn't. I don't mind sharing. Except that
I forgot shoes. But none of my shoes would fit her anyway. I tried to
give her mine yesterday, but her feet are still bigger, even though she's
my size. That's probably 'cause she's older."

Damon didn't know what to think. On one hand he was grateful
Belle was willing to share, but on the other, he wasn't looking forward
to replacing the items. And who was this Jennie Anne anyway? For all
he knew, she could be a youthful manipulator, taking advantage of
Belle and her innocence.

He opened his mouth to question his daughter further, but
suddenly Mickelle opened her arms and pulled Belle close. "I am *so*
proud of you," she said emphatically. "I think it's a wonderful thing
you've done. You're a wonderful friend. And as soon as I'm well, you
and I will go together to find some shoes for Jennie Anne."

Belle grinned, her tears vanishing so quickly that Damon
wondered if they had been contrived. It certainly wouldn't be the first
time Belle had used tears to get out of a bind. But what was Mickelle
doing supporting her actions? Sitting on the couch and staring back
and forth between them, he felt as though there was much he had
missed in this conversation and in the days that he and Mickelle had
been apart. He met Mickelle's eyes. "This little girl really needs help?"

She nodded. "Definitely. A lot. She— Oh!" Her hand went to her mouth. "Jennie Anne's supposed to come over today to play with Belle after school! Well, every day, really. And I'm supposed to help her with her reading."

"We're paying her to come," Belle added importantly.

Damon blinked several times in silence. "Let's get this straight. You're watching a little girl every day *and* paying her to come and learn? *And* Belle is providing a new wardrobe?"

"It's a long story," Mickelle offered, giving him a crooked smile that made him want to take her in his arms.

"Well, that's okay. It's a long drive to Belle's school. Maybe she can tell me about it. And then you can fill in the gaps later."

"Be glad to," murmured Mickelle. She winked at Belle.

"I know some of it," Tanner volunteered. "I'll tell you on the way. But if we don't go soon, I'm going to miss all of my first class instead of just some."

Damon eased off the couch. "Somehow I think I'm going to enjoy this." He had a rough picture of it already: Mickelle's heart had gone out to a needy child in Belle's class. How impressive! Even amid panic attacks and problems with romance, she was able to see outside her own needs and get things done. On the other hand, he hadn't been able to finish even half his normal work load!

I'd better marry her quick, he thought. *Before I ruin my business.*

He was smiling as Belle asked worriedly. "Jennie Anne can still come here, can't she?"

"I don't know," Mickelle responded. "We'll probably have to tell her aunt about the change, but that's kind of hard when she's supposed to come home from school with you." She glanced up at Damon. "You don't think we can just bring her here, do you? And then tell her aunt about the change when we take her home?"

"Well . . ." He would hate having someone take his child anywhere without prior knowledge. "We could call her."

Mickelle was already shaking her head. "I don't know her number. And she doesn't know ours." She paused and then added thoughtfully. "Or where we live, either."

Damon shook his head, unable to believe that any child would be allowed to go somewhere without contact information. "Well then, if this

Jennie Anne is supposed to be with Belle, and the aunt doesn't know where that place even is, I don't think it matters much where she ends up."

Mickelle frowned. "That's exactly what I'm afraid of," she whispered in a barely audible voice, "to see where Jennie Anne will end up."

Damon bent down and kissed the top of her head, which looked as though it might hurt less than her face, and then squeezed Belle's shoulder. "We'll talk about this later," he said confidently. "We'll work something out."

He felt their eyes on him as he led Tanner out to the garage, and he wondered if he could live up to all his promises.

CHAPTER 16

Mickelle had a quiet and relaxing morning. She saw the live-in housekeeper, Mrs. Mertz, several times as she went about tidying the kitchen, and was more than happy to put down her book when the woman approached. The older lady was tall and strong-looking, with short, gray-streaked blonde hair and a pinched face that was considerably more appealing when she smiled.

"Mr. Wolfe tells me you'll be moving in," she said a bit hesitantly. "Does this mean you won't need my services any longer?"

"Not at all," Mickelle assured her. "I wouldn't even know where to begin with a house this size. I'm happy to have help. Tell me, which of the empty rooms do you think would be best for my boys? They'll want their own, of course, and I'll want them close enough to be able to check on them."

"You'll be in the master bedroom?" asked Mrs. Mertz.

Mickelle felt herself color, though she certainly had done nothing of which to be ashamed. "Yes. Eventually, that is. When Dam—Mr. Wolfe and I are married."

"Well, there are two more rooms in the wing that he and Belle share, although you might not want them that close."

"Oh, I do." Mickelle grinned, and then admitted sheepishly, "I'm a bit overprotective right now. You see, I lost my husband and . . ."

"And then last night," the older woman finished. She shook her head, pinched face abruptly full of sympathy. "You'll be safe here." She hesitated, twisting the dusting cloth in her hands, before adding in a much softer voice, "My husband died two years ago. So I . . . I know what it's like."

"What did he . . . ? Do you mind me asking?"

Mrs. Mertz gave a wry smile. "Old age. He was fifteen years older than me. He smoked, too, which never helped anyone." She sighed. "I miss him a lot. It helps, finding the gospel."

"You're a member?"

"Not yet."

"But you're thinking about becoming one? Please, if you don't mind, I'd love to hear about it. I'm a bit bored just lying here on this couch."

Mrs. Mertz nodded, but didn't sit. "I was working for Mr. Wolfe when he joined more than a year ago. Thought he was nuts when he said he was going to quit smoking cold turkey. I didn't think he could do it. But he did. And then I saw the change in him and . . . well, it's taken some time, but I'm seeing the missionaries now." She grimaced as though she had confided too much. "I'd best get back to my job." She nodded at Mickelle. "If you need anything, just holler."

Mickelle watched her leave. The old woman had been extremely reticent the only other time Mickelle had seen her, and Damon had mentioned that she was a bit stern and occasionally short with the children. When she had asked why he kept her on, he had replied, "Because I don't believe she has anywhere to go. I've offered to pay her return flight to Anchorage, if that is what she wants, and two months severance, but she says she likes it here. She was only coming temporarily to help us get adjusted, but now . . . Well, whatever else, she's a very good housekeeper. Besides, I'm kind of used to her being around."

Mickelle smiled to herself, suspecting that Mrs. Mertz was a wonderful person, using gruffness and a sour face to hide the fear and insecurity eating at her heart. *Maybe now she'll see there's nothing to fear except the fear itself.*

Mickelle laughed softly. She wasn't afraid, not anymore. At least not at this minute. Oh, she knew that she should feel violated, as many victims did when their homes were broken into. But she *knew* her attacker and that his motives were revenge and greed. She could deal with that a whole lot better than if it had been someone she didn't know. They would catch him eventually, and that would be the end of it.

Meanwhile, if he came back as promised, he would be in for a very big surprise.

Mickelle fingered the romance novel she had been reading. It was interesting, but a little more passionate than she felt she should be reading—especially since she and Damon weren't yet married. She already found him irresistible, and didn't need the encouragement.

An urge to explore came upon her, to immerse herself in the house that would become her home with Damon, but she was so exhausted from her ordeal that she contented herself with surveying her immediate surroundings. As always, she marveled at the immensity of the conjoined kitchen and family rooms. The entire top floor of her own house could fit in this space, with room to spare. Besides the standard dishwasher, refrigerator, and stove, the kitchen boasted numerous oak cabinets and cupboards, two ovens, a large upright freezer, a garbage compactor, a long eating bar, and blue-flecked counters that went on forever. The floor was fine blue ceramic tile, and overhead was a high ceiling with expensive lighting. A long banquet table with padded chairs graced the far end of the kitchen, where a large alcove had been built for that purpose, though she knew there was also a formal dining room.

What a joy it would be to cook in such a kitchen! She had thought so many times before, but now it was a reality. If she didn't feel so weak, she would begin right that minute.

The family room was equally impressive, dominated by huge, curtainless floor-to-ceiling windows. Through these she could see the outdoor pool, the indoor pool house, and the tip of the tennis court beyond. The green lawn was carefully manicured, with pink dogwood trees that still carried a few of their fall leaves. The built-in wall unit completely covered another wall, reaching high to the thick, elaborate molding that ran around the tall ceiling. This place was all too like a movie. Did people really live like this? Well, she was about to find out.

Mickelle took a sip from the glass of water Damon had set on the elegantly carved coffee table, digging her bare toes into the plush carpet that felt like a caress on her skin. She sighed as she snuggled more comfortably into the blue leather sofa. Despite the aches of her body, her heart sang with the joy of her love.

The soft beeping of the phone on the coffee table called her attention. "Hello?" she answered quickly, hoping it was Damon.

"Hi honey, how are you feeling?" It was Damon!

"Better. Well, still tired. But it's a bit lonely. I know Mrs. Mertz is here but I've only seen her a few times. What time does the cook come?"

"Not until about five, but she may not be much company. She's a little peeved with me for missing so many of her dinners the past month or so."

"When you've been with me and the kids?"

"Yeah." He sounded rueful. "I told her to just leave it in the refrigerator or oven. And I always ate the food for breakfast and took it for lunch as well. Somehow that didn't seem to comfort her."

"Well, I'll talk to her about a schedule," Mickelle offered. "But I really feel odd having someone do what I can very well do myself."

"I know, but please at least wait until you're better before starting to cook. Besides, if you're going back to school, cooking on the weekends might be enough."

"You have a point."

"I just don't want you to overdo things. I know only too well what that's like."

Mickelle had another, more intimate reason for keeping the services of the cook. She wasn't getting any younger, and if she and Damon wanted to have their own child, perhaps a little girl as she had always dreamed, they would have to try for a baby soon after the wedding. And she knew from experience that she wouldn't feel up to doing anything while pregnant.

"Besides," Damon was saying, "you might want to get involved in something else. Maybe charity work. Who knows?"

Mickelle had ideas in that direction as well. With Damon's resources she could do something for the community, perhaps for children like Jennie Anne, or others who didn't even have an aunt to care for them. She and Damon could donate to others who were helping children as well. They could pray for opportunities to present themselves.

The voice at the other end of the phone had grown quiet. "What?" she asked, wondering what she had missed.

"I've been talking to the police, and I also checked out the bank where your insurance funds were kept. It's all gone."

"Gone?" She had expected as much but the reality was unsettling.

"Yes. Apparently his name was on the account also. There's nothing we can do about it because the bank has a paper saying that you approved him. Did you sign anything like that?"

There was a sinking feeling in her heart. "I signed some papers Colton brought. They were bank papers, but I only scanned them. They seemed straightforward enough."

"It was probably embedded in small print or in legal jargon that takes normal people a dictionary and few hours' time to understand." Damon's voice was gentle. "I really am sorry."

"Did the police find him yet?"

"No. His apartment is deserted. They think he's skipped the state."

Yeah, with my ring and my money, Mickelle thought bitterly.

"Don't worry," Damon consoled her. "It's not your fault. He has practice at this sort of thing. He tells people what they want to hear. Like all that stuff he told you about his missionary service. He's not even a member, so he didn't go on a mission. At least not for our church. Or any other, if I had to bet."

"Was he even married?" she wanted to know.

"No. At least not from the information I have."

"Then the story about his twins drowning—it was all a lie."

"Sounds like it."

"He must have known that would touch me because of Brionney's twins."

"Well, in the notebook you guys found, he had written a note about using that story. Not to mention a lot of Mormon terms and such. He had been planning this for weeks. Probably already knew he could get you your money."

"He must have had inside help."

"Possibly. Or he broke in and took the records."

Mickelle gripped the phone with increasing anger. Looking back, there had been signs that she had neglected to see. The fact that Colton knew Belle had only a father before she had said anything, that he always seemed to know about all her friends, that he remembered details of things she mentioned only in passing.

She shifted the portable phone to her other ear. "He cried while telling me that story about the twins. And all along it was just something he'd probably read in the paper." Of course that meant it had happened to someone. Mickelle felt a deep sadness for those parents, and an ever growing fury toward the man who had so callously used their story for his own gain. "I'll bet he never lost his father, either."

"I don't know. Do you want me to find out?"

"No, it doesn't matter." She did wish she had kicked Colton harder last night, or that she had remembered the pepper spray he had given her, still in her purse. Of course, she wouldn't have been able to reach it during the attack.

Mickelle took a deep breath. "When are you coming home?"

"Right now. I'm going to pick some stuff up at the office, and then I'll be there."

"Good, because there's something else I've been meaning to discuss with you."

"Can't you give me a hint?"

She smiled, though he couldn't see her. "Okay . . . it's about a nursery."

She expected him to laugh, and perhaps to tease, but instead he was so quiet that she thought the line had gone dead. "Are you there?"

"I'm here."

"What's wrong? Don't you want another child?"

"It's not that. It's . . . Mickelle, I don't know how to tell you this. My wife . . . well, her cancer came back at the end of her pregnancy with Belle. Because of the pregnancy she had to delay her treatments. We knew it was the right thing to do for the baby, but I was so upset that I had surgery so it wouldn't happen again. Another baby, I mean. I couldn't bear for her to die because of me."

"Did it make a difference?" For some reason that was important to Mickelle. "Her delaying the treatments, I mean."

"The doctor couldn't tell us for sure, but I think so. She fought hard, but three years later she was dead. I've never thought about the surgery since, not even when I joined the Church. At the time I believed it was right for Charlotte. Another baby might have killed her much earlier." He heaved a long sigh. "Not that it mattered much. She and I were never really together after Belle was born. She was too sick."

"I'm sorry," Mickelle said in a small voice.

"No, *I'm* sorry. This just brings home the fact that you never know how your decisions will affect your future."

Mickelle didn't reply. She felt as though she had been punched in the stomach and couldn't find her breath. So many of her recent daydreams had focused on having a child with Damon, despite her almost thirty-seven years and the gap it would create in her children's ages. Now she was being forced to reevaluate everything.

"Kelle," Damon's voice was beseeching, "does it matter that much?"

"I don't know," she replied honestly. "I just don't know."

Damon was silent. "Maybe it can be reversed. All I know is that I love you."

"I love you, too." But Mickelle felt suddenly distant and a little numb. Would loving Damon force her to give up her dreams? Hadn't she had enough of that with Riley?

There was no easy answer.

"I'll be home soon," he said. "We'll talk then."

"I'll be here." Mickelle hung up the phone. From her comfortable place on the couch, she stared out the window to the sky beyond.

CHAPTER 17

Mickelle and Damon didn't talk when he came home because Mrs. Mertz informed them that the security man was waiting for Damon in his study. He felt a sense of relief when Mickelle smiled at him and suggested they talk later.

When he had finished with his business Mickelle was asleep on the couch, her honey-blonde hair falling across her face. He stroked the locks softly before returning to his study to work, waiting until it was time to pick up Belle and Jeremy at Forbes Elementary. He would have to collect Bryan as well from Brionney's, where he was supposed to wait after school. He hoped Bryan wouldn't cause any trouble.

Mickelle was still sleeping when Tanner returned on the school bus. "I'm going to get Belle and the others now," Damon told him. "Keep an eye on Mickelle, huh?"

Tanner promised that he would, but even so, Damon went downstairs to alert Stan, the security guard, that he would be out. The basement room Stan had been allotted was being furnished with monitors that would soon connect to the security cameras he had been installing all morning, cameras that scanned the entrances to the mansion and the surrounding estate. His presence was overkill, Damon was sure, but he wasn't taking any chances. He knew he should tell Mickelle about Stan's continuing presence in the basement, especially since she already knew that he was beefing up security, but he didn't want to call it to her attention yet. She might worry, something she didn't seem to be doing just now.

At the elementary school Belle was waiting in front with Jeremy and a small girl he didn't recognize. She had straight dark hair, a face spotted with numerous freckles, and a wary expression in her somber brown eyes. Around one of the eyes were the greenish brown remains of a bruise. She was dressed ordinarily enough in jeans and a long-sleeved shirt that seemed vaguely familiar.

"This is my dad," Belle announced proudly. Her friend studied the ground and remained silent.

Damon couldn't remember the girl's name so he said, "Nice to meet you."

"I told you Mickelle couldn't come get us, Jennie Anne," Belle reminded the other girl. "'Cause she got hurt."

Jennie Anne backed away. "You are coming, aren't you?" Damon asked. "Mickelle's looking forward to seeing you. She says you guys are working on reading or something? I promise, I won't bite."

Belle giggled. "Of course not, Daddy."

"Can we play basketball tonight?" Jeremy asked. "Please?"

"Sure, but let's get going. I thought we'd stop at, uh, Jennie Anne's to make sure her aunt doesn't mind that we go to our house instead of Mickelle's."

"She doesn't!" Jennie Anne said suddenly. "Uh—and she's not home anyway. I heard her say that she was going somewhere."

Damon read the fear in her eyes and wondered what it meant. "Even so, we should stop and make sure. Maybe her plans changed."

He was worried the child wouldn't follow him to the car, but Belle pulled her friend along. "Don't worry," she whispered loudly. "My dad's not afraid of your aunt."

When they drove to the girl's house, Damon was dismayed at the dilapidated old place. Even the discussion he had with Belle and Tanner that morning had not prepared him for the condition of Jennie Anne's home. "Wait here," he ordered the children. Everyone obeyed, even Jeremy, who had already removed his safety belt.

At the front door, no one answered his ring, or his knock. He was almost certain that someone peered at him from behind the dirty windows, but when he studied the panes, only half of which were curtained, he saw no further movement.

Back at the car he said, "No one was home," watching Jennie Anne carefully. She was noticeably relieved.

"Are you going to leave a note?" Belle asked.

Damon looked at the house again, shaking his head. "No. I'm not."

The children didn't appear to think this strange, but to Damon it was a big step. He was now as committed as Mickelle was to helping this child.

They went to pick up Bryan at Brionney's, but he wasn't there. "He's over at the house," Brionney told him. "My dad came and got him a half hour ago. Said they were going to fix a door, or something. I'm not sure what that meant exactly, but Bryan seemed to."

"Then I'll go there." Damon started to turn on the porch. "We have to get some things for the boys anyway."

"Wait!"

Damon stopped, raising his brow questioningly.

"Bryan. He was caught fighting at school today. They tried to call Mickelle, but she wasn't in. They called me instead. I didn't want to worry Mickelle so soon after last night's attack, so I thought I'd wait to talk to you."

Damon's heart sank. "What happened?"

"I'm not sure, really. They say that one of the other boys said something about a basketball game in gym. Bryan got mad and slugged the boy. The boy hit him back. They had to be torn apart by two teachers. I talked to the principal quite a bit on the phone and explained what happened to Mickelle last night, and of course he knows about Riley's death. Because of all that, he was willing to go easy on Bryan this time. But if it happens again, he'll be suspended."

"Thank you. I'll have to talk to Mickelle about this."

Brionney grimaced. "I'm sorry. Stepparenting won't be easy, but for what it's worth, I think you'll do a great job. Already are."

He nodded his thanks, wishing he felt as confident as Brionney sounded.

* * * * *

Bryan knew he shouldn't have hit that loud-mouthed jerk. Then again, Chris shouldn't have made that crack about him playing like a girl. Bryan knew he wasn't that good at basketball, but heck, neither were any of the other seventh graders. Still, Bryan hadn't meant to hit

Chris; he just sort of exploded at the taunt. The next thing Bryan knew, a teacher was yanking him from the floor where he was rolling with Chris. His jaw and chest ached, but there wasn't any blood, at least not his. Unfortunately, Chris had a bloody nose, which had earned him sympathy.

"When it's dry, I'll let you sand it," his grandfather said, breaking into Bryan's unpleasant reverie. "And then we'll paint the whole thing white."

Bryan almost jumped at the voice. He had forgotten where he was. "Today?" he asked.

Terrell shook his white head. "Nope. Have to be another day. The putty around the wood piece we put in has to dry at least overnight."

"Looks good. Real smooth."

Terrell chuckled and lifted his tall, thin frame from his crouched position. "That's the idea. But it'll still need a bit of sanding."

There was noise at the front door, and before long Jeremy came running down the hall. "Grandpa? Grandpa? Oh, there you are!"

Terrell hugged Jeremy, lifting him a foot from the ground. Bryan remembered how that felt: like flying! Terrell had done the same thing to him when he was little. Suddenly, he missed it.

As though somehow knowing how he felt, his grandfather set Jeremy down and slung a companionable arm around Bryan's shoulder. "We just finished fixing the door. Wasn't too hard. And before that we put in the new glass I bought earlier for your mother's window. Couldn't have done it without him."

Jeremy stared at Bryan with a mixture of envy and admiration. "Too cool."

The proud smile on Bryan's face died when he saw Damon moving down the hall. "Hello, Terrell," Damon greeted. He smiled at the older man, and then his gaze slid past to Bryan, seeming to bore into his heart.

He knows, Bryan thought. *Aunt Brionney must have told him.*

Belle and her new friend had arrived with Damon, and Belle's voice filled the space in between them. "Hello, Grandpa!" Since Belle didn't have any living grandparents of her own, she had adopted Bryan's upon first sight. At first it had bothered Bryan, but when he saw how it pleased his grandparents, he had changed his mind.

"Hello, Belle," Terrell said, lifting Belle the way he had Jeremy. "Who's this?"

"She's Jennie Anne." Belle turned to her friend. "Jennie Anne, this is Grandpa. He doesn't have any other name for us, so you have to call him that. You don't mind, do you, Grandpa?"

"'Course not." Terrell shook Jennie Anne's hand. She was smiling, but when she glanced at Bryan her face froze, just as it had when he passed her the night before after he fought with his mother in the kitchen. The strange stillness made Bryan shiver. He looked away quickly. Too creepy.

"Hey, kids," Damon said, "I think you had all better go feed Sasha. Maybe let her out to run around for a while. We won't have the new pen up at the other house for a few days, and she's going to get lonesome."

Bryan turned to go with the others, but Damon's voice stopped him. "Not you, Bryan. Terrell and I need to have a talk with you."

Bryan gave Damon his best dirty look, but he didn't seem to notice.

"What's going on?" Terrell asked.

Damon sighed deeply and leaned against the wall in the hall. "Bryan here's been fighting at school."

"It's none of your business!" The words seemed to burst forth from Bryan's lips without his permission.

"Bryan!" his grandfather said sharply. "Please be respectful."

"This isn't about me, Bryan," Damon said. "This is about what happened to your mother last night and the fact that she can't take any more problems right now."

"Then don't tell her."

"I have to."

"What happened?" Terrell asked.

Bryan told his grandfather, and was relieved when he nodded and said, "I can see why you got upset at that boy, but fighting is not the way to handle your emotions. You'll have to be punished . . . grounded or something."

Bryan wanted to tell his grandfather that it really didn't matter since Damon's house was too far away for him to hang out with his regular friends anyway, but he only nodded. "Okay, I'll be grounded.

And I won't do it again. I promise." He meant it. He was mad at his mother, but he didn't want to evoke that terrible sadness he had seen in her eyes yesterday, or the exhaustion he had glimpsed this morning.

"I trust that you won't do it again," Terrell said.

Damon's eyes didn't leave Bryan. "We'll still have to tell your mother."

Bryan scratched his jaw, and felt the bruise near the bone where Chris had landed a deft punch. It didn't hurt half as bad as the blows to his chest, but he wouldn't tell that to his grandfather, or Damon.

"Could we just not tell her this once, or at least not right now?" Bryan asked.

His grandfather and Damon looked at him and at each other for a few moments. They must have come to some understanding, because Terrell nodded. "For now. At least not for a few days. But I don't want to hear about this again. If you have a problem, you either work it out or go to an adult who can help."

Again Bryan nodded, relieved. He was angry at his mother for moving to Damon's, and especially for agreeing to marry him, but she did look terrible this morning. And last night . . . no, he wouldn't think about that.

Bryan waited to hear what Damon would say, but he remained silent. After a while Terrell began picking up his tools. "I'd best get home. I promised your grandmother I'd be home early." He looked at Damon. "We'd like to come out to the house tomorrow to see Mickelle, if she's feeling up to it."

"I'm sure she'd like that. I'll let her know."

That was it? Bryan almost laughed at how easy it was to get out of the trouble he had caused by fighting with Chris. Not that he would do it again. He put his hand in his pocket and fingered the money wadded there. Things were looking up.

"Get your stuff together, Bryan." Damon said quietly. "We'll be leaving soon."

As the men went down the hall together, Bryan turned back to his room to decide what clothes to take. When he had finished filling two duffle bags and a large plastic sack, he walked out to the front porch. Damon was by the rose bushes, and Belle and Jennie Anne were practicing cartwheels on the lawn. Jeremy was nowhere in sight.

"Who did this?" Damon reached down and lifted a handful of pink rose petals. "Someone deliberately tore these off."

Bryan swallowed with difficulty, suspecting this deed was as bad as fighting at school. Maybe worse. He would be grounded so long that he would spend his eighteenth birthday in his room. He clenched his jaw, determined to remain silent.

Belle came over from the lawn and took the petals from her father's hand. "Oh, Daddy, I'm sorry. I did it. I mean, not all. Some were already on the ground, like around these other bushes. But I was sitting here yesterday, and I was talking and thinking and playing that game, you know, 'he loves me, loves me not.' I had to get it just right, see? I must have—boy that's a lot of petals. I'm sorry. Do you think Mickelle will get mad? Can I buy her some more roses to make up for these?" There were tears in her eyes, and if Bryan weren't so astonished, he would have laughed.

Damon did laugh. "It's okay, ma Belle. Turn off the waterworks. I'll bet Mickelle's done that flower thing a time or two. I've even done it myself. We can stop and get her a bouquet on the way home to make up for it. But don't do it again."

"I won't. I promise. Besides, I'll bet dumb old Bryan here wouldn't let me." She stuck her tongue out at Bryan.

"Belle!" Damon warned. "Get out to the car. Now!" He looked at Bryan. "Sorry about that. I'll talk to her, believe me."

Belle skipped over to the Lexus, but when Damon turned his back to talk to Jennie Anne, she winked. Bryan winked back, and pretended to rub his nose to hide his smile.

* * * * *

Damon drove back to Alpine in relative silence. He wasn't sure if he and Terrell had handled Bryan's fighting at school severely enough, but what could he do? He wasn't sure exactly what discipline he should give the boy, or even if it was his right or duty. He felt that it was, but something inside reminded him that he wasn't Bryan's father, no matter how much he wished that he was. Mickelle was the boy's mother, though, and her feelings and desires toward her son had to be considered first.

But I can't tell her now. He would wait a few days until she was feeling stronger. It was unlikely that Bryan would do something similar before then. His repentance seemed to be real, though he continued to treat Damon with resentment. Damon tried to store the ugly thought away.

"You know, we're going to have to think about changing schools after the term," he said as they turned into the driveway of Wolfe Estates. "Now that you no longer live in American Fork. It's just too much driving for Mickelle."

Jeremy shrugged. "I don't mind."

"Can Jennie Anne come?" Belle wanted to know.

Bryan, of course, said nothing, but his glare deepened.

"I don't know. We'll see." Damon glanced at the child in question and saw that she was staring at her hands in her lap, her jaw clenched unnaturally tight. "It's still a long way off," he added. At that Jennie Anne seemed to relax, but only slightly. Damon sighed, wishing Mickelle were there to ease this transition. He knew nothing of this homely little girl, except that she seemed to touch a core of protectiveness inside him that was as basic as the protectiveness he felt for his own family.

When they entered the house, Mickelle was awake and sitting up talking with Cammy Warnock, the cook. Cammy was young and pretty, with long curly dark hair, lively brown eyes, and a ready smile. Like many good cooks who loved to sample their own wares, she was a bit round, and from the conversation, she was about to grow even more.

"I've been trying out a lot of low-fat recipes at home," she was saying to Mickelle.

"I hope you'll try them out here too," Mickelle said. "We could all stand to eat better."

Cammy laughed, a high, clear sound. "Well, with the baby coming, I'm going to have to watch my weight."

"Congratulations, Cam!" Damon called from the kitchen. She had worked for them since before her marriage, and he had always called her by her first name. She still seemed too young to be married, and now she was having a baby. He glanced at Mickelle to see what effect this news had on her, but she was focused on the children.

"Jeremy," she said, hugging him. "And Belle, come here. I've been so lonely without you all today. Since I couldn't get up, the day just dragged by. And Jennie Anne—I'm so happy you could come over."

Jennie Anne gave a wide grin and her dark eyes sparkled. If Damon hadn't been watching the child's face, he wouldn't have believed the transformation. Had he really thought this child homely?

"These flowers are for you, Mickelle," Belle said, proffering the two dozen pink roses they had stopped for on the way home. Her head bowed penitently. "To make up for the ones I tore off your bush. I'm sorry."

Mickelle looked relieved as she accepted the roses and breathed in their fragrance. "Thank you, Belle. I'm glad to know what happened. I saw all the petals there yesterday and I wondered." She glanced at Bryan, and Damon wondered if she had suspected her son. That had been his first thought when he found the destruction. "And don't worry," Mickelle continued, "the ones on the bush will grow back next year."

"That's a relief." Belle was all smiles again.

"Bryan." Mickelle held out a hand. "Come give me a hug."

The boy hefted the duffle bags and plastic sack in his hands. "Can't I put this somewhere first?" Damon noticed that he kept his face averted, though he couldn't see why. Other than a barely noticeable red mark on Bryan's jaw, there didn't seem to be any damage.

Mickelle's smile faltered only slightly. "Sure. Mrs. Mertz tells me there are two empty bedrooms in the same wing where Belle has her room." She glanced at Damon and he nodded.

"That's really the best place," he said. "There are more rooms in the north wing where Rebekka stayed—one even has an entire sitting room and small kitchenette—and then there are quite a few more in the basement where Tan and Mrs. Mertz are sleeping, but it's kind of far away."

"I'd feel better with them close."

He smiled at her teasingly. "Does that mean you're going to sleep in *my* room?" He blinked innocently for emphasis. "So you'll be close to check on them."

"I hadn't even thought about it." She lifted her chin. "But I suppose I may as well sleep there, since you aren't. Shall we help you pack?"

Damon laughed heartily. "Why not?"

"Is everyone staying for dinner?" Cammy inquired, her face bright at the prospect.

"Yes, I guess we are." He surveyed the group. Boy, it felt good to have them all here! Even with Bryan glowering like that.

During the few minutes they had been talking, Jennie Anne had sidled closer to Mickelle. "Does it hurt?" she asked in an almost inaudible voice as she observed Mickelle's bruised face in fascination.

"Not anymore. At least not much." Mickelle put her hand gently on the girl's arm. "And the person who broke into my house last night is gone, and the police will catch him. That's what they do with people who hurt others. They catch them and take them away—or sometimes they help them learn not to hurt others. But they aren't allowed to do it again."

Jennie Anne's eyes grew wide. "You called the police?"

"Yes, I did."

"Well, I hope they catch him," Jennie Anne said vehemently.

"They will." Damon tried to sound sure, but Jennie Anne didn't take her eyes from Mickelle's face, as though mesmerized by the damage she found there.

"Well, let's go see the rooms," Mickelle suggested. She shrugged off her blanket.

Damon helped her stand. "Do I need to carry you?"

"No you don't need to carry me!" But she leaned on him heavily all the same. Not that Damon was complaining. This was exactly where he wanted to be.

He led them up the main staircase to the south wing. The boys' new rooms were on the left with a splendid view of the backyard. Belle's room was the first on the right, taking up the top part of one of the turrets.

Damon showed the boys to their rooms and then took Mickelle to see Belle's, arriving before the girls, who had dawdled on the stairs.

Mickelle peeked inside. "Wow, Damon, this is really something!"

Damon grinned with satisfaction. He had hired a decorator specifically to make this space resemble a medieval castle. There was a canopied bed, a faux fireplace, stone facing on the wall, hanging tapestries, a rustic-looking wood floor with thick rugs, and lighting that resembled torches along the wall. Even the large wooden chest, the small table and chairs, and the bookshelves appeared authentic. Damon had been rather pleased with the result. And Belle had been thrilled.

"I always *thought* this place was a castle!" Mickelle exclaimed. "I love it!" He gave her an awkward little bow.

As they were drawing away, the girls arrived and entered the room, ignoring them as though they didn't exist. Mickelle returned to the door, and Damon followed her. "I want to see Jennie Anne's reaction," she whispered.

Though the door was now partially shut, they could see Jennie Anne walking to the middle of the room where she stared slowly around her. A smile filled her thin face, and she clapped her hands. "Oh, Belle, it's a princess room! It's so perfect for you—you are a princess! You're always so sweet and nice to me. I'm so, *so* glad you have a room like this." Tears came out of Jennie Anne's eyes, and Damon felt an odd loss in his heart, one he couldn't describe. Suddenly he wanted to make a room just like this for Jennie Anne. He glanced at Mickelle and saw a mirror of his emotion. As one, they looked back into the room.

Belle watched her friend, puzzlement on her face, then she threw her arms enthusiastically around Jennie Anne. "You deserve it too, Jennie Anne. I'll give it to you! It can be yours—all of it—whenever you come over."

"Really?" Jennie Anne's mouth gaped in amazement. "Do you mean it? We can share?"

"Of course! We'll both be princesses. Bear and Horse will be our servants."

"And your dad and Mickelle are the King and Queen, right?"

"Yes, and my brother's the prince and so's Jeremy. Not Bryan, though, he's too mean. He can be an outlaw or something."

"I like Jeremy," confessed Jennie Anne softly.

"Then you can marry him. *I'm* going to marry Bryan."

"I thought you said he's mean."

Belle smiled secretively. "He is, but not to me. I'm the only one he likes. We pretend not to like each other. It's fun."

Damon raised his eyebrows at this. He didn't put it past Belle to have Bryan wrapped around her finger just as everyone else in her life, and obviously there was much he didn't know about Bryan.

"Let's go," Mickelle whispered.

"Wait a minute." Damon tapped on the door, opening it wider. "Hey, Belle, remember the rules."

The girls started, as though surprised. "Oh, yeah," Belle said. "I forgot. He means we have to leave the door open. We always do when friends are over."

Damon shrugged at Mickelle's questioning glance. "I like them to know that I could pass by at any moment to check on them. Keeps them honest."

"Not a bad idea."

He led her down the hall. "Well, working in the hospital industry I've seen a lot of things that could have been avoided by a little intervention, from sexual abuse to accidents, and I just want to keep tabs on things. Though I have to admit it's a little difficult in a house this size."

As he spoke, he reached for the doorknob to the room next to Belle's. "And here, my dear princess, is *your* suite." He opened the door for Mickelle with a flourish.

He watched as she stared at the large vaulted room that was furnished with a king-sized, four-poster bed, a matching dresser, a few paintings, and a white marble dog. There was also a fireplace with an exquisite white wooden mantel built into the wall opposite the bed. He had always considered the paintings, the burgundy bedding, and even the fireplace a little feminine for his taste, but now with Mickelle standing there, it was perfect.

"It's very nice," Mickelle offered.

"There's a sitting room too, through here, and closets over there, and the master bath."

She took it all in quietly. Too quietly.

"Mickelle, is something wrong?" he asked anxiously.

She shook her head, but the tears in her eyes belied her words.

He turned her to face him, and touched a tear beneath her eye. Then he kissed the spot tenderly. "What is it?" He felt a fear inside him. Was it because he might not be able to give her another child? He had thought the baby stage was behind them, but apparently Mickelle had other ideas. And how did he feel about that?

I would give her anything, if I could. I like kids.

"It's just—" She broke off, hiccupped slightly, and then said, "Everything is *so* wonderful! It may sound stupid, but I feel like Cinderella."

"That's good, right?" He still wasn't sure how to read this reaction.

She nodded. "But then I had a terrifying thought. He's coming back, and what if he somehow takes it all away?" She began to cry softly.

Damon pulled her close. Tears streamed down her face as he held her. He had worried about the reality of the attack hitting her, had been warned by the doctor at the hospital that it might happen, but Mickelle had seemed so sure that it was over, so ready to put it behind her. Thank heaven he hadn't dumped Bryan's trouble at school on her today!

"I think he wanted to kill me," she whispered. "He was that mad. But first he was going to make me suffer."

"You didn't let him!" he reminded her.

"I fought."

"You did."

"I should have kicked him harder." Her watery smile came as quickly as the tears.

"Mickelle, I'm doing everything in my power to make you safe. There is *no* way he can come here. He'd be crazy to try."

She sniffed. "I know that—logically. He's got everything of monetary value that I had. And he's got to be long gone, running from the police. But somehow I'm suddenly . . . scared. I know it's stupid, but there it is."

"It's not stupid; it's a normal reaction. But you know, you're wrong about something." He paused for dramatic effect. "You still have this." From the pocket of his suit coat, he pulled out a small box and opened it.

She gasped and then hugged him. Exactly the reaction he had planned. "You found the ring!"

"Well, actually it's another one." He slid the thick band with the heart-shaped diamond onto her finger. "It took some doing, getting it here today, but the company bent over backwards. They found it in one of their stores in another state and had an employee fly it to Utah."

She held her hand out to admire it. "They did?"

"Well, they do those things when you get in that price range. Especially when it's the second one you've bought from them."

"What range are we talking about?"

He shrugged, but she grabbed his hand. "Oh no, you aren't getting out of this. How much?"

"It's insured."

"How much!"

"A few hundred . . . uh . . . thousand."

"A few hundred thousand . . . That's way too much."

"The other ring was also insured. Don't worry, we can afford it."

More tears slipped from her eyes, and she wiped at them impatiently. "I must be the biggest bawl-baby in the whole world!"

"After what you've been through, you've a right." He grabbed her hands. "If I could give you the moon, I would do it."

"I don't want the moon. I just want you."

He grinned. "Should I take it back?"

His lips met hers, but drew away as she winced at the pressure. "Sorry," he muttered. "I keep forgetting."

Mickelle continued, "And I'm suddenly feeling guilty. We have so much, and then there are people like Jennie Anne—"

"I saw where she lived," said Damon.

"Terrible! And I'm almost certain she's being abused in more ways than one. Do you mind—" She stared at him earnestly. "I'd like to help her."

"I would too."

"It shouldn't be too much money . . ."

"Use as much as you like. I would be happy living in a shack as long as I have you." He half laughed, half snorted, and then said quite seriously, "But with my luck, the land under the shack would have an oil well."

She giggled. "I know, I know. Everything you touch turns to gold." She wrapped her arms around his neck. "Now, what I want to know is whether I'm going to become gold."

He searched her blue eyes. "You, Kelle, are much better than any gold."

"Good," she said, swaying against him slightly, "because if you don't mind, I'd like you to carry me to that couch in there." She pointed through to his sitting room.

"Are you feeling okay?"

She tried to hide a grimace. "Well, actually, I thought you needed practice."

"Practice?"

"For after we're married. If I remember correctly, the groom has to carry the bride across the threshold."

He picked her up. "And up the stairs too, no doubt."

"Why not?"

"Why not indeed? You're light."

"I haven't always been. When I was pregnant with—" She broke off, and Damon instinctively tensed. They had promised to talk, but so far had avoided the issue.

He set her carefully onto the tan sofa, expecting her to continue. She didn't. Instead, she reached for the remote lying on the arm of the couch. "I think I'll watch just a little bit of this nice TV here while you go and pack. Coming up the stairs is about all the excitement I can handle tonight. I believe I'll also have to eat up here on a tray. Okay?"

He smiled uneasily, but was all too ready to let the issue slide for now. They had a lot to deal with as it was. "Sure. The kids can eat downstairs and you and I can eat here in front of the TV." As he moved to the door her voice stopped him.

"Damon?"

"Yes?"

"I love you."

Warmth filled him. "I love you too."

CHAPTER 18

Mickelle's scrapes and bruises faded gradually over the next few weeks. The fear she had admitted to Damon faded as well. Except that sometimes when she was alone in Damon's room the events of that terrible day came rushing back, utterly real and terrifying. She wished he could stay with her, but neither wanted to compromise their principles by the appearance of impropriety. Besides, she was never really alone because Mrs. Mertz was home during the day, and the children were home at night. Damon also spent most of his off-hours at the house. He was always around at bedtime for the children, so that he could read Belle and Jeremy a story.

Mickelle's happiness grew. She became accustomed to the vaulted ceilings, and the openness no longer gave her the feeling of being outside and unprotected. At first she passed the time by focusing on her recovery, and then suddenly she had nothing to do. The housework was taken care of by Mrs. Mertz, the dinner by Cammy, and the outside by Old Bobby, the weathered groundskeeper. Damon urged her to take a hand in everything, but she preferred to hold off until she felt more at ease with his employees.

Instead, she concentrated on the children, who flourished—especially Tanner who had been so long without a real mother, and Belle who had never really known her own because of the cancer. She took them shopping, talked to their teachers and friends, and was home for all their comings and goings.

Jennie Anne continued to come to the house after school and on Saturdays as well. The child had changed drastically during her time with them, though she continued to curl into herself in misery each time she had to return to her great-aunt's. Mickelle thought constantly about Jennie Anne on Sundays, when her aunt refused to allow her to come over, and had taken to packing food in her backpack on Saturday nights. The bruise on Jennie Anne's face disappeared, and Mickelle saw no signs of further abuse. Even so, it took all her courage to drive Jennie Anne home each Saturday evening and leave her. And she couldn't help wondering why Jennie Anne rejected any overture to talk about her home life.

Only Bryan was unhappy, despite Mickelle's increased attention, and he made every attempt to annoy her and Damon. Mickelle also noticed that while he and Belle often exchanged name-calling, she usually escaped his real torture, as did Jeremy, who rarely took offense at anything. Bryan completely ignored Jennie Anne. But Tanner, formerly his idol, had become a victim for every taunt, every harsh word, and a few well-aimed basketballs. As a result, Tanner would no longer play basketball with Bryan unless Damon was present, and when Damon played, Bryan refused to join the game. Mickelle didn't know what to do about his attitude, but begged the others to have patience. Tanner, to his credit, held back and hadn't given the younger boy the beating he likely deserved.

A few days after the attack Damon had told her about Bryan's fight at school, and they had agreed to let it go without further discussion as long as he continued to uphold his part of the bargain. Mickelle did talk briefly to Bryan about it, just to let him know that she was informed and concerned, and he had promised that he would never do it again. He had accepted his five-day grounding silently, but his anger and sullenness seemed to boil just under the surface.

Mickelle's relationship with Damon deepened, until it was almost a physical pain to bid farewell to him each night as he left for her sister's house. Knowing that she wouldn't see him until the following evening was pure torture. Had she ever loved anyone so much?

And yet the subject of a baby continued to loom over them like an ominous shadow. Mickelle didn't know if she could *or should* give up one dream to obtain another. So she simply didn't face the problem, and though Damon constantly brought up their pending marriage, she avoided setting a date.

Soon, she told herself.

On Saturday morning, more than two weeks after the attack, she used the treadmill in Damon's—now hers—personal sitting room. She felt good, if not completely well. Only a few deep bruises remained on her upper arms and on one cheek, yellow-green now, and fading fast. After exercising she took a hurried shower. Damon was on his way over from Brionney's, stopping first to pick up Jennie Anne, and she wanted to be ready when he arrived.

She was in the kitchen making blueberry pancakes on the large electric griddle when Damon finally entered. Jennie Anne was with him, and something else she had not expected.

"What's that?" she exclaimed, bending over to hug Jennie Anne.

Damon staggered over to set his burden down on the counter. "It's a pumpkin. What do you think?"

Indeed, it was the most monstrous pumpkin Mickelle had ever seen. "But we have pumpkins." Mickelle and the kids had gone over to her house after school last week and picked the pumpkins and other produce in the garden, saving them from certain frost. Today was the Saturday before Halloween and they were going to make jack-o'-lanterns.

Damon grinned at her, his amber eyes shining. "Hey, if we're going to have this pumpkin seed fight that Jeremy keeps talking about, I am going to be armed."

"Yes, but . . ." Mickelle shook her head. "Where did you get it?"

"I know people," he said mysteriously.

She rolled her eyes.

"We got it from a guy selling vegetables at the side of the road," Jennie Anne volunteered. She sniffed the air appreciatively. "Those pancakes sure smell good."

"They're blueberry. If you'll go get the others in the game room, we'll eat. They're watching Saturday morning cartoons."

As Jennie Anne left the kitchen, Damon took Mickelle into his arms and kissed her soundly. Mickelle laughed softly as white-hot sparks crawled up her spine. "Good morning to you too."

"I missed you," he whispered huskily.

"I missed you." She lifted her lips to be kissed once more.

Their brief tête-á-tête was interrupted by running feet and

screams of "pancakes!"

"Great," Mickelle muttered. "I can never get them away from the TV on Saturday morning, but *this* morning they come running."

Damon gave her another grin. "It's the seed fight I tell you. It's causing all sorts of havoc."

"Oh, should we cancel then?" she asked innocently.

"Not on your life. This is one of your traditions I'm going to perpetuate—because I am going to win!"

Mickelle reached behind her and drew out a pair of scissors. "We'll see."

"What's that for?"

"Your hair. We are not carving one hole into any of these pumpkins—especially not your inferior-though-large pumpkin—until you get a haircut. I did Tanner's last week and you are in for it today."

Damon grabbed at the yellow hair on his temple, pulling it up for a look. "Yeah, I guess when a guy can see his hair like this, it's time for a cut. At least I've kept my moustache nice and trim."

Belle giggled from her stool in front of the breakfast bar. "I can cut your hair, Daddy."

"Uh, I think I'll let Kelle do it this time. Maybe when you're older."

Belle wasn't offended at the refusal. She held out one of the plates that Tanner was passing around. "A pancake please."

"First the prayer," reminded Mickelle. She scanned the children, wondering who to pick. Her eye caught Bryan's but she knew better than to put him on the spot.

"I'll say it," offered Belle.

"Okay, Belle," Tanner said with a groan, "but can we at least eat while the pancakes are still warm?" Belle had a tendency to bless everything and everyone during her prayers.

"Tan," Damon warned.

Tanner sighed, but bowed his head.

Belle was uncharacteristically quick with her prayer, though still blessing most everyone she knew. Afterward, Mickelle set a plate of pancakes on the counter and everyone reached for them. She noticed that Bryan served Belle before himself because her little arm didn't quite reach the plate. Mickelle helped Jennie Anne, who still held back during most family activities, before returning to the griddle. For a moment there was blessed silence as everyone munched happily.

Before long, breakfast was over, and Damon was sitting on a chair with a towel around his neck as Mickelle expertly trimmed his hair. She enjoyed the opportunity to run her hands through the wet locks that smelled clean from his shampoo. At one point he pulled her to his lap and kissed her until her lungs begged for air. "You're getting hair all over me," she complained lightly.

He only tightened his hold.

She blew some hair from his forehead and it stuck in his thick eyebrows. "Hey, you're getting it in my eyes," he protested.

"Serves you right." Mickelle threw back her head and laughed, her heart feeling almost too small to contain her emotions. She landed a kiss on his nose and resumed cutting.

An hour later a pall was cast over Mickelle's day in a way she hadn't anticipated. They had unanimously agreed to set up the contest on the patio outside the game room, and giggles soon filled the air. The day was beautiful for late October, and the warm sun shining down on them went a long way toward mitigating the brisk chill in the air. On a newspaper-covered table, they went to work slicing into and cleaning out their chosen pumpkins, with Damon's arm and entire head disappearing inside his as he scraped the bottom with a kitchen knife. Mickelle laughed so hard at the sight that she nearly cut herself. She ran inside to get her camera.

That was when she noticed Bryan by the sliding glass door, arms crossed as he scowled at everyone. "What wrong?" she asked. "I thought you were helping Belle."

"This is stupid."

She studied him silently for a few seconds. "You never thought so before. You always loved carving the pumpkins."

He grimaced at her and said nothing.

Mickelle retrieved her camera, trying not to let Bryan's attitude bother her. When Damon saw what she was doing, he stopped to set up his video camera on a tripod. In minutes they were carving faces into their pumpkins.

Jeremy threw the first seed, or so Belle claimed later, but Mickelle was so busy making sure the knives were out of the way that she didn't notice. She did notice when Damon came toward her with his cupped hand full of seeds and squishy pulp from his monstrous pumpkin. "Oh, no you don't!" she shouted, ducking around him and grabbing a handful of seeds herself, sending them hurtling toward him.

Splat! They landed right in his face, one clinging to his blonde moustache. The kids giggled furiously.

"Oh yeah?" He threw his seeds, which hit Mickelle in the chest and slopped down her old sweater.

After that it was a melée, with everyone slinging seeds and laughing themselves helpless. Even Sasha got in on the action, barking excitedly as she ran around the patio. When they were spent, they each plopped down on the ground or at the table, breathing heavily and grinning at each other. Damon looked as though he had received the worst of the blast, and Mickelle suspected she came a close second. Jennie Anne was the least touched, though she had joined in a good share of the mess and now picked seeds from her jeans.

"How wonderful!" Damon exclaimed.

"What?" Mickelle asked, trying to get a seed out of her ear.

"I haven't had so much fun since our first soccer game together." He reached over and combed some of the seeds from her hair with his fingers.

Mickelle returned the favor by picking off a small mound of sticky pulp from his sweatshirt. "What's wonderful is that you have three oversized water heaters and enough bathrooms for us to all clean up at once."

She redeposited the pulp from his sweatshirt on Damon's head, under the pretense of kissing him.

"Hey," he said, scooping the mess from his hair.

"You're it." She grinned, and the play began again.

When they were thoroughly exhausted, the children left to bathe, while Damon and Mickelle cleaned up the patio. Bryan had vanished, though Mickelle was sure she had seen him earlier staring through the sliding glass doors.

Damon got out the hose and directed the water onto the patio, forcing the pumpkin seeds into the grass. "Oh, I did pay Jennie Anne's aunt." He shook his head and sighed. "That old woman . . . I don't know how a person can be so greedy."

Mickelle paused in gathering up the newspapers from the table. "I know . . . except then I kept thinking how desperate I felt after Riley died. Not having a sufficient income makes you feel mean and greedy inside. Maybe we should give Nedda the benefit of the doubt."

"And the bruises?"

Mickelle frowned. "That I don't know about. But there haven't been any since. At least not that I can see."

Damon took her hands in his, which felt cold from the water. "Jennie Anne hasn't been around her enough to provoke an attack."

"I know. I've thought the same thing myself. Is it possible that Jennie Anne really did fall into something?"

"It's always possible." He sighed, rubbing her hands. "What does your heart tell you?"

A lump as big as Damon's pumpkin seemed to grow in her throat. "My heart tells me that someone has hit her."

"Then we've got to do something about it."

"I know. We are, aren't we?"

"Yes, but it doesn't seem fast enough."

Now it was Mickelle's turn to sigh. "My feelings exactly." She let go of his hands and began to roll up the newspaper in front of her, first pushing the remaining gooey pulp toward the middle so it wouldn't fall out. "She seems a part of our family already."

Damon paused in picking up the hose, allowing it to drop once more onto the grass next to the patio. "Our family," he repeated. "Yes, she does. I never thought I'd have any more children." His glance held a trace of guilt.

Abruptly, Mickelle's heart was pounding in her chest so hard that she suspected a panic attack, though she hadn't experienced a full-fledged attack since she and Damon had become engaged. This discussion now bordered the unsaid words between them, and she wasn't sure if she was ready to face the consequences—whatever they might be.

To her relief, Damon retrieved the hose and resumed cleaning. "I just remembered. We're having a reception for some of our clients at the end of next week at the Marriott, and I wanted you to come. It's going to be a real posh event—you know, evening wear type of thing. I was thinking that we'd let Tanner watch the kids and take the cell just in case they need us. We'll have a night out for a change. What do you think? Brionney'll be there."

"I wouldn't begin to know what to wear." Caught off-guard, Mickelle had blurted out the truth. The pounding in her heart continued furiously, and she sat down on the bench, breathing deeply.

Damon turned off the water and started to coil the hose. "We'll get you something new, of course."

She blinked at him. *But what?* she wanted to say. *Where?* The last time she had picked out a nice dress had been for her wedding to Riley, and her mother had been the one to choose the stores. Mickelle doubted if her favorite store, Wal-Mart, carried any formals. *That's stupid,* she thought. *There's always the mall.* But even that idea daunted her.

Did her reluctance to go shopping alone have anything to do with the attack? Probably, but she wasn't willing to be a prisoner in her own home—or Damon's.

Damon came to her side; put his arms around her. A pumpkin seed clinging to his sweatshirt fell onto her sweater. "What's wrong?"

His eyes and face radiated so much concern and love that Mickelle felt she could tell him. "I guess it's just . . . I feel so uneducated. I don't even know where to go to buy a formal, though I do need new clothes." Even while attending church in Damon's ward, where she and the children had been very welcome, she had felt decidedly frumpy compared to most of the other women.

"Ah, Kelle." He shook his head slowly, eyes roaming her face. "You're smart and funny, widely read. You speak well. You may not have a college degree, but you have likely earned the equivalent. Heck, I only have a bachelor's degree. And I used to feel very awkward around others who had more education, but you know what? I've discovered it doesn't really matter. An education does widen your world—and that's one of the reasons I support you going back to school—but it doesn't make you a person worth knowing. That comes from the heart."

She hugged him. "Thank you. Thank you for that." But even as she said it, she felt awkward, as though she were a child, constantly needing reassurance. Would she ever feel as secure as he did? She believed so, but it might be some time in coming.

"You know Kelle," he said in a low voice. "You have changed my life so much, and given me so much, that I could spend the rest of my life trying to make it up to you and never be able to. So I don't need thanks. I'm the one who should thank you."

His comments made her feel immensely better. Perhaps she *did* help and reassure him as well. Wasn't that what a partnership was all about?

Damon led her through the glass doors, where they removed their shoes, and then into the kitchen where Tanner was making hot cocoa.

"Damon," she said, returning to their conversation. "I have to admit that I'm a little nervous to go out and shop in unfamiliar territory. I don't know why—well, I do, really. I'm afraid . . . what if Colton . . ." She let the words trail off.

His eyes brightened momentarily with a fury she knew was not directed toward her, but in the next second the emotion was buried. "I know someone who can help you get a dress," he said, voice steady and gentle. "In fact, she can help you pick out a whole bunch of things. Right from the house. It's what I do with Belle and Tanner for school stuff." He grinned as he took down a bag of marshmallows from the cupboard. "Besides, isn't that what women are supposed to do when they get married? Get a new wardrobe—what do they call it—a trousseau?"

She made a face. "I do need a new swimsuit. I mean, that is if we're going to need it where we're going on our honeymoon." He had refused to tell her where they were going, but had maintained that she would love his surprise. She wasn't so sure.

"You'll need one for here, anyway. Or get two," Damon suggested.

"So when *are* you guys getting married?" Tanner asked as he handed a steaming mug of hot chocolate to Mickelle.

She set the mug on the counter, heart agonizing over the question. It would be so easy to name a date, any date. But she had already buried herself once in a man's wants and needs, and this time she wanted to be sure that she married on her own terms. When she decided what she was willing to sacrifice, she and Damon could talk more seriously about dates. "You know," she said, "I'd better get cleaned up. Do you guys mind? I feel like Peter Pumpkin Eater's wife right now."

Damon's laugh was noticeably tense. "By all means. While you're gone, I'll use the shower down here. I'm feeling rather like I've been inside a pumpkin myself."

"You were," Tanner said with a smirk.

Mickelle burst into laughter.

The laughter hid her other feelings. Why couldn't she just let go of her dream of having another child, a dream that was really being fulfilled by Tanner and Belle anyway? She had seen Belle in her vision the night of her husband's funeral—before she had ever met Damon and his children. And in that vision she had been the mother of the child. Of Belle. At the time she had thought she was expecting a long-awaited daughter, and it had temporarily given her hope. When she discovered it wasn't true, she had blamed Riley for taking even that opportunity away from her. Then into her life came Damon, Tanner, and little Belle—the girl in her dream. So why wasn't that enough? Why was it suddenly so important for her to have Damon's baby?

Am I jealous of his first wife? she wondered.

She shivered as she slunk up the back stairs to Damon's suite. No, she didn't envy his first wife. Charlotte had died after a long, torturous bout with cancer. She didn't envy that.

She did envy the fact that Damon had loved her.

But I loved Riley, she thought. *And what I felt for him has no bearing upon what I now feel for Damon.*

Of course, Riley had been emotionally abusive, so maybe it wasn't the same at all.

Yes it is. I loved him despite his faults, despite the fact that we weren't really partners. And Charlotte was ill all the time. Neither Damon nor I had a chance to be truly one with our spouse. Until now. A spreading warmth in her heart gradually eased her shivering. The truth was that she and Damon would likely grow to love and depend on each other even more than they had ever dreamed possible. They would love each other more than they had loved their first spouses.

So if it didn't bother her that he had once loved Charlotte, and had still loved her enough to have her sealed to him last year, then what *was* the problem?

Sealed.

Was that it? Did it bother her that Damon was sealed to another woman in a ceremony in the holy temple? A ceremony that bound them together even after death?

Mickelle stepped into the shower, thinking deeply. How could that possibly bother her when she was also sealed to Riley?

"No," she said aloud, lifting her face to the warm water. The peppering spray felt like a massage on her body. "I don't think the sealing is what's bothering me."

Damon had told her repeatedly that he was positive they would be together forever. And she believed it. She also believed that just in case it wasn't true, that if in the end Damon was with Charlotte and Mickelle was with a changed Riley, they would still be happy—all of them. She trusted in this with her whole heart. Heavenly Father would arrange things to work out so that each worthy person was happy. Yet if she strongly believed this, what *was* her problem? She loved Damon with her very soul, so why wouldn't she set a wedding date?

Then it came to her in a bright, clear flash. *I just want something that's his and mine. Only ours.*

There, that was it. A shared child, a new being that was part of each of them, would bind her and Damon together in a very unique way. No matter what happened after this life, they would have a child, born out of their love.

Tears formed beneath Mickelle's closed eyes. She was grateful for the fact that Damon couldn't see her tears, for the warm water that would eliminate all signs.

She took a breath. So what now? Ask him to reverse the surgery? Even if it worked, which she doubted, was it fair to ask him to undergo such a thing? Besides, not only was she past the age when doctors encouraged pregnancy, but neither of them were very young. Taking care of a newborn required a lot of energy, not to mention sleepless nights. Then there was also the continuing effort it would take to merge their two families. Mickelle didn't fool herself into thinking there wouldn't be problems. Even big problems. She only had to look at Bryan to see that. So was she ready for the combined challenges of a new baby and a step-family situation?

I could do it, she thought.

But she wondered if having a child was right for her and Damon, or whether she was being driven by her fears to forever have a piece of the man she loved.

Would Damon understand?

CHAPTER 19

Bryan dragged himself into the kitchen when he smelled the hot chocolate Tanner poured into large mugs on the bar. His mouth watered as he sat on a stool. Though he had planned to stay completely aloof from this familial tradition because the Wolfes were *not* family, perhaps he had already made his point. He really loved hot chocolate. Had his mother bought buttery croissants to go with it? Ever since his uncle had first served a mission in France, the croissants had become part of their family jack-o'-lantern party.

"Have some chocolate, Bry," Damon encouraged from the other end of the bar.

Bryan felt resentment bubble inside him. Why did Damon have to be here? He was horning in on Bryan's family, and he wished there was some way to stop it. He felt like a child trying to stick his finger in the hole in the dike, only to feel the dike crashing down around him.

He chose to ignore Damon, and folded his hands angrily on the countertop. Tanner set a hot mug of chocolate in front of him, and despite his better intentions, Bryan put his fingers around the mug.

Belle and Jennie Anne came clattering into the kitchen, Belle talking a hundred miles an hour, Jennie Anne quietly listening. Both wore white leotards and some kind of poufy skirt that reached clear to their ankles.

"Look," Belle said, doing a pirouette. "Mickelle sewed these outfits for us while we were at school the other day. Aren't they cute? Turn around Jennie Anne, so they can see you better."

"Mine's pink 'cause that's my favorite color, and Jennie Anne's is blue 'cause that's hers. And this is how they stick out so far." Belle lifted a transparent cloth, woven with gold thread, and an under layer of pink material. Beneath these were several rows of white netting which gave the outer layers fulness. The skirt was tied on like an apron with a thick shiny ribbon. "And she made 'em 'cause we're princesses."

Bryan thought to himself that Belle looked more like a fairy than a princess. Her eyes shined as she twirled before him.

"Very cute, Belle," Damon said, "but try not to spill chocolate on them."

"Princesses don't spill, do they Jennie Anne? We know how to eat." Belle climbed onto a stool, but then quickly jumped off. "Oh, I forgot!" She ran to one of the cupboards and extracted several packages of croissants. Placing them on the table she met Bryan's eyes and, after making sure that no one was watching, winked. "Mickelle forgot these when we were at the store, but I remembered before we left."

"That's cool," Jeremy said. "It wouldn't be a good seed-fighting party without those."

Belle's laugh tinkled throughout the room. "I know, you and Bryan told me a hundred times."

Bryan felt a stinging behind his eyes. His mom forgot, but Belle remembered. Belle was okay. She was more than okay. Not like Tanner, who was quickly becoming a copy of stuffy old Damon. Why had he ever thought Tanner was so cool?

Everyone reached for a croissant except for Bryan. *I don't care if I have one,* he thought.

Belle scooted two croissants near his mug of chocolate, chattering to her father about her costume for Halloween next week. Bryan was sure no one noticed her move, so he grabbed one of the croissants and held it under the counter, occasionally tearing off pieces and shoving them furtively into his mouth. Ha! With Belle's help he could eat and still make Damon and his mother feel sorry for all the torture they were putting him through!

"So is everyone clean?" Mickelle asked as she entered the kitchen. Her hair was wet and her blue eyes seemed to stand out in her oval face. As usual, she found a stool by Damon. She glanced at Bryan briefly, and he saw a momentary sadness, but it didn't bring him as much satisfaction as he had expected.

She doesn't care about how I feel, he told himself. *And she never loved my dad. Maybe that's why my dad killed himself.*

The thoughts made him even more angry.

"Oh, did I tell you?" Damon said into the brief pause. "Jennie Anne's great-aunt gave permission for her to come to church with us tomorrow."

"Yay!" shouted Belle, clapping her hands and nearly falling from her stool. Bryan's arm shot out and grabbed her just in time. Belle smiled at him gratefully, showing her dimples, but didn't say anything aloud. He was glad she didn't. Her smile made him feel warm inside, just like he felt when he and Jeremy played soccer in their backyard. *Their* backyard, not Damon's. Bryan scowled.

"I can't believe it!" Jennie Anne said in a voice more excited than Bryan had ever heard her use. "Wow! I've been wanting to see what your church is like."

"Don't you ever go?" Belle asked.

Jennie Anne shrugged. "Sometimes, but we only stay for a little while. I don't get to sit with any kids."

Bryan watched as his mother put her arm around Jennie Anne. "Looks like Damon's winning your aunt over."

"I wish I could stay here all the time!" Jennie Anne flushed with embarrassment the moment she had spoken, but Mickelle sighed.

"So do we, Jennie Anne. So do we. You fit right in with our family."

Bryan wanted to jump up and yell at them all. He wanted to remind them they weren't a family, not yet, and that his dad was dead in the graveyard. Nothing could change that; it always came down to that. *I'm the only one who remembers him.*

Fury grew in Bryan's chest, and suddenly he couldn't sit there and watch *that man* step into the place that rightfully belonged to his father. He shoved himself from the stool and stalked out of the room. *It's all her fault,* he thought. *Mom's a betrayer. All she cares about is him. Him, and Tanner, and that dumb Jennie Anne!*

"Well," he heard Damon say as Bryan stomped loudly down the hall, "who's up for a game of table tennis?"

Bryan was amazed. No one had even acknowledged that he was angry at them. Especially not Damon!

I hate him! Bryan knew then that he had to get out of this house once and for all. If his mother and Jeremy wouldn't come with him, he would go alone.

* * * * *

Mickelle watched Belle, Tanner, and Jeremy follow Damon from the kitchen, heading toward the game room. Her heart felt heavy. Damon had wanted to go after Bryan, but she knew he wouldn't unless she gave her permission. She was no longer certain how to handle her son. With Riley, tears had worked after a period of calming down, but she was never going to fall into that rut again. *She* was in charge of her emotions, and she wouldn't allow Bryan to force her to be unhappy.

But I want him to be happy, too, she thought. Why did everything have to be so complicated? She had known there would be problems joining two families, but Bryan was quickly becoming uncontrollable. His comments, when he deigned to speak at all, were almost always derogatory, especially toward her and Damon. Only Belle was immune from his wrath. Bryan reminded her of Riley. Too much. *Way too much.*

She forced her thoughts to follow a different path. Not difficult since Jennie Anne was still on her stool, watching Mickelle.

"Jennie Anne," Mickelle began, sitting beside the child. "You remember when that guy broke in my house and hurt me?"

"Yes." Jennie Anne's gaze briefly met hers, then fell to the counter.

Mickelle studied her profile. Jennie Anne had come so far these past weeks, but at any hint of conflict she would revert to this sad, withdrawn child. "Well, you know it was wrong for him to do that, and when the police find him he will go to jail."

"And what if they don't?" asked Jennie Anne. "They haven't yet."

"No, but since they're searching for him, he won't dare show his face around here again. He can't hurt me. Do you understand that?"

Jennie Anne nodded, still not looking at Mickelle. She traced a pattern on the blue-flecked countertop.

Mickelle went on. "Sometimes people do things like that to their own children. And it's still wrong. The police will make them stop.

Do you understand that? It's wrong for people to hurt kids, and no matter what the person says to the child, no matter how they threaten or scare that child, it can't go on. The police and other nice people like their school teachers will make them stop even if the person hitting them is a parent . . . or an aunt."

Jennie Anne continued to say nothing, so Mickelle reached out and gently touched a place on Jennie Anne's arm. The girl had been wearing long sleeves earlier, but now the short-sleeved leotard couldn't hide the new bruises there. Deep bruises.

"The books fell on me," Jennie Anne said. There was fear in her voice.

"Jennie Anne, I want to help you. If the books really fell, then that's okay. But if someone did this to you"—Mickelle's voice broke—"then I won't let it happen again. You need to trust in me. *Tell me.*"

Jennie Anne lifted her eyes. A tear spilled over and ran down the freckled cheek. "The books fell on me," she repeated slowly.

Mickelle's heart was breaking. She felt that Jennie Anne was lying, but why?

"Okay," she said. "But when you're ready to tell me, I'm here. I'm not going anywhere."

Jennie Anne nodded. Then she slipped from the stool and left the kitchen silently on her bare feet.

Mickelle put her head on her arms, wanting to talk more with Jennie Anne, but knowing that it would do no good. On Monday she would call Social Services. Jennie Anne couldn't protect herself so she would have to do it for her.

A noise startled Mickelle and she looked up to see Bryan, a full backpack slung over his shoulder. "Where are you going?" she asked, following him to the mudroom where he put on his shoes.

He reached for the phone by the door. "I'm leaving. Doug'll let me stay with him." He punched in the numbers.

"Put . . . that . . . down." Mickelle enunciated each word, hoping he would bow to her authority.

Bryan kept on punching. "I'm not staying here with *him*. Or with you. You're a betrayer."

His word stabbed into Mickelle's heart, but she warned herself to be cool. Grabbing the phone from him, she said, "You're not calling anyone."

"Fine!" Bryan lifted his chin, brown eyes lit with fire. "I won't call anyone. But I'm still leaving. I'll live in the street if I have to. Or maybe I won't live at all. Then let's see how happy you'd be with *him*."

Mickelle wanted to believe he didn't mean that last threat, but she remembered too vividly the last time Riley had left the house. She had never expected him to die either. To commit suicide. Either way, the street was no place for a thirteen-year-old boy.

Galvanized into action, Mickelle threw herself between him and the door. "You are not going anywhere except back up into your room! And you are grounded."

His eyes glinted and his jaw hardened. He took a deep breath and Mickelle noticed how solid he had become. Solid and strong. *Like his father.*

Bryan tried to pull her from the door.

"No!" She remained firm.

He hit her then, the blow coming at her stomach without warning. Not even Riley had hit her, though she had been afraid he would, near the end. Perhaps he would have succumbed to physical abuse eventually; by killing himself he had shown that he was capable of violence.

Mickelle cried out as Bryan continued to alternately pull her out of the way and punch her. The blows were painful and accurate, and she held up her arms to fend them off. But she didn't give up her place. No matter what, she would not allow Bryan to leave the house. Suddenly, Mickelle found herself lying on top of the short wood shelf where they stored their shoes. She felt the wood splinter under the impact. Pain shot through her upper thigh and then knifed through her skull as it cracked the ceramic tile.

Everything then seemed to happen at once. A man Mickelle didn't recognize shot into the mudroom, pulling Bryan from her. Damon was close behind, and he rushed to Mickelle's side. "I'm okay," she muttered, though her body throbbed with pain.

Bryan let out a feral growl. The strange man continued to hold onto him, but in an effort not to hurt the boy, he was losing ground. Damon sprang to his aid.

Mickelle watched as her son, her firstborn, struggled with the two men. Her heart was torn in two. Never had she expected to suffer abuse from her own son! Never! Especially not physical abuse. She had not even been remotely fearful of such a thing—until that first heartbreaking punch. If she had believed that her husband Riley would hit her, or endanger her life or that of the boys, she would have left, found a shelter to hide from him. She wouldn't have been able to excuse threats or physical abuse as she had tried to excuse the emotional abuse for so many years. But what did you do when the physical abuse came from your thirteen-year-old son?

One thing she did know: it could not be allowed to continue. She refused to be a victim—again.

She reached for the phone, lying where it had fallen in the fray. The receiver had come apart, exposing the wires, but she pushed it together. Miraculously, it still worked. She dialed 911.

Her eyes lifted to see Jennie Anne standing in the doorway, one hand to her mouth, her eyes radiating terror. She had changed her clothes, Mickelle noticed, and was wearing one of the new outfits they kept at the house for her. She had chosen long-sleeved. *To hide the bruises,* Mickelle thought. *There's too much hiding here.*

The person on the other end of the phone answered and Mickelle spoke, her voice gravelly. "My son hit me. They're holding him down now, but we need assistance."

Damon glanced at her sharply as she spoke, then nodded his approval. As she gave the address, Bryan began to calm. The other man let go of him and retired to a corner, but Damon kept his grip. There was fear in Bryan's eyes now, and Mickelle longed to go to him. But she couldn't. She *wouldn't.* Her heart hurt even worse than her injuries.

Her eyes shifted to the other man, still lurking in the corner of the mudroom. He had light brown hair and was of average height and build, but looked as hard as a piece of steel. The grey eyes in the intent face seemed to note everything. He wore jeans, a sweatshirt, and tennis shoes. Who was he? Obviously, he was known to Damon, and she was grateful for his help, but she felt uncomfortable having him there to witness such a personal trial.

Damon saw her stare. "This is Stan," he said. "He's the guy doing our security work."

"I thought the security system was already in place."

Damon's angular face wore a mask of discomfort. His moustache twitched. "It is, but Stan is also watching the camera monitors. He has a room in the basement."

"He has a . . ." Mickelle couldn't believe it. "He's been living here?"

"Well, working really."

"He has cameras?" Mickelle's mind was dredging up all sorts of images that she didn't like one bit.

"Around the outside of the house," Damon hastened to say. "The only inside ones are by the doors. That's why he came when Bry . . ." His eyes pleaded for understanding. "I meant to tell you. I didn't want you to get upset. It was only going to be for a while, but then the police never caught Colton . . ."

Mickelle glared at him. "You should have told me." She struggled to her feet, ignoring the pounding in her head. "I can't believe you didn't tell me!"

She limped past him and out the door where all the other children had gathered. She felt, more than saw, Damon shove Bryan at Stan. "Hold him."

Bryan started struggling again, and it was all both men could do to contain him without hurting him. Mickelle was almost glad when the police arrived. They filled out a brief report before heading to the door, taking Bryan with them, even as Belle and Jeremy begged them not to.

"Mom," Bryan said, sounding like her son again. His eyes bored into hers—begging, pleading.

The ice around Mickelle's heart softened. "We'll come get you soon." The officers were taking him to juvenile detention for the night. She prayed with her whole being that she had made the right decision. At least in custody he couldn't hurt anyone . . . or himself.

After they left there was silence in the family room. Stan, the security man, had disappeared after talking to the police and promising to make a video copy of the disturbance.

Disturbance, Mickelle scoffed. She wished she were alone so that she could cry. But the children were watching her earnestly. Instead, she sat stiffly on the blue leather couch and wiped the tears seeping from her eyes. "You should have told me about him," she scolded

Damon. "I hate it that you didn't tell me." There was venom in her voice, but at that moment she didn't care.

Damon put a hand on Tanner's shoulder. "Take the girls and Jer to the game room, okay? Kelle and I need to have a little talk. And shut the door. Don't worry, everything's going to be just fine."

Mickelle was glad he had remembered the children. Her heart was feeling too betrayed and desolate to think coherently. She forced a smile for the kids. "Go on, really. I'm okay. We're okay. Everything will be fine."

Jeremy and Belle looked relieved, but she could tell that Jennie Anne didn't believe her. *Jennie Anne and I are too much alike.* The thought surprised Mickelle, though perhaps it was true.

When they were alone once more she said, "To think that he's been here in the house this entire time. It's creepy! That's what's wrong with living in a house this size. Someone can live in your basement, and you don't even hear them!"

Damon sat on the edge of the love seat, elbows on knees, head inclined in her direction. "You think I'm going to leave you here unprotected? If you remember, the police haven't caught Colton yet—if it was Colton that night, which I really doubt."

"I thought you had an alarm!"

"But I wanted someone to be here in case the alarm went off! I knew I couldn't stay because it would look funny." He grimaced. "Although for some reason a perfect stranger can live here without it being frowned upon. And so I did the next best thing. I hired Stan to be here when I wasn't."

"You hire everything out!" she yelled at him.

"So?"

"So it's a waste of money—the gardening, the cooking, washing the car . . ."

"It's not a waste. Most things I hire out so that I can be with you and the kids. Isn't that more important?"

She blinked, realizing that everything he was saying made a lot more sense than her comments. "I'm just not used to all this," she whispered. "Money was always so tight, and . . ." There was nothing more to say, since she didn't really know what was wrong with her anyway.

Damon was next to her in an instant, his strong arms enfolding her like a familiar warm blanket. "Bry will be okay," he said, pinpointing her real despair. "I'm sorry that this happened, but for what it's worth, I think you made the right decision. And somehow we'll work through this. You'll see. We'll be a family yet."

"There were signs. His arguments with Tanner, always throwing the ball, his anger toward me and you. Mostly to me. His fighting at school. I should have seen it coming. I *did* see it coming, just not in this way. I should have guessed."

"No," Damon shook his head. "We couldn't have. Don't blame yourself."

"My poor little boy." She sobbed against his chest. "I was so afraid he'd leave. That he'd hurt himself. I couldn't let him. I didn't matter at that moment—what he did to me didn't matter. I just had to save him."

"I know."

Damon held her for a long time, and Mickelle's anguish slowly spent itself. The terrible pounding that had begun when her head hit the tile, relaxed marginally. "I've been praying so hard that he'll come around," she murmured, wiping the tears from her eyes and cheeks.

"Maybe this is Bry's way of coming around. Maybe this is the only way we can get him the help he needs."

A similar thought had crossed her mind. Sometimes a person had to be brought to the depths of humility before he was ready to change his life. Of course, some people wimped out at that point. Like Riley. *"What doesn't kill you makes you strong,"* she quoted silently.

They sat together mutely until the evening shadows crept into the room and then she said, "Don't you ever hide anything from me again. I can take it. I want to know about *all* the Stans. Every single one." She jabbed her finger into his chest, accentuating the last three words.

"Okay," he promised. After a brief moment of silence, his voice took on a teasing note as he said, "I suppose that means you want to know where we're going on our honeymoon, too."

"I won't go that far." She gingerly touched the place on her thigh where she had fallen on the shoe shelf. There was a swollen mound there now, as large as her open hand, protruding like a large half grapefruit. Another bruise to add to her collection.

He grinned. "Oh, I don't mind. We're going to Europe. I know you've always wanted to. I thought we'd hit Italy, Spain, Greece, Germany, London, and of course France, so you can see your brother and his kids. We can even go to Ireland if you want."

She stared at him with increasing surprise, her mouth agape.

He hesitated. "You're catching flies." His hand gently caressed her jaw, and she shut it with a snap.

"Catching flies . . ." She shook her head at him, then winced mentally as her head renewed its throbbing with the motion.

"It's okay that the surprise is ruined." He grinned at her, eyes sparkling. "I thought since we were going to be gone so long, you might want to help plan the trip anyway. Maybe the kids could even join us for the last leg of the journey—if you want."

Mickelle hugged him, and he hugged her back. She couldn't believe that everything in her life, while still difficult and agonizing, was suddenly manageable. Her burden was shared.

"When I asked you to marry me," Damon whispered in her ear, sending delicious shivers through her body, "I meant that we were in this together. And I believe that together is the only way we can do it right. And the same goes for anything we face. If there's a bridge, we'll cross it together—somehow."

She knew he was talking not only about Bryan but also about her desire to have his child.

But there was something that had to come before that: Jennie Anne's welfare. "It's not just Bryan," she said softly, reluctantly. She adjusted her position so the swelling bump on the side of her head wouldn't touch anything. "I mean the situation with him is bad enough, but I noticed when Jennie Anne changed into that leotard today. . . it had short sleeves." She swallowed hard at the sudden dryness in her throat.

"Noticed what?"

"She has more bruises. What are we going to do?"

* * * * *

To Jennie Anne's dismay, Damon came in with her when he drove her home. She didn't want him to come, always worried that he would discover her secret and that her aunt wouldn't let her go to his house anymore. So instead of walking into the house as she did ordinarily, she rang the bell to give her aunt warning. That was especially important if Troy was around.

"What? Huh? Oh, it's you." As Jennie Anne slipped past, her aunt focused on Damon. She even smiled. Though it was probably because of the money he gave her, Aunt Nedda seemed to really like Damon.

Jennie Anne tried to peer over the stacks of junk in the front room to see if Troy was home. It was no use. She just wasn't tall enough. Damon, though, would be able to see from the door—maybe. And if Troy was home, there might be big trouble.

She peered down the path through the piles to the couch. He wasn't there. The relief didn't pour through her yet. First she had to peek into the kitchen.

Sighing with relief at last, Jennie Anne crept quietly back to the front room to hear what the adults were saying. *Oh, please, oh please, don't let him talk about the bruises. I hope Mickelle didn't tell him about the bruises!*

She was too late to hear what they had said. Damon was already leaving, and Jennie Anne watched him go, feeling suddenly lost. She wanted to run after him and beg him to take her back to Mickelle where she would be safe.

The problem was, she didn't know if she would be safe, even with Mickelle. She had wanted to confide in Mickelle about the bruises, especially when she talked about the police. But those same policemen hadn't found the man who had hurt Mickelle yet. Jennie Anne knew that if he decided to, he could still hurt Mickelle.

And I can still be hurt. The police will never know.

The police *had* taken Bryan away when he had tried to hurt Mickelle. So maybe sometimes it worked. Was it worth the risk?

No, better to keep quiet. At least she spent most of her days away from this horrid house.

She smiled, thinking of Belle's castle room. Magic happened there. She was no longer Jennie Anne, but a powerful princess, who never had any bruises. Of course, Belle was kind of bossy, always telling her to play this or do that, but it was okay, really. She loved Belle fiercely. Her only friend, the one who had opened her heart, and, perhaps even more importantly, the doors to reading—to a whole world she had never imagined.

There was a sound in the bathroom, and Jennie Anne's blood ran cold. Her heart seemed to quit beating. She huddled up to a stack of magazines, taller than her head. The stack swayed slightly, but was kept in place by the surrounding piles of junk.

Troy didn't notice her. "So who was it?" he growled. Jennie Anne knew he was waiting for that pretty man to come back. She had seen him twice since that day when her uncle had first driven off with him. Both he and Uncle Troy had bruises around their blue eyes. Jennie Anne wondered if they had fought, and if so, why they continued to be friends. She had gloated just a little, in the safety of the Wolfe home, that Uncle Troy had a black eye. A mean little part of her hoped it hurt him as bad as her bruises hurt her.

"Just the rich guy. None of your concern."

"He give you more?"

"No, and I didn't ask." Nedda's chin jutted out.

"I think he'll pay more."

"So? I got enough. And more coming next month. You better stay away from her."

"What—I ain't touched her!"

"You left bruises all over her arm."

"Did he mention them?"

"No, but he knows. I know he knows. He as much as said I wouldn't get more if she was hurt. You'd better lay off. "

Troy sneered at her. "I do what I please. *You* lay off! I'm going to get me a chunk of that rich snob's money one way or another. And I don't give a crap what happens to Donna May's whelp. Don't matter to me at all. Not one little bit."

Jennie Anne shivered. Her arm ached where he had grabbed it a few days ago. He had been so angry when he'd come home. Something to do with money—it was always money with him. When she hadn't been quick enough to clear a chair for him to sit, he had told her how lazy she was . . . and then gave her the bruises to remember to do better the next time. She had been careful not to let Mickelle or Belle know about how bad her arm hurt, like her aunt said, but it wasn't easy.

She had slept in her aunt's room since Troy came back, instead of in the kitchen. She was glad because sometimes before when he had stayed with them, she had awakened in the night and found Troy watching her as he downed a beer from the fridge. His eyes had been dark and ugly, and she had been afraid. This time he had been back for longer than she could ever remember him staying at one time; she hoped he would leave soon.

Jennie Anne tried to slink past them, but Troy caught her arm painfully. "Did you tell them about the bruises?" he demanded.

She was trembling violently and her knees threatened to give out. Without mercy, his fingers dug into the bruises he had made before. *It hurts so bad!* She couldn't say the words aloud; he might do even worse. He had before.

"Books fell on me," she said in a frightened whimper.

Troy laughed and let go of her so quickly she almost fell. The intense pain subsided.

"Go to my room," Nedda ordered under her breath, shoving her in that direction.

Jennie Anne fled.

They fought more, as they always did. Jennie Anne knew it was bad to want people to die, but she hoped that Troy would.

CHAPTER 20

As Mickelle left the church building, she felt her spirits, so uplifted by the services, plunge into a deep melancholy. Jennie Anne hadn't been allowed to come with them after all. When Damon had stopped by to pick her up, an unshaven man had met him at the door and told him she wasn't going—wasn't feeling well. Damon had asked to see her, but the man had refused.

"I don't know who he is," Damon had told her, his frustration showing through, "but he seemed too young to be Nedda's boyfriend."

"The son maybe? She said he came around occasionally."

"Could be."

"What'd he look like?"

"Brown hair. Longish. Not sure about the eyes. Not very tall but he had some good-sized muscles. Looked mean, too. I think he enjoyed telling me no."

"Didn't you see Nedda?"

"Not a sign. I bet I could have gotten around her."

Mickelle had hated the idea of Jennie Anne returning to her aunt the night before, and had only agreed to allow Damon to take her because mentioning any other alternative had thrown Jennie Anne into a fit of anxiety. Now she wished she had kept the child, even against her will.

Bryan's absence made things worse. Mickelle kept wondering if he was all right, getting enough to eat. They were going to see him after lunch. She had the option of taking him home today or waiting another, but she hadn't made any decisions yet. She was fasting and praying hard to know what would be best for her son—and for their family. He wasn't like a husband she could leave, but her own precious child. A part of her flesh. Calling the police yesterday had been the hardest thing she had ever done.

* * * * *

Damon slammed the door of his green Lexus, and took Mickelle's arm as she limped toward the juvenile facility where Bryan had stayed overnight. The lines on her forehead and around her eyes were etched deeper than he had ever seen them, as though she hadn't slept well. He hoped Bryan could see the change, too. *I'll make him see it,* he thought.

Bryan was brought into the room, and his eyes lit up momentarily, though the rest of his face showed no expression. They sat around a small table awkwardly, glad for the privacy they had been allowed.

"Are you ready to come home?" Mickelle asked.

Bryan's jaw tightened. "To *our* home, yes."

She ignored the implication. "It'll have to be on my terms, Bryan. What you did yesterday was wrong and it cannot happen again."

"It won't."

"How can I be sure?"

"It never happened before."

"No, but you have been heading in that direction for a long time."

Bryan didn't reply.

"We brought a contract for you to sign. It states that you will not leave home without our permission, and that you will address us with respect—among other things."

His eyes flicked over the paper. "Whatever."

"It's not whatever. I want you to read it and sign it. I want you to promise me that you'll behave."

Bryan stood up so fast his chair tipped over. "You want, you want, you want!" he sneered. "What about me! Look, I don't want to come home—ever!" He turned and walked toward the door.

Mickelle stared at Damon helplessly. They had thought Bryan would be miserable and want to come home; in fact, the counselor they had talked to assured them that most first-time offenders were immediately repentant and many never repeated the offense. They had hoped Bryan would be more compliant.

Damon stood to go after him.

"Wait," Mickelle said. "He'll calm down. He always does."

Damon gazed at her beseechingly. "I've got to start being his father sometime, Kelle. And I need to go after him now."

For a second, she hesitated, then with a nod, she let him go.

He walked quickly and arrived at the door as Bryan did. "Excuse me," Damon said to the aide outside the door. "We need to talk privately. Is there any other place?"

In another empty room down the hall, Bryan glared at him, folding his arms across his chest. Neither sat in the vacant chairs. "I don't want to talk to you," Bryan said through gritted teeth.

"Well, that's too bad."

"I wish you'd just back off. Leave us alone."

"I love your mother."

"So? A lot of people do. People better than you."

"I suppose by that you mean Colton Scofield."

Bryan shrugged. "He was cool."

"Cool, huh? You think he's cool after what he did to your mother?"

"He might not have. You said so yourself."

"Oh, and your mother's money just disappeared on its own?"

Bryan didn't answer.

"Well, let me tell you what I know for sure that Colton Scofield *did* do to your mother earlier that same day. And I know it for a fact because I came over after he'd been there and she had the marks on her wrists."

Bryan said nothing, but Damon could tell he had his interest.

Suddenly Damon walked up to Bryan, using his larger frame to push him backward. "She didn't want you to know, but maybe it's time you did." He kept talking as he walked, his voice calm and even. He didn't stop pushing Bryan until his back was against the door. "He took her to your house when she was alone and pushed her up against the sink. He grabbed her hands like this."

"Hey, stop!"

"Then he forced them down to her side and told her she had to go see his friend to invest her money. He was angry, you see, because he and his buddy had a plan to have the investment go bad. That way he could take the money without the police tracking it to him. She tried to get away, but he held her still. How does it feel, Bry, to be so helpless?"

Bryan's jaw jutted angrily. He tried to free himself, but Damon held fast.

"She looked away, but he grabbed her face like this. His fingers pinched into her skin, her head was immobilized. Can you move, Bry? How do you feel? How do you think your mother felt?"

"Stop it!" Bryan's voice rose an octave.

"That's what she said, but he didn't. She tried to pull his hand away with her free one, but he grabbed it again, came closer . . ." Damon gripped Bryan hard without really hurting him, seeing the fear in his face, the tears welling up in his eyes. He released Bryan abruptly and backed away, feeling that he shouldn't push further.

"Luckily, your mom's friend came over just then. The door was open. If it hadn't been . . . well, I don't know what your friend Colton would have done to your mother." He let the thought seep in. "The truth is that Colton Scofield is a user. He would have hurt your mom, like he's done so many other vulnerable women. He did steal her money. Is that the type of person you want to be? Is it?" He paused so that the next words would stand apart from the others. "Still, even after that little episode with Colton in the kitchen, your mother didn't have to take pain medication for the goose egg on her head, or limp from the huge grapefruit-sized bruise on her leg. That's what *you* did to her. To your own mother."

Damon could see that Bryan was fighting tears, though he still looked furious. But Damon had thought about this all night and there was much more to be said to the boy he wanted to have as a son.

"But none of this is really about Colton Scofield, is it? It's about your father."

"I don't want to talk about him."

"I'm sorry you had to see your father emotionally abuse your mother."

"Go away!" Bryan was still backed up against the closed door though Damon stood more than an arm's length from him.

"And I'm sorry you were abused."

"I wasn't!"

"He manipulated and controlled you, Bry. That's abuse. But you need to know that real men don't take out their frustrations on the women and children in their lives. They find better ways to deal with their anger."

"So my father wasn't a man?" Bryan's chin lifted, though his voice wasn't as defensive as before.

Damon sighed heavily. "Your father had medical problems, and I believe the Lord will take that into account. But no matter what he was going through, he shouldn't have treated your mother any less than a queen. And just because he didn't, doesn't mean you have the right to follow in his footsteps. No right at all. And as long as I'm alive, you will never touch her again. *Never.*"

Bryan remained quiet so Damon continued, "Now it's up to you, how you decide to behave. I love your mother very much. More than anything else in this world. And I love you and Jeremy, whether you believe it or not. Regardless, I am going to be a part of your life. You don't have to like me, but you do have to put up with me. And you do have to show your mother the respect she deserves. In turn, I can promise you that *I* will never hurt your mother. I *will* try to make up for the years of hurt she has endured. I know that you love her, too, and I hope you are man enough to act like it. I think you are."

Damon didn't know what more to say. His anger and urgency had drained away with the words. He didn't know if what he said had made the situation better or worse. How did any parent know? But he believed in setting limits, and Bryan had finally been given his.

Leaving Bryan in the room, Damon went out to the hall where Mickelle and the aide waited. Mickelle's turbulent blue eyes searched his. He shrugged, not knowing what to tell her. He wanted to say that it wasn't Bryan's fault, not really, but his father's. The pain in her eyes made him hold his tongue.

* * * * *

Tears slipped from Bryan's eyes. He hated what Damon had said to him about Colton and about his father. Worse, he knew it was true. He felt it deep in his gut. And it hurt.

What about his mother? She *had* walked in today with a limp. Was that really because of him? He didn't know. Yesterday, he had simply become so furious at her, so entirely enraged that he hadn't been thinking straight. He had wanted her to hurt as much as she was hurting him.

It's all Damon's fault!

The thought came with less conviction than before. The truth was, he didn't know whose fault it was. Somehow everything had spun out of control.

Now he would have to stay here another night, maybe more, listening to people talk about how wrong he had been, how stupid. The boys here weren't what he was accustomed to either. He didn't belong.

He wiped at the tears on his face, but more sprang to take their place. He couldn't let anyone see him like this, or they would tease, push him around even more than they already had.

The ache inside him grew so big that he wondered if there was anything in the world large enough to fill it. His family was gone, and there was nothing left for him. For a moment he wanted to die. Like his father. Except he really didn't. *He wouldn't.*

The next thing he knew, warm arms came around him. He immediately recognized his mother's smell, though he had tried to recall it last night in his strange bed to no avail. Sobs burst through his mouth, sounding like an animal in pain.

"There, there," his mother said, holding him tightly.

Bryan never wanted her arms to leave. "I'm sorry," he choked out.

"I know. I am too. I am *so* sorry."

Bryan wondered what part she was sorry for, but decided it didn't matter. "I want to come home. I want to sign that contract."

"Okay. Let's go get your things."

She helped dry his eyes as she had when he was little. Instead of triumph at his surrender, there was a beaten aspect in her manner that he remembered seeing so often when his father had been alive. As she limped to the door, a powerful remorse filled his being. *I'm so sorry,* he told her silently.

He still hated Damon—that hadn't changed—but he now hated his father even more.

CHAPTER 21

They were arguing again and Jennie Anne thought it best to stay in her aunt's room. She couldn't help going to the open door to listen. After all, it did concern her.

". . . and you went behind my back and said she couldn't go. Now he'll never give me more money."

"Not true. I only showed him who's boss. That we control whether or not they see Jennie Anne."

"I told him he could take her."

"And I told him no. Trust me, I know what I'm doing." There was a pause. "You might even be able to afford better food—this stuff is crap."

"What do you mean?" Nedda's voice was worried, and that made Jennie Anne feel uneasy.

"You don't need to know about it, hear? I've got it taken care of."

"You and that pretty boy, you mean?"

"So? What of it? You didn't mind the money he gave us."

"I only saw what he gave me. What'd you do with the five hundred you say he gave you?"

"Ain't no concern of yours. I got expenses. Now leave me to eat in peace."

"I won't have you hurting her again."

There was a crash, and then a silence. Jennie ached to go to see if Nedda was all right, but her sore arm throbbed in protest. She sank down by the closet in terror. Her senses urged her to hide, but she knew it would be of little use. He would find her. He would find her anywhere she could run, except maybe at Wolfe Estates which was so big not even Belle would find her if she hid. Then again, maybe Belle would help her hide. She could stay in the basement like Stan.

She clung to the thought as she heard her great-aunt moan from the kitchen. Well, at least Nedda wasn't dead. Jennie Anne would be sorry for that, she really would. Nedda didn't hit her.

"This is my house," she heard Nedda say.

Troy laughed. "So, call the cops, Mommy."

Nedda didn't say anything, but a short time later she came into the bedroom and closed the door. She sat on the edge of the double bed they had shared for the past few weeks. It was the closest they had ever been since Nedda never hugged her. Not like Mickelle, who hugged everyone.

"Get your things together," Nedda said evenly. "Not everything. Just what you really need. But don't let him see."

Jennie Anne studied her great-aunt from her crouched position by the closet. Her aunt's eyes looked smaller and meaner than she had ever seen them, her face more droopy and old. The terror in her heart returned, but she tried not to show it. Showing the fear always made it worse. At least this way she could pretend she didn't care.

Jennie Anne nodded and moved down the narrow space to the far side of the bed. All her belongings were in a corner, between several boxes filled with who-knew-what and a huge mound of clothes that she had never seen Nedda wear. She pulled out her yellow backpack with her school books and stuffed in the old photo album that had been her mother's. Next, she put in the small box with the silver necklace that Mickelle had given her last week. She didn't wear it around the house because one never knew when Troy would show up in a fit, or when Nedda would decide to save something for one of her summer yard sales.

That was Nedda's excuse for keeping all this junk around, most of which was given to her or found at the city dump. "One man's junk is another man's treasure," Nedda was fond of saying. Jennie Anne had never found much that interested her in Nedda's junk, and the few things she did like were sold to people who came to look down their noses at the stuff piled on boards and blankets in the yard. She had stopped asking Nedda for anything but the old clothes which usually didn't fit well or had stains and holes.

Belle, of course never wore secondhand clothes. Jennie Anne almost laughed at the very idea.

A sigh from her aunt, now standing before a closet as jam-packed with junk as the rest of the house, pulled Jennie Anne back to the task at hand. She put the small heart-shaped box that carried the rest of her personal treasures—small rocks she liked, a piece of a robin's egg, a length of wire, an old coin. This stuff she knew had no value to Nedda or the people who came to the garage sales, but to Jennie Anne they were special treasures.

On top of this she put two of her new pairs of jeans and several pairs of socks. That was it. Nothing more would fit if she wanted to use the zipper. At least she was wearing the nicest dress Belle had given her, donned in anticipation of going to church. Of course, that meant she had to put on the new stiff church shoes instead of the comfortable tennis shoes—both gifts from Mickelle and Damon. And what should she do about that sweater Belle had given her, and all the other clothes? Jennie Anne gazed in amazement at her mound of belongings. She couldn't bear to leave any of the clothes behind, not when they were so new and pretty. She suspected that if it had been summer, she might have lost many of these clothes to a yard sale, so she had meant to enjoy them while she could.

"Here." Nedda shoved a large bag at her, made of bright green cloth. "Put some of them clothes in. You're going to need them."

With relief, Jennie Anne filled the bag, carefully storing most of the items she had been given since meeting Belle. The tense pit in her stomach eased slightly. If Nedda was letting her take all this stuff, then wherever they were going couldn't be so bad.

A sudden thought brought tears to her eyes. Would she ever see Belle and Mickelle again?

Behind her the door slammed open, knocking into the piles of stuff between the door and the wall. Clothes, papers, books, and knickknacks went flying. Under cover of the commotion, Jennie Anne pulled the edge of a blanket from the unmade bed to cover the green bag and her backpack.

Troy scanned the room, but apparently didn't see anything out of the ordinary. Jennie Anne could see why. The clothes Nedda had taken from the closet and folded in a stack on her bed really didn't stand out from the crowded piles of junk around the room.

Troy snorted in disgust, tossing the dull brown hair on his head. "Geez, Mom, you can hardly fit in here for all this stuff."

"What do you want?" Nedda's voice clearly showed her anger, and Jennie Anne crouched even further down by the bed in anticipation of another fit. Why couldn't Troy just leave them alone?

"Look, Mom, I'm sorry. I shouldn't have done that. But don't get me angry, see? Once I get the real money, I'll give you some. Maybe move you down to Arizona or someplace hot."

Nedda's face said, *I don't want no part of it, you creepy excuse for a son. Now get out before I call the cops.* What came out of her mouth was, "Okay, Troy. Whatever."

He grinned at her. "Well I'm gonna shave and then take care of some business. By tonight I'll know more. This is going to be big."

He went to the bathroom and they heard the water running. Nedda sank down on the bed, staring into space, her plump arms folded across her belly. Jennie Anne craned her head to see her expression. Did that mean they weren't going after all? And why did that suddenly seem even more frightening?

They sat in silence, listening to Troy in the bathroom. Forever clicked endlessly by until he emerged and the outside door slammed behind him. When the sounds of his old Chevy truck faded into the distance, Nedda arose and walked into the kitchen. With Troy gone, Jennie Anne felt secure enough to follow.

". . . I know it's an inconvenience," Nedda was saying into the phone, "but I'll pay you. It's just to the airport. Thanks. I owe you one. Thanks a lot."

So they were still going!

Nedda went back to her room, but Jennie Anne stared at the phone on the wall. The numbers to Mickelle's old phone number and the new one to the Wolfe Estates collided in her mind. She wanted more than anything to call Mickelle, to say good-bye. But what if she came running over? What if Troy hurt her?

Mickelle would wonder, though, what happened to her. She would be sad.

Jennie Anne decided to call the old house. They had installed an answering machine, and went there occasionally to move their belongings to Wolfe Estates. They would get her message within a day or two, and she would get to say good-bye.

"Hi, it's me, Jennie Anne," she said when the machine picked up. "My aunt's taking me away and I wanted to say good-bye. Don't worry about me. I'll call. Bye." She wanted to say, "I love you" or even "Please come and get me" but this first stuck in her throat and the other was too dangerous.

Then, because she couldn't bear to go without at least hearing Mickelle's voice one last time, she dialed the other number. The ringing sounded three times before a voice answered.

"Hello?" It was Belle.

Tears slipped out of Jennie Anne's eyes. She quickly hung up the phone.

"Whatcha doing!" Nedda grabbed her bruised arm and pulled her away from the phone.

"Nothin'—I . . . Ow!"

"Ooh, you're making this hard on me!" Nedda exclaimed. She raised her hand as Jennie Anne cowered, but no slap came. "Just don't call nobody," Nedda said. To Jennie Anne's surprise, she hugged her.

Jennie Anne's emotions tumbled about inside her like a twig tumbled in the water when she tossed it into the creek. She stood there, unmoving, but feeling so much.

Her aunt drew away. "There now, Franny'll be here in a minute. Get your stuff. I'll keep a lookout for Troy."

Jennie Anne obeyed. When she was finished, Nedda told her to watch for Troy while she retrieved her money from the secret place under one of the piles in the bedroom. Jennie Anne knew where it was, but she had never touched it.

While Nedda was gone she went down the pathway to the couch, deciding that she could hear Troy's truck just as well from there. Resentment built up inside her with each step. Troy had ruined everything. He had stolen her sleeping place and had hurt her repeatedly. She wished she could hurt him back, especially since he was planning bad things for Mickelle and Damon. Not for the first time she wondered if that beautiful man had anything to do with the plan. She had thought he was Mickelle's friend, but now she wasn't so sure. He had never come to see her, even after Mickelle was hurt. Jennie Anne had tried to talk about him once to Belle, but her friend refused to listen, saying that she hoped he fell off a cliff. Since Jennie Anne was forbidden by her aunt to talk about him anyway, she had let it go. She didn't even know his name.

Her eyes fell on something under the couch—a suitcase, similar to the large one in which Nedda had packed her clothes. It had been squished flat to fit in the six inches of space where Jennie Anne kept her treasures when Troy was away. Jennie Anne pulled it out, driven by a fascination she couldn't explain. They were leaving Troy behind, and he would never know she had touched his things.

She opened the suitcase, empty except for a few items of clothes. One of the inner pockets bulged. With a trembling hand, she reached in and pulled out a sheaf of bills. Her eyes opened wide. She knew those numbers now on the first bill, and it was as large as most of the first graders knew how to count.

"Jennie Anne!"

She jumped at her aunt's sharp voice, but she didn't put back the money.

"You was supposed to be watching out the door. What if Troy had come—" She broke off as Jennie Anne wordlessly handed her the bills.

"Why, there are thousands of dollars here," Nedda said after a moment of counting. "Ten at least, maybe more. Why that dirty sneak. He's been holding out on me. He never told me it was this much." She seemed to debate for a minute, before tucking it into her purse. "He owes me this and more, and I'm going to take it. He ain't going to be any madder than he already is when he finds us gone. And by then it'll be too late. Makes up for all I'm leaving behind for the landlord, too." Nedda stared a little misty-eyed at the stacks around her. With one hand, she fluffed her short curly locks, which were showing gray near the scalp. Jennie Anne knew that now she would have enough money to get her hair done. That would make her happy.

A sound of an engine outside galvanized them into action. Thankfully, it was only Franny, and in minutes they were ready to leave. As Franny sped away, Jennie Anne fixed her eyes on the sad old house and Nedda's rusty car. She felt heartsick when they faded from view, but didn't know why, since she wouldn't miss any of it except the willow tree where she had spent many hours swinging on the branches.

The new coat Mickelle had bought her when she had taken her to Wal-Mart suddenly seemed to weigh a ton.

Belle! her heart said. But even more deeply it cried, *Mickelle!*

* * * * *

Mickelle asked Damon to swing around to the old house to pick up a list of things she had been needing—especially her box of roses now that her curio cabinet had been restored and sat in a perfect place in Damon's main sitting room. She couldn't wait to set them out, and hoped that doing so would cheer her up.

Bryan immediately disappeared into his room to collect more of his belongings. He had been quiet all the way home, and while things weren't perfect between them, at least he had not interjected his negativity into the conversation.

There were other items, like her cookbooks and her special spices that she also wanted. As she packed them, she listened to the phone messages. The last one made her heart nearly stop. She had only missed it by a half hour. "Damon!" she called out the door.

He sprinted in from the car where he had taken her roses. "What?"

"A message from Jennie Anne . . . on the phone." She pulled him along as she ran back to the kitchen. She punched the replay, then impatiently sped up the tape. Finally, Jennie Anne's voice came through, sounding thin and scared.

Damon started for the door. "There might still be time."

"Bryan, we're leaving," Mickelle shouted. "Hurry! Or we'll come back for you." She ran for the car, pain shooting up and down her bruised thigh.

Bryan came hurrying out, a box in hand. "What's going on?"

"It's Jennie Anne. Her aunt's taking her away. We have to see if we can stop her!"

Damon shoved his Lexus into gear as they slammed the doors. He sped the three blocks to Jennie Anne's as Mickelle sat praying. Her head had begun to hurt again. "That's why they wouldn't let her go this morning, I'll bet," she said.

Damon's mouth tightened, but he concentrated on his driving.

"Did she try to call the other house?" asked Bryan.

Wordlessly, Damon handed over his cell phone, and Mickelle dialed quickly. "Hi, Tanner, this is Mickelle. Did Jennie Anne call?"

"Not that I know of. Belle answered the phone once, but nobody was there."

"Check the Caller ID, would you?"

There was a pause and then Tanner said, "Yes, she called. Maybe it was her when Belle answered."

"When was it?"

"A half hour ago. What's going on?"

"I'm going to hang up now. We'll explain when we get home."

Had Jennie Anne needed help?

They arrived at the old house. The rusty car was still there, and everything appeared as it usually did. Mickelle was out of the door before the Lexus had come to a full stop. She half ran, half hobbled down the broken sidewalk. Damon reached her as she knocked on the door.

No answer.

They alternately rang and knocked for several minutes. Mickelle tried the door. "It's locked."

"I'll try around back."

Mickelle listened at the door, but heard nothing. She tried to peek through the window to no avail. In a few minutes, Damon returned, shaking his head.

"Locked."

"I should have called the police about the bruises."

He gathered her in his arms, but Mickelle's heart was so broken that she refused to be comforted.

"We'll find her." He was so confident, so in control. Sometimes it made her angry.

"What if we never do?" That would be worse, the not knowing.

"Come on."

Damon led her back to the car, where Bryan stood uncertainly. Mickelle didn't look at him. Everything just hurt too much.

* * * * *

"I got to stop someplace first," Nedda said to Franny. She glanced back at Jennie Anne. "To drop off Jennie Anne."

Jennie Anne couldn't contain her gasp of dismay.

"Now don't get upset, girl; you know I was never much of an aunt to you. I'm too old and ornery. Can't take you with me or Troy'll catch up to me. He'll be looking for an old lady with a kid. Can't have that. He's crazy. He'd kill me."

Jennie Anne only knew that leaving her behind meant that Troy would find her. "I want to go with you," she choked out.

"No." Her aunt shook her head. "I got it all planned. Right now I got to do what's best for me."

Jennie Anne wrapped her arms around herself in misery. What would happen to her now?

She paid little attention as Franny drove. Scrunching down to reach her backpack, she pulled it onto her lap and thought hard. She couldn't let Troy find her. Without Nedda, things would be much worse.

She decided to jump for it. As soon as the car stopped, she would jump out and run. Old Nedda and her friend wouldn't be able to stop her. Of course, she would have to leave behind the green bag with most of her clothes. Carefully, so as not to alert her aunt, she unlocked the car door.

The car stopped at a red sign which Jennie Anne now knew said "stop." *Jump,* she told herself, but her legs wouldn't work.

She closed her eyes and clutched the backpack. *I got to do it.*

Twice more the car slowed, but Jennie Anne still didn't jump. Finally, the car stopped, and Jennie Anne sprang out. What she saw stopped her in mid-stride, jaw gaping open. It couldn't be! It couldn't be!

"Give them this note," Nedda told her gruffly. "It explains it all." Her mouth twitched a little as though she had something caught in her front tooth and was trying to worry it out with her tongue. "Bye, girl."

There was no hug, no explanation, but there wasn't need for either. Jennie Anne understood, as surely as if her aunt had spoken, that Nedda loved her. Maybe not as much as her mother had, or as much as Mickelle, but this time it was enough.

* * * * *

Mickelle tried to gain her composure on the drive home. She felt as though a piece of her was missing, the same way she had felt when Bryan had left with the police the night before. *Poor Jennie Anne.* She wondered what the child was thinking and where she was at that very moment. Would they ever learn what happened to her? Would Mickelle spend a lifetime wondering?

"We'll find her," Damon said for the third time. He had already talked to someone on the phone about it, and Mickelle realized that he was good at giving orders—not a bad thing as long as he used the talent wisely. She bet that Bryan's refusal to comply with his desire ate at him more than he was willing to admit. So far he had been fairly patient.

At least Damon had the resources to search for Jennie Anne.

They drove up the long driveway in silence. "Well, look who's here," Damon said in amazement.

Mickelle gazed out toward the house, and gasped in surprise. "Jennie Anne!" She began opening the door.

"Wait a minute! I'll stop in front. No need for you to have to run across the driveway—your leg."

Mickelle was out the minute he stopped. Forgetting her sore leg, she ran up to the front steps where Jennie Anne sat with a paper in her small hands. Her battered yellow backpack was at her feet and a large green duffle sat next to her on the step. She seemed calm enough, but her freckled face was pale and splotched with tears. Luminous brown eyes, rimmed with red, lifted to Mickelle's. In the next second Jennie Anne was in Mickelle's arms, and began sobbing uncontrollably, her former calm completely dissolved. Mickelle resisted her own urge to cry in an effort to soothe the little girl. She held onto Jennie Anne tightly, rocking her like a small baby. "It's okay. I promise. It's okay now. You're never going back. Not ever."

After Mickelle had calmed her down, Jennie Anne drew away slightly, and pressed a now-rumpled note into her hands. "I sat here to read it. I can't read all the words. It's messy."

Mickelle's eyes scanned the scrawled message, her breath coming more quickly.

> *I'm going away. Won't be back. Take good care of*
> *Jennie Anne. She's yours now.*
> *Nedda Chase*
>
> *P.S. I never hit her. It was Troy.*

So bare and abrupt, but it was everything Mickelle could have hoped for. She hugged Jennie Anne again. "I love you," she told her fiercely.

Damon came up next to them. He read the note, then held out his arms. "Well, don't I get a hug, too?"

Jennie Anne gave him a tremulous smile and then hugged him tightly. A lone tear slipped out of her eye.

"This calls for a celebration, don't you think, Kelle?" Damon asked, winking at her with one of his marvelous amber eyes. "Now that we have all our kids back at home. And it's high time we introduce Jennie Anne to my famous Sunday chocolate chip cookies." He picked Jennie Anne up high and set her on his shoulders. "How about helping your mother with Jennie Anne's bags, eh Bry?"

As they bent for Jennie Anne's things, Mickelle marveled at how quickly her mood had changed. One moment everything was desperate, and then a miracle occurred.

She was about to follow the others into the house when she felt an odd sensation. *As though I'm being watched.* Her eyes went instinctively to the camera she knew was hidden in the light near the front door. *Of course,* she thought. All the same, she scanned the driveway with her eyes. There was nothing out of the ordinary.

With a shake of her head, she entered the house.

CHAPTER 22

Troy studied the man who sat across from him in the cheap motel. Two days had passed since his mother had stolen his cash and cut out on him. But now this man before him, the educated fancy boy he had grown to detest over the past few weeks, was going to give it back to him—one way or another.

"I'm sure it's your niece," Colton Scofield said. "Your mother and a friend dropped her off."

"She handed the brat over just like that?"

"Appears so. I've been watching the house. Can't get too close, though. They've got cameras."

"So what's the plan? They ain't gonna give *me* the kid. Not for the asking, anyway." Troy knew the other man had a plan, no question of that. The ten thousand dollars Colton had already given him might be gone with his no-good, stealing cheat of a mother, but there would be more where that came from. A lot more. Only they wouldn't be able to extort money from the rich guy for Jennie Anne's custody as they had first intended. So what else was there?

"The school." Colton sat back in the squeaky chair and steepled his hands on the formica table top. "We'll grab her at the school. And not just her but Wolfe's daughter. We leave a little note, and they pay up. Simple."

"What about the cops?"

"Relax. I'll take care of the planning. They won't call in the cops. They'll be too worried about the kids."

Troy shrugged. He didn't give a hoot what happened to the kids, just as long as he got his money. With enough he'd go to Mexico and lay low for a while—live like a king. There was nothing connecting this mess to him. The word on the street was that they were searching for fancy boy, not him. So after he was sure he was in the clear, he would go find his mom and get back his money. Or what was left of it.

"Look." Colton leaned forward. "The only thing you have to do is nab the girls. Get them to the van. Then we drive to this vacant farm I've arranged to use. The rest—the note, the ransom—leave it all to me. I figure we can get a million at least."

"I get half."

"You get a quarter."

"I get half or I'm walking." Troy put on his mean face. "Remember it's me who took all the risks with that broad. Me who got kicked. And plugged in the eye. You didn't tell me she was such a strong witch. Didn't expect it since she's such a looker." Troy had punched fancy boy in the eye for that when they had met up later, just to even stuff up a bit. "And that guy of hers—if I hadn't found that rock to clobber him with, I'd be back in the slammer. Bottom line—I deserve half after what I went through."

They stared, each mentally weighing the other. They had similar builds—short for men, but with strong, well-proportioned muscles. Troy knew, though, that he was stronger physically, and harder in his resolve where it really counted; for all his boastful scams, Colton was weak. It was this weakness Troy planed to exploit. Big time. When he walked away from the entire mess he would have *all* the money, every single penny. With any luck, his former partner would be in jail.

"Okay," Colton muttered.

Troy grinned to himself. "So when we doing it?"

"Friday. I need a few days to get things planned."

"I need some cash."

"I gave you ten thousand."

"I got expenses." Same thing he had told his mother. He still couldn't believe she had found the money and split. No way would he admit that to this fancy boy. "Anyhows that rock I got you was worth more than ten times that."

"Okay, but this advance is coming out of your share."

Troy almost laughed at the irony. "Sure. Whatever."

He watched as Colton counted out three hundred dollars from his wallet.

"I'll wait to hear from you." Troy began whistling as he started for his Chevy.

* * * * *

As good as his word, Damon had made an appointment with someone to outfit Mickelle. A very young-looking woman appeared on her doorstep Tuesday morning, dressed in a smart cranberry suit and carrying a large briefcase. "Are you Ms. Hansen?" she asked, her black eyes sparkling in the outside light.

"Call me Mickelle. Would you like to come in?"

"I'm Cindi Hecho—Cindi with an I."

"Hello, Cindi." Mickelle led the short, dark-haired woman into the sitting room. "Hecho—what nationality is that?"

"Well, my parents are from Korea originally," Cindi said, seating herself gracefully next to Mickelle on the couch. "But I was born here. My, that's a beautiful piano."

Mickelle glanced over at the adjoining music room which had been built in the bottom half of a turret. "Yes, it's a Steinway. Handmade."

"Nice. Do you know how to play?"

"I'm taking lessons. My, uh, Damon's former wife played."

"I see. I don't play at all. But I do enjoy listening." Cindi opened her briefcase. "Well, I guess we should get right down to work. From what Mr. Wolfe said, you need quite a few things."

"Just a dress really," protested Mickelle.

"Let me tell you how this works." Cindi placed a large stack of laminated four-color brochures on the coffee table. "I'm what you call a fashion consultant. Together we look over these and decide what you need and then I go get it from my suppliers. Some basic items I already have out in the van, and some I'll bring back later. If anything needs adjusting, I'll either do it, or have it done. If you want something made just for you, we can do that too, though we'll need a few weeks notice on something like that."

"Something ready-made will be fine." Mickelle felt a trifle overwhelmed, but she knew that agreeing to be a wealthy man's wife would mean changes. Her wardrobe was a place she could begin.

The bell sounded, and Mickelle stood, trying to move graciously as she had seen Cindi do. At least her limp was gone, though her leg still sported the ugly bruise from her fight with Bryan. "It's probably my sister. I hope you don't mind, but I asked her to come over and help."

"Oh, no—the more the merrier."

Brionney was at the door, for once without the twins and Rosalie. "Mom agreed to watch them," she said with a grin. "Imagine! Shopping in your own home. Can you believe us?"

They giggled together as Brionney scanned the entryway. "Gosh, I always forget how big this place is until I come here."

"I know just how you feel. We have fifteen thousand square feet—I don't see how we could ever use more. I didn't even know there were houses this big in Utah."

"I know, but from what I've seen, Damon actually lives quite modestly compared to a lot of rich guys."

"I agree." Mickelle hesitated before adding, "I hate to admit it, but I have really fallen in love with the turrets. It's like living in a castle."

Brionney gave a long sigh. "Ah, a fairy tale come to life. You can't beat that. And to think it was all my idea."

"Yeah, right. Come on, my consultant is waiting." They burst into laughter again. Mickelle was very glad that Brionney had come.

Cindi smiled at the newcomer as they entered the sitting room. "Hello. You're just in time. I thought we might start with wedding dresses."

"What?" Mickelle arched an eyebrow. "I bet Damon put you up to that."

A telltale flush spread over Cindi's olive skin. "Well, yes, but if we begin now, you can have the dress specifically made for you."

"Well, let's get to it then." Brionney enthusiastically reached for a brochure.

They spent a wonderful morning planning and picking out Mickelle's wardrobe. Several times Cindi went out to her grey van for sets of clothing which Mickelle tried on in front of the full-length mirror in the downstairs bathroom. There were no prices, and Mickelle didn't ask.

She enjoyed herself thoroughly. Cindi had brought all sorts of clothes in her size and Mickelle was surprised to see how wonderful the outfits looked on her. She chose several pantsuits, a few suit dresses, and a blue and white Sunday dress that brought out the blue in her eyes. Then, with encouragement from Brionney, she added four pairs of shoes, sweats, two new swimming suits, three sweaters, and a pair of designer jeans. For her dinner date with Damon she opted for an off-white, two-piece-look dress that featured a close-fitting beaded top and a long, full satin skirt.

"You've got just the right height for that dress," Cindi said. "It doesn't look half as good on people my size."

"Tell me about it," moaned Brionney. "And now that I'm weaning the twins I've gained a few pounds."

"I've got something here for you, too." Cindi pulled out another brochure from her seemingly endless supply. "You just need this type of dress. See how it curves inward at your feet? And that cut diminishes the waistline."

"I do like it," Brionney said admiringly.

So in the end they both bought a dress, though neither was able to keep it since Cindi didn't have Brionney's size and Mickelle's dress needed hemming. Mickelle felt like a princess when trying on her dress and swirling around in the full skirt. She could hardly wait until Friday night!

She had tentatively chosen a wedding dress as well from one of the brochures, but wanted to put off a final decision for a few weeks. The dress was a close-fitting column dress, made with white satin and a white lace overlay. It had long sleeves, and once hemmed it would just brush the tops of her matching satin shoes. The wedding dress was nothing like the bulky one she had worn with Riley, but simple and elegant. Her excitement grew as she thought about wearing it in the temple with Damon as they exchanged vows.

"I'll bring that wedding dress and a few similar models when I return on Friday morning with your dress," Cindi promised. She held out an invoice for Mickelle to sign. "This just means that you received these items. A copy of this plus the itemized bill will go to Mr. Wolfe. He said to tell you this was his wedding gift."

"Thank you," Mickelle said.

Cindi grinned. "Not me—him. Although it has been a lot of fun, hasn't it? I love my job."

After Cindi was gone Brionney sighed and gave Mickelle a hug. "Well, I'd best get going as well. Those kids are a handful for Mom. Thanks for inviting me. I've never spent so much money on one dress, but boy, am I going to look good." She strutted out the door while Mickelle laughed.

Brionney stopped and turned as she reached the steps. "Oh, so when *are* you and Damon getting married anyway?"

"I—I don't know yet. I'm sort of waiting to see how everything gets settled with Jennie Anne."

Brionney stared at her for a long time before shaking her head. "No, that's not it. You love him. You wouldn't let that stand in your way. His lawyers'll take care of Jennie Anne. What's really wrong?"

"I never could hide much from you." Mickelle leaned against the door frame. Then, remembering the cameras by the door, she motioned her sister back into the house.

In the family room, she felt secure enough to speak. "You know when Riley died how I thought I was pregnant—hoped that I was pregnant? Well, I thought now Damon and I could . . ."

"Have a baby."

"He had an operation."

"Sometimes they can be reversed."

"It's not just that. I don't think he really has the need for another child. Not that he wouldn't love one if I got pregnant. But I don't want to do it just for me. I want his baby, but I want us to do it together."

"Have you told him how you feel?"

"We haven't talked about it much. But we will. Things keep getting in the way."

Brionney nodded sympathetically. "How is Bryan?"

"Sullen. But at least he's not acting out. The contract helped, I think. He hasn't said much to anyone, though."

"Damon's a good man. Bryan will come to see that."

"I hope it's soon."

* * * * * *

Mickelle pondered her dilemma as she went to pick up the kids from school. The more she thought about it, the more positive she felt that she had to talk with Damon soon. *We will work it out.* She felt confident in her new maroon pantsuit, and grateful that Cindi had given her a little speech on *not* saving the outfits for a special day, but to enjoy the clothes immediately. "Too many women save things for a special day," she said. "But why not make every day special?"

She arrived at Forbes early enough to help with Jennie Anne's reading group. Twice weekly she had been coming in to read with them, and was pleased with both Belle and Jennie Anne's progress. In past weeks Jennie Anne had surpassed most children in the class in all areas of learning except the social aspect. Her mathematical abilities continued to delight and impress her teacher, though Jennie Anne refused to say more than two words to Mrs. Palmer personally. So far, she spoke only at reading time, or to answer questions. Nothing more. But today the teacher hurried over to Mickelle. "I can't believe the change in Jennie Anne," she whispered. "She talked to me today. She talked!"

"What did she say?"

"She asked me if I like the color blue."

"Her favorite color," Mickelle murmured. She glanced at the child, busily writing on a piece of paper like all the other students in the class. "I hoped that she would open up to you, now that she's with us."

Mrs. Palmer smiled. "You were right." They stood in silence watching Jennie Anne for a minute before the teacher added, "Oh yeah, and the school counselor also had a chat with her as we discussed. He'll be contacting you personally, but he asked me to let you know that he will speak on your behalf in the custody hearing, if you like."

"That would be great. We feel certain they'll let her stay with us, but we plan to track down the aunt to get her signature on official papers. We've got somebody on that now."

Mrs. Palmer's eyes gleamed with approval. "I'm so glad. She deserves it. And I keep thinking that if it wasn't for Belle and you, she would have ended up . . ." She blinked the tears away. "Well, you know as well as I do."

"I feel a little guilty that I thought it was her aunt," Mickelle confessed.

"Well, it could so easily have been."

"I still don't know what made her leave."

"Jennie Anne hasn't said anything to you?"

"Just that her uncle was back. I don't think Nedda told her much. And every time we talk about it, Jennie Anne gets nervous."

"Well, who can blame her? I'm sure that over time she'll open up." Mrs. Palmer raised her voice. "Okay, class, it's time to divide for our reading groups."

After school let out Mickelle drove by her sister's to pick up Bryan. In order to save her an extra trip to American Fork he had agreed to wait there every day after school. She planned to move all the children to a closer school after she was married, but meanwhile it was a lot of driving—two times in the morning to take first Bryan and then the younger children, and another trip in the afternoon. She had also toyed with the idea of moving back to her own house, since Colton was likely long gone, despite his threats, but Damon would hear none of it.

"We don't know that he won't come back," he had insisted last night.

"But seriously, Damon. What have I got that he could possibly want?"

He nuzzled her ear. "Everything. Besides, Belle would be heartbroken."

So she had agreed to stay at Wolfe Estates. She admitted to herself that it would be difficult to move back into her small house, with no housekeeper or cook to make dinner. *I'm spoiled,* she thought. *Who would have ever expected that? Me, a woman who could barely afford a washing machine last May.*

Bryan greeted her with stoic indifference as he had since she had brought him home from juvenile detention, but she noticed that he loosened up with his brother and Belle. Especially Belle.

She smiled. Bryan might not know it, but Belle could be the answer to their deadlock. Mickelle knew firsthand that cute, intelligent, exasperating, darling, annoying Belle could change attitudes by doing nothing more than just being herself. In fact, she had been a big factor in Mickelle's decision to trust Damon in the first place.

Once at home the children scattered. Mickelle went up to her room to finish hanging up her new clothes in the walk-in closet, and clean out the worn or outdated outfits she had clung to out of necessity. She sang as she worked, feeling content. Her earlier confidence had remained, and she believed she was finally ready to get on with her life.

Cammy rang the intercom to let her know that she had arrived. "Don't worry, Tanner let me in. I just wanted to tell you that dinner will be ready at six-thirty sharp. But I'll have to leave right after, so if Mr. Wolfe is late . . ."

"He won't be. But if so, I can take care of it," Mickelle assured her. Lately, Cammy had been staying to put the food on the table and to watch their reaction to her low-fat creations.

Finished in her room, Mickelle wandered down the hall to see what the girls were up to, knowing she would probably find them in the bedroom they now shared. The door was only partially open, but when Mickelle tried to walk in, the door refused to open further. "Belle, what—?" The door gave and Mickelle fell into the room.

The scene before her was more astonishing than anything she had ever beheld, even after living with two boys. Every toy Belle owned was off the shelves or out of the large wooden chest. The closet was also gaping open and clothes were strewn about. Only occasional patches of the wood floor and throw rugs were visible.

Mickelle picked her way through the jumble. "Belle, what's all this?"

"I was deciding what to wear for Halloween tomorrow."

"Where's Jennie Anne?"

"She and Jeremy are playing *Candyland*. I didn't want to play."

"I thought you already decided to be a princess."

"Yeah, but what kind of princess? I could be Cinderella, Snow White, Sleeping Beauty, Belle from Beauty and the Beast—I should be her 'cause that's my name, but the Cinderella costume is much more beautiful."

Mickelle bent and picked up a pair of stretch pants. "Why are these out?"

"It's pretty cold at night, you know." Belle sounded as though she were speaking to a toddler. "Dad's gonna make me wear stuff under the dress."

"Well, that's wise." Mickelle knew that Belle was excited. In Anchorage, Damon hadn't felt comfortable allowing her to go trick-or-treating, since he hadn't personally known many of his neighbors, so this was Belle's first time.

Mickelle was still scanning the room when her eyes came to rest on the mixing bowl in Belle's plastic kitchenette. It was caked with a watery flour mixture, and there was flour dusting the floor and the entire kitchenette. Belle was also powdered, as were her stuffed bear and her plastic horse. Despite the huge mess, Mickelle stifled an urge to laugh at how adorable the child looked.

She and Damon had disagreed over whether or not Belle should be allowed to have this sort of thing in her room. He had maintained that there was no fun if you couldn't use water and real "stuff" to play with, and Mickelle had finally agreed to allow it if Belle was held responsible for the cleanup. This would be a *big* cleanup.

"Well, Belle, dinner will be ready in an hour and I think that you had better get cracking."

"Cracking?"

"Cleaning up."

"Mrs. Mertz can do it."

"Mrs. Mertz is off now."

"Then tomorrow."

Mickelle shook her head. "That wasn't the deal. Mrs. Mertz is not your personal servant."

"But Dad pays her to clean."

"The house, not your room. Not a mess like this anyway."

"But she always cleans it when I do this."

"Not anymore."

Belle's lower lip jutted out. "I don't have to obey you 'cause you're not my real mother."

The unexpected words were like a blow to Mickelle's heart, though she knew from other stepparents that it was inevitable. She forced herself to be calm. "I know that I'm not your *real* mother, but I love you like a real mother does, and like it or not, after your father and I get married, I'll be the only mother you've got."

"Well, I don't need a mother!" Belle shouted, her round face turning rosy with ire.

Mickelle was beginning to feel angry herself. In an instant of exasperation, she said, "No? Well, maybe I should just leave! Would you like that? Maybe I should just get out of your way." She doubted she was making the situation any better. *Control,* she told herself. Aloud, she added, "But you better think about it hard, because I bet if you think *real* hard, you'll decide that even I'm better than no mother at all. Aren't I? Well? Don't you love me just a little?" Mickelle held her breath. Belle was temperamental. She might tell her to get lost and then where would she be?

Boy, had she ever been right about the challenges of joining two families! First there was Bryan's trouble, and now this run-in with her darling Belle.

Belle glared at her, brow creased. "Humph!" she said after a long pause. "I guess I still do like you a tiny little bit." She raised her thumb and forefinger to show Mickelle just how small. "But I don't have to do what you say!"

"How about we do it together? And then maybe after dinner we can make real cookies. What do you say?" She wouldn't have used this tactic with the boys; she simply would have demanded that they obey or else. But that never worked with Belle. The other alternative was to threaten Belle with the horse her father had promised her if she behaved, and Mickelle didn't want to do that, either. She wanted Belle to obey out of love.

She wasn't fooling Belle, not for a minute. Belle understood only too well that making the cookies still required her to clean her room. Silently, Mickelle prayed for guidance.

"All right," Belle said with a disgusted sigh. "I guess so."

They bent to the task, Mickelle purposefully slowing her efforts so that Belle did most of the cleaning. As they worked they talked about Halloween, and what princess Belle should be. At last everything was back in its place and relatively clean, except for the mixing bowl Belle held in her hands to take down to the kitchen.

"There." Hand on her hips, Mickelle surveyed their work. "Now that looks like a princess's room, don't you think?"

"I guess it does look kind of good."

"Shall we go downstairs?"

"Yeah."

At the door, Belle paused and stared gravely up into Mickelle's face. "I really do like you a lot, Mickelle. And I don't want you to ever go away."

Mickelle felt terrible for even having made the suggestion. Since Belle's birth she had been with nannies—and they had all eventually left. *How can I have forgotten that even for a moment?*

She knelt down in front of Belle, seeing again a glimpse of the vision she had seen so many months before, on the day of Riley's funeral. "I shouldn't have said that, Belle. I would never leave you. You know, I love your Daddy very much, but even before I met him, I dreamed about you."

"Me?"

"Yes. I saw you in a dream. I was holding you, and I knew that you were going to be my little girl. I knew it from the moment I saw you."

Belle was obviously impressed, but then her brow furrowed. "So when are you going to get married? I miss daddy being here."

Mickelle realized how unfair she'd been to hold everyone in limbo. "How about at Thanksgiving time? That's only a month away."

Belle shuffled her feet excitedly. "Oh, I can't wait to tell Dad!"

"No!"

Belle gazed at her sharply.

"I mean, I should be the one."

"Okay." Belle gave Mickelle one of her angelic smiles before walking down the hall.

Mickelle followed her, feeling almost giddy with her new commitment. This was the right thing. So why did she feel so nervous?

CHAPTER 23

Cammy glanced up as Mickelle came into the kitchen. "My special meatloaf is nearly ready; it only needs a few minutes more in the oven."

"I can take it out," Mickelle offered. "You go if you need to. And I'll also take a plate down to Stan. Mrs. Mertz is out, but we'll leave hers in the fridge." Even when she was home, Mrs. Mertz preferred to eat her dinner in her own large room in front of her TV set.

Cammy smiled and began removing her apron. "Thanks. I really do need to get going. Tonight's Aaron's birthday, and I want to have a surprise ready for him when he comes home from class."

"Go right ahead. Hope it works out."

"It will." She started for the door, but paused and faced Mickelle again. "How are you feeling? I mean, your leg and all?"

For a minute, Mickelle had to stop and think what she had told Cammy about her thigh. She certainly wasn't advertising that her son had gone berserk on her, but she had let the staff know she had been hurt. Most assumed she had tripped on the shoe shelf in the mudroom. "My leg? Oh, it's good. I still have a whopping bruise, but the swelling's gone way down."

"I noticed you weren't limping."

"Nope. Thanks for asking."

"I—uh . . ." The woman still hesitated, tugging at the elastic band that held back her hair.

"What is it?"

Cammy shifted nervously. "It's just that Aaron is graduating in December. He got a job back in Minnesota where my family is from.

It's a good thing with the baby coming and all—we can live in my parents' basement apartment. There's even an old couple next door who would hire me to cook part-time."

"So you're giving me notice?"

"Yes." She gave a sheepish nod. "I hate to do it, you know. Damon's been so good to me and Aaron. I don't know what we'd have done if I hadn't found a job like this—dinner five times a week plus the grocery shopping. It's really not a lot of work for what he's paying. And I've enjoyed it. It's been good since the pregnancy, too, since I'm only sick in the morning."

"You don't have to feel bad, Cammy. You need to do what's best for you and your family. I think I'll be able to handle things."

"I knew you could. It's just—I didn't want to leave you in the lurch, what with the wedding and Jennie Anne and all. But everything should be taken care of by December, don't you think?"

"Sure. That's just great. I'm happy for you. It's good to be near your mother when you have your first baby."

"I think so, too." Cammy backed toward the door. "Well, I'd better go. Good-bye."

"Good-bye!" Mickelle called after her. "And enjoy yourself!"

Mickelle hummed as she put dinner on the table. She knew many women didn't enjoy this chore, but she derived a satisfaction from the ritual. Secretly, she was glad Cammy had given notice, though she would miss her company.

Mickelle walked over to the intercom that would send her voice throughout the house. "Kids, dinner's ready!" She knew it would be a few minutes until they all gathered, and by then Damon should be home.

Two strong arms crept suddenly around her from behind. For a brief, terrifying moment, Mickelle was back in her small house fighting a masked intruder. Her heart banged fearfully inside her chest.

Then warm lips caressed her neck.

"Damon!" she exclaimed with relief.

"Who else would it be?"

She didn't reply, but he read the truth in her eyes. "I'm sorry. But you're safe here."

"It's okay. I'm okay." She hugged him, and lifted her lips to his. Instant electricity flowed through her body, causing every nerve to tingle in anticipation. She pushed herself closer to him and their kiss deepened.

"Daddy, Daddy!"

Mickelle sighed, but Damon chuckled and said in a low voice, "It's just as well. They keep us honest."

"Daddy!" Belle threw herself into his arms. "Isn't it wonderful? I can't wait to be a flower girl!"

"What?"

Belle looked anxiously at Mickelle. "You did tell him, didn't you?—that you're getting married by Thanksgiving."

"I hadn't gotten around to—" Her words were choked off by Damon's hug. He picked her up and spun her around.

"Thanksgiving, Thanksgiving," sang Damon. "I'm going to be married by Thanksgiving! Oh, Kelle." He kissed her again in front of their growing audience.

Belle and Jennie Anne clapped, while Tanner and Jeremy made catcalls. Bryan walked stiffly out of the kitchen. He didn't say a word, but Mickelle saw his angry glare.

Damon's smile faltered only slightly. "I'll go after him."

Tanner was already out the door. "Let me," he called over his shoulder. "You guys go ahead and eat."

* * * * *

Anger welled up inside Bryan until he wanted to burst out with every swear word he knew. He clenched his fists. His rage made him so furious that he wanted to break things or punch someone. Anyone.

Even your mom?

Even the thought left a nasty taste in his mouth. No, he didn't want to hurt his mom. It was Damon he wanted to kill, but if he made one false move, they would call the cops and he would have to go back to juvenile detention. He shivered, though he still felt flushed with his rage.

"You want to hit someone?" a voice challenged.

Bryan swivelled on his heel to see that Tanner had followed him into the game room.

"If you do, then you'd better try me." Tanner's lean face looked mean, without a trace of his usual good humor.

"I just don't want to eat. What's it to you?"

"I'll tell you what," Tanner said. "It's your mother. I hate the way you glare at her. And I still can't believe that you hit her. Your own mother."

Bryan shook his finger at Tanner, forgetting for a moment that the older boy had nearly a foot and twenty pounds on him. "You stay out of this. It's none of your business!"

"It is my business," Tanner returned, his voice increasing in volume. "You heard them, they're getting married. Duh! That means we're going to be a family."

"No we're not! Just because *they* get married doesn't mean *we're* family."

"It does to me."

"I'll never accept Damon!"

"So? Who cares? Not me. You're the one with the problem."

"My dad's dead!" Bryan yelled, not knowing where it fit in the conversation, but somehow needing to voice the thought.

"Well, my mother's dead!" Tanner retorted. "I watched her get sick and die. When all the other boys were playing with their moms in the park, or their mothers were cheering for them at baseball games, my mother was in bed dying of cancer. She couldn't even get up to make dinner." Angry tears started down Tanner's face and he wiped them impatiently away with the backs of his hands. "Sometimes I can almost remember a time when she wasn't sick, but then it's gone, and I see her lying on that stupid bed, getting skinnier . . . losing her hair. And I would stay awake in bed at night hearing her cry and wish there was something I could do for her." Tanner paused for a breath before rushing on. "I wish like anything that she was here, but she can't be! She can't! You ought to be grateful you even have a mother. But instead you hit her." This last was delivered with a scorn that ate into Bryan's heart.

"And I don't care how you feel about my dad," Tanner continued, "but you better stop hurting your mother—I won't let you hurt her. Not even her feelings. She's wonderful . . . and so's my dad, but you're just too stupid to see it. Why don't you grow up and realize that you're not the only one who matters here?"

"Leave me alone," Bryan muttered.

"I will. We all will. But you're the one who's losing out. Man, don't you see it? We have a chance to make something great! Something that really means something! But, no, you're too selfish."

Bryan watched Tanner leave the game room, banging the door on his way out. For a moment, Bryan felt lost. Once he had so admired Tanner, had considered himself lucky to have him as a friend. What had gone so terribly wrong?

Hot tears burned the backs of his eyes and bitterness stung his throat. *My dad's dead.*

So was Tanner's mother. He had watched her die.

What's more, Tanner wished his mother was here. Could Bryan say the same about his father?

Bryan tried to see his father's face, to remember what he looked like, but he couldn't get a clear picture. What he did see was a series of images—playing Game Boy on the couch, fishing on the lake, soccer in the yard. Then came a vision that was more clear than the rest: his father yelling at Jeremy for opening a drawer.

Bryan doubled over with anguish as he recalled the instance, sinking to the floor by the pool table. *Jeremy had finished eating and wanted to draw a picture of Pikachu, his favorite Pokémon, but Dad was still eating dinner at the bar. He sat in front of the drawer holding the markers. Jeremy reached in to get a marker and Dad slammed the drawer, narrowly missing Jeremy's fingers. Dad began to yell. Mom put her arms around Jeremy, comforting him, hustling him away.*

More about his father came to the surface of his memory, disjointed bits that weren't as clear as the scene with Jeremy. *Mom's face. Empty, yearning, wanting. Tears in the night, sobbing. His father's scornful voice . . . degrading . . . shameful.*

Bryan clutched his stomach, willing the images to fade. They refused to leave, but instead narrowed on the times when his father's wrath had turned on him. *Dad's face going red as he yelled at him for scaring away the fish, for not being quiet when Dad wanted to watch TV. Yelling . . . always yelling . . . or sneering. Disgust. And always the question: why doesn't my Dad love me? What's wrong with me?*

Bryan closed his eyes against the memories.

"Bryan, Bryan?" The soft voice penetrated his visions. Small fingers slid along his arms. "Bryan, are you okay? Tell me you're okay!"

He forced his eyes open to see Belle kneeling before him where he crouched by the pool table. "I'm okay," he managed, his voice sounding like rocks grinding together.

She put her arms around him and Bryan hugged her back. Her love flowed throw him like a river of water, dousing the flames of his hurt and shame. "I'm sorry you're mad," she whispered. "I wish you wouldn't hate my daddy."

"I just wish mine wasn't dead," he answered, though suddenly he wasn't sure it was true.

"I don't remember my mom much," Belle said. "She was sick all the time. But I love Mickelle. I want her to take care of me until I go back to heaven with my own mommy."

"I know." Bryan vowed then that he would try to fight the anger and confusion inside him, if only to make Belle happy. He only hoped he could succeed.

* * * * *

Fortunately, dinner was saved by Belle, who disappeared halfway through the meal and returned with a subdued Bryan. Mickelle didn't know what had transpired between any of the children, but she hoped they could all survive the growing pains. Only Jeremy seemed completely oblivious to the undercurrents of emotion.

After dinner, Damon took Mickelle's hand and they went into his study and shut the door. "Okay," he said. "We need to talk."

"I'm not sure where to begin." She settled on the black leather sofa next to the bookcase. Damon sat with her.

"You want another child, isn't that it?" His tone wasn't accusing, but concerned.

"Yes, and you don't."

"It's not that."

"I know. You just never thought about it. You don't feel a lack in your life."

He took her hand. "Why does it mean so much to you? Can you help me understand?"

"I've thought a lot about this." She met his gaze, willing him to feel her sincerity. "At first I thought it was because I craved another baby. You know, the miracle of the birth, the new baby smell of them. The little clothes. The hugs." She sighed. "But it's not that at all. I don't crave having a baby so much as I crave having something that's yours."

"You have my heart." He touched the ring on her finger.

"I know, but after . . ."

"You're worried about our sealings to Charlotte and Riley, aren't you?"

Mickelle tried to explain. "It's not that." She held him with her eyes, willing him to understand. "I love you so much. It almost scares me how much. It fills me—my whole heart." She made a circular motion over her chest with her hand. "And if I go by what's happened between us so far, my feelings are only going to increase."

"But that's good—that's exactly how I feel about you."

She took a breath. His amber eyes were so startling, so expressive. She loved him so much. "I know that we hope to be together forever, but we don't know about Riley and Charlotte. They . . . they will have their chance to progress to gain eternal life, and what if . . . Well, I feel now that we'll be together, but if things work out that we are with them instead of each other—" He tried to interrupt, but she held up her hand. "No, let me continue. I believe that the Lord will give us happiness, no matter what. I *know* He will. Even though it hurts so much to think of not being with you." Tears gathered in her eyes now and she tried unsuccessfully to blink them away. His features were unclear, but she still felt his eyes boring into hers, holding her in place. Supporting her. "I think why I want a baby so much is because I want something that is yours and for you to have something that is mine—no matter what happens in the next life."

Damon's eyes showed his understanding, but he shook his head. "I can't think of an eternity without you, Kelle. I just can't. You're a part of me. But regardless of what happens after this life or whether or not we have another baby, I'll be raising Jer. And Bry, too. I will laugh with them, play with them, cry with them. There will always be a piece of them in me, and me in them. I will always be interested in their welfare. The same holds true with you and Belle and Tan. We will raise these children together. They are ours."

When he put it that way, Mickelle could hardly argue, except the yearning inside didn't go away. She took his hands. "I know all that with my mind, but in my heart. . . I want something even more, something that is *only* yours and mine, not Riley's or Charlotte's—not one tiny bit." She shrugged. "I know it sounds selfish, but I want something together that we won't share with them or with anyone else. A bond that will never end."

His eyes searched hers. "Oh, Kelle. We have that, don't you see? I love you, and I'll love you forever. We'll always share a unique connection. I promise you that. What more can I say? If having another child makes you believe, then let's do it. I'm willing to try, to have surgery, if that's what it means. Anything." His tongue wet his lips nervously as he waited for her reply. She followed the motion with her eyes.

"Give me a little time. I want to think about it some more. Pray."

"We're still getting married?" His eyes suddenly reminded her of a little boy.

She smiled and placed a playful kiss on his lips. "Of course! How about a few days after Thanksgiving so that we won't miss sharing the holiday with the kids?"

"I have a better idea. How about we get married a few days before Thanksgiving, and we delay leaving for Europe until after the holiday?" He lifted her hand and kissed it, beginning at her fingertips and working his way up her arm. By the time he arrived at her neck, Mickelle agreed that his plan was definitely better than hers.

"Okay, you're on," she squealed, as his breath caused goose bumps to shudder throughout her body.

"Yoohoo!" Damon shouted in triumph. He sprang to his feet and started for the door.

"Where are you going?"

"I'm going to round up the kids and take a swim." He flexed his arms several times. "Yes, I think I definitely need to work off some steam."

She laughed. "Good, because I bought two new swimsuits today." Now was as good a time as any to overcome the aversion she had to the pool house. Damon loved swimming and so did all the children.

He pulled her to him one last time, kissing her thoroughly. *This is heaven,* Mickelle thought. *What could possibly go wrong now?*

* * * * *

From a group of close-growing trees on the neighboring property, Colton Scofield watched the family play in the pool through large glass windows covering one wall of the pool house. His warm breath made white clouds in the cold air. He lowered the binoculars. Mickelle seemed so happy.

He frowned. She had been happy with him, too.

Wiping his hands on his black outfit, he ran across the yard and down the long drive to his car, his path illuminated by the bright moonlight. A dog barked in the stillness.

"She made the wrong choice," he muttered. "The wrong choice." He would show her just how wrong.

CHAPTER 24

On Halloween night Damon and Mickelle took the younger kids trick-or-treating, while Tanner and Bryan stayed home to give out (and eat) a huge bowl of treats. Belle and Jennie Anne were adorable in their princess costumes—Cinderella and Snow White—and Jeremy made a very believable Harry Potter. Mickelle had made the black costume herself last week and already it was showing wear from Jeremy's constant use.

The evening was cold, but bearable, and the kids had fun. The biggest tragedy was Jeremy losing the magic wand he had so carefully painted. To stave off tears, Mickelle and Damon promised to help him make a new one. Back at home they ate chili and hot chocolate before digging into their bags of treats, carefully checked over by Mickelle and Damon.

Jennie Anne ate only three of her candies, and stored the rest in her room. Mickelle noticed that she had a tendency to save everything, but in light of where she had spent the past few years of her life, that wasn't a big surprise. The counselor Jennie Anne was seeing assured Mickelle that the phase would pass. Until then, he advised Mickelle to allow Jennie Anne to hoard anything she wanted.

They hadn't yet found a trace of Nedda Chase, except a plane ticket to Arizona. There, she had completely disappeared. Their attorney didn't think her absence mattered since there was a clear case for abandonment, and the note proved Nedda's intention to transfer guardianship. They were undergoing the state scrutiny now, but Mickelle was sure it was only a matter of time until they were granted full guardianship. Maybe then they could look into something more permanent.

Life was full of possibilities.

* * * * *

"Everything ready?" Troy asked. His nerves were tight and were growing tighter with each passing moment, but the rest of him felt good. Real good. He had tossed back a couple of shots of straight whisky and was ready for action. He flexed his fingers, then cracked the knuckles.

"Yes, everything's perfect," Colton replied brusquely. "Just get them to the van. You'll have to time it right."

"I know, I know. But you sure that broad ain't going in?"

"It's Friday, isn't it? She only goes in on Tuesday and Thursdays. The other days she waits out in the car. You have to get them before they reach it. I'll provide a distraction if it's needed."

"What if she goes in anyhow?"

"She won't. She's been doing the same thing every day since she moved."

"There's always a chance."

"Then we abort and do it on Monday. But she won't, you'll see."

Troy got up from the chair and went to the bathroom. In front of the mirror, he adjusted the false beard he had purchased the day before. With the beard and a hair inset that made him look mostly bald, he doubted anyone could identify him even if they saw him grab the brats. Just in case, he would wear a thick jacket and dark glasses. That should be enough. He was ready.

* * * * *

Friday morning Mickelle awoke with a nervous twinge in her stomach. She knew the feeling was due to the fancy dinner being held that evening, where she would be introduced to all of Damon's most important clients and business associates. She! Damon's fiancée—it was almost too much to believe.

She shook her head, recalling all of the times Damon had found her with grass stains on her pants from playing soccer with the boys, dirt on her cheeks from working in the garden, or wilted hair from a water accident. She prayed that tonight she wouldn't mess up by dropping something down her front or tripping on her long dress.

Damon would pick her up at five-thirty and drive her to the hotel in Salt Lake. The dinner wasn't scheduled until six-thirty, but they would need to arrive early to be sure everything was perfect and to be on hand to greet the guests as they arrived. Despite the butterflies in her stomach, Mickelle was excited about the evening because tonight would be her first official appearance as Damon's fiancée. She was also glad that Brionney, as the wife of Damon's partner, would be by her side.

Cindi arrived at Wolfe Estates before lunch with most of Mickelle's ordered clothes, including the dress she would wear that night. "Try it on," she ordered. "I want to make sure it's right."

The dress was perfect, and as Mickelle spun before Cindi's admiring stare, she knew she was beautiful and that Damon would appreciate the dress.

"I wish I were as tall as you," Cindi moaned.

"That's funny, I always wanted to be short." Mickelle had always been on the tall side for a woman, like her grandmother.

"You should get your hair done."

"I'm going to. I have an appointment at Chloe's in American Fork at two. My sister goes there, and I've decided to give it a try."

"Well, good. I'm glad for that. I mean, you look really great, but a swept-up hairdo will take his breath away."

Mickelle bid farewell to Cindi on the front porch where Old Bobby was trimming off the drying miniature roses on the porch railing. She felt sad as he pruned off her favorite blossoms—the ones with the vivid red on the outer part of the petals and bright yellow on the inner portions. Of course, they would grow again next spring, along with all of the other miniature roses planted along the porch, but she hated to see him cut them off and sweep them away.

"What are these called, Bobby?" she asked the old man, rescuing a tiny rose that wasn't as wilted or dried as the others. "These are my favorite."

The groundskeeper straightened from his work and smiled appreciatively at her dress. The action revealed startling white teeth in his tanned and weathered face. He scooped up one of the red and yellow blossoms and twirled it in his gloved hand. "You don't know? Why, this here's a Jennie Anne."

"A Jennie Anne?"

His eyes crinkled as his smile widened. "Pretty, aren't they? Red and bright on the outside, soft and yellow on the inside. Just like our Jennie Anne, or like she will be."

Mickelle held the rose in her hand as Old Bobby went back to his work. *Jennie Anne,* she thought, *Jennie Anne.* Had the child been named after a rose? Had Jennie Anne's mother shared Mickelle's love of these flowers?

She could hardly wait to tell Jennie Anne. "Let's plant more of these in the spring, Bobby. Lots more. I want them all around the tennis court and by the patio."

Old Bobby nodded his gray head, never one to speak unless he was spoken to, and then only if he had something to say.

"Thank you."

Mickelle went inside the house to change back into her chocolate-colored pantsuit. With it she wore the pair of dark thick wool socks Damon had given her more than two months ago, his first gift ever, resulting from her first visit to his house. That day she had removed her shoes and found an embarrassing hole in her sock. Damon had laughed and shown her the even bigger hole in his. They were two of a kind, even from the beginning. Now every time she wore these socks, she felt his love as tangibly as if he were in the room.

A while later, after her appointment at Chloe's, Mickelle drove the Mercedes to Forbes to pick up Jeremy and the girls. She was in plenty of time to find a nice parking place out to the side of the building, where parents drove in to pick up their children. Parking quickly, her mind danced ahead to Brionney's where she would collect Bryan and then on to the house where she would change for her special date.

She hoped Tanner and Bryan wouldn't find something to fight about while she was gone. Since their conversation the other night at dinner, there was a new wariness between them that hadn't been there before. At least Bryan hadn't snapped at Tanner for a few days. *Count your many blessings,* she thought with a smile.

Jeremy reached the car first as he always did. Belle would still be in the classroom, chatting with her friends and Mrs. Palmer, while Jennie Anne urged her to hurry.

There's plenty of time, Mickelle thought, checking her watch. If she went in, she would likely get involved talking with Mrs. Palmer, and she couldn't do that today. She hummed as she waited, tapping her fingers on the steering wheel.

She loved this car, and had since the moment she had first sat inside—especially the hint of Damon's scent that still lingered in the comfortable leather seats. In fact, she hadn't driven the Metro but once since she had moved onto Wolfe Estates.

"Mom, that guy is staring at you."

"What?"

"Over there. The guy with the hat." Jeremy pointed to an old brown van four cars to their left.

"He's not."

"Well, he was."

Mickelle went back to her drumming, playing out the coming night's events in her head. She couldn't wait to see Damon's eyes when he saw her in that dress. Tonight she was going to the ball!

In the mirror, she checked her hair, swept up and teased into curls at the crown. It had turned out perfectly, but she wondered if she would ever be able to copy the style. Maybe she and Brionney could practice on each other.

Without thinking, she turned her head in the direction of the brown van. The driver's eyes met hers across the large space. She couldn't see what color they were or even the color of his hair. He glanced away immediately, but something about him was familiar. What?

She looked at him again, but he had donned dark glasses, though it wasn't particularly bright outside. Where had she seen him before? The odd impression left her unsettled.

Probably just one of the parents at the school.

But then the answer came to her like a revelation. "Colton!"

"What?"

"It's Colton!" Her heart had gone into overdrive in the space of one beat. "What could he—the girls! Jeremy, lock the door and stay right here until I come back!"

As she sprang from the car, she saw the driver of the brown van do the same. He yelled something across the narrow parking lot. Following his gaze, Mickelle saw a short, bearded, balding man in a big jacket near the door to the school. He had a hand on both Belle and Jennie Anne. When Belle saw Mickelle, she began struggling valiantly. She gave the stranger a sharp kick and pulled away. Screaming at the top of her lungs, she dashed toward Mickelle.

The car seemed to come out of nowhere, hurtling at Belle. With a dull thump, she flew into the air. The car jerked to a stop.

Mickelle ran to Belle, expecting that she would have sustained a few small bruises. To her horror, she saw Belle's limp body lying on the blacktop, arms askew. *Dear Father, no!* Mickelle prayed.

Belle still wasn't moving. "Call an ambulance!" she screamed, but someone in the gathering crowd was already doing so. She checked Belle's pulse and was relieved to find a strong heartbeat.

The driver crouched down next to Mickelle. "I'm so sorry. She came out of nowhere. I wasn't even going fast."

Mickelle nodded but was too frightened to speak. Belle seemed to be breathing. Why wouldn't she awake?

Then she heard Jeremy at her side. "Mom! Mom! Jennie Anne!" His blue eyes were wide, and he was having trouble speaking. Instead, he pointed at the brown van.

Mickelle jumped to her feet, feeling torn in two. Was this how Colton had felt when he tried to save his twins? But no! He had made that up. This was real.

She had risen in time to see the brown van driving over the curb and into the street. "Stop!" she screamed, running a few feet. "That man took my daughter! Help! Oh, help!"

There was a rush of questions that Mickelle tried to answer as best she could, her mind whirling, her heart aching. Someone called the police. She sat by Belle in the parking lot and wondered if she would now lose both the girls she had come to love as her own.

"Is there someone I could call for you?" a voice asked. It was Mrs. Palmer, the girls' teacher. By habit, Mickelle gave her Brionney's number.

The ambulance arrived and the EMTs pushed back the crowd as they began to work on Belle. The day of Damon's near drowning flashed vividly in Mickelle's mind. *Oh, please don't let her die!*

The police arrived next and Mickelle talked with them briefly as the EMTs placed Belle into the ambulance. She described the brown van, the balding man, and Colton Scofield. Her heart hurt so badly, she didn't know if she would live for one more minute. Only Jeremy's presence forced her not to give in to despair.

Mickelle was glad to see Brionney arrive. She clung to her sister for a moment, drinking in her strength. "You stay with your aunt," Mickelle told Jeremy. "I'll see you very soon." She climbed into the ambulance and reached for Belle's limp hand.

The ride to the Utah Valley Regional Medical Center in Provo took longer than Mickelle liked, but the ambulance personnel assured her that the nature of Belle's injury required the capabilities of the larger hospital. "We suspect some serious internal injuries," they told her. "And she's having trouble breathing."

Mickelle closed her eyes and prayed with her entire being. Against the back of her lids she relived the frightened look on Jennie Anne's face, and the way Belle had pulled away, screaming, from the stranger. What could she have done differently? Guilt lay like a heavy burden on her heart.

On arrival at the hospital Belle was rushed into emergency surgery, and Mickelle was left alone. In the sudden silence, Mickelle finally had a chance to call Damon.

* * * * *

Damon answered his cell phone. "Hi, honey," he said cheerfully when he heard Mickelle's voice.

But Mickelle began sobbing. "It's Belle," she mumbled through her tears. "And Jennie Anne. She's gone, and Belle . . ."

"Are they missing? They've done this before. Or Belle has. Remember? She's probably rebelling about not being able to go to the dinner tonight, and I'll bet she made Jennie Anne go along with her."

"No!" Mickelle's voice was tortured. "Belle was hit by a car at the school. They took her into surgery. They can't tell me—it doesn't look good."

The realization of what Mickelle was saying bore down on him, bringing with it a terrible pain . . . and fear. "Where are you?"

"In Provo."

"I'll be right there."

It was only after he hung up and was in the Lexus that he realized he hadn't found out what had happened to Jennie Anne. Was she missing?

Mickelle met him in the emergency room. Her hair was beautifully swept up on her head, like a tragic heroine in a film, but it was the haunted look in her red-rimmed eyes that held his attention. "I haven't heard anything," she said as he hugged her.

He held her back to peer into her worried face. "What about Jennie Anne?"

"Colton took her. Oh, Damon, it was so terrible!" Her voice rose an octave. "There was Belle lying on the ground and that man taking off with Jennie Anne. He would have taken them both, if he could. He tried, but Belle fought and got away!"

"Tell me slowly." Damon listened as she recounted the events, feeling helpless to aid either the girls or Mickelle, whose guilt nearly leapt out of her face as she spoke. Horror, fear, anger, and a host of other emotions battled for preeminence in his heart.

"The worst was knowing that I couldn't help either of them." Mickelle tried to wipe away the tears on her face, but more took their place. "I could never have made it to Jennie Anne in time, or to Belle before the accident. There was *nothing* I could do!"

They clung to each other as though to a lifeboat in a storm, watching and waiting. Mickelle's family arrived, and the bishop in Damon's ward had also come, bringing Tanner with him. They had scarcely greeted each other when several police officers arrived to talk to Mickelle.

"We have a license plate," one of them said. "We should have something for you soon. The next few hours are crucial, as I'm sure you know they are in any kidnapping. Of course, the FBI has also been called in since kidnapping is a federal offense. They'll be here soon."

In ten minutes the officers were gone. They had still received no word about Belle.

Damon felt a numbness begin in his heart and spread throughout his body. He couldn't imagine life without his Belle. She had kept both him and Tanner going when Charlotte had died. She had been their very reason for living.

Of course, he had the gospel now, and with his heart and soul, he knew that if she died, Belle would go to heaven and wait for him there, that they would be reunited one day. Yet he was unprepared for this terrible agony slicing into his heart, unprepared for the bleakness of life without her smile, without her hugs, without her tiny hand in his. He leaned forward and put his head between his hands, closing his eyes against the devastation.

Jennie Anne. The idea that she was being held by desperate men was even worse than Belle's accident. They might never see her again, might never know what unspeakable things she suffered.

Mickelle took his hand, and only then did he realize the extent of the fear she had experienced at his near death. No wonder she had been so afraid of loving him! He gripped her hard, wanting to keep what he had left from slipping away.

The FBI Special Agents came and went long before the doctor finished with Belle's surgery. When he did emerge, his young face was drawn and weary, and his sandy hair was matted to his scalp. Damon and Mickelle rose to meet him.

"I've done everything I can," he told them gravely. "Right now your daughter is stable, but I—her chances aren't very good. She was bleeding profusely from nearly all the major organs in her abdominal cavity. The surgery stopped the bleeding, for now, and we just have to see how well things heal. They may start bleeding again, and there's a high risk of infection. It's hard to predict. The best thing she has going for her is her age. I'm sorry I can't give you better news. They're taking her to the ICU now, and you can see her. I don't know that she'll wake up . . . She woke up briefly before the surgery, and she was in extreme pain. I had to give her a high dosage of painkiller. And she'll have to keep taking it. It's just too much trauma for her body." He hesitated. "You might call her whole family and . . . say your good-byes."

They all started crying, but Damon managed to say, "We want to give her a priesthood blessing."

The doctor inclined his head. "Of course. It might make the difference we need. There is always hope. My prayers will be with you—with her."

So with the bishop, Jesse, Mickelle's father, and Mickelle's two other brothers-in-law, they went into Belle's room and surrounded her bed. Jesse anointed her. Then they laid their hands on her head. Damon began the blessing, but halfway through he couldn't continue. There was so much he wanted to say, but he was having difficultly separating his will from the Lord's. So much depended upon this moment, and the responsibility didn't lay easily upon his shoulders. The group stood in silence around Belle's inert figure for long moments, until at last Jesse resumed in Damon's behalf, pleading for Belle's life and asking that the Lord's will be done.

Damon nodded his thanks, his heart so full of torment that he wondered if he would ever be completely happy again.

CHAPTER 25

From the dilapidated couch Colton alternately studied his companion in crime and the little girl they had abducted. He wished he could roll back time to before he had paid Troy to attack Mickelle, that he had skipped town after stealing the insurance money.

Of course, then he wouldn't have the money from Mickelle's diamond ring.

He sighed. If only she had made it easier for him, if she had fallen for him like the others. Then he wouldn't have needed to come up with a plan to get more, to make her pay for her betrayal. She *should* have loved him. Then he could have left town with the money, the ring, and the good feelings he normally enjoyed after these exploits.

Most certainly he wouldn't be at this deserted farmhouse freezing his toes off. This was also Mickelle's fault.

If things had gone differently he might not have split Utah at all, for a while anyway. He and Mickelle could have had fun together, maybe even gotten married—never mind the other wives he had left behind in three other states. It wasn't like he would ever go back to them. Especially to Terry. She didn't want him anyway after what he had let happen to their sons that dreadful night ten years ago. If they hadn't drowned, his life would have been much different. He wouldn't have to keep moving to stay ahead of the loathsome reality, the all-encompassing pain.

Mickelle had been the first one in all these years to whom he had admitted the truth. He knew she would understand because of her nephews, and he had been right. And even though she hadn't loved him, her comments about the afterlife had temporarily assuaged his horrendous guilt. Could any of it be true?

The little girl they had kidnapped was huddled on the floor by the wood fireplace where Troy had started a fire, an untouched hamburger on her lap. She cradled her left arm with the right, her freckled face pinched white with pain. Her silky skirt, now stained with dust from the floor, puddled around her. Colton suspected her shoulder was broken from when Troy had thrown her into the van yesterday. She had whimpered then, until Troy had threatened her with his fist.

Now Troy was pacing the floor, hitting his fist into his hand repeatedly. Colton wanted to yell at the overgrown monkey to sit still, but he didn't want to start anything. Not now when he had to think.

What was he going to do?

He remembered Mickelle's face when he had seen her in the pool and from the van yesterday. She had looked good, really good. She had recognized him too, at the end. What had she felt? Did she miss him at all? She must know about the insurance money.

It's all her fault.

The situation continued to nag at him. He had stolen money more times than he could count, along with a good number of female hearts. He had been a burglar, a con-man, and a tax evader.

But for the past ten years he had never been directly responsible for hurting a child. He had made sure of that.

Except that now Belle, the pretty, rosy-cheeked angel Mickelle adored, could be dead, and this little girl by the fireplace needed medical attention.

He wanted out.

"It's over," he had told Troy when they had driven a few blocks from the school yesterday. "Let's just let her off at the next corner and get out of here."

Troy's face had lunged at him over the seat. "It ain't over till I say so. Now keep driving!" Then he had pulled out the gun.

Colton had little choice but to obey and hope the man came to his senses. What had begun as a scheme to get a little cash had now turned into a fiasco. There was no way the police wouldn't be involved, not with one child dead and a million witnesses. They were facing big time jail sentences. He realized belatedly that he should have planned better, but his impatience to punish Mickelle had proven too great a temptation.

He could cut out, of course, but that would leave the little girl with Troy, and somehow he couldn't stomach that. It wasn't right, leaving her defenseless. After receiving the ransom money, Troy would just as soon let her remain here to freeze to death as return her to Mickelle.

Colton was a lot of bad things, but despite his tragic past, he wasn't a murderer. Or a child abuser. Troy seemed to have the potential for both.

He had to try again. "I think we ought to get out of here. They've called the feds by now."

Troy whirled suddenly and shook his fist under Colton's nose. "You're a wimp. And we do it my way. Understand? Where's the note?"

Colton knew Troy thought of him as spineless and weak, but that was perfectly all right with him, since he considered Troy crude, unlearned, and stupid.

He smiled. Stupid. Now that he could get around.

He pulled on his gloves and removed a tiny envelope from his jacket pocket. "Here it is."

"You go deliver it. Then I'll go get the money," Troy commanded.

Colton smirked darkly inside himself. Troy was so brainless that he thought Colton would actually trust him to go for the money.

"Okay." He pocketed the note. "But don't move her. Shoulder's broken."

Troy shrugged his indifference. "Just hurry. They'll be waiting to hear—I'm anxious 'cause it's been so long."

As Colton stood, Troy grabbed the front of his jacket and pushed him up against the wall. His unshaven face was inches away, and Colton could see the bulge of the gun in his pocket. For a moment Colton thought Troy was going to hit him as he had the night he had stolen the ring from Mickelle, but the man only sneered, "And don't try to put one over on me, fancy boy. Or you'll be sorry." With a few heavy curses to accentuate his threat, Troy released him.

Colton fastidiously straightened his jacket and walked over to the little girl. "Don't give him any trouble," he muttered in a low voice. "Just hang tight. It'll be over soon."

She said nothing, not even raising her head to look at him. Her eyes were fixed on her left arm. Colton had only felt like this much of a rat twice before—once ten years ago and again more recently, when he had seen the damage Troy had done to Mickelle the night he stole the ring. He shouldn't have hurt her that badly. And the attack alone should have been revenge enough, but Colton had been too angry and hurt to see it then.

It's still her fault. She could have chosen differently.

He left the farmhouse, driving a new car he had rented under one of his aliases with a stolen credit card. Without Troy's intense gaze, he felt more confident, more sure of what he would do.

Two blocks away from the flower shop he put on his disguise, thick clear glasses, a hat with blonde hair, loafers with a tall heel. Pulling on his gloves once again, he took out the small envelope. He removed and tore up the old ransom note inside. Then he took out a small sheet of paper and wrote a new message. Smiling in grim satisfaction, he sealed the envelope before walking to the flower shop.

"May I help you?" asked the matronly woman behind the counter.

"Yes, I'd like to send some flowers. A dozen yellow roses. Preferably dark yellow—almost gold."

"Will these do?"

"Yes. Perfect. And I'll want them delivered."

"How about this vase?"

He nodded and watched as she expertly arranged the roses with baby's breath and several greens, tying it with a yellow ribbon. "If you'll just fill out the address where we are to deliver it," she said, placing a form before him, "I'll ring it up. Oh, and here's a card to write a note."

"I got one when I came in earlier." He showed the note in his gloved hand. "I wanted to think about what I was going to say."

She smiled, obviously approving the action. Colton paid for the roses with a stolen credit card. "Thank you," the woman said, not checking the signature on the back. Of course, even if she had, the signatures would have matched to the untrained eye. He was good at what he did. It was too bad the cards weren't good for more than a few uses, and then only up to a paltry amount. Not like a hundred thousand dollars insurance money or a heart-shaped diamond ring.

Colton left the shop, walked back to his car, and drove away. If he was lucky he could be free of Utah by nightfall.

* * * * *

Friday night, and all day Saturday, Mickelle and Damon stayed at the hospital with Belle. The only change was for the worse when an infection set in. The antibiotics had halted the advance of the infection, but didn't seem able to get rid of it completely. Her life hung in the balance. The doctor had tried lowering her pain medication so that she would awaken, but she exhibited such stress that he put her under once more.

At least her abdomen had not filled again with blood—yet. That was another reason to keep her sleeping and unmoving while her organs healed. Only the monitors and the slight up and down motion of her chest showed that she still lived.

Periodically Mickelle and Damon kissed or patted the soft, feverish cheeks, unmarred by the accident except for a small scrape by her left temple, and begged her to come back to them. The doctor had told them that whether or not she awoke, either to say good-bye or to get better, would depend not only upon how quickly her internal injuries healed, but how hard her spirit fought for survival.

Mickelle knew that Belle was a fighter. She always had been. But was she strong enough for this?

They heard nothing from Jennie Anne's kidnappers, though Mickelle's parents had gone to the Wolfe Estate with the boys to await a ransom note. The FBI and the police had turned up nothing except the brown van, deserted in Lehi a short distance from the freeway. Their phone was tapped, and an FBI agent had joined Stan in the basement, where he would be notified at once if anyone came close to the house.

"You two need to go home and take a break," Brionney said to Damon and Mickelle late Saturday afternoon. "Just go home, take a shower, be with the kids, have a good dinner and sleep. I'll stay right here with her. I have your cell number, and I'll call you the instant anything happens."

Mickelle frowned at Damon's haggard face. Her sister was right; he looked as though he hadn't slept in a month. He needed rest. However, Damon shook his head. "No. Thanks anyway."

Brionney didn't give up easily. "Go on home. Neither of you slept at all last night. The doctor said there wasn't likely to be any change this evening, didn't he? Until he lowered her medication. So come back in the morning. Then you'll be ready to stay the whole day, to be here when she really needs you."

Damon shook his head again, and Mickelle knew exactly how he felt—that if they stopped focusing on her for one instant they would lose her.

Like Jennie Anne.

Damon cleared his throat. "The specialists I found—"

"Won't be in until tomorrow," Brionney interrupted. "I know it's hard to leave her, but I'll take care of her." She hesitated and added, "Mom called and told me the boys are really upset. She thinks they need to see you both home right now, if only for a while. Jeremy wet the bed last night."

The implication was clear: Jeremy always wet the bed when he was emotionally disturbed. Mickelle exchanged glances with Damon. She saw the suffering in his eyes . . . and something even worse—resignation. She knew he didn't believe Belle would live. He rubbed a hand over his worn face and through his yellow hair. The lines around his eyes and on his cheeks seemed to have deepened overnight. "Okay," he agreed finally. "We'll go home for bit." His eyes pinned Brionney's. "But you must promise to call us if there is even an insignificant change. Any change at all could be important."

"I will, I will. Don't worry. I'll guard her as though she's my own."

Mickelle and Damon spoke little on the way home, but as they pulled into the garage, she put her hand on his. "There's still hope, Damon. We must have hope."

He nodded and gripped her hand, pulling her to him as though he would never let her go. There was no passion in his intent, only an urgent need for comfort.

Inside the house, the boys were waiting in the family room with Mickelle's parents. Jeremy threw himself at her, and Tanner likewise went to Damon. Only Bryan continued to sit on the blue leather couch and stare at his hands. Mickelle settled Jeremy on the couch and sat between her sons. Tentatively, she placed her arm around Bryan's shoulders. He turned and hugged her, quiet sobs shaking his body. Mickelle tightened her hold and rocked him gently.

"Have you eaten yet?" asked Irene, her clear blue eyes showed concerned. Her short, white hair was as carefully styled as ever, and her slender frame looked elegant in her black silk pantsuit, but there was an unmistakable sadness in the fine lines of her mother's face that Mickelle hadn't seen for a long time. Not since the day Mickelle had confessed to her about Riley's abuse.

"No, Mom, we haven't." Mickelle couldn't remember when she had last eaten, though she vaguely recalled a cheeseburger and a drink. She was hungry. But how could she eat under the circumstances?

"Well, your father and I will get you something. Terrell?" Irene looked at her husband, who clasped Damon on the shoulder in a heartfelt gesture of sympathy before following Irene into the kitchen. Damon and Tanner settled on the love seat, legs touching, as though they needed to know the other was nearby.

"Is Belle going to die?" Jeremy asked, squeezing even closer to Mickelle on the couch.

Mickelle stroked his hair. "We don't know yet."

"What does the doctor say?" Tanner asked.

Mickelle saw the desire to protect his son in Damon's eyes, but also the reluctance to lie to him. "He doesn't know," Damon said finally. "We just have to wait and see."

Bryan stood abruptly, fists clenched. "This can't be happening! Belle—Jennie Anne—it just can't!"

Before anyone could speak, he ran into the bathroom and slammed the door, locking it behind him. Jeremy began to cry, and Mickelle pulled him onto her lap. "It's okay," she soothed. "It's okay."

"I want Jennie Anne," he cried. "I want Belle."

"I know." There was nothing she could do but rock him until he fell asleep in her arms. Then she laid him gently on the couch and pulled a blanket over him.

Her parents brought a plate of food from the kitchen, and Mickelle was grateful because she felt too emotionally and physically exhausted to move. She had taken only one bite when Stan and another man she didn't know burst into the room. They were an incongruous pair, one dressed in jeans, the other in a dark suit.

"Heads up," Stan announced. "We've got company. Looks like a flower delivery, but it could be the ransom note."

The knots in Mickelle's stomach doubled in size. "What should we do?"

"Wait here," the other man said. "We'll take care of it. It may be nothing."

Mickelle set her food on the coffee table, her appetite vanished. Damon managed a few more mouthfuls before he too set his plate aside. They waited tensely.

Irene settled on the arm of the couch where Mickelle sat next to the sleeping Jeremy. Her mother's calm and stately presence in the midst of this entire crisis brought strength to Mickelle's heart, for which she was grateful.

Bryan came from the bathroom, his face red, but his emotions under control. He sat on the floor by the couch, as though afraid to be too close to Mickelle. She wasn't offended because she felt the same way; each time she neared Damon, she wanted to collapse into a weeping bundle.

Mickelle's father dropped to the floor next to Bryan, but didn't touch him, as though understanding his need to be apart. He explained the new situation to Bryan in a few succinct words. "We're waiting to see who the flowers are from—if it's flowers." Bryan nodded, but didn't speak.

At last, the strange man she assumed was with the FBI returned to the room carrying a bouquet of dark yellow roses. Mickelle stiffened when she saw it, immediately recalling the flowers Colton had pretended to give her. Damon's flowers.

"This means something to you then?" he asked, seeing her reaction.

"It could be him."

He sat on the leather chair between the couches and pulled on thin transparent gloves. Everyone crowded around as he carefully slit open the envelope with a small knife and drew out the card, holding it at an angle so they could see what was written.

> *The girl is at an abandoned farmhouse with the kidnapper. Be careful, or you won't get her out alive. He is armed. See map on back.*
>
> *C*

Mickelle shook her head in disbelief. "Why would Colton help us? I saw him driving the van."

The FBI Special Agent put the note and envelope in a plastic bag. "My guess is he's having second thoughts. Either that or he wasn't a willing participant from the beginning."

Damon grunted in disbelief. "Could be a trap."

"Could be. But I would be surprised since they're both amateurs—at least in kidnapping. We'll take every precaution."

"Who brought it?" asked Tanner.

The agent shook his head. "Florist. Stan is holding the delivery guy for the police to question—they'll be here soon—but it's likely the flower shop knew nothing. Still, we might be able to trace the buyer."

"Colton. It was Colton." The words exploded from Mickelle. "But why did he back out?" Nothing made sense.

"He's scared, that's all." The agent pulled out a phone. "I'm telling my partners. Do you have a fax machine? The sooner we get this map to the police station, the sooner we can have an exact location. Might take awhile. It's hand drawn and we don't know how well he knew the area."

"I have one in my study," Damon said, coming to his feet. Tanner hesitated a moment, and then followed them from the room.

Time passed slowly and still they heard nothing. Mickelle's worry for Jennie Anne increased. She knew that with each passing second the likelihood of finding the child decreased. As they waited, Damon called the hospital three times to check on Belle, but there was no change in her condition. Tanner and Bryan began yawning. "Why don't you all go to bed?" Irene asked. Tucking Jeremy's blanket more securely around him. "I know it's early to sleep, but you were up all night."

No one moved.

"Well, at least let's get Jeremy into bed. He'll wet the couch."

Mickelle hesitated, thinking of her small son upstairs alone. "He needs someone to stay with him Mom."

"Your father and I will be there. Don't worry." Irene gently laid a slender hand on Mickelle's arm. "We won't leave him alone for a minute."

Mickelle hugged her mother, feeling her ready tears come to the surface. "Thanks," she whispered, blinking hard to clear her eyes.

Terrell gently scooped Jeremy into his arms. "Bryan, how about you show us where he sleeps?" Bryan didn't reply, but stared off into space.

"I'll show you," Tanner volunteered.

Mickelle carried her uneaten plate of food to the kitchen. When she glanced back, Damon was leaving. She followed him down the hall to his study. "Damon, are you okay?" Stupid question, she knew, but what else could she say?

"I have to go back," he said, turning to her. The tears she hadn't yet seen him shed were falling rapidly, glistening over his cheeks. "I can't bear to leave her to face this alone."

Mickelle held out her arms and he fell into them. "I keep asking myself, why them?" Damon muttered in her neck. "Why my precious Belle? Why little Jennie Anne who hasn't had a fair shake her whole life. Why now when everything is going so well?"

"I don't know. But I do know that we must never give up hope—never! Despite what the doctor says. We are a people of miracles. Our God is a God of miracles. I believe He can heal Belle." This last she said because of the resignation in his eyes . . . and the terrible emptiness. Both frightened her.

"This is my first real trial since my baptism," he said slowly. "And I have to tell you, Kelle, that despite my faith, this is so . . . hard."

She knew the word was a vast understatement. "I know."

"I have to go back to the hospital. You see that, don't you?" He rubbed his chin hard. "I've been taking care of her since she was a baby."

"One hour then. We'll go back in an hour."

"You should stay with the boys."

"My parents'll be here. They'll be okay."

She pushed him toward the black couch. "Now you lie right here and try to rest just for a moment. I'm going to take a quick shower, check on Jeremy, and then we'll go." She kissed his brow gently as he clung to her in the dark.

"I love you so much," he whispered. "I don't know how I would get through this without you."

"You must have hope. Please don't give up! Don't let your fear deprive you of hope and faith, the way I nearly let my fear deprive me of your love." He didn't reply, but after a while, his grip relaxed. Mickelle slipped from the study, hoping he would sleep.

As she went back down the dimly lit hall and into the wide entryway, she caught sight of the huge oval wine glass that she had half-filled with water and left on the wall table in front of the elaborate gilt mirror. In it floated the flower she had rescued yesterday and saved to show Jennie Anne. Had it only been yesterday?

Oh, Jennie Anne, my little rose! And Belle, my beauty!

With a stifled sob she ran up the main staircase. Jeremy was still sleeping under the watchful eyes of her parents, so she headed toward her own suite. Instinctively, she stopped at the room the girls shared. Thanks to Mrs. Mertz, the castle room appeared as though no child had ever set foot inside. Not a toy was out of place, not a piece of clothing was on the floor. Mickelle remembered the flour mixture Belle had made and cleaned up earlier in the week. How she missed the mess now!

Wrapping her arms around herself, she stumbled over to one of the twin beds and grabbed the pillow, then to the other bed for that pillow. Holding them against her breast, as she longed to hold the girls, she cried. Cried as she hadn't been able to do with Damon because she had to be strong for him—because he had even more pain to deal with. And as she cried, she prayed.

* * * * *

Damon wondered if Mickelle had been listening to the same doctor he had. The prognosis had not improved with the passing hours; in fact, if anything, it had grown worse. In the eyes of both the nurses and the young doctor, Damon saw that they didn't expect Belle to live. What little hope they offered was only for the parents. For him and Mickelle.

Damon stared at the dark ceiling, afraid to close his eyes. When he did, he saw Belle's face as it had been over the years—laughing, crying, sleeping . . . and now dying. And he could smell her, feel her touch.

Hope. What had Mickelle meant?

He hadn't been able to give Belle a blessing.

She'll be happy in heaven with her mom.

No! Oh, Charlotte, no! I know you would love to have her, but . . .

But what? What was it he was trying to say?

His eyes closed, borne down by his deep weariness, one that he felt in the very marrow of his bones.

What had Mickelle meant?

Hope. Faith. The evidence of things not seen.

Was he giving up too soon? Was he playing the role of a martyr without reason?

He slipped from the couch, twisting so that he landed on his knees. Prayer. He wanted to pray, but the words tumbling around in his mind wouldn't form sentences. There was too much emotion all at once, too many thoughts rushing for utterance. He had to funnel them, and the only way he could think of to do that was to state them aloud.

"Dear Father," he began. "Dear Father." His voice broke and for a time the emotions overcame him. When at last he could speak, he felt as though the words were ripped from his very soul. "I don't know why this has happened, and I'm so scared that I will lose my little Belle. Please don't let that happen. Please." He thought for a moment, and then continued because he knew that his faith required more. "But I accept Thy will. I will not accept the doctor's words nor my own pragmatic view, but I will have faith in Thee. You can save Belle, or . . . or You may have other plans. I bow to Thy greater wisdom, while at the same time I plead with Thee for her life. I understand now that there is hope because You live."

There was more, much more. "And Jennie Anne. Please bring that special spirit back to us. Protect her from the man that would abuse her. Help her to be strong and to . . . to have . . . hope. Yes, hope." He prayed more for Jennie Anne, letting the words rise silently from his soul.

"And Bry, please bless Bry. I know he's suffering and I pray that I can comfort him, and that he will understand how much I love him and his brother . . . and Kelle."

He realized then that while much of what he loved hung in the balance, much that he loved rested safely in his home. He let his gratitude for these blessings rise to the God he felt so near by. "In the name of Jesus Christ, Amen."

He had to return to the hospital now. He had to pray over his daughter there, to heal her if it was the Lord's will, or to ease her transition to heaven.

CHAPTER 26

But I love Mickelle. I want her to take care of me until I go back to heaven with my own mommy. The words kept replaying in Bryan's head. Did that mean that Belle was going to die? He thought it did. She must have sensed that her time was short.

His mind rebelled. She was so bright and happy, and she loved him better than even her real brother Tanner who teased her constantly, and Jeremy who most times acted younger than she did. Bryan loved her, too. He loved the way she asked his advice, the way she always thought to include him, and the way her cheeks dimpled when she smiled. She was the best little sister he could ever imagine. Oh, sure, she got on his nerves, but not nearly as much as Jeremy, and she was so cute that it was hard not to love her anyway.

And now she would be gone. Gone. Just like his dad.

Everyone had disappeared somewhere, and Bryan was alone in the family room. He hated being alone, though he couldn't share his feelings with them. He felt too exposed, too betrayed. He wandered from the room, hoping to find his mother and feel her comfort.

He heard her in the study, speaking in a low voice with Damon. What was she saying? Something about hope. Had Damon given up hope? Was Belle even worse off than he had been told? Was she perhaps already dead?

"But I love Mickelle. I want her to take care of me until I go back to heaven with my own mommy."

No! She couldn't go to heaven. He wouldn't let her. God couldn't take her.

God had taken his dad.

No, Dad made his own choice.

He knew there was a difference, though it mostly felt the same to him.

Someone was coming from the darkened room, and Bryan shrank into the shadows, glad it had grown dark enough for him to hide. He watched his mother disappear into the entryway, heard her going up the stairs—probably to the room she would soon share with Damon.

The bitterness didn't come to choke him as it usually did. Bryan knew Damon was suffering, but it didn't make him happy. Belle was not something to use against Damon. Never.

A mumbling took him by surprise. He recognized Damon's voice, and edged closer to the partially open study door, more for the contact of another human, than to eavesdrop.

Damon was praying for Belle, and the words made the tears return to Bryan's eyes. The prayer left Belle decidedly in the Lord's hands, but Bryan wasn't sure that was the best place for her. Couldn't Damon just demand that God return Belle to them?

No, that wasn't how it worked.

But Bryan couldn't do the same thing. He couldn't say "Thy will be done." He could only repeat in his head, "Please don't let her die. Please don't let her die."

Damon continued his prayer, talking about Jennie Anne. The words he said aloud were short, but then he was silent for such a long time that Bryan thought he must still be praying. Or maybe he had fallen asleep.

Suddenly, he was surprised to hear Damon speaking his name, or at least the shortened version Damon always used—Bry. Praying for him! But there was nothing wrong with him—why would Damon waste his breath? He waited to see if Damon would pray for Jeremy and Tanner, too, but he didn't.

So why had Damon lumped him with Belle who was dying and with Jennie Anne who was missing?

Sobs came from the room then, loud, raucous sobs that bit into Bryan's heart. He felt compelled to enter the room. Almost immediately Damon became aware of his presence. His sobbing ceased.

"She's going to die, isn't she?" Bryan said.

Damon rubbed his hands over his face. "She may. But that doesn't mean we give up hope. It's in the Lord's hands now."

Bryan said nothing for a moment as his eyes further adjusted to the room that was even darker than the hall. Damon was still on his knees. Bryan reached out a hand and clasped Damon's shoulder as his grandfather had done earlier. It was a manly thing to do, but Damon starting crying again. Bryan lifted his other hand and found his own face wet.

Damon stood and reached out to him, and Bryan let himself be pulled into a bear hug, reveling in the comfort, but not returning the hug. Bryan's silent tears became sobs. "I don't want her to die. Please don't let her die."

"Will you pray with me, Bry?"

Bryan nodded, and felt some regret when Damon pulled away. He kept hold of Bryan's hand, though, which felt awkward and wonderful all at once. They knelt on the carpet and bowed their heads.

My father never prayed with me, Bryan thought with regret.

First Damon thanked the Lord for his blessings, from Bryan's mother to Mrs. Mertz, the housekeeper. He was thankful for things Bryan had never thought about, like the sunset and the rain. Then he prayed with feeling about Belle and Jennie Anne, as though he had not already done so a few minutes earlier.

When Damon finished, he said, "It's your turn."

Bryan hadn't expected that. He even resented it a little because it was God's fault that Belle was hurt, wasn't it? And that Jennie Anne was missing. Belatedly, Bryan felt a deep sadness for Jennie Anne. He didn't know her well; he had never really tried. But he liked her. *I wish I had played with her more. I wish I had been nicer to her.*

So he prayed, asking for Jennie Anne to come home and for Belle to get better. In his heart he promised the Lord that he would change. He would never hurt anyone again.

"Thank you, Bry." Damon's voice was rough. He hugged him again and this time Bryan hugged him back. It felt warm and good and right.

He wanted to say he was sorry for how he acted, but the words that came out were, "Did you really mean it when you thanked God for everything. Aren't you mad at Him?"

Damon didn't answer right away, as though he was really considering the question. Bryan knew from experience that Damon wouldn't answer lightly about something so serious, but all the same he was reassured to see Damon actually thinking about his response.

"God doesn't cause accidents, Bry. He allows them to happen. And maybe sometimes it's because we're not being faithful, but mostly it's because we need the experience. We need to learn and grow. The Lord tests those He loves. Never forget that. But also never forget that He will be right there with you. And that He will help you through." Damon made a sound, which vaguely resembled a wry chuckle. "I forgot that today. I almost gave up. But your mother helped me remember. Now I know that no matter what happens with Belle at the hospital, the Lord loves us and He will make it right if we turn to Him with our whole hearts. He will take our burdens, if we let Him."

That sounded good to Bryan, and miraculously, his heart did feel lighter, though that might also be because of Damon himself, and the way they were talking. As though they were father and son. As though there was nothing wrong with Bryan at all. *My father was wrong*, he thought. *I'm not stupid or dumb or lazy.*

"And there's something else," Damon continued. "You and I may not always agree, but I will always be here for you. And I will do my best to be fair."

"I know." And suddenly Bryan *did* know.

Damon climbed to his feet. "I need to get back to Belle."

Bryan's anxiety returned, though not as heavily as before. "I want to go with you." He ducked his head slightly, half expecting a negative answer, but after a moment, Damon nodded.

"I'd be glad to have you come. Thank you."

A wonderful warmth entered Bryan's heart. He smiled through his tears.

* * * * *

In the end, everyone returned to the hospital except for Jeremy, who was still sleeping with Grandma and Grandpa close by. Bryan couldn't wait to see Belle, to talk to her. On the drive over, his mother called the police station for news about Jennie Anne.

"They've located the farm, they think," she relayed. "But they're studying their options. They don't want to endanger Jennie Anne." She hesitated before adding, "Apparently, her kidnapper has a very bad history of beating people up, including a few officers. They don't want . . . well they're trying to do what's best for Jennie Anne. If she's still there. He might have moved her."

Bryan felt nervous as they arrived in the ICU waiting room. Everyone in sight seemed to be in a somber mood. He wondered if that was because the patients in this wing were so close to death.

They couldn't all visit Belle. In fact, visitors were still limited to Damon and Mickelle, or to Aunt Brionney if they had to leave. Bryan was upset that he wouldn't be able to see Belle, but Damon talked to somebody, and Bryan and Tanner were given permission to go in one at a time with a parent. Tanner and Damon went first, and when they came out, Bryan and Mickelle went inside.

After kissing Belle and telling her how much she loved her, his mother waited near the door, giving Bryan a chance to talk to Belle. She seemed to know he wanted privacy.

Belle looked tiny in the big bed. Her round cheeks were no longer rosy, but pasty white except for two red fever spots, and the position of her limbs was stiff and contrived. Her normally curly hair limply framed her delicate face, and there were dark circles under her eyes. Oxygen hissed from a tube in her nose as an IV solution dripped into her arm. He wished she would open her eyes so that he could know she was still inside.

He leaned down close to her. "Belle," he whispered. "It's Bryan. I know I haven't been to see you before, but they wouldn't let me in yesterday, and then Grandma took us back to the house. But your dad let me come to see you now. He made them let me in even though I'm not really your brother. And, well, I wish I was your brother. That's what I wanted to tell you. And I thought you would be glad to know that I made up with your dad. I really did. We prayed for you. So now you need to come back because . . . because . . . well, I just need you to. We all do. I promise I won't say mean things about your dad anymore. Or Tanner. We'll be a family like you wanted. I'll even tell Mom that it was mostly me who ripped up her roses. Of course, I might tease you a bit just so the others won't think I'm playing favorites, but you'll always be my favorite. Please don't leave us. Your mom can wait a lot longer to have you with her, 'cause time is different in heaven, you know. Earth life is like a blink of an eye there. Or something."

He straightened, wanting to say more, but not able to think of anything in particular. Instead, he kissed her cheek as his mother had done, wishing she would wake up and smile. He studied her for a minute before backing away from the bed. Tears again were slipping from his eyes, despite his efforts to hold them back. "Good-bye, Belle."

His mother put her arm around him and led him out the door. Bryan felt her love suffuse him, and for a minute the pain of maybe losing Belle lessened. "Mom," he said, "I'm sorry. I'm really sorry. I've been so angry. I don't know why." He paused. "Sometimes I hate dad."

She blinked in surprise. "I didn't know you felt that way. I used to feel that way a lot. But . . . Bryan, maybe we ought to go back to the counselor we saw after your dad died. I think maybe it might help us both. Would you come with me?"

"Yeah, he was cool. I'd go." Bryan felt a big relief that his mom didn't think it wrong for him to hate his dad. He hadn't known she had felt the same way.

"Mom, there's something else."

"What?"

"Uh, Colton, he gave me this." Bryan pulled a fifty-dollar bill from his pocket.

"He gave you . . . When?"

"That day you came to Aunt Brionney's to talk to me. He told me if I'd be nice to you, he'd give me this money. And more when I needed it. But I don't want his money anymore. Not after what he did."

She looked aghast. "He paid you to be nice?"

"Yeah. I feel really bad about it. I did then too, but I guess I didn't care 'cause I wanted the money. I don't now." The bill seemed to burn his hand, like a lie in his heart. "So what should I do?"

"You could donate it to the hospital. I bet they have a system set up to help needy people pay their bills. How does that sound?"

He sighed with relief. "Good."

Maybe things would work out after all.

* * * * *

Jennie Anne was glad when Troy put more wood on the fire. She was cold and her shoulder ached terribly whenever she moved, sending shots of pain throughout her entire arm. Her stomach was also growling. The hamburger the beautiful man had given her was long gone. She didn't know if Troy had more food and was afraid to ask.

For the most part, Troy had ignored her, but as time passed and the beautiful man didn't return, he began to talk aloud to himself, and sometimes to her, though he never required her to say anything in return.

"Dumb fancy boy probably got himself caught. He better not spill the beans on me, or I'll have his pretty face cut up big time. I ain't going back to the slammer. No way! That spineless little jellyfish. Got him an education so he thinks he can order me around. Just wait till he gets back here. I don't need him to pick up the money. Like to see his expression when he finds out he ain't going anywhere. I'll tie him up, that's what. Cops'll have a heyday." He laughed and continued his diatribe.

Jennie Anne quit listening after a while. He was nothing but contemptible, according to the school counselor. Contemptible. Though she wasn't sure what the word meant, she really liked the way it sounded on her tongue. She practiced it under her breath. Concentrating on it helped her keep her thoughts away from the pain.

She wondered where Belle was and what she was doing. Did she get away? When Troy grabbed them Jennie Anne had gone stiff and silent with fear. Not brave Belle. She had hollered and kicked until she got free. After seeing her success, Jennie Anne tried to follow her, but Troy had dragged her and thrown her inside the van. Her shoulder had given a loud pop, and the pain had enveloped her.

She thought she had glimpsed Mickelle's face, but wasn't sure if it really happened, and if so, when she had appeared in the sequence of events. Everything was hazy through pain, except the word contemptible.

Contemptible.

Was the beautiful man coming back? She wished he would because he had looked at her with those nice blue eyes, and when he smiled, that marvelous happy-looking dimple had appeared. But if he did return, then Troy might hurt him, and she wouldn't want that, even if he had driven the car that brought her to this freezing place. He had still been nice. Before he left, he had promised it would soon be over.

Or had she imagined that part?

And did he mean it would soon be over because Damon would pay the ransom, or had he meant something else? His blue eyes had almost seemed like they held a secret, especially the way they had darted to Troy and then away.

Jennie Anne turned her other side to the fire so it could get warm. If she kept turning she wasn't too cold. She wished she had a coat, but she had left it inside the school. Her legs were especially cold because the skirt she wore was silky and didn't seem to do much to warm her.

She accidentally bumped her left arm on the raised hearth and gasped at the pain rippling through her shoulder—like a hundred sharp needles.

"Hurts you, does it?" Troy suddenly loomed over her. "Serves you right, brat. You should've done what I said."

He backed away and she breathed easier. "Your mother was always that way. Had to do things her own way. We told her to get rid of you, but she wouldn't. Said she loved you." He snorted. "That love got her really far, didn't it? She still got pneumonia and died." He laughed gleefully. "Of course if it wasn't for my dear old cousin, I wouldn't have all this nice money coming to me. Ha! Dear smart, snooty old cousin did good for me in the end."

He started to pace again and worry aloud about the ransom and the "fancy boy." He was like a wound top, ready to spin out of control.

Jennie Anne realized then that the beautiful man wasn't coming back. Maybe he had gotten the money already, or maybe he had skipped town. Either way, that meant Jennie Anne would pay. Troy would probably kill her, or at best leave her here to starve to death. Or freeze.

Tears stung her eyes. She thought of the castle room she shared with Belle, and the identical one Damon had promised to build for her very own. She thought of the piggyback rides he gave her, of Mickelle's hugs, and Tanner's teasing. When she got to Jeremy and Belle, the tears slipped out and down her cheeks.

I have to get away.

There was only herself to depend on. She tried to get to her feet, but the pain in her shoulder blinded her.

What now?

Slumping next to the brick hearth, she contemplated her options. She could pray. According to Belle, who had once prayed for a mother and a horse—one of which she was getting and the other of which was promised—you could get anything you wanted by praying.

So Jennie Anne shut her eyes and prayed. She had listened to Belle and the others enough to know how, and had practiced in private, though she had never said a prayer aloud when people could hear. Occasionally during her prayer she opened one eye, just to be sure where Troy was, and that he wasn't watching her. After she had prayed for what seemed like a long time, he added another log to the fire, muttered something about taking a pee, and left the room.

Jennie Anne remembered something she had learned in school, a fable that told how Hercules, the Greek god of strength, once advised a wagoner that he should try to get his wagon out of the mud first before asking for help. Was this the answer to her prayer? Was she supposed to help herself? What good then was God?

Of course, Troy *had* gone to the bathroom, which she knew was out of order from her own short visits earlier when the pretty man had been here. The last time it had stunk pretty bad. Had God sent Troy there so she could escape?

She arose. The pain in her shoulder jumped to life—sharp instead of the continuous dull ache—but this time she wasn't blinded by the pain.

Maybe God is helping me.

She kept moving, slowly and silently through the front room to the long kitchen, as though she were playing a hiding game with

Jeremy and Belle. Her breath sounded loud in her ears and she tried to hold it. What little light there was came from several lanterns Troy had lit in the house. There was unidentifiable debris on the ground; she stepped around it. At last she reached the back door, smiled grimly when she saw that the knob was missing. She had only to put her finger in the hole and pull.

It was harder than she thought because opening the door with her right hand meant taking the support from her left arm. A whimper of pain escaped her lips before she clamped them tight and tried to swallow the sound.

The hinges creaked. Had Troy heard? She shivered as she thought about what he would do to her, and the fear almost froze her feet as the pain had not.

Keep going. She forced herself to continue.

Outside, the cold made her shudder. The stars beamed so brilliantly overhead, it wasn't hard for her to believe that they were faraway suns. She kept walking. Surrounding the farm, she saw nothing but long empty fields. There were no neighboring lights, not a single glow to give her hope. She might freeze before she found another house.

Or Troy would find her.

Disappointment flooded her body. God hadn't helped! She had tried, but *He* hadn't done anything!

Choking back sobs, she took a step toward the house. Her teeth chattered with the cold. Could she get back before Troy found out she was gone? If not, what excuse could she use?

Tears obscured her vision.

She ran into something soft. A person! Excruciating, piercing pain from her shoulder once again washed over her. A bright light shone in her eyes.

A voice came through the pain. "Stupid brat!"

Troy had found her.

She shut her eyes and gave herself to the pain, grateful when the dark took away her consciousness.

CHAPTER 27

Damon had given Belle a father's blessing when he and Tanner had gone in to see Belle. A comfort spread through his heart. He had done all he could do mentally, emotionally, and spiritually. The rest was left in the Lord's careful hands.

After the initial visits he and Mickelle had stayed alternately with Belle and with their sons in the waiting room. They were not alone. Other families were also gathered, and took turns with their critically injured or sick loved ones. One particular couple caught Damon's attention. Their three-year-old daughter was near death, caused by a fall from a balcony. His heart went out to them and to the grandparents who had also gathered. The girl was the couple's only child, which increased Damon's gratitude for Tanner and for Bryan and Jeremy. And for Jennie Anne, though that was a difficult direction for his thoughts to take. They had still heard nothing from the police.

All the families in the waiting room prayed in their huddled groups, and talked quietly of hope and the hereafter. Hours ticked by.

Near midnight Mickelle emerged from the corridor leading to Belle's room, and Damon arose for his turn. Neither he nor Mickelle was willing to let Belle be alone for very long . . . just in case.

She hugged him, and she felt warm and alive in his arms as he breathed the scent of her freshly washed hair. "No change," she said wearily.

He wondered how long they could keep up this schedule. How long it would be until one of them would have to go home to take care of the other children. How long before Belle awoke. Or died.

"Mom!" Bryan's voice penetrated Damon's thoughts, urgent and demanding.

In his arms, Mickelle stiffened. Her hand went to her mouth and then fluttered to her side. Damon turned. "Jennie Anne!" Mickelle's voice was a strangled cry. She ran across the room to the elevator where two police officers had emerged, one carrying a blanket-wrapped Jennie Anne in his arms. Damon hurried over.

"Mickelle!" Jennie Anne said weakly.

"Careful," one of the men urged as Mickelle reached for the child. "Her shoulder's dislocated. She needs to go to the emergency room, but we knew that you would want to be with her. You'll have to hold her on this side."

They gingerly made the switch. Mickelle cradled Jennie Anne in her arms, kissing her and then pressing her face against the little girl's head. "Oh Jennie Anne, you're safe! Thank you, oh, thank you, Father." Her eyes focused on the officers. "And you—thank you for finding her."

One of the men shook his head. "It was her who found us, ma'am. We were outside the farmhouse, wondering how to get inside without endangering her, and then she comes wandering out, running away from what we can gather. We gave her a little fright sneaking up on her, but we didn't want to risk the kidnapper hearing. He did come out of the house. Almost got her, too. But we were quicker. We have him in custody now. He's going away for a long time."

"She fainted," added the other man. "Though that was probably because her shoulder hurt so bad. On the way here she kept muttering something about a wagoner and Hercules, or something. Couldn't make sense of it."

Jennie Anne nuzzled closer to Mickelle, then moaned with pain. Damon caressed her forehead with his hand and kissed her. "Good girl, Jennie Anne. You did good. Really good. We're proud of you. What a strong girl you are!"

She gave him a smile that was strained, but that showed her contentment.

Damon looked at Mickelle. "Why don't you go down with her, and I'll stay here with—" He stopped, not wanting to talk openly in front of Jennie Anne until she had been prepared for the news of Belle's accident.

Mickelle nodded. "We'll be back as soon as we can."

She turned to leave, but Jennie Anne's good arm shot out to Damon. "Why don't you call me a nickname like everybody else?" she asked.

It was true. Damon used a nickname for everyone close to him—Tan, Belle, Jer, Kelle. He even called Bryan Bry. For Damon, the shortening had come naturally, so why did he still call Jennie Anne by her full name? It was probably the nature of her name—two complete words. She was not Jennie, which could be shortened to Jen, or Anne, which was already short. She was Jennie Anne. But how could he explain this to her?

Jennie Anne's eyes fixed on him, awaiting his answer. Silently he tried out the possibilities. Jen Anne. No still too long. How about J.A.? He grimaced mentally at the thought. That simply didn't describe this freckled-face angel who had been tougher than anyone he knew.

"Well, you know," he said at last, "some people are just too special to have a nickname." He saw the disappointment in her eyes, and quickly amended his statement. "What I mean is that it takes a long time to come up with the perfect name because they're so special. So I have to think and think of a name that will be just right for you."

In her brown eyes he saw that she wanted to believe him, but didn't quite. So he searched for something to help her believe. "I think I need to wait a little longer to settle on a special name, and I was wondering if I could tell you on a special day, the day Kelle and I become your official parents. Two specials in one."

Joy sprang to life in Jennie Anne's eyes, scattering the disbelief. "Okay," she agreed happily.

Mickelle smiled at him, her eyes shimmering. She mouthed, "Thank you."

Damon watched them go, feeling much happier than he had felt since the ordeal began. Jennie Anne was back and safe. He directed a prayer heavenward: *Thank you, Father.*

Leaving Tanner and Bryan in the waiting room, he went to sit by Belle's bed. He couldn't wait to tell her about Jennie Anne. They hadn't mentioned her before, not wanting to upset her in case she could hear them, but the good news should only improve her chances of recovery.

Just inside the ICU, Damon stopped to get a drink from a fountain in the hall, then froze as he heard a scattering of murmuring voices. "She's gone . . . nothing more we could do . . . didn't expect it so sudden like this . . . . usually more warning . . . tell the parents . . . not looking forward . . . they've been here so long . . . just left her side for a few minutes . . . faithful . . . praying . . . wish we could have done more . . ."

Damon straightened as a doctor and a nurse rounded the corner. They came toward him, every step sluggish as though slowed in a sports replay. Damon's attention riveted on the doctor. Ever so slowly he continued his approach, solemn at the news he would be forced to divulge. Damon saw the dark stubble on the man's face, the harsh pain in his eyes, the finality, and his gut tightened with fear, although he knew it was already over. All that remained was the pronouncement. The doctor took a few more steps. He seemed to go so slowly, it made Damon angry. "Tell me!" he wanted to shout. "Just tell me!"

But the torturous steps also made him glad. *Slowly! Walk more slowly! Don't tell me my daughter's dead!*

Their eyes met. A brief, acknowledging smile appeared on the doctor's face . . . and then . . . he walked past Damon.

Damon turned, following the doctor's progress with his eyes. He saw the couple with the injured three-year-old daughter come through the wide door from the ICU waiting room, no doubt on their way to sit with their daughter. Damon held his breath, willing the doctor and nurse to walk by them as well.

The doctor stopped. Damon was too far away to hear their voices, but he saw the instant agony on the couple's faces, and felt it profoundly; only seconds earlier he had lived their pain.

The nurse was comforting the distraught couple, and Damon forced himself to look away, to turn the corner. He made it a few steps to a single chair that seemed to have been placed against the wall just for such an occasion. He felt a tremendous urge to run to Belle's side, to assure himself that she was breathing, but his limbs had lost all strength.

A nurse came down the hall, her face similar to all the many other kind faces he had seen in the past two days. "Ah, Mr. Wolfe, I've been looking for you. Your fiancée asked me to stay with your daughter until you traded places. But guess what? Your daughter's showing signs of fighting to wake up despite the medication, and her color is really good. That means the infection is possibly leaving. I'm going to get the doctor now to see what he says, so keep your fingers crossed. If the tests check out, I think he'll want to lower the dosages and see what happens. If we can get her awake and fighting . . ."

Damon's heart beat heavily and painfully for several seconds before he realized he was hearing good news. Belle was getting better, not worse—she wasn't dead!

Damon felt tears of relief and joy streaming down his face. He recalled the other parents who sobbed in each other's arms around the corner. The roles could have been reversed so easily. His Belle could have been the one to die. His heart filled with a thankfulness that knew no bounds. Not one, but both of his daughters had been saved!

He felt a deep compassion toward the couple who had not been so fortunate. They were good and worthy people, who had loved their daughter as much as he loved Belle. He prayed that they would find comfort, and felt that they would.

"Please," he said to the nurse through his tears of relief. "Can you help me up? I seem to have forgotten how to walk."

She smiled and pulled him to his feet. "Come on, I'll help you to your daughter's room. You'll want to be there in an hour or so when she wakes."

* * * * *

Jennie Anne's dislocated shoulder had scarcely been returned to its proper place when a nurse appeared in the room to speak to Mickelle. "Mrs. Hansen?"

"Yes?"

"Your sons are out at the desk asking for you. They say it's important."

Mickelle's heart seemed to stop. Did Bryan and Tanner have news of Belle? She glanced at Jennie Anne, whose eyes silently begged her not to leave. "Could you tell them we'll be right out? The doctor went to write a pain prescription."

A short while later Mickelle carried a nearly sleeping Jennie Anne out of the emergency room.

Bryan and Tanner sprang up from their seats. "It's Belle!" Tanner said, nearly shouting.

Bryan grinned from ear to ear. "She's waking up! Damon told us to come tell you."

Mickelle hurried to intensive care with the boys, excitement and gratitude renewing her energy and her spirit. Jennie Anne was asleep when they arrived, and she arranged the child on the couch in the waiting room, tucking a blanket around her sleeping form.

Admonishing the boys to watch Jennie Anne, she hurried past the nurse on ICU duty and down the hall to Belle's room. Damon met her halfway across the room, his arms going around her in a triumphant hug. "She was awake just now—I talked to her! The doctor says she's going to be okay. Her insides are healing better than he'd hoped."

His lips met hers in an urgent kiss that spread like fire through Mickelle's veins. "I love you so much," he murmured, "and I want to do anything to make you happy. To make our family happy. Beginning with the surgery."

Mickelle laughed until the tears came. "But Damon, don't you see? Jennie Anne is ours together! *She* is what I need—my special rose that only you and I share. I just didn't see it until you told her that we were going to adopt her!"

"Of course we are going to adopt her—weren't we always? But Jennie Anne or no Jennie Anne, you have to believe that I will always love you."

He kissed her again, and suddenly there were no doubts in Mickelle's heart. Whatever happened next, wherever they ended up, she knew they shared a love that would exist forever.

EPILOGUE

The weekend before Thanksgiving, Mickelle and Damon were married for time in the Timpanogos Temple. Mickelle felt beautiful in her new dress and so full of happiness that she kept wanting to pinch herself to make sure she wasn't dreaming.

After a brunch with all the family and close friends, they left for home, where they had decided to spend an uneventful and quiet weekend before the rush of Thanksgiving. The children were being taken care of by relatives, and all the help, including Stan and his cameras, had been given the weekend off. They had postponed their trip to Europe for a few months to make sure the girls were safely healed. Mickelle didn't mind; she was too happy to worry about anything but loving her new husband and her children.

Damon picked her up outside the front door and carried her into the house. "Are you sure you haven't gained weight?" He kissed her to show he was teasing.

She playfully cuffed him. "Better save your breath, that staircase is pretty long."

He kissed her again, and every inch of her body tingled with his touch. "Wait," he whispered, setting her down.

From the front closet he retrieved a white box about five inches square, topped with brilliant red and yellow ribbons.

She eagerly tore off the ribbons and lifted the lid. "Oh, it's beautiful!" Inside was a colored glass replica of a rose in full bloom. But not just any rose. This one was bright red on the outer half of the petals and sunshine yellow on the inside. A Jennie Anne.

"I love it," she said simply, recognizing that the message no longer referred only to their soon-to-be daughter, but to their eternal commitment.

They put the blossom in her curio cabinet with the rest of her collection, next to the gold-dipped rose he had given her so many weeks before. Then he lifted her again and carried her up the stairs.

* * * * *

Wrapped in Damon's arms, Mickelle dreamed of a golden bridge. *A long, wide, glorious bridge spanned an immense gulf. She stood at the mouth of the bridge. She couldn't see what was on the other side, but she wanted to be there, for she knew it held all the hopes of eternity. She looked around, and was grateful to see Damon beside her. He took her hand. She smiled. Behind them Tanner, Bryan, Jeremy, Belle, and Jennie Anne followed, skipping and laughing. Occasionally one would stumble and fall, but the others would help, and the trip across the wide bridge continued.*

Mickelle stopped and gazed out over the vast emptiness the bridge spanned, marveling at the impressive structure. Who could have created such an amazing bridge?

Damon pulled her along, grinning. She felt his love as though it were in her own heart. They were one.

Abruptly, they came to the end of the bridge. Her foot nearly slipped off the edge. She gasped, struggling for balance. "Oh, no! What do we do now?"

Damon steadied her and stared sadly at the darkness below. The children crowded around in dismayed silence.

Their destination was still obscured, but it called to Mickelle even more strongly. She desperately wanted to go on, but to continue meant certain death. There was no choice but to return to the mundane existence they had left. What disappointment!

Then Damon grabbed something out of the air and placed it at the end of the bridge. The object became part of the bridge. He put on yet another piece and then stepped forward. The bridge held! He motioned for her to come with him.

Mickelle stepped forward. Something moved in the air, a flash of light. She reached out and it solidified in her grasp. Together, she and Damon placed it on the end of the bridge. They laughed and stepped forward, searching for another piece of light.

"We're the ones building the bridge," she said. "The bridge to forever."

* * * * *

Thanksgiving Day found Mickelle and Damon leading Belle and a sling-wearing Jennie Anne around on the family's new cream-colored horse. Belle's face radiated happiness at finally obtaining her heart's desire, while Jennie Anne's sparkled with newfound confidence.

"Is it my turn yet?" Jeremy asked from his perch on the wood fence, where he sat with Tanner and Belle.

"I can see we might need to get another horse," Damon said with a sigh.

Mickelle laughed. "Let's see how well they take care of this one first."

After everyone had a ride on the horse, the children gathered in the family room to play a game of *Phase 10*.

Mickelle went to the adjoining kitchen, followed by Damon, who began to carve one of the two turkeys. She put the rolls in the oven before saying, "They'll be here any minute. Are there glasses on the tables?" They had set up another table to accommodate all of her family. She was excited because this was the first time she had ever hosted a family holiday. From the moment she had first entered Damon's house, long before they fell in love, she had known it would be perfect for such an event, but had never believed she would really see it happen.

Mickelle Wolfe, she thought. *Perfect.*

Damon had paused in his work and was observing the children. "We may never find him, Kelle," he said after a few minutes. There was no need to name the man who had so disrupted their lives.

She sighed. "I know. And I have to let it go. At least he gave us back Jennie Anne. I'm grateful for that. There was something good in his heart after all. I wish him well. I hope he finds happiness some day."

"For that to happen he'll have to change."

"A step at a time, I guess."

Damon's eyes rested on Jennie Anne. "I can't wait to tell her."

"Me either."

Her family were not the only ones invited to the feast. Mickelle's single friend Brenda and her four daughters were coming, along with the banker, who had managed to overcome his cautious nature enough to ask Brenda to marry him. Happily, she had said yes. Mrs. Mertz had also agreed to forego her usual meal in front of the television and join them instead. Mickelle thought her decision might have something to do with the fact that Damon would be baptizing her in two days.

Mickelle and Damon waited until all the guests had arrived and were seated around the Thanksgiving tables to tell their good news. Damon stood and tapped his wine glass, full of sparkling apple juice. "Before I offer the blessing on the food, I'd like to make an announcement."

Everyone grew silent, even Forest—the twin who was never quiet. Mickelle was sure that was a good omen.

"After a bit of searching my attorney has located Jennie Anne's great-aunt, and she has signed papers permitting us to adopt Jennie Anne." Damon held his hand up to quiet the resulting cheers. "We still have to appear before a judge to make it official, but it is merely a formality. So"—he lifted his cup—"Jennie Anne, welcome to our family. We love you and are so grateful that everything worked out the way it did. Now—" He paused expectantly, and Jennie Anne glanced at Mickelle hesitantly. Mickelle gave her the thumps-up sign.

"Now," Damon continued, "you all know I have the habit of using nicknames."

"Annoying habit," inserted Jesse.

Damon inclined his head. "An annoying habit of using nicknames," he amended. "And now that Jennie Anne's an official part of our family, it's time she got hers. I have to admit that this was not an easy call, but at last I've figured out a name that is to be used by me and no one else."

"Good, 'cause I like the name Jennie Anne," Belle said.

Damon walked over to Jennie Anne's chair and put his face close to hers. "This name is even more special because Nedda told me your mother used it." He smiled and winked. "It's Jenna. You're my Jenna."

He lifted her from her chair and hugged her tightly. "Welcome home, Jenna." Jennie Anne beamed, and her eyes grew teary.

With Jennie Anne still in his arms, Damon extended a hand to Mickelle. Momentarily, she again saw the glorious bridge from her dream, and felt their love flowing between them like a rushing river.

She reached out and grabbed a piece of light.

About the Author

Rachel Ann Nunes (pronounced *noon-esh*) knew she was going to be a writer when she was 13 years old. She now writes five days a week in a home office with constant interruptions from her five young children. One of her favorite things to do is to take a break from the computer and build a block tower with her two youngest. Several of her children have begun their own novels, and they have fun writing and plotting together.

Rachel enjoys traveling, camping, spending time with her family and reading. She served an LDS mission to Portugal. She and her husband, TJ, and their children live in Utah Valley, where she is a popular speaker for religious and writing groups. *Bridge to Forever* is her eleventh novel to be published by Covenant. Her *Ariana* series is a best-seller in the LDS market.

Rachel enjoys hearing from her readers. You can write to her at P.O. Box 353, American Fork, UT 84003-0353, send e-mail to rachel@rachelannnunes.com, or visit her website at http://www.rachelannnunes.com.

BENEATH

the

SURFACE

The phone woke Hannah Dennison who had fallen asleep on the floor, her chin resting on an open book. Years later she would remember that phone call—and the discovery of the body in Lake Shiloh—as the end of her childhood and the false shelter of her own innocence. The second ring caused Hannah to lift her head slightly and stare at the page of Shakespeare framed by her elbows and arms, one forearm stacked on top of the other—it was the balcony scene of *Romeo and Juliet.* She used the cuff of her sweatshirt to rub off the little grease smudge her chin had left on the page. Her waist-long hair spread like tendrils of wild ivy over her plush bedroom carpet. During the third ring, Hannah unfolded herself from her tortured position. Her legs had been stretched out into Chinese splits in an unbroken line from her hips; her torso pressed flat on the floor above them. Madame Karanaeva had recommended that all her advanced ballet students sit in this position for fifteen minutes each day to perfect their turnouts and keep their muscles flexible. Hannah squinted to see the time on her clock radio. *Midnight.* She had held the painful position for more than three hours.

On the fourth ring, Hannah stood, testing her weight on her wobbly, overflexed muscles, and tottered over to the phone by her bed. On the fifth ring, wincing and moaning, Hannah picked up the receiver.

"Hannah? You okay?" came a gruff male voice from the phone. "It's Dale Farley."

"Yeah, Chief, just . . . suffering for my art," she replied, sitting gingerly on the edge of her bed, biting into the knuckle of her thumb.

"Your folks out of town again?"

Hannah looked at her clock again and realized that a phone call after midnight rarely brought good news. Suddenly she knew exactly why Dale Farley had called. "Have you got Gabe at the station, Chief?" She grimaced again, this time from having to deal with the antics of her twelve-year-old brother whom she had last observed sleeping soundly in his bedroom down the hall.

"Fourth time this summer, Hannah. Every time your parents go to one of them Christian pep rallies, Gabe seems to think he can do as he pleases. You need to call your Aunt Kate or get Jared or someone to bring you down to the station." Jared was Hannah's next-door neighbor who was old enough to drive. Aunt Kate lived across town.

"Can't you just send Gabe home in a squad car like you did last time?"

"I'm not going to do that, Hannah. I'm filing paper work on him for his own good. First step toward a juvie record, Han. He's too young to be hanging out down here on that college campus. You know how it gets over Labor Day weekend with all them college students coming back."

"So exactly what crime has Gabe committed, Chief?" she asked, protectiveness bristling up through her annoyance.

"I haven't actually caught him doing anything other than breaking curfew, but it's just a matter of time till I figure out what he's up to. We want to keep Gabe out of serious trouble, Hannah, so let's get your folks in on this and nip this midnight wandering thing in the bud."

Hannah was touched by the genuine worry she heard in Dale Farley's voice. The Chief had been a member of her father's church for as long as she could remember; most of his patrolmen were members too. In a concerted effort, they had kept Gabe's mischief off the police blotter, and the Dennison family name had remained unsullied all summer long.

Her father's church functioned as the center of the social and religious life in the small town of Griggsberg. His non-denominational house of worship called The Church on the Hill stood on the high end of Bennigan's Bluff; the stained-glass figure of Christ could be seen from anywhere in town. The church was the loom on which the threads of all their lives were anchored, then woven into a tidy, predictable pattern. *Loom.* That was a good word. In addition to providing its foundation, the church loomed over the town like a watchful presence.

Behind the forty-foot-high bluff snaked a good-sized river called the Little Blue. Between the Bluff and the town, a glistening lake curved like a kidney bean, meeting the river at both ends of the lake. Before it had accidentally flooded years before, the lake basin had once been a dusty limestone quarry. After the quarry flooded, forming the lake, Midwest Christian College had moved its campus from downtown Kansas City to Griggsberg. The shiny new college campus and the magnificent church above it had transformed Griggsberg into a bustling, prosperous college town.

Hannah had fallen silent as she considered how she would get down the Bluff to the police station to claim her brother without the whole town finding out he was in jail. "Okay, Chief, I'll throw on some clothes and find a way down there." She hung up the phone and massaged her calf muscles through the large holes of her favorite dingy-white, wooly leg warmers. Scattered on the floor by her bed were the five Shakespearean plays she had been reading over the summer for her honors English class. The test was on Tuesday, the first day of school. *Maybe Gabe will settle down once school starts up again,* she thought wearily as she stacked her books.

Without changing her grungy San Francisco Ballet sweatshirt that she always wore to bed, Hannah stepped into a navy blue pleated skirt and buttoned it at her slender waist. She couldn't find her Doc Martens in her cluttered room, so she grabbed her leather dance slippers with the black elastic bands from her dance bag. She snugged these on, then wove her unruly ash blonde hair into a single messy braid, secured it with the inky rubber band from the morning newspaper, and tossed it over her shoulder. From the glass dish on top of her father's dresser, Hannah picked up a large ring of keys and found the one to his Ford Taurus. No sense in bothering anyone at this hour. Although Hannah was still two months shy of her sixteenth birthday, she'd been driving the family car for more than a year whenever her parents left on one of their frequent trips to speak and sing at church conferences, to participate in political rallies, or to appear on Christian television shows. *How else can I get bags of groceries up the steep roads of the Bluff?* she always thought to herself whenever she took the car. *Do they expect me to make a nuisance of myself whenever I need to haul anything home or get Gabe and me where we need to go?* She wasn't going to let a few pesky laws keep her from doing what she needed to do. Over the last year, Hannah had developed a secret pride in her ability to run a home and look after her brother during the frequent absences of the adults who lived there. She thought of these self-taught skills as her personal contribution to the family ministry. Knowing how to survive and get things done had freed up her talented, charismatic parents so they could go out and save the world.

Without turning the headlights on, Hannah backed the Taurus out of the garage and headed down the hill. *No sense in waking the neighbors.* In the rearview mirror, she caught sight of Gabe's wide-open bedroom window on the second floor of the house. One of his royal-blue curtains with the rows of red and yellow superman logos flapped in the breeze like a wagging tongue. She noticed for the first time how close the branches of the elm tree had grown to her brother's window, and made a mental note to get the saw out and chop them down. *Time to bust Superman out of jail,* thought Hannah bitterly as she rumbled over the wooden floorboards of the covered bridge. She switched on the headlights and drove toward the police station.